Praise for

A CASE OF REDEMPTION

"Mitzner's courtroom drama is Grisham-like in suspenseful before-the-bench action. The book is plot-driven, and it's a wicked ride, with more loops and flips than Coney Island's Cyclone, right up to the surprise-and-bigger-surprise denouement. . . . *Law and Order*–like twist-and-turn, moral-quandary suspense needing only the echoing cell door sound effect."

—*Kirkus Reviews*

"Compelling. . . . Head-and-shoulders above most [in the genre]."

—*Publishers Weekly*

"Ah, the crucible of the courtroom! Adam Mitzner understands its appeal so very well. Devotees of legal suspense will find themselves happily at home, zinging with the intrigue, reeling with the twists, and ultimately well fed with a satisfying (if shocking) resolution. And if you've been away from the fictional halls of justice for too long, *A Case of Redemption* is where you need to come back."

—Jamie Mason, author of *Three Graves Full*

A CONFLICT OF INTEREST

"Mitzner's assured debut compares favorably to *Presumed Innocent*. . . . His strength lies in his characters and his unflinching depiction of relationships in crisis. This gifted writer should have a long and successful career ahead of him."

—*Publishers Weekly* (starred review)

"This is a capably written, well-plotted legal thriller. . . . Miller is a nicely drawn character. It's a solid debut effort, definitely recommendable to legal-thriller readers."

—*Booklist*

"The story keeps pulling you in deeper and deeper. . . . The characters are well thought out and very well developed. . . . It's hard to believe this is Mitzner's first novel. I highly recommend it to anyone who loves a legal suspense thriller. You will not be disappointed."

—seattlepi.com

"With more twists than a California cloverleaf interchange, Mitzner takes readers on a thrilling legal roller coaster ride."

—*Bookreporter*

"The epitome of legal thrillers."

—*Community Bookstop*

"A heady combination of Patricia Highsmith and Scott Turow, here's psychological and legal suspense at its finest. Adam Mitzner's masterful plotting begins on tiptoe and morphs into a sweaty gallop, with ambiguity of character that shakes your best guesses, and twists that punch you in the gut. This novel packs it. A terrific read!"

—Perri O'Shaughnessy

"Adam Mitzner combines the real world insights of an experienced litigator with the imaginative flair of a fine novelist to produce a page-turner with deeply flawed heroes, sympathetic villains, and totally unexpected twists. I loved it!"

—Alan Dershowitz

"Intriguing, exciting, and packed with suspense, mystery, and shockers you couldn't even imagine heading your way. . . . Mitzner is fresh, inventive, and original. . . . He integrates diverse and infinitely complex flawed and relatable characters into a powerful drama, delving into their lives, their emotions, and their dark, sinister motivations, making *A Conflict of Interest* a deliciously satisfying read."

—themysterysite.com

"A masterfully woven suspense thriller that'll keep you reading for hours; if you're able to put the book down at all."

—*True Crime Book Reviews*

Also by Adam Mitzner

A Conflict of Interest

A
CASE OF
REDEMPTION

ADAM MITZNER

POCKET BOOKS

New York London Toronto Sydney New Delhi

Pocket Books
A Division of Simon & Schuster, Inc.
1230 Avenue of the Americas
New York, NY 10020

This book is a work of fiction. Any references to historical events, real people, or real places are used fictitiously. Other names, characters, places, and events are products of the author's imagination, and any resemblance to actual events or places or persons, living or dead, is entirely coincidental.

Copyright © 2013 by Adam Mitzner

All rights reserved, including the right to reproduce this book or portions thereof in any form whatsoever. For information, address Gallery Books Subsidiary Rights Department, 1230 Avenue of the Americas, New York, NY 10020.

First Pocket Books paperback edition January 2014

POCKET and colophon are registered trademarks of Simon & Schuster, Inc.

For information about special discounts for bulk purchases, please contact Simon & Schuster Special Sales at 1-866-506-1949 or business@simonandschuster.com.

The Simon & Schuster Speakers Bureau can bring authors to your live event. For more information or to book an event, contact the Simon & Schuster Speakers Bureau at 1-866-248-3049 or visit our website at www.simonspeakers.com.

Manufactured in the United States of America

10 9 8 7 6 5 4 3 2 1

ISBN: 978-1-4516-7480-4
ISBN: 978-1-4516-7481-1 (ebook)

For my wife, Susan

Gonna stop you when you sing,
gonna give it til you scream;
don't like what you said,
gonna go A-Rod on your head.

—LEGALLY DEAD, "A-ROD"

"Where should I start?"

This is what my clients would say, back when I had clients. And they'd say it with the utmost sincerity, as if they truly didn't know how to explain the circumstances that gave rise to their seeking out a criminal defense lawyer who charged a thousand bucks an hour.

It wasn't that they didn't know when the facts concerning the crime began, but they wanted to emphasize that there was a context, a preface to all that followed. By telling me they didn't know where to start, they were indicating that something came before they crossed the line into criminal conduct, and that was important, too.

So, where should *I* start?

Everything in my life—the one I have now—starts at the same point. Nearly two years ago, my wife and daughter were killed in a car accident. I've learned it's best to just come out with it like that. No amount of prefacing prepares people for the shock, and so I say it straightaway. I also tell them that the other driver was drunk, because if I don't, they invariably ask how it happened. And to cut off the next question, I volunteer that he also died at the scene. I keep to myself that the driver's death is but small solace, because it was instantaneous, which means that the son of a bitch didn't suffer.

Shortly after, I calculated how many minutes I'd been alive up to the exact moment of the accident. I used the calculator on my phone to go from the 1,440 minutes in a day to 43,200 in a thirty-day month, and then to the 525,600 in a non–leap year. My forty-one years, three months, four days, six hours, and twenty-nine minutes meant that I'd been alive for 21,699,749 minutes at the time of the accident, and up until that point nearly everything in my life had gone exactly according to plan. I'd gotten good grades, which led to acceptance at an Ivy League college, then a top-ten law school, a coveted judicial clerkship, employment at a top-tier law firm, and then the Holy Grail of partnership. My wife was beautiful and whip smart, and my daughter was, in a word, perfect.

And then, in the 21,699,749th minute, my life was shattered. Broken so utterly that it was impossible to know what it had even looked like intact.

That is the context, although obviously not all of it. Suffice it to say, when I met Legally Dead, the up-and-coming hip-hop artist accused of murdering his pop-star girlfriend, I was legally dead, too, and looking for someone or something to put life back into me.

1

The siren felt like it was inside my brain. My first thought was that it must be the vestige of a nightmare. That's how I normally wake up these days, in a cold sweat. But then I felt the aftereffects of at least two drinks too many. My tongue felt coated, my throat hoarse, and my eyes drier than both. And seeing that I'm not usually hungover in my dreams, I concluded that I must be conscious, although perhaps just barely.

The god-awful sound wailed through my head again. It was only then that I realized it was the ringer on my phone. I must have at some point changed it to the horrible all-hands-on-deck emergency sound. I wouldn't have answered it at all, but I desperately did not want to hear that shrillness again.

"Hello," I croaked.

"You sound like you were hit by a truck," said a woman's voice.

"Who's this?"

"It's Nina." Then, after a slight pause, "I was calling to say that I'll be there in fifteen minutes, but it sounds like you might need more time than that."

"Nina?"

She laughed, a soft lilting sound that struck a chord of recognition.

"Rich's sister," she said, just as I recalled it myself. "We talked last night at the party. I told you that I'd be coming by your place today at nine."

I squinted over at the clock on the cable box. Eight forty-five.

"I'm sorry," I muttered. "I didn't—"

She laughed again. "No apology necessary. You're doing me the favor."

Favor? It felt like trying to reconstruct a dream. Shards of recollection were out there, but I couldn't pull them together in any type of coherent way.

Neither of us said anything for a moment, and then, as if she had just gotten the punch line of a joke, she laughed for a third time. "You don't remember anything from last night, do you?"

That was not entirely true. I recalled showing up at Rich and Deb's annual Christmas party in jeans and a sweatshirt, unshaven, while everyone else was dressed to the nines. I didn't care about looking more or less like an aging hipster, however. I hadn't wanted to go at all, much preferring to spend the evening as I did most nights, in the company of my closest confidant these days, Mr. Johnnie Walker. But Deb had been Sarah's closest friend since middle school, and that gave her a sense of familial entitlement to invoke Sarah's will, claiming that my deceased wife would be very disappointed in me if I didn't attend her best friend's annual Christmas party.

So, there was that.

And I remembered meeting Nina. Although what

we'd discussed was still a mystery, a clear image of what she was wearing came into view—a low-cut, sparkly silver cocktail dress, three-inch pumps that brought her to eye level, and a pendant hanging midway through her deep cleavage. But, let's be honest, even a dead man would have remembered that.

"Rich warned me that this might be the case," Nina said, sounding somewhat amused by my hangover. "Last night you agreed to come with me to visit with Legally Dead. He's being held at Rikers."

I didn't have the faintest recollection of even discussing Legally Dead, much less agreeing to visit him in prison. But at least now I knew the what. Unfortunately, the why was still a mystery.

I was tempted to just ask her—after all, she said I was doing her the favor here. But I decided the better course was not to let on how little I remembered from the previous evening, just in case something I'd said or done was too far over the line.

So I offered her the most noncommittal-sounding "Okay" known to man.

"Jesus, you really don't remember, do you? How much did you drink last night, anyway?"

There's no good answer to that question, and so I said nothing.

In the voice you'd use to talk to a second grader, she said, "Okay, let's review. I'm a third-year associate at Martin Quinn. We do work for Capital Punishment Records. That's Legally Dead's label. With me so far?"

"Yes," I said, trying not to sound either annoyed or

embarrassed, although both emotions were coursing through me.

"Good. So, at one of the team meetings, I heard that Legally Dead wanted to switch counsel, and that he wanted the guy who represented Darrius Macy. That would be you. Remember, I told you that story about how Legally Dead first said, 'Get me the dude who represented O.J.' And when he was told that Johnnie Cochran had been dead for about ten years, he said, 'Then get me that guy who got Darrius Macy off.'"

I had no recollection of that story at all. Fortunately, Nina didn't wait for me to acknowledge my alcohol-induced amnesia before continuing.

"Steven Weitzen, he's the big hitter in the litigation group at Martin Quinn, called over to Taylor Beckett, and someone there told him that you'd left the firm and that you weren't practicing anymore. End of story, right? But I knew that you were Rich and Deb's friend and I'd see you at their party. At first you were trying to make excuses, everything from thinking he must be guilty to you, and here I quote, not being a lawyer anymore, but I explained, rather persuasively, I thought, about how there was no evidence against him and how this is mainly a racial thing. White pop princess, black rapper. And you agreed."

And I agreed? I must have drunk even more than I thought. Even as far removed from life as I'd been lately, I still wasn't in deep enough to believe that Legally Dead's arrest for murdering the pop star known by the one-name moniker of Roxanne was mainly a racial thing. All you needed to do was turn on a radio for fifteen minutes and you'd hear "A-Rod"—a song written and performed by Legally Dead in which he rapped about beating a singer to death with a baseball bat. Coincidence of coincidences, that was precisely how Roxanne was murdered.

I'd never declined taking on a client before because he was guilty. In fact, in my previous life, I would have jumped at the opportunity to insert myself into a high-profile case without a moment's hesitation. Now, however, I saw a million reasons to decline.

"Listen, Nina, I'm really flattered, but I can't even think about taking on something like this . . . I'm . . ."

I didn't finish the thought. There were so many words that might have completed the sentence that I found it hard to pick just one: depressed, suffering, in pain, mourning, and how about just plain old drunk a lot of the time.

"I'm not having the same conversation we had last night all over again," Nina said forcefully. "I heard all your reasons then, and after you heard mine, you said you'd come with me today. That, my friend, is known in the law as a binding contract, and I'm holding you to it. Besides, as I told you last night, and as I'm sure you don't remember today, I've met with Legally Dead a couple of times already. He's a very sweet guy, and I absolutely believe him when he says that he's innocent."

I wondered if I'd asked her last night if he said that

in a song, too, or if he reserved his music for threats of murder, but given my compromised brain function, I just wanted this conversation to end, even if it meant capitulation on my part. Although spending the morning visiting a murderer in jail was not necessarily my idea of fun, it's not like I had anything else on my agenda that day. Or any other day that month, for that matter.

"Okay, you win. But it's going to take me . . ." I couldn't even remember how long it took me to get ready in the morning. "A half hour, maybe forty-five minutes."

"That's fine. I'm relatively sure that Legally Dead isn't going anywhere. Just remember, you promised me you'd wear a suit and shave."

I did? Christ.

The shower helped relieve my headache, and the mouthwash removed the stench of my breath, which was so putrid it even bothered me. Then I scraped off my stubble, trying to remember how many days' growth it represented.

When I opened my closet, the first suit that caught my eye was my best one, a charcoal-gray Brioni. It was the one I wore the opening day of the Darrius Macy trial. My go-to suit. The one that, once upon a time, gave me the most confidence.

It was also the last suit I'd worn, on the day of the funerals.

It fit much more snugly than the last time I'd worn it. I didn't know exactly how much weight I'd gained, but twenty pounds would have been a safe bet. The jacket pulled across the back, and the inside pants button was a lost cause. It was yet another reminder that I was a different man now.

Before I left the apartment, I stopped to assess last night's damage in the hallway mirror. I'd been seeing my father's face in my reflection more and more these days. He died three months after my daughter was born, and for a while it was something of a macabre race as to which event would occur first.

There are worse things to see, especially on the morning after an evening during which I'd had too much to drink. My father was very handsome, almost to the point of distraction. We share the same pale complexion, long straight nose, and strong chin. It's around the eyes, however, where I see the strongest resemblance, for better and for worse. My eyes have always been among my better features, large and deep blue, which contrasts with my jet-black hair. More than one person had commented, back in my younger days, that I looked a bit like Superman. Now, however, all I saw was sallowness, which reminded me of the way my father looked after the chemo ended, when all hope was lost.

2

Rikers is a jail, not a prison. The distinction is that it's operated by the city and the inmate population hasn't been convicted yet, but is awaiting trial. For that reason, it houses less-hardened criminals than you might find at Sing Sing, for example, one of New York State's prisons. But that doesn't mean it's a bed-and-breakfast, either. Just a few years ago, one of Rikers's guards was indicted for running a program in which handpicked inmates operated as enforcers, beating prisoners at the guard's command.

It was below freezing outside, and not much warmer inside. It wasn't just the air that was cold. The cinder-block-gray walls were bare except for the painted-on name of the institution and the official photos of the president and New York City's mayor in cheap, black plastic frames. The floor was even more barren, without a stick of furniture or a rug, just scuffed gray tile that might once have actually been white.

We waited in line to show our credentials to a heavyset woman sitting behind what I assumed to be bulletproof glass. Just beyond her was a small courtyard where two inmates shoveled away last night's light snowfall while under the supervision of two guards.

"Inmate name," the woman behind the glass barked when it was our turn at the head of the line.

"Nelson Patterson," Nina said. Seeing my confusion, she whispered to me, "You didn't think his parents actually named him Legally Dead, did you?"

"Purpose of your visit?" the heavyset woman said.

"Counsel," Nina replied.

Nina slid her business card through the small slot in the window, and then said, "My colleague forgot his, but he'll write out his contact information if you'd like."

The woman behind the glass eyed me suspiciously. No wonder Nina had told me to wear a suit.

After I scribbled down my home address and cell phone number, the woman pressed a button that caused a loud buzzer to sound. Simultaneously, a large metal door beside the bulletproof glass slid open. Nina and I walked through the doorway only to find another large metal door locked in front of us. When the first door closed behind us, the buzzer sounded again, indicating that the second door was now opening.

We were immediately hit with a wave of almost paralyzing stench, the unfortunate by-product of hundreds of men living in extremely close quarters. In front of us stood a guard who looked barely older than twenty and was as big as an NFL linebacker. The smell didn't seem to faze him in the least.

The guard led us down a maze of hallways until we arrived at a bank of phones. They looked just like they do on television cop shows. Each station was a mirror image of a black phone on the wall and a single metal chair, the two sides separated by thick glass, which, again, I presumed to be bulletproof.

There were only two other visitors. One looked like an attorney, if only because he was wearing a suit. The other was a woman, a girl, really, likely still in her teens. Her arms were covered in tattoos and she was holding an infant up to the glass.

"You'll have a little more privacy over here," the guard said to explain why we were being assigned to the phone on the end.

The baby was now crying. The top-of-the-lungs shriek that only infants can muster.

As we waited for Legally Dead to arrive, my thoughts turned to the reason why he was here in the first place: Roxanne. More accurately, I remembered that my daughter was a big fan. In fact, Roxanne may have been the first popular recording artist Alexa ever mentioned. One day she was singing the theme song from *Elmo's World,* and the next she was yelling from the backseat of the car that she wanted me to play Roxanne on the radio. Sarah laughed that our daughter thought the car radio worked like an iPod, and we could conjure at will whatever song we wanted to hear.

That memory merged seamlessly into a less happy one. An interview of Roxanne's mother I'd seen only a few weeks earlier. She didn't look much older than me, and was weeping to Katie Couric about how Legally Dead had murdered her precious angel.

When you're in law school, you spend a lot of time in legal ethics classes discussing how everyone is innocent until proven guilty and therefore entitled to a lawyer. You read *To Kill a Mockingbird,* for maybe the third time, and think someday you'll be a hero lawyer like Atticus Finch, representing unpopular causes, either because you believe in them, or just because you have that obligation.

It took about five seconds after I'd joined Taylor Beckett for me to realize that's not the way it works at a large law firm. Although everyone may be entitled to a lawyer, you couldn't hire one at Taylor Beckett without paying a six-figure retainer. And even then, Taylor Beckett had a committee that reviewed every new representation to ensure that the firm wouldn't lose future business by taking on an unpopular client.

My most famous client, Darrius Macy, was a case in point. There was resistance from certain partners to the firm representing an accused rapist. The head of the corporate group laughed—actually laughed—when I tried the everybody-is-entitled-to-a-defense line. "Maybe so," he had said, "but everybody's not entitled to Taylor Beckett representing him."

"You really think this guy's innocent?" I asked Nina.

"I do," she said without even a flicker of doubt.

"Statistically speaking, it's the boyfriend or husband like seventy percent of the time, and in a hundred percent of those instances, the boyfriend or the husband hasn't written a song explaining how he was going to commit the murder."

"Are you stuck on the song still?"

"Me and everybody else in the English-speaking world."

Nina sighed. "I told you this last night," she said, and then quickly added, "but I've got to remember that means absolutely nothing to you. I'm going to start treating you like the guy from that movie who has no short-term memory. I'll let Legally Dead explain it, but the song isn't about Roxanne at all."

She smiled at me, and was it ever a smile. It actually felt as if it generated heat. It also reminded me that it had been a long time since I'd been in the company of a woman who didn't look at me with abject pity.

"So tell me, what's in this for you?" I asked.

"You mean aside from wanting justice to prevail?"

She flashed that smile again.

"Yeah, aside from that."

"I'd like to second seat."

"Will your firm . . . where did you say you were at again?"

"Martin Quinn."

"Right. Will they let you do that?"

"No," she said with a self-satisfied grin. "But I'm going to quit."

"Really? You'll quit a big law firm job in this economy?"

"You obviously have forgotten what the life of a third-year associate looks like," she said. "My days are filled staring at a computer screen reviewing—and I kid you not—something like sixteen million emails. My job is to sort through all the garbage, all the 'all hands' notices about team meetings and corporate-speak and whatever else, and make sure that there's no email that could possibly suggest that the client knew that his thingamabob would explode if it was ever placed on a radiator." She stopped, and then added, "And, of course, the partner in charge made it abundantly clear to me and my fellow document grinds that if we miss anything, we'd be fired. So, the way I figure it, this is a win-win for me. I get out of an intolerable work situation, I get to represent someone I believe in, and I get some real lawyer experience."

"So is this something of a job interview?" I said with a grin.

"If you'd like. I don't have my résumé here, but I'm law review out of Columbia, three years of big-firm experience, I know the case, and the client loves me."

And the client loves her, I thought. Of course he did. He was a man locked away with other men, and then someone who looks like Nina comes to visit and says she believes his story. Who wouldn't love that?

"Well, you are the first candidate I've spoken to," I said, playacting the role of an interviewer.

"If you're thinking of hiring me, that at least means you're seriously thinking of taking the case, doesn't it?"

She was right. I was thinking about taking the case. I had to admit that it felt good to be a lawyer again. A lot better than the other one-word descriptions that would have applied to me over the past eighteen months—widower, drunk, bum.

3

A few moments later, Legally Dead entered the room on the other side of the glass. He was wearing the jail's standard-issue dingy gray canvas jumpsuit, and his gait was lethargic. He was taller than I had expected, as tall as the guard who accompanied him, who I pegged to be about six foot two. He looked strong, too. Even in the baggy clothing, you couldn't help but think it was possible for him to have beaten a woman to death.

Or not, as I'm sure Nina would have argued.

The guard on his side of the glass pointed to the seat across from us. Legally Dead did as he was told, slowly settling into his seat and then even more slowly reaching for the phone. He wiped off the receiver with the sleeve of his jumpsuit before putting the phone up to the side of his face.

Nina took the phone on our side off its hook. "Hi," she said excitedly. "How have you been holding up?"

Legally Dead mouthed what I thought began with "fine," but then went on to something else. I got the impression that part of what he was saying was to ask just who the hell I was.

"This is Dan Sorensen," Nina said, "the lawyer who represented Darrius Macy. I spoke with him yesterday and told him that you wanted to meet him. I want to tell you up front that Dan's not sure he wants to take your case, so be your usual charming self. Okay?"

Nina flashed her smile, and I was beginning to see that she used it like a wand, getting the recipient to do what she wanted. It seemed to work, because Legally Dead reciprocated with an equal-size grin.

Then she handed me the phone.

Even through the heavily scratched glass, I could see that Legally Dead was a handsome man. His skin was a dark chocolate color, and his head was shaved smooth, so much so that there wasn't even a shadow where hair had once been.

"Hey, man," he said. "Thanks. For meetin' me. Really appreciate your time."

Legally Dead's tone and demeanor surprised me. Everything about him suggested a gentle nature. The smile, the softness of his voice, and even the sadness in his eyes, which reminded me a little of a lost boy, were all incongruous emanating from the man who had graced the cover of *People* magazine under the headline: "The Most Hated Man of All Time."

Even though the man on the other side of the glass didn't match my preconceived impression, it's the oldest lesson in criminal defense law that looks can be deceiving. If you're coldhearted enough to kill someone—especially someone you were romantically involved with—you're capable of anything, even faking human decency.

"Nice to meet you, too," I said. "Before we start talking about the case, what should I call you?"

"What?" he said, as if he'd never been asked the question before.

"I know your given name is Nelson. Should I call you that? Or . . . Legally?"

"L.D. That's what my friends call me. L.D."

"L.D. it is, then," I said with a smile, trying to suggest that we'd already accomplished something significant. "So, tell me about you and Roxanne."

"Not much to tell," he said. "Roxanne was my girl, you know? She was everything to me."

You can tell a lot about how a client will do on the witness stand by the way he answers open-ended questions. Some find it an invitation to tell you everything that pops into their heads on the subject. Others answer with the most limited amount of information they can get away with.

Legally Dead was apparently in the latter group. As far as testifying went, that was the better group to be in. But it made getting information from your client that much more difficult.

"L.D.," I said, "even though I'm not committed to be your counsel yet, this conversation is still subject to the attorney-client privilege. So I need you to be comfortable telling me the truth. And I need to hear it all, okay?"

"A'ight," he said, which made me smile because it was the way the drug dealers talked on *The Wire*. I wondered whether the TV show copied it from real life, or if it was the other way around.

"So how long had you and Roxanne been together?"

"Few months. After I upped with Cap Pun, befo' my

first track even dropped, Matt Brooks calls me up and axes if I can do him a favor. He says Roxanne's still got ten shows to do, but her opening act was all fucked up on some shit, so will I open fo' her? You know, he don't have to ax twice. Imma go from fucking nowhere to playing twenty-thousand-seat arenas. Sign me up, man."

L.D. didn't explain who Matt Brooks was, but there was no need. Even someone as removed from the rap world as me knew that he owned Capital Punishment Records. The Silver Svengali they called him, on account of his hair and the unqualified devotion exhibited by the acts he signed. He stood out in the rap world by his age (midfifties) and his race (Caucasian), but otherwise he had the accoutrements you'd expect from a music mogul—a $250,000 car, Gulfstream jet, Hamptons estate, and supermodel wife . . . another person who went by only one name: Chiara.

"Okay, so that's how you meet Roxanne. What happens next?"

"Use your imagination 'bout what happened next." He laughed, and then, as if he realized that humor was severely misplaced under the circumstances, he stopped himself abruptly and said, "I'm not gonna disrespect the girl, you know. It wasn't like that. The thing is, I really loved her."

Not just him. Everybody, it seemed, loved Roxanne. She'd been the It girl for three years running. Her popularity was based on the usual post–Britney Spears factors—a virginal face, torrents of blond hair that were almost certainly extensions, the figure of a Barbie doll.

But if he thought that by telling me how much he loved her I'd be less inclined to think him capable of murder, he was off by 180 degrees. Call me a cynic, but I would have been more convinced of his innocence if he'd told me he really didn't give a damn about her.

"Where were you on the night Roxanne was killed?" I asked.

"My crib."

At least I understood what that meant. He said it flatly enough to suggest the answer to my next question, but I still had to ask it.

"And I take it you were home alone?"

"Yeah. Roxanne wouldn't come to my hood, you know?"

No, I didn't know. "Where do you live?"

"Brownsville, man. Tilden Houses projects."

Well, that explained why Roxanne never visited him. Brownsville was probably the most crime-ridden neighborhood in the five boroughs.

"Can anybody give you an alibi?"

"You think I'd be sitting in here if somebody could?"

"I just thought that, I don't know, you'd have an entourage or something with you at the time."

"You mean like Vince and Turtle and Drama? Fuck, no. I ain't Hollywood, man. 'Sides, you gotta remember, when this shit happened my record had just dropped, and it wasn't on the way to goin' platinum or nothing, neither. All I'd done was opened a few shows for Roxanne and was, you know, wit her and such, but

I wasn't getting any money out of it. Shit, I still haven't seen a fuckin' nickel from Cap Pun, you know?"

I looked over at Nina, but because I was the one on the phone, she apparently hadn't heard Legally Dead's claim of poverty. I wondered if her commitment to the cause included working for free.

"Marcus Jackson was representing you pro bono?" I asked.

"Pro what?"

"For free. You weren't paying him?"

"Can't give the man what I don't got."

"So why do you want to switch lawyers? Marcus is a very well-respected guy, and he's not charging you."

"The thing is, Marcus be tellin' me that I gots to plead guilty. Don't matter how many times I say I'm innocent, he keeps sayin' that Imma get convicted, and I gots to make a deal." Legally Dead shook his head, lamenting the injustice of it all. "I know that some of this shit don't look good, but I didn't kill her. I swear I didn't."

"I hear you," I said, the lawyer's noncommittal response. I wasn't saying that I agreed, just that I understood the words he was saying.

Legally Dead was apparently smart enough to recognize the distinction. He turned away from me, staring at the floor, shaking his head again.

So I decided to throw him a bone. "For what it's worth, L.D., I was home alone that night, too, and I don't think I could get anyone to alibi me either."

Of course, I wasn't Roxanne's boyfriend, nor had I written a song describing how I'd murder her if she ever got out of line. But for the moment, those were pesky details, and I wanted to gain his trust, if for no other reason than to try to get the truth from him. Or whatever his version of the truth might be.

He resumed eye contact. It was enough encouragement that I continued.

"I have to confess, I really don't know much about the hip-hop world—"

He interrupted me. "I do rap. Hip-hop and rap ain't the same thing, man. That's lesson number one."

"What's the difference?"

L.D. chuckled. "You ax a hundred people, you get a hundred answers. But fo' me, it's simple. You can hear the difference. What I do is rap. Spoken poetry to music. Eminem, Fitty, Dre, Snoop, that's rap. Damn if I know what's hip-hop, but I know what I do ain't it."

I smiled back at him. "Fair enough," I said. "Where I was going with this, however, is that, from what I understand of it, mainly from Nina and what I've read in the press, the prosecution's theory goes something like this: you were her boyfriend, which put you at the top of the suspect list, right off the bat." I realized the unfortunate word choice as soon as I'd said it, but decided it would only make things worse to call attention to it. "Second, you wrote the 'A-Rod' song, in which you talk about killing a singer by beating her with a baseball bat, and the forensics folks are saying that the murder weapon was a baseball bat."

Both Nina and L.D. started talking at the same

time. "Hold on," I said to L.D., and put up my index finger as I pulled the phone away from my ear to listen to Nina.

"They don't know the weapon for sure," she said. "They never found it. They're assuming it was a bat because Roxanne had a bat in her bedroom from singing at the World Series or something, and now it's missing. And because of the song, it obviously helps the prosecution if the murder weapon is a bat."

I gave Nina a not-too-subtle eye roll, although I was careful to turn my head sufficiently so Legally Dead didn't see it. "But I'm assuming that the wounds Roxanne suffered are consistent with a baseball-bat beating, right?" I said. "I mean, I get that the murder weapon could be a two-by-four and not a Louisville Slugger, but it's not a knifing case."

"Right," she said, conceding my point.

I wasn't sure how much of that L.D. heard, but when I turned back toward him, he looked more agitated than he had before. "The song ain't fuckin' about Roxanne!" he shouted into the phone. "I been saying that from day one, but nobody's fuckin' payin' it no mind. You gotta listen to the lyrics."

Apparently recognizing that his flare-up had not helped his cause, he smiled again, but the damage had already been done. If nothing else, L.D. had revealed himself as the kind of man whose emotions could turn on a dime.

He began to rap, swaying from side to side as he did, as if he were onstage before screaming teenagers, rather than behind a bulletproof glass wall talking to a lawyer.

> *"We were blood bros and now this;*
> *the ultimate dis.*
> *Gonna stop you when you sing,*
> *gonna give it til you scream;*
> *don't like what you said,*
> *gonna go A-Rod on your head."*

When he was finished, he looked at me as if that resolved everything.

"I'm sorry, L.D., you're going to have to explain what you mean."

"The song ain't about no shorty, it's about a fuckin' dude." He rapped again: "'We were blood bros'—*brothers*. It's 'bout these gangbangers and one wants outta the game, and the other guy says if you talk shit about me, I'm gonna go A-Rod on your head. So everybody be sayin' that because the lyric is *sing* it's gotta be about a singer like Roxanne. But no fuckin' way. It's about . . . you know, like them old movies and shit, when people talk to the cops and they be singin' like a canary."

I felt like saying: *Well, with an explanation like that, I'm surprised they even arrested you,* but didn't think I could summon enough sarcasm to give the thought justice. It was apparent I'd need to study not only the "A-Rod" lyrics but the entire Legally Dead songbook.

I had a momentary vision of translators in the

courtroom debating the meaning of the lyrics, the way it sometimes happens when you have foreign-language interpreters arguing over the nuance of language in different regions of the country. *No, it's* phat *with a* ph, *so it means cool, not obese.*

I did a recap in my head. No alibi. Check. Sketchy, at best, explanation on the song. Check.

Next on my agenda was motive.

"How were things between you and Roxanne on the day she died?"

"We all good."

"What I've read is that the prosecution thinks Roxanne had recently . . ." I searched for a word that was gentle, and then decided that my offending him was the least of his worries. "She dumped you. Right before Thanksgiving. They claim that you couldn't handle the rejection and so you killed her."

He shook his head, as if the theory was so ludicrous as not to warrant even a response. It came off arrogant, and I made a mental note that he'd have to work on that expression if he was ever before a jury.

"So what's the story there?" I asked.

We stared at each other for a good thirty seconds. It was obvious we were taking each other's measure.

He blinked first.

"I saw my baby girl over Thanksgiving. I was never gonna go to Roxanne's mama's house."

"Baby girl?" I said.

"Yeah."

"Another girlfriend?"

He laughed, a real from-the-belly laugh. "You think I'm talkin' a whole different language, don'tcha? No, man. Baby girl. She a real baby. My daughter, Brianna. She's five."

This took me by surprise. Nina hadn't mentioned that part.

L.D. was showing me his broadest smile yet, framed by two perfect dimples. I recognized it all too well as a father's smile. There was no doubt in my mind he was telling me the truth, at least about this. He had a five-year-old daughter.

"You got any kids?" he asked.

It's a question that I still don't know how to answer. Technically, I suppose, the answer is no, but that would suggest that I've never experienced fatherhood. Sometimes I give a fuller explanation—*I had a daughter, but she died*—but in situations where I don't want to discuss it, I go with one of the two shorter options, both of which seem equally true and untrue: yes or no.

This time I said, "Yes."

"How old?"

"Six," I said, which would be the answer I'd give for the rest of my life. And then I added, "A girl."

"Good," he said. "Then you know why I gotta get outta here. Think about it fo' a second. How'd you feel if you gonna be separated from your little girl fo' the rest of your life fo' somethin' you didn't do?"

I didn't answer, but instead looked over to Nina. From the sadness in her eyes, I knew she understood what we'd been discussing.

4

On the subway back from Rikers, I shared with Nina Legally Dead's portion of the conversation. I did it without invoking his name or saying anything that would reveal privileged information about the world's most notorious murder suspect to the other riders on the train. It's something lawyers become quite adept at—speaking in pronouns and euphemisms, so someone eavesdropping has no idea what's being discussed.

The first thing I raised with her was the money.

"He doesn't have a pot to piss in. Apparently, his employer never paid him. Are you still up for doing this pro bono?"

The disclosure didn't seem to surprise her.

"It won't be pro bono, Dan. He'll have money. He just doesn't have it right now. I hate to say it, but he's going to earn millions from . . ." She looked around the train. "On that one thing alone."

She meant the "A-Rod" song.

"Blood money," I said.

She shrugged. "Not if he's innocent."

It was ironic, albeit in a tragic way, but I didn't care about the fee because I was living off my own blood money. At Sarah's insistence, when Alexa was born, we took out a large life insurance policy on both our lives. It made sense to insure me that way because we depended on my income, but going back to work wasn't in Sarah's short-term plans, and in any event, magazine writers just didn't pull in the kind of money that mattered to maintain our lifestyle. But Sarah insisted that the policies be of equal amount, and made me promise that if anything ever happened to her, I'd leave Taylor Beckett and take a job that permitted me to spend more time with Alexa. "I want you to be the richest lawyer at the ACLU," Sarah would joke every time I groused about paying the premiums to insure her life.

So money didn't matter to me, either. Of course, that didn't mean it didn't matter to Nina.

"So you'll do it without payment?"

"Yes," she said, with a conviction I couldn't help but admire. "There'll be money down the road, I assume, and even if there's not, this isn't about getting paid for me. It's about making sure an innocent man doesn't go to jail for the rest of his life."

I was tempted to say that I thought she had a better chance of getting paid than that L.D. was innocent, or that he'd be acquitted, for that matter, but I didn't. From the look in Nina's eyes, I knew it would have been like telling a child there was no Santa Claus.

"He tell you anything else I should know?" Nina asked.

"As a matter of fact, he told me he has a daughter. Did you know that?"

"I did," she said. "I thought telling you that might be laying it on too thick."

"But you made sure to tell him to mention it," I said.

"Maybe," she said, and then flashed that smile of hers.

After we got aboveground, we stopped off at an Italian restaurant near my apartment. It was really not much more than a glorified pizza place, but it served individual pies, which came in handy when you were always dining alone.

When the waitress came over to take our order, Nina answered quickly—a salad of some sort—but I deliberated slightly longer, wondering if it was too early to order a drink. I decided that these days it was never too early, and asked for the fungi pizza and a scotch.

I thought I saw a subtle frown from Nina, but perhaps it was my imagination.

When the waitress left, I started rattling off the pros and cons of taking on the case. It wasn't long before Nina cut me off.

"C'mon, Dan. What's it going to be? Yes or no?"

Before I had a chance to answer, the waitress returned with our drinks, and without hesitation I took a deep mouthful. As the scotch rolled down my throat, I let my mind wander to what it would be like if I said yes, visualizing my standing on the courthouse steps addressing hordes of reporters, and then delivering closing arguments before a packed courtroom.

"Dan?" Nina said, pulling me out of my daydream.

My hand had begun to quiver, which was why Nina had called my name. I reached for the scotch to steady myself.

Nina leaned across the table. Her emerald-green eyes locked on to mine. I stared into the flecks of brown and blue, which reminded me of a flame, the way closer inspection reveals a myriad of colors.

In a soft, reassuring voice, Nina said, "I really believe that he's innocent. And it's not just going back and forth over the evidence. It's a little bit like religion. We could talk all day long about whether this miracle or that actually happened, but at the end of it, it's just a matter of faith. I have that kind of faith in him, and so I'm willing to do whatever I can to help him."

"I wish I felt that way," I said in a quiet voice, as much to myself as to Nina. "Not just about our prospective client, but about . . . anything. Maybe there's just some genetic defect in my DNA with regard to matters of faith."

Nina's expression told me that she understood my comment was a reference to my wife and daughter. "You have to let yourself believe before you can believe," she said. "Sometimes, in a leap of faith, the leap's got to come first, and then the faith follows."

I was considering the metaphor, actually envisioning myself leaping from one cliff to another, not unlike the way the Road Runner and Wile E. Coyote did in the cartoons. And then I thought of L.D.'s daughter. In my mind, she had her father's dimples and warm smile. She likely wore dresses, I thought to myself, because all five-year-old girls favored them over pants. At least Alexa did.

Had, anyway.

I drained the last of my drink. Then with a fluid motion, I signaled to the waitress for a refill.

When my eyes reconnected with Nina's, her look of disappointment was unmistakable.

"Do you mind if I'm totally honest with you, Dan?"

"You mean you've been lying to me until now?" I said, trying to sound lighthearted, knowing full well that was not where she was heading.

"I've been honest, but now I'm going to get personal. I think you need him as much as he needs you."

"How do you figure that?"

"I've only been around you for . . . what, four hours? And this must be the sixth scotch I've seen you down. If you don't do something to put yourself on a different course, you're going to be stuck on this one, and I think you know that continuing in that direction is going to end very badly."

I knew this, of course. In fact, I'd been saying the same thing to myself for more than a year. At the same time, there was a part of me that reveled in the downward spiral, in the morbid fascination of contemplating the depths to which I could actually fall.

And besides all that, there was Legally Dead to consider, too. If he was innocent, didn't he deserve someone whose skills were a bit sharper? Someone who was truly up for the kind of fight that a high-stakes murder case requires?

"Nina, all posturing aside, I haven't been in a court-room in a year and a half, and this is going to be a very big case. I just don't know if I'm up to it."

"The client certainly thinks you are. Isn't that what matters?"

I chuckled, not sure if she was truly that naive. "The client," I said, "doesn't know anything about how I've spent the last eighteen months. He doesn't know what's been going on in my head. Christ, he doesn't even know that I don't have a job."

"Consider this, then, another instance of faith," she said softly. "I believe you can do this. Look, he al-ready had Marcus Jackson in his corner, and you saw how he felt about that. I don't have any doubt that your skills in the courtroom will still be there. Plenty of top-flight trial lawyers go years between trials, so that's hardly an excuse, Dan." She looked at me hard, and then continued, "Let's make a rule, just between us, that we'll try to be honest with each other. I get that you're scared about doing this, about pulling your life together and rejoining the living. That's what's really holding you back. This idea that maybe you're not good enough anymore? That's not even worthy of discussion, because you know as well as I do that it's just not true. So, the question for you, Dan, is whether you want to change your life. If the answer to that is yes, then you really have no excuse, because this case is the best hope for you to do that. But if the answer is no, then you've got no reason to give it even this much consideration."

Even though I knew it was empty, I reached for my glass of scotch, a Pavlovian response to pain I knew all too well. I sucked on an ice cube and spit it back into the glass. The very act reinforced Nina's point that my current course was not going to end well.

I read this book once about an elite section of the navy SEALs that's deployed only to rescue other navy SEALs lost at sea during hurricanes. The SEALs parachute into the ocean from above the storm. As they fall, the SEALs can't differentiate between the rain-soaked air and the ocean. The only way a SEAL knows he's even hit the water is when he stops descending.

This is the most apt metaphor for grief that I know.

It actually sometimes feels as if I'm falling, with that same weightless, untethered sensation. Like with the navy SEALs, all my hopes are pinned to the belief that one of these days I'll realize that I've stopped descending, and then, maybe, I'll be able to rise again.

"Do you really think that taking on Legally Dead offers a happier ending for me?" I asked.

"How could it not? You'll be saving his life, and you'll be giving your own a sense of purpose."

And that was really the heart of it, wasn't it? If taking on the case could stop my descent, how could I possibly decline?

5

They say that you're never more yourself than when you grieve. I suppose that's why I've mainly mourned alone.

Even when Sarah and Alexa were alive, I was never much of a people person. I'm not comfortable with the superficiality of small talk, and the last thing I wanted to do after they were both gone was to share my grief with others. Maybe this is unfair, but it felt as if general interest in what happened to me was only a thin veneer away from voyeurism, and I wanted no part in allowing people who had never been touched by tragedy to experience it vicariously through my suffering.

But I think about them, and how they died, all the time.

The jury had acquitted Darrius Macy two days earlier, and Sarah thought that meant I might now take a little time off and spend it with her and Alexa at our summer home in East Hampton. She did not understand when I told her that I couldn't.

"This is ridiculous, Dan. You've been working nonstop on the Macy case for months," Sarah said. "Now that it's finally over, and especially given that you *won*, the firm should at least let you have a few days off to spend with your family. The place won't collapse without you."

"You grossly overestimate the familial concerns of the partnership," I replied, only to see a stare down that told me this was a far more serious issue than my comment suggested. "I'm sorry, but I just can't. I have clients besides Macy. Do you know how many phone calls and emails I have to return? Besides, I've blocked out two weeks in August for us to be away."

"Oh, come on. You think I haven't heard this song before? By August you'll be neck-deep in some other crisis, and we'll be lucky if we get you for Labor Day weekend."

We'd been having this fight for more than a decade now, and Sarah was right that I had been engaged in a constant exercise of moving the goalposts. The first few years, I told her that seventy-hour weeks were like boot camp for young associates, with the billable-hour benchmarks used to weed people out. After that, the recession made midyear associates expendable, and so the long hours were necessary for survival. Then I was in the homestretch, and if I wanted to make partner I had to show that nothing was more important in my life than the firm. The case I was working on when I made partner, a huge antitrust matter, didn't suddenly stop once my title had changed, and so I continued to churn out the same hours for the next two years. That case morphed seamlessly to the next, and then the next, and then, ultimately, to Darrius Macy.

The year Sarah and Alexa died, I was on pace to bill more than three thousand hours. That translated to, on average, sixty hours a week, which, in turn, meant that I was in the office more like seventy, when you counted lunch and the time I couldn't charge to any client. Or, put in the terms that mattered to Sarah, I was at the office about twelve hours a day, Monday through Friday, and about ten hours over the weekend.

The last time I spoke to Sarah, she was at the beach, which made the cell phone reception less than ideal. For the first time all week, however, she sounded happy. Every prior call had been tense. She had gone to the beach on Wednesday, without me, and the fact that she was there and I was in the city was the obvious source of her discontent. But I promised her that I'd be coming that afternoon, and that was seemingly enough to change Sarah's mood.

"Alexa was so funny today," Sarah said, laughing into the phone. "She's spent the better part of the day jumping into the waves and then running back to the blanket to look at her feet. I finally asked her what she was doing, and she told me, 'You said that I should be careful of something under my toe.'"

"Mommy, *Mommy!*" I heard Alexa exclaim.

"Alexa, please wait a moment. Can't you see that Mommy is on the phone? I'm talking to Daddy."

"Look at these shells I found!" Alexa said, oblivious to what Sarah had just told her. "Which one is your favorite?"

"They're all beautiful, sweetie. Do you want to tell your father about them?"

"No," Alexa said. I couldn't help but smirk.

"Then tell him that you love him."

"*I love you, Daddy!*" Alexa screamed this into the phone, as if she believed she had to raise her voice to be heard because I was so far away.

An hour later, Sarah pulled out of the beach parking lot, and at the next intersection a black Escalade ran the light and plowed into our car.

Based on the wreckage, the paramedics presumed both Sarah and Alexa died on impact, even though they were wearing seat belts. The Escalade's driver was found twenty-five feet from his car, almost completely decapitated.

I was sitting in my office, stuck on a conference call with no end in sight, when my assistant came in and told me that someone from the East Hampton police was on the line, and that it was urgent. Nearly everything that followed is a blur. Just people dressed in black and platitudes about tragedy and God's plan, whatever that was.

One thing that I distinctly recall from that period is my first day back at the office after the funerals. After making an appointment with his assistant, I walked into the office of Taylor Beckett's managing partner, Benjamin Ethan, closed the door behind me, and told him that I was going to resign my partnership.

Ethan looked at me like I was completely insane. The only reason a partner ever voluntarily left Taylor Beckett was to run for statewide office or to accept a presidential appointment. Bereavement was just something you eventually got over.

"There's no need for that, Daniel," Ethan said in his smooth baritone. "Of course, I cannot begin to understand what you are going through, but I do understand what it is like to be under tremendous strain. What we do here is counsel people under that type of pressure. And even though you have not asked me for my counsel, I'm going to give it to you anyway." He smiled. "Free of charge, of course."

Although he's not yet sixty, Benjamin Ethan always seemed to me to be a man of an entirely different era. He wears bow ties and calls everyone by his full given name, and everyone calls him Benjamin. Sometimes clients call him Ben, and to Ethan's credit he never corrects them, or opposing counsel would drop his name to boost their credibility with me—*tell Ben Ethan I said hello*—but the effort to demonstrate familiarity only proved they didn't actually know him very well. In this case, his formality required that I give my assent before he provided me with the unsolicited advice he was offering.

"Thank you," I said, even though I knew what he was going to tell me, having said it to myself more than a dozen times already.

"There's no need for an official resignation, Daniel. Instead, why don't you take a leave of absence? It can be open-ended, for as long as you want. When you're ready to come back, just call me. We'll still be here. We've been here since 1869, and we'll be here when you're ready to resume your career."

"I appreciate that, Benjamin, I really do. As you

know, I've devoted my professional life to this firm. My wife would have said that I devoted my *entire* life to this firm."

He gave me a knowing smile, surely recognizing where this was heading. "Daniel, I know how hard you've worked, because it's as hard as I've worked, and as hard as every single one of our partners has worked. And as many hours as we have all logged, it probably is roughly the same amount of time as put in by the world's best surgeons, and pianists, and writers, and athletes. The others in our lives—spouses, children, friends—they all get a little less because of the commitment we have to make to practice law at our level. And you've just established yourself in that topmost echelon with the Macy verdict. Don't throw all that away, Daniel. Instead, why don't you take some time to think about how you want the rest of your career to look, and then call me when you've made a decision."

"I appreciate the offer, Benjamin. I do, along with everything you've done for me over the years, but I've made up my mind. I'm done with this." I could have left it there, but I wanted to make it crystal clear that this was final, and well considered. "And since you brought up the Macy case, you need to know . . . it's not a reason for me to stay, it's a reason for me to leave."

I knew that he wouldn't try to talk me out of it any further. "I see," he said in a measured voice. "Best of luck to you." And then he shook my hand.

And that was it. I hadn't spoken to him or anyone else at Taylor Beckett since that day. Even though I'd known many of my coworkers for twenty years, I didn't get a single telephone call or email. I was just as much to blame for the silence as my former colleagues, as I hadn't reached out to them, either. The expression *out of sight, out of mind* doesn't apply anywhere more than at a large law firm. It was all very Orwellian; I was wiped from the institution as completely as if I'd never worked there at all.

But now, this afternoon, and after all this time, I dialed Benjamin Ethan.

His assistant, a woman named Janeene, answered his phone. When I worked at Taylor Beckett, I spoke to Janeene so frequently that she joked about wishing her husband called her half as much as I did. But when I gave her my name and asked to speak to Ethan, she was all business, asking me to hold while she told "Mr. Ethan" that I was on the line.

"Daniel. Long time, no talk," Ethan said when he finally picked up, after I'd been on hold for the better part of two minutes. "What has it been, two, three years?"

"Eighteen months, actually."

"Time. Where does it go?"

I chuckled to myself. You'd think that a guy who billed $1,250 for every sixty minutes would have a better sense of time.

"How have you been?" I asked.

"You know, a slave to the billable hour. But I can't complain. What can I do for you?"

"I'm ready to get back into practice."

"I'm glad to hear it. But, well, you know the way this place runs. It's not up to only me, and after so much time . . . I just don't want you to get your hopes up, that's all. I'll certainly advocate for your return, but I don't know how the other partners will feel about it."

This was hardly a surprise. I'd long suspected that Ethan's grandiose "you're always welcome back here" when I'd left the firm was classic lawyer BS. The last thing that anyone at Taylor Beckett wanted now was for me to return. Nature might abhor a vacuum, but a big law firm devours it. My cases had been reassigned, and my clients were now firmly under another partner's control. Even my office was occupied. My return would upset the natural order of things, and that is something a large law firm simply can't abide.

"I'm afraid I wasn't clear," I said. "I don't want to come back to the firm. I've got this one case, and I'm going to handle it with a friend. I'm calling to ask if I could use some of the firm's resources—an office or two, maybe some light secretarial help."

Even over the phone, I could tell that Ethan was letting out a sigh of relief.

"I don't see why not," he said. "Besides, it would be nice to see you around the office again. So what's the case that's so interesting it brought you back into the game?"

"It's a big one, actually. The rapper named Legally Dead."

"Really? A front-page murder case. Well, you're not easing back into it, now, are you, Daniel?"

"No, I guess not."

"Do you mind my asking how you came to represent him?"

"No, not at all. A friend's sister, she's an associate over at Martin Quinn. Or at least she was before we agreed to take on Legally Dead. Anyway, she knew the client from her time there and took an interest in the case. He'd heard about the Macy case, and I guess he figured since I got one celebrity acquitted for rape, why not another for murder, and so he asked her to make the introduction."

I expected some pithy comeback, but Ethan didn't say anything. When the silence became noticeable, I said, "Is something wrong, Benjamin?"

This time I actually heard him let out a deep sigh. "I'm afraid so," he said in a somewhat pained-sounding voice. "I hate to say no to you, Daniel, especially because I just said yes, but unfortunately I have to rescind my offer of office resources."

"Why's that?"

Again there was a pregnant pause. Ethan had the kind of mind that was patient and deliberate. Whereas most of us fill our uncertainty with stammering and verbal tics, Ethan never did. If he didn't know precisely what he wanted to say, he was silent.

"I'm afraid Taylor Beckett cannot be seen to be supportive of your client's objectives. Please do not misunderstand me: I am not making a moral judgment as much as relating a business reality. You know better than most that our clients are hardly saints-in-waiting.

But *your* client, I am afraid, is someone we just cannot be associated with publicly."

This was hardly a shock. In fact, I found it more surprising that Ethan initially agreed to my proposal without delving more into the nature of my represen-tation. I assumed he figured it was some insider trad-ing or accounting fraud case, and therefore there'd be little institutional resistance. A murder case, however, was a totally different thing at Taylor Beckett. That much I knew from the opposition from certain part-ners to the firm taking on Darrius Macy, and at least then, the firm was getting paid.

"I understand, Benjamin. I'll just make other ar-rangements."

"Daniel . . . would you mind if I asked you a per-sonal question?"

"Of course not."

"Why do you want to take on someone like him? Like this Legally Dead character? I would think you of all people . . ."

I laughed slightly into the phone, a defense mecha-nism to get him to stop from finishing the thought. "'Someone like him,' huh? This from a man who once said that the only mission of a law firm is to make money for its partners."

"I never said that, Daniel."

"Then it was something pretty close to it."

"Well, is that the answer, then? Is it for the money?"

"No. It's not the money."

"Then my question still stands: Why, Daniel?"

"Isn't the pursuit of justice a sufficient reason?"

Ethan chuckled. "I hope you know, Daniel, that I have always had a special fondness for you, which is the only reason I am intruding in this way. Given your experience with Darrius Macy, I would have thought—"

I tuned out what he said next, knowing full well what he thought about my experience with Darrius Macy. What he didn't understand, however, was that far from viewing my representation of Legally Dead as a repeat of that experience, I saw it as my last chance to get out from under all that.

6

Before the accident, I'd wake up most mornings at six so that I could go for a run. On days when I was pressed for time, I'd do two loops of the reservoir in Central Park (3.2 miles), but my preferred route was the inner loop of the park (5 miles), and if I was feeling particularly strong, I'd do the park's outer loop (6.2 miles).

I'd be back home by seven, which was when my daughter would be sitting down to breakfast. The twenty minutes I'd spend with Alexa as she chomped on crustless toast smothered in strawberry jam was the only time I'd see her during the workweek, as I always came home well past her bedtime.

At 7:20 a.m., Sarah would take Alexa to school, which, although less than ten blocks away, was nevertheless a half-hour walk for six-year-old legs. Then I'd shower, shave, and dress, and be out the door myself by eight.

Here's what my morning routine was after they died:

I got up around nine, often after some type of bad dream had jolted me awake. It would take me a moment to get my bearings, and then my entire meaningless existence would flood back to me in an instant. My wife and daughter were still dead, and I had nowhere I needed to be. The end.

Filling the day, or even half the day, became a challenge. Sometimes I'd go to the movies or, less frequently, to a restaurant, just to get the hell out of the apartment. I'd read more than I ever had before, although found that I rarely finished a book, usually putting it down somewhere at the midpoint. I drank too much, even on the days I vowed to take it easy. And on the few occasions I put on my running shoes and headed to the park, I couldn't go even half a mile. The moment I felt the slightest bit of struggle, I broke stride.

One of the cruelest ironies of my postwork life was that when I was gainfully employed, there never seemed to be enough hours in the day to get done what I wanted to get done, at the office or at home. But now the opposite was true. There was far too much time.

The day after our meeting with Legally Dead, Nina arrived at my apartment at ten a.m. with a large bag over her shoulder and a tray with two cups of coffee in her hands.

"Howdy, pardner," she said, and gave me that smile.

I'd called Nina the previous evening and told her I was in. She said Legally Dead would be very pleased and she was looking forward to our working together. I said that I was, too, but she must have thought I didn't mean it because she said, "Trust me, Dan, you won't regret doing this."

Stepping inside my apartment, Nina examined the space. "It's beautiful, Dan. I never would have guessed you were so into modern furniture. It's like Don Draper's apartment from *Mad Men*."

After the accident, I sold the apartment on Park Avenue I'd shared with Sarah and Alexa and our house in East Hampton. Rather than put down permanent roots, I rented a one-bedroom in Tribeca that purported to be a loft solely because it had high ceilings. It was less than half the size of the place on Park Avenue, but square footage was not something I cared about any longer. I took it because of the view, forty-two floors above the city, and the terrace off the bedroom. On more than one night during the summer, I'd fallen asleep out there, a bottle beside me.

One of the benefits of downsizing is that the furniture you're left with is only the good stuff. Virtually everything else I owned went to storage, which included all of Sarah's and Alexa's possessions. It was somewhat selfish of me, in that I knew I'd never have any need for their clothing or Sarah's jewelry or Alexa's toys, but I just couldn't imagine giving away anything that they'd ever touched.

"Sarah was the modernist, not me," I said.

It was a quirk of my apartment's design that it had both a dining room and a breakfast room. The dining room contained an oval Saarinen table, six plywood Eames chairs, and a midcentury credenza behind them, while the breakfast room opened from the kitchen's other entrance and had a smaller Saarinen table, this one round, although still in white marble, and four acrylic Eros chairs in red.

Nina put the coffee on the table in the breakfast room and settled into one of the Eros chairs. "They remind me of that ride in Coney Island called the Whip," she said. "You know the one? It was this red thing with a high back, and you'd sit in it and then it would spin."

"These swivel," I said with a smile, and then gave her chair a twist.

She pulled one of the coffee cups out of the tray and passed it to me.

"I prepared my coffee at Starbucks, but I didn't know how you take yours," she said, "so I left it black."

I would have added milk, but if I had any in my refrigerator, it would have been well past its expiration date, so I made do without. "How do you take yours?" I asked as I sipped.

"Milk and Sweet'N Low."

"Okay, then. Now that the most important matter has been settled, I guess the next thing on the agenda is to figure out where we're going to work. I called Taylor Beckett but, unfortunately, there's no room at the inn."

"I don't mind working out of here," Nina said. "One of us can work at this table, and the other one on the dining room table. I've got my laptop, and that's all I need. Besides, it's not like we have a client who's going to be visiting the office."

"That sounds like a plan. So, I guess, the first thing we should do is prepare a notice of appearance. We should hold off on filing it with the court until right before we have to appear in person next week. No need to start the media feeding frenzy if we don't have to. A few days of work under the radar will be nice."

"How bad will it be?" she asked.

"If the Macy case is any guide, reporters won't be going through our garbage or investigating whether you smoked pot in junior high school, but we'll probably have a paparazzo or two in front of the building from time to time, mainly on days we're due in court. The truth is, they get better pictures in front of the courthouse, so that's where they usually stake out. We'll also get a lot of requests for interviews. On the Macy case, any time any idiot had something to say about Darrius, they'd call me looking for comment."

She looked a bit concerned. "You okay with that?" I asked.

"Yup. I didn't even smoke pot in junior high school," she said with a sudden change of expression.

"Okay, because you looked a little worried for a second."

She laughed. "Oh no, I was thinking about something else."

"Care to share?"

"When I draft the notice of appearance, I'll need to identify our little law firm's name, and I was wondering whether it should be Sorensen and Harrington or Harrington and Sorensen."

I laughed with her. "I take it, then, that you've rejected out of hand the Law Offices of Daniel L. Sorensen or Daniel L. Sorensen and Associates?"

She looked crestfallen, apparently taking my effort at humor seriously. "I'm joking, Nina. Whatever name you want."

"Okay, because I was joking a little bit, too. I realize I'm being a bit presumptuous to assume that you're going to put my name next to yours, given that the client wanted you and I really have very little clue what I'm doing unless all of a sudden the DA's office dumps a bazillion emails on us."

"No, we're partners, Nina. I'll likely do the lion's share of the stand-up trial work because I'm more experienced, but you'll see how quickly you'll pick things up, and I'm going to rely on you almost exclusively for the legal arguments. Besides, our client may have asked for me, but he *loves* you."

She rolled her eyes at me. "I'm going to go with Sorensen and Harrington," she said, "in deference to your age and experience."

"That's very generous of you."

"I try."

While Nina worked on the notice of appearance in the breakfast room, I took my coffee out to the dining room and put a call in to Marcus Jackson. Protocol was that prior counsel should hear he's being replaced, rather than get an email notification from the court system.

The woman who answered the phone at Jackson's eponymous law firm told me that Jackson would not be able to return my call for a few days, as he was engaged in "several serious matters" that required his immediate attention.

"Does he have voice mail?" I asked.

"I'm it."

"Okay, my name is Dan Sorensen. Please explain to Mr. Jackson that I'm sorry to leave this in a message, but if he's really not going to be able to return my call for several . . . days, I guess I have no choice. I've met with Legally Dead—Nelson Patterson—and he wants to substitute us in for Mr. Jackson."

I'm not sure what type of reaction I expected, but the loss of the firm's marquee client should have engendered some comment. All I got, however, was a very bored-sounding, "What is your number and could you spell your name, please."

Next I called Matt Brooks's office at Capital Punishment Records. It was a rerun of my call with Jackson's office. Brooks's assistant told me that Brooks was out of town but would get back to me shortly. Like with Jackson, I wasn't going to hold my breath.

"Well, I'm done for the day," I said when I came back into the breakfast room less than five minutes later. "I left messages for Jackson and Brooks. Want to bet which one calls back first? Or if either one ever bothers calling back?"

"So what do we do now?" Nina asked.

I paused for a moment, making a mental checklist of the things we'd need to represent Legally Dead. "Well . . . since we're flying under the radar for now, I don't want to call the prosecutor just yet. But we could start to think about lining up an expert. We'll need a forensic guy."

"The only MEs I know are on television," Nina said with a smile.

"I have a list somewhere of the guys we used at Taylor Beckett. Since you're a little more up to speed about our client and his music, why don't we divide things up like this—you call the potential MEs and line up some interviews, and I'll do some work on Google and find out what I can about Legally Dead?"

Less than a second after I typed "Legally Dead" into Google, over three million hits popped up. Even limiting it to "Legally Dead rapper" or "Legally Dead Roxanne" or "Legally Dead murderer" didn't significantly reduce the number.

I clicked on the first site listed and began to read.

The first thing I learned (aside from L.D.'s penchant for being photographed shirtless) was that he acquired his moniker when he was fifteen. A drug deal he was involved in went bad, and he ended up getting shot four times—once each in the neck and upper thigh and twice in the torso (above and below the rib cage). For a guy who seemingly never caught a break in his life—no father, mother dead of a drug overdose before he could walk, in and out of foster care—it was nothing short of a miracle that none of the bullets pierced anything vital. The story is that one of the paramedics at the scene pronounced him "legally dead," which didn't make a lot of sense to me because it's a phrase with no medical significance, but when he survived, the nickname stuck.

From there I went to L.D.'s Wikipedia entry. A

section labeled "Recordings" listed his one and only album as *First Kill All the Hos*. Lovely, I thought to myself. Another thing we'd have to deal with. The album "dropped" on October 30, less than a month before the murder, and had fifteen songs—"A-Rod" among them.

The full lyrics to "A-Rod" were printed. Three readings later, I still couldn't tell if it was about Roxanne or gangbangers or something else entirely. It was like a Rorschach test; the listener would interpret it according to preconceived prejudices—those who thought L.D. was guilty would immediately think it was about Roxanne; anyone who believed he was innocent could find a half-dozen alternate interpretations.

The entry about Roxanne's murder was the longest at five paragraphs, but the information it contained I'd already learned from Nina—the alleged pre-Thanksgiving breakup, which led to his allegedly being disinvited to Stocks, South Carolina, for Thanksgiving, which led to the alleged post-Thanksgiving confrontation upon Roxanne's return to New York, which led to L.D.'s allegedly grabbing the baseball bat Roxanne had been given for singing the national anthem at the World Series, and then allegedly beating her to death with it before he allegedly got rid of the murder weapon.

I surfed through another ten or so websites, but found nothing new. Interestingly, none of the sites mentioned that L.D. had a daughter, which gave me some faith that not everything was publicly available in cyberspace.

When I reentered the living room, Nina was still on the phone, but smiling. She held up her index finger, telling me that she wouldn't be long.

"Okay," she said into the phone. "I understand. And thank you. Good-bye."

When she put down her cell, I said, "Does your smile mean we have an expert?"

"Sure do. The three names you gave me were all noes. One claimed to be too busy, and the other two said there was a conflict. But the last guy told me to call a guy named Marty"—she looked for her note-pad—"Popofsky. He just left the ME's office."

"And he's willing to consider coming aboard?"

"Better than that. He'll be here at four."

7

As we waited for Popofsky to arrive, I got an unexpected call.

"Hold one moment, please," a woman's voice replied after I said hello.

The next thing I heard was "This is Matt Brooks."

My first thought was that I was being punk'd. That's how unlikely I found it that Matt Brooks would be returning my phone call.

"Thanks for calling, Mr. Brooks," I said, somewhat tentatively. "I reached out to you because my partner and I are about to come in for Marcus Jackson as counsel of record for Legally Dead."

"Let me stop you right there, Counselor. You need to call me Matt, okay?"

Brooks's voice was confident and encouraging. It was more than just a pleasant surprise. It was something of a shock, actually. Not only did I not expect him to return the call but I had imagined that if he did call back, he'd be hostile, considering that our client stood accused of murdering his label's biggest star.

"Of course," I said.

"I've checked up on you a little bit, and I must say, L.D. is very lucky to have you in his corner. I know you did wonders for Darrius Macy."

There was a time when someone knowing your

professional accomplishments in a first phone call was disconcerting, like they'd run a background check on you, but now all it takes is plugging your name into a search engine, and voilà, instant biography. Anyway, I was reasonably sure I knew a lot more about Matt Brooks than he knew about me.

"I'm hoping I can help L.D. the same way," I said. "He's an innocent man."

It was the first time I'd said it out loud. The words flowed easily, as if I actually believed what I was saying, which made me wonder if, at least on some level, I did.

"So, what can I do to help you in your noble endeavor?"

"I'd like to meet with you, Mr. . . . Matt."

He didn't hesitate. "Sure thing, Dan. Right now I'm in Atlantic City. My man Looming Large is performing at the Borgata tonight, and I got to represent, as they say. Unfortunately, I'm getting on a plane right after the show, and I'm not going to be back in the country until after the New Year."

No wonder he called me back. I had little doubt that when I called him after the New Year, he'd string me along for a few more weeks before finally telling me that, upon further reflection, it was bad PR for him to help out L.D.'s defense. No hard feelings, right?

"Can we fix a definite date to meet upon your return?" I asked, awaiting some excuse about how much was up in the air or whatever he came up with.

But he surprised me. "Why put it off, Dan? Can you come down here tonight?"

I looked at my watch. I'd need an hour, maybe two, with Popofsky, and figured the drive to Atlantic City would be about three hours.

"I've got a meeting starting in about ten minutes," I said, "but we could drive down right after that. Depending on traffic, I think we could be there by nine."

He laughed. "Traffic?" And then he laughed again. "You know that line in *Back to the Future*?"

"What?" I said, although I understood him.

"At the end of the movie *Back to the Future*, Michael J. Fox? The inventor guy says, 'Roads? Where we're going, we don't need any roads'?"

"Yeah, I remember," I said.

"Well, you go down to the heliport on Wall Street. My Sikorsky will be there. Takes less than an hour."

He didn't expand on what his Sikorsky was, but I figured it was a helicopter, seeing that we were meeting him at the heliport.

"Okay. Thank you. I'm also going to be bringing my partner, Nina Harrington."

"The more, the merrier. Looking forward to meeting the both of you. Come find me at the poker tables."

Marty Popofsky was at my door exactly at four.

An expert willing to come over upon request was always a good sign, because it meant he didn't have a lot of other things to fill up his day. The more hungry for paying work, the more likely the expert will give you the opinion you want, because he knows that if he doesn't, you'll find someone else who will.

As soon as I opened the door, however, I realized that no matter what came out of Marty Popofsky's mouth, we had some work to do before he'd be ready for prime time. He was wearing a New York Mets baseball cap and a suit that looked like it had been slept in. When he took off the hat, he revealed a comb-over that he smoothed into place with his hands.

"Thanks for making time to meet us on such short notice," I said, extending my hand.

"My pleasure," Popofsky said. "I figured, no time like the present, right?"

At least his voice was good, deep and confident. How an expert sounds makes up a lot for how he looks. The initial impression of his appearance lasts a second, but then the jury hears what he has to say for hours.

The meeting was more like a first date than anything else, just getting to know each other. I told him the basic facts of the case that had appeared in the press, none of which he seemed too familiar with. I chuckled at the thought that he'd be our ideal juror—the last man on earth who did not have preconceived prejudices about the case.

"We're looking for a full-service guy," I said, "to give us an opinion on cause of death, analysis of blood spatter, the whole nine yards. The prosecution's theory is that the murder weapon is the baseball bat Roxanne had in her bedroom, but the police never found it. So we'll also need you to analyze splinters, if there are any."

"If they haven't found the bat, why do they think it's the murder weapon?" Popofsky asked.

"Because of the song," Nina said.

From the blank look on Popofsky's face I could tell that he had no idea what she was talking about. Nina pulled out her iPhone. A few touches later, the pounding beat of L.D.'s music was blaring, and then his staccato rhyming began.

> Gonna stop you when you sing,
> gonna give it til you scream;
> don't like what you said,
> gonna go A-Rod on your head.

Popofsky didn't even blanch. It was as if he didn't fully understand what the words meant, and then it occurred to me that he just might not.

"'Going A-Rod'," I said, "is a reference to beating someone with a baseball bat. A takeoff on Alex Rodriguez, the Yankee third baseman, who's known as A-Rod."

"Oh, I got that part," Popofsky said, "even though I'm a Mets fan. Although the way that guy's been playing lately, it just as well could mean that he swung and missed." Popofsky chuckled at his joke, and then said, "But the thing I don't get is, why'd she have a baseball bat in her bedroom? That's kind of strange for a woman, isn't it?"

"Not really," Nina answered. "She sang at the opening game of the World Series, and the teams presented it to her. It was signed by the players or something."

"Oh," he said. "I saw the game, but I guess I didn't

pay much attention to who sang the national anthem. I never heard of any of those pop stars, anyway."

"So, is this all something you can help us with?" I asked.

"I don't see why not," he said cheerfully. "It's all within my area of expertise. In fact, I can tell you right now, if the murder weapon was a baseball bat, there probably won't be any evidence of it in the victim's skull. Major-league bats are made out of northern white ash, and they just don't splinter when they come in contact with a human skull." He shrugged. "That's the kind of information you acquire from twenty-plus years in a coroner's office. Sad to say, this won't be my first baseball-bat murder. So I'm pretty confident that I'll be able to tell you everything that good ol' Harry Davis tells them."

"Who?" Nina asked.

Popofsky chuckled. "I guess he's not a household name outside of the forensics world. Harry Davis is the head of the city's medical examiner's office. And I tell you, a bigger SOB you'll never meet. The guy was my boss for twenty years. And don't ask me how I lasted that long."

"How does he come off in front of a jury?" I asked.

"He's very smart. Even more arrogant, though. Product of the New York City public school system, something I bet you he mentions within the first thirty seconds of his testimony. He's very proud of that. For the past . . . I don't know how long, Davis's main job function has been to serve as a professional witness. Others in the office, which up until a month ago included me, do the work, and when it's showtime, Dr. Harry Davis steps out in front of the cameras and reveals the findings."

"Here's my first bit of legal advice, Marty. You don't have to outexpert him. All we need is for you to fight him to a draw. If the jury's not going to be able to tell which expert is telling the truth, we'll be awfully close to reasonable doubt."

"I'll do my best," Popofsky said, now looking less confident than I would have preferred.

It was time to explain the facts of life.

"One thing that you may not have experienced when you were at the ME's office," I said, "is that there's a difference between a testifying expert and a consultation expert. Right now, we're going to retain you solely to provide consulting advice to help us as part of our legal representation. That means that what you tell us will be covered by the attorney-client privilege. Later on, we may choose to designate you as our testifying expert, at which time we'll also have to waive the privilege. That's when the real work begins, and we'll be spending a lot of time with you, preparing for testimony."

"I get it," he said with a knowing smile. "Just because I'm new to the private sector doesn't mean I don't know how the game's played. If you like my opinion, I'll be your expert. And if you don't, you'll find someone else."

Spoken like a man who's seen the light.

8

At the time, I thought Darrius Macy was going to be the case of my career.

It wasn't without good reason. Darrius Macy was that year's Cinderella story of the NFL. He'd begun the season as a walk-on at the Jets' training camp, and ended it as the Super Bowl MVP. A full-on superstar, and one with all the trappings, he was on the Wheaties box, hosted *Saturday Night Live,* and hawked half a dozen products on TV, in magazine ads, and on billboards.

And then, when it seemed like there was nowhere to go but up, the bottom fell out. A waitress named Vickie Tiernan, who worked at a fancy New York hotel, claimed that two months after his triumph, Darrius Macy, America's Mr. Everything, and a married father of three, invited her up to his hotel room and raped her.

The confluence of events that fueled Darrius Macy's meteoric rise and even greater fall began when the Jets' starting quarterback went down during the preseason, moving Macy up from third to second string. Ahead of him, however, was a former All-Pro named Michael Ross, who led the team to the playoffs with a 10-6 record. The Jets advanced through the playoffs, getting a huge break when the top-seeded Patriots fell to the wild-card Raiders, making the Jets the favorite in the AFC Championship Game. They won by ten, and headed to the Super Bowl against Chicago.

But from the Super Bowl's opening kickoff, which the Jets fumbled, it was clear that it wasn't going to be their day. In the first half, the Jets were within striking distance only once, and that drive ended with an end-zone interception that the Chicago cornerback ran all the way for a touchdown.

The score was 24–0 when, about five minutes into the third quarter, Ross was crushed under more than a thousand pounds of Bears, and left the game on a stretcher. That's when Darrius Macy came in to take his first NFL snap.

In the next twenty minutes, Macy threw for three touchdowns, bringing the Jets within three. With four and a half minutes to go, the Jets had the ball on their own twenty, when Macy engineered a final drive that left them sixteen yards from victory, with twelve seconds to go. It was enough time for one more play from scrimmage. Touchdown, and the Jets would be world champions; fail, and they'd call a time-out and go for the game-tying field goal.

That one play, however, made Macy the most famous football player in the world.

He faded back to pass, and must have seen a receiver open, because his arm shot forward, releasing the ball. But the pass was swatted at the line of scrimmage and, as if God Himself had a wager on the Jets, the ball fell back into Macy's arms.

Macy turned on a dime and scrambled to the other side of the field. By the time he was able again to look upfield for receivers, the clock read double zero—meaning that the game would end on this play. There'd be no game-tying field goal. It was now or never.

I was watching the game in my living room. For most of it, Sarah was reading, periodically asking me the score, usually after I'd shouted at the screen. But for that last drive, she was keenly focused, and even Alexa, who had been coloring on the floor for most of the second half, seemed interested in the outcome.

It was Sarah who first said, "He's going to run."

When she said it, Macy was around the twenty-yard line. "Nah, that's too far away," I said, sounding as if I was far more expert about football than I actually was.

As was usually the case when Sarah and I disagreed, she was right. Almost as soon as the words left my lips, Macy darted forward.

I've seen the play fifty times by now, and yet I could see it fifty more times and still not look away for a second. It was unbelievable, electrifying. The Bears defenders, who must have seemed miles away when Macy made the decision to head for the end zone, closed in a flash. From the camera angle, it looked as if Macy was alone in taking on the entire Bears defense. He shot to the left, and then juked to the right, like a slalom skier, weaving in and out of 350-pound men as if they were stationary gates.

Seconds before, all seemed hopeless for New York. Now it actually looked like he was going to make it. He hurdled one linesman, spun around another, and literally flew over the last two, landing safely on the other side of the goal line.

"*Yes! Yeeeeeeeessssss!*" I screamed, standing in front of the TV now, and even Sarah shouted something, because Alexa said, "What just happened?"

"The man on the television just scored a touchdown, and the Jets won the Super Bowl!" I exclaimed.

"Oh," Alexa said, putting the event in some perspective, as Sarah howled with laughter.

The next time I thought of Darrius Macy was nearly three months later, when Benjamin Ethan called me. It was a Thursday night, and as usual on Thursday nights, I was still in the office at ten p.m.

"Have you ever heard of a football player named Darrius Macy?" Ethan asked.

I remember thinking that it was almost like asking, *Have you ever heard of a president of the United States named Barack Obama?* Of course I'd heard of Darrius Macy.

"Yes" was all I actually said.

"Well, he's in lockup down at the Tombs, awaiting a seven a.m. arraignment tomorrow on rape charges. It'll be yours if you feel like meeting him down at 100 Centre Street."

"Sure," I said. "You going to meet me there?"

"No, Daniel, you'll be flying solo on this one. That all right?"

"Better than all right. How come?"

"Sadly for Mr. Macy, and, I suppose, luckily for you, he is something of a spendthrift. I'm told he can scrape together about two hundred grand, but his first priority is putting as much of that as he needs toward making bail. That means there's not going to be enough left over to pique my interest, especially to represent a rapist. But it would be great exposure for you. Lawyer to the stars, and all that."

I had no qualms about representing a rapist. He had me at "lawyer to the stars."

"That sounds great," I said.

"Well, it's not set in stone yet," Ethan said. "I suspect there'll be some pushback from the powers that be at the firm about conflicts, and, you know, the corporate guys would prefer we not represent any criminal defendants unless they're investment bankers, but if you're up for it, I'll do what I can to make it happen."

"I'm definitely up for it, Benjamin."

"Then good luck."

When I arrived the next morning at 100 Centre Street, the Manhattan Criminal Court building was bursting with reporters. They were camped outside the entrance, in the corridors, and right in front of the courtroom door, with a lucky few getting past security to have the honor of watching the proceedings.

I didn't even have the chance to introduce myself to Macy before the judge, the Honorable Jordan Ringel, a longtime fixture on the criminal bench, asked that I state my appearance for the record.

"Daniel Sorensen, of the law firm Taylor Beckett, Your Honor."

"Taylor Beckett. Nothing but the best for Mr. Macy, I see," Judge Ringel said. "So, let's see if you're going to earn your keep, Mr. Sorensen. What say you regarding the issue of bail?"

"We respectfully request that Mr. Macy be released on his own recognizance, Your Honor. Mr. Macy has a very bright future ahead of him, and there is no way he would jeopardize that by attempting to flee the jurisdiction. And as a practical matter, Mr. Macy may very well be the most recognized man in this country. There's nowhere for him to hide, and the charges against him will be known by every airport ticket taker and border patrol agent, so there's no possible way for him to flee the country. In other words, even if he were inclined to flee, which he is not, he couldn't do it."

"How do the people feel about that?" Judge Ringel asked.

The assistant district attorney handling the calendar call was someone I'd never met before. She was in her forties, and seeing how the calendar call duties usually go to a more junior lawyer, she was undoubtedly there solely for Macy.

"Nancy Wong, for the people," the prosecutor said. "Given the seriousness of the crime and the potential of a long incarceration, the people request that bail be set at five million dollars."

Most bail bondsmen require 10 percent of the bail amount down, which meant that Macy wouldn't make bail at all if I didn't get it down to $2 million.

"Your Honor," I said, "as the court well knows, bail is not punitive, but merely to ensure the defendant's appearance at trial. I am informed that Mr. Macy does not have access to considerable funds. Perhaps if bail were set at one million dollars, that would satisfy the court."

Judge Ringel laughed. "If I were Solomon, I'd split the difference. But alas, I'm not blessed with such wisdom. I'm only a lowly New York State criminal justice. That said, this justice is inclined to believe Mr. Sorensen's pitch, and so I'm going to set bail at one million dollars."

Two hours later, I left the courthouse with my newest client. We headed straight to Taylor Beckett's offices.

Macy's wife, Erica, was with us, and he insisted that she sit in on the meeting. My normal practice was to exclude spouses because they usually inhibited getting to the truth, and that went double here. No one is going to admit to a rape, or even use the defense of consensual sex, with his wife sitting next to him.

No one except Darrius Macy, that is.

"Look, I know I screwed up really bad," he said, alternating his gaze between his wife and me. "But . . . that woman, she followed me up to my room and . . . basically threw herself at me. I should have said no, so I know I'm not without blame, and it's all on me for hurting Erica and my kids, but, I swear, I did not rape her."

After Macy had denied the charges against him about ten different ways, I told Erica that I needed to spend some time alone with her husband. When she left the room, I gave him the standard criminal-defense-lawyer speech.

"It is my job to represent you zealously no matter what the facts are, Darrius. So if you're innocent or you're guilty, it doesn't change my job one way or the other. My only responsibility is to protect you. But I can't do my job unless I know the truth. More people go to jail for lying to their lawyers than for committing crimes." (Needless to say, I doubted that was actually true.) "I wasn't in the hotel room with you, and I don't have the ability to ask Vickie Tiernan what happened, so the only version of events I'm going to hear before trial is from you. And based on that, I'm going to fashion a defense and make arguments to the jury. If one fact ends up being proven wrong, then the whole defense collapses like a house of cards. Jurors, like everybody else, don't like being lied to, and they often conclude that if a defendant lies to them about *anything*, no matter how small, that means that same defendant is probably lying to them about *everything*. So if there's anything—anything at all—that you lie to me about, the odds of your being convicted go up exponentially."

"I understand," he replied calmly.

"Good. So in light of that, is there anything you

want to tell me that's different from the facts you provided when Erica was in the room?"

"No. It happened exactly like I just told you with
her here."

And I believed him. Not a little bit, either. Completely and totally—the same way Nina believed Legally Dead.

9

Nina and I arrived at the Wall Street heliport by six, and just like Matt Brooks had said, we were inside the Borgata less than an hour later.

There were ten or so poker tables on the main floor of the Borgata. Each was populated mainly by senior citizens who looked as if they had to borrow money to make the minimum bet. A far cry from the high rollers I imagined Brooks counted as his crowd.

"Is there a more private area for poker?" I asked a scantily clad cocktail waitress who was passing by with a tray full of drinks.

"Straight through those doors are the no-limit games," she said without stopping.

I had expected the high-roller area to look different from where the schnooks play, but it didn't. The carpeting was the same, and the dealers were all still wearing cheesy gold vests and red bow ties. The cocktail waitresses looked older, likely a result of a system that rewarded seniority, but they were just as scantily dressed as the younger women on the main floor. Even the gamblers seemed pretty much the same: out-of-shape men wearing tracksuits, interspersed with old ladies. Casino Royale it was not.

Amid this crowd, Matt Brooks was easy to spot. He was in the back of the room, sitting at one of the no-limit tables, attired in his trademark dark, double-breasted suit, tie, and matching pocket square. He was playing blackjack, which surprised me a bit because he'd told us to meet him at the poker tables, but he was also playing all five spots on the table, which seemed consistent with everything I'd read about him.

Even at first glance, it was obvious that Matt Brooks was the big dog in every sense of the term. It wasn't his size—even though he was seated, I could tell he was an inch or two under six feet tall—but there was something about the way he carried himself that left no doubt he was the man in charge of every interaction in which he engaged. He could fairly be described as handsome, with a swarthy complexion, strong jaw, and eyes that suggested a sharp intelligence resided behind them.

Brooks's rags-to-riches tale was something of a legend. The official history on Capital Punishment's website had it that Brooks and a guy named Ronald Johnson, whom everyone referred to as Rojo, were childhood friends from West Philadelphia. Rojo was the first act that Brooks signed, and they were fifty-fifty partners in the business. Fast-forward ten years, and just as Capital Punishment was hitting the big time, Rojo was found dead in his hotel room, likely of a drug overdose, although there were conspiracy theorists online who claimed everything from a government plot to silence his music to Brooks killing him to acquire the business.

After Rojo's death, Brooks expanded Capital Punishment, signing more mainstream acts, like

Roxanne, as well as diversifying into other businesses: a clothing line, video games, and more recently, movies. Capital Punishment was now something of a juggernaut, and likely to get even bigger, as an IPO was rumored to be just around the corner.

"Mr. Brooks," I said, "I'm Dan Sorensen. This is my partner, Nina Harrington."

Brooks lifted his eyes from his cards. He glanced fleetingly at me, and then his gaze went up and down Nina's entire body.

I had extended my hand, but he didn't take it. For a moment, I assumed it was because he didn't recognize who I was.

"We spoke earlier today," I went on. "We're counsel for Legally Dead."

He laughed. "Don't let the gray hair fool you, Dan. I'm not senile. In fact, I'm thinking maybe you have a bit of Alzheimer's, because I distinctly recall telling you to call me Matt, didn't I?"

He said this with the broadest of smiles, as if he were teasing a longtime friend. He grabbed my hand with a confident grip and pumped it.

"It's great to meet you, Dan. And you, too, Nina." Then, with a sweep of his arm, Brooks said, "Care to sit in for a few hands?"

I looked at the little plaque in the corner of the table. It read: "Minimum Bet—$1,000."

"It's a little rich for me, I'm afraid."

"Oneil," Brooks said, turning to the dealer, a thirty-something man who wore a name tag that said he was from Ocho Rios, Jamaica, "deal my friend in a hand, and I'll play the other four."

Brooks placed a single yellow chip into the small box in front of the stool on the end, which presumably was for me, because he then organized two neatly formed stacks, five yellow chips high, in each of the other four boxes. My quick math indicated that he had forty thousand dollars riding on this hand. Forty-one, if you counted the hand he was staking for me.

Oneil dealt all five hands. He was showing a six up, which gave me a little lift because, even with my limited knowledge of blackjack, I knew he'd have to hit sixteen. I was holding eighteen.

Brooks studied his cards like a general reviewing battle plans. He didn't make a commitment on any of his hands until he had seemingly decided what to do on all of them. Then, in rapid-fire succession, he said, "Split the eights and hit them both," and as each one turned into an eighteen, he gestured with his hand, holding it flat, palm down, which must have meant he didn't want any more cards, because then he said, "Double down," and pushed another ten grand into the box next to the two-card eleven. Oneil pulled the next card out of the shoe, which was a ten of clubs, giving Brooks a three-card twenty-one, but Brooks didn't let out even a hint of a smile. Then he repeated the hand signal to hold over his last two hands, an eighteen and a two-queen twenty.

"Sir?" Oneil said to me.

"No, I'm good," I said.

"You need to use a hand signal, sir. If you want to

decline another card, then hold your hand over them."

I mimicked the motion I'd seen Brooks perform, glancing over to Brooks to confirm if I was doing it correctly. He paid me no heed, however, and instead seemed transfixed by Oneil's cards, as if he could change them through the sheer power of his concentration.

Oneil turned over his hole card. The jack of hearts, which gave him sixteen.

"Dealer hits," Oneil said, and then he flipped over a deuce. "Eighteen."

In a swift movement, Oneil clicked a stack of yellow chips against Brooks's two eighteens and my own, and then paid out on Brooks's two winning hands.

"You'd already counted that one in your pocket, didn't you?" Brooks said to me, chuckling. "But that's the thing about life, isn't it?"

"What is?"

"Nothing's ever for certain."

"I suppose that's right," I said.

"Mind if we take a break," Brooks said to Oneil, without the inflection of a question. "Keep the table clear, will ya."

"Whatever you want, Mr. Brooks," Oneil answered.

Brooks got up and led us to another blackjack table nearby. This one was empty.

As we sat down, I looked up at the ceiling. Brooks must have been reading my mind, because he said, "Don't worry. Even though they record everything, it's video only. They won't know what we're saying. That's why you need to use hand signals when you're playing."

"Thank you for meeting with us," I said, "and, of course, thank you for the ride."

"Like I said, whatever I can do to help. I really appreciate that you two are willing to take on L.D." He shook his head. "I mean, talk about getting killed in the press. It's like the presumption of innocence just doesn't apply if you're a black man or a rapper, and unfortunately for L.D., he's both."

I nodded along with Brooks's comments on the racial insensitivity of our judicial system. He shook his head ruefully. "And I got to be honest with you, I feel like part of his situation is my fault, because I was the guy who told him to include 'A-Rod' on the album. You know, if he hadn't, he might not be in this mess. Or at least it wouldn't be so bad."

"Can I take that to mean that you believe he's innocent?"

Brooks grimaced slightly, followed by a subtle shrug. "How can anyone really know if someone harbors that kind of rage? So I can't tell you that. But what I can tell you is that I've always liked L.D., and the public doesn't really know the real man, if you catch my drift."

I looked over at Nina to see if she understood. The blank look on her face told me that she didn't.

"I'm not sure that we do," I said.

He let out a deep sigh, suggesting he was worried this might be a problem. But then he said nothing more, waiting for us to ask him directly.

Nina did the honors. "We've met with L.D., and he's explained his side of things. There was nothing he said that caused us to think he wasn't being candid."

Brooks seemed startled by the sound of her voice. When he turned to her, he gave her a particularly wolfish smile, and then said, "Maybe you didn't ask the right questions."

I looked at Nina, who didn't betray any reaction. When I met Brooks's eyes again, I didn't get the leer he'd just given Nina, but a contemptuous grin that belied his claim of liking L.D.

"Did you ask to see his scars?" Brooks asked.

"Excuse me?" I said.

"The scars from when he was shot four times and left for legally dead?"

"No, we didn't. Why?"

"Because there aren't any," Brooks said with a satisfied smile. "The thing is, when I met the man, his name was . . ." Brooks's pupils rolled back in his head, as if he was searching for the information in his brain. "Calvin . . . Mayberry, I think? Definitely Calvin Something-or-Other. Anyway, he was this suburban kid from outside Boston. His mother was a schoolteacher. I can't remember what his father did, but they were regular middle-class folks. Now, the kid could rap, but I told him, in this business it's as much about the backstory as it is the rhymes. And that was especially true for L.D. because his raps were hard-core, about gangs, thug life. Real throwback stuff to Tupac and Biggie, which was great, but I couldn't sell Calvin from the Boston suburbs doing that. So we did a whole character creation. Calvin Something-or-Other ceased to exist, and in his place came Nelson Patterson, more famously known as Legally Dead."

Brooks seemed far from finished, and I was content to let him talk for as long as he wanted before asking any questions, but the shock of what he was telling us was too much for Nina not to jump in. "Are you saying that everything about him is a lie?"

Brooks laughed. "I hate to break it to you, but the tooth fairy ain't real, either."

"With all due respect," I said, "every newspaper reporter and blogger is digging into L.D.'s past, and nobody's come up with this. Wouldn't there be people from his Boston past running to *TMZ* or the *National Enquirer* with the real story?"

"You don't know me, Dan, so you're going to have to take this on faith, but when I do something that I don't want people to find out about, then they don't find out about it. Simple as that. His parents are dead, and he told me he didn't have any family, so who's going to put it together? Besides, what possible reason would I have to lie to you? If L.D.'s real life goes public, it's not going to help my brand any."

"Then why tell us at all?" Nina said, making it clear that she was not buying Brooks's story, despite the logic he had just laid out.

Brooks smiled at her, a patronizing gesture that I was sure was not lost on her. "Because I know L.D. won't. He thinks once it gets out that he isn't who he says he is, that he's not some guy who was shot four times in a drug deal and left for legally dead, he's finished in this business. And the thing is, that may well be true, but he's got to see the bigger picture here. He's twenty-five years old. He's got his whole life ahead of him, and there was never any guarantee that he was going to make it in this business anyway."

I'd said this very thing to more clients than I could remember. Perhaps because the truly worst-case scenario in a criminal prosecution is beyond what most people can envision, they fixate on lesser ramifications, like losing their jobs. Those with the most to lose financially are often the worst offenders. I must have gone over this with Darrius Macy a half-dozen times, telling him that if he never got another endorsement deal again, but stayed out of jail, it would be a great result.

"We'll talk to him about that," I said, trying to make it sound as if I had no concern L.D. would tell us the truth, despite the fact it seemed like that ship had already sailed. "Another thing we wanted to raise with you was that L.D. said he hasn't received any of his royalties from the label."

"That's right," Brooks said, as if it ended the matter.

"Why not? He's earned them, right?"

"Look, as I'm sure you know, we're heading toward an IPO, and Roxanne's murder has already depressed our value. Last thing we need now is to pay L.D. for bragging about killing her."

Brooks shrugged, suggesting that this was his cross to bear, only making $5 billion rather than $10 billion. The hypocrisy that Capital Punishment was all too happy to profit off the song, so long as L.D. didn't get his share, didn't seem to matter much. It reminded me of a line from *The Godfather*—it wasn't personal, this was strictly business.

I was sure Brooks knew there was no legal basis to withhold L.D.'s royalties, but like the old saying goes, he with the gold makes the rules, and if Brooks wasn't going to pay L.D. his royalties, then we weren't going to get paid. After the trial, L.D. could sue and, after a year or so of delays by Brooks's legal team, there'd be some type of settlement, most likely involving the payment of a fraction of what was actually owed.

"What did you know about his relationship with Roxanne?" I asked.

"Not much more than anybody else. You know, none of my business, right?"

"So you don't know if they had broken up?" Nina asked.

"Do you tell the owner of your company every time you break up with a boyfriend?" Brooks waited a beat. "Same thing in our business. I only know what I've read in the papers, and I know enough never to believe what I read in the papers."

A very large man walked over to us. A bodyguard, no doubt. He whispered something in Brooks's ear.

Brooks stood, a silent statement that this meeting was over. "I'm afraid that's all the time I have this evening," he said. "Thank you for coming down here to talk with me. Both of you. As I told you, I'll be away for the holidays but will be back in my office right after the New Year, in case I can be of any further assistance."

Oneil must have been watching us, because within seconds he was in front of us. "Excuse me, Mr. Brooks, but are you ready to resume play?"

"I'm afraid I'm done for the evening, Oneil. These two just wore me out." He gave Nina a wink, and me a smile. "But let me ask you this, my friend: What's the biggest tip you ever got?"

"A thousand dollars, sir," Oneil said.

"Here's an early Christmas present for you, then."

Brooks reached into his suit-jacket pocket and pulled out two of the yellow chips. Two thousand dollars. He tossed them to Oneil.

"And the next time you see that guy who gave you a thousand, you tell him that Matt Brooks says he's a cheap bastard. You got that?"

"Yes, sir," Oneil said. "And thank you very much, Mr. Brooks."

Having uttered his exit line, Brooks walked away. I followed him with my eyes as he strode across the casino floor. He stopped intermittently to shake some hands, but didn't look back at us.

When I turned back to the table, I was met by Oneil's ear-to-ear grin. He was fingering the chips between his thumb and forefinger, almost as if they were Aladdin's lamp and by rubbing them, more good luck would come his way.

"So, who was the cheap bastard who tipped you only a thousand dollars?" I asked when I was confident Brooks was too far away to hear me.

"Mr. Brooks, last night," Oneil said, still grinning.

10

Nina had previously joked that one advantage of working out of the apartment was I could show up in my pajamas, but I decided that part of my new lawyer life meant I needed to dress the part, even if it was only for Nina. I didn't take it to the extreme of putting on a tie, but a suit and dress shirt did the trick of making me feel like a professional.

So when I woke up the morning after our trip to Atlantic City, the first thing I did was make coffee. Then I showered and got dressed, just like a respectable citizen. I even ran out for milk and Sweet'N Low and made it back before Nina arrived.

The noise level in the helicopter on the ride home didn't allow for much conversation, and with Matt Brooks's personal pilot sitting just inches from us, that was more reason to not even try. We arrived back in the city at close to eleven, both of us tired, and so we decided to sleep on what we'd heard and talk about it in the morning.

The one thing I did upon returning home, however, was scour the internet looking for a picture of L.D. that showed his scars. Even if I'd known what bullet scars looked like, it wouldn't have mattered; given that he was so covered in tattoos, any scars would have been well hidden.

Apparently our time of reflection had yielded different conclusions about what Brooks's disclosure meant. Even before she'd taken a sip of the coffee I'd just handed her, Nina started telling me how she thought what Brooks had told us was really good news.

"The way I see it, one of the biggest obstacles we had in this case was that everybody thinks L.D.'s the kind of guy who would do something like this," she said. "And the reason they think that is because of his supposed background as a true-life gangster, which, in turn, causes everyone to assume that his lyrics are autobiographical, and that leads directly to them thinking that 'A-Rod' is a promise to kill Roxanne. But if it's made up, all of that goes away. He's not a natural-born killer; he's just some kid from the suburbs who's never been in trouble with the law before. You know, we can also play up the Brianna angle, show him as a good father, maybe."

I'd thought of this as well, and it made a lot of sense. At the same time, Brooks's disclosure bothered me, for reasons that Nina hadn't addressed.

"Why do you think L.D. didn't tell us about all this himself?" I asked.

"I guess for the same reason that Brooks said: he's worried it'll end his career."

"So it doesn't bother you that the guy lied to us?"

She smiled at me, but it wasn't the captivating one I'd seen before. This smile suggested only that I was being naive.

"I don't believe he's a murderer, Dan, but that

doesn't mean I think he's an altar boy. And when good facts are handed to you, I prefer not to look them in the mouth. This is a good development. It's even better than that. It's a veritable cause for celebration. Our client's not a thug, and the crazy rantings in his songs don't describe his real-life experiences. So is that technically a lie? Sure. But that's also the music industry, I think."

I felt as if I was about to take the first step down a very slippery slope—believing our client when he proclaimed his innocence, even while we knew he'd lied to us about other things. It's a road I'd traveled down before, and I'd vowed not to take that path again.

"Once we file our notice of appearance, there'll likely be no getting out for us," I said. "One counsel switch a judge will let go, but two and they think the defendant is trying to delay."

Nina didn't respond, at least not at first. She took a long sip of coffee, as if she was waiting for me to say something else.

When I didn't, she said, "If you want out, that's your call."

"I frankly expected a much harder sell from you than that."

"Like I said to you the other day, there are lots of reasons to take this case, one of them being that he's innocent. But that's not the only one. And even though I believe him, you need to have your own reasons, because I don't want you to have any regrets about doing this. Life's too short for that, right?"

I couldn't help but wonder whether Nina intentionally used that phrasing to invoke Sarah and Alexa, but decided that sometimes a cigar is just a cigar, and not everything has a deeper meaning. Which brought me back to why I was taking the case in the first place. Whether he was called Legally Dead or Calvin Mayberry, he was still my best, maybe last, chance to put my life back on track.

And so, at exactly 3:00 p.m. that afternoon, Nina hit the send button, which transmitted our official notice to the court system that the law firm of Sorensen and Harrington would substitute for Marcus Jackson as counsel of record for Nelson Patterson.

As I expected, within minutes the feeding frenzy began. My phone was buzzing nonstop, and by the time I checked my BlackBerry at 3:10, I'd received more than a hundred emails. I let the calls go directly to voice mail and looked at enough of the email messages to assume they'd all be exactly the same—the sender identified him- or herself and the news agency at which he or she was employed, and requested an interview, either on or off the record.

I didn't respond to any of them. Although sometimes playing the press is to a defendant's advantage, it usually doesn't work that way. At least not beyond a single statement proclaiming your client's innocence, which is what I'd be doing in court the next day, when we made our first in-person appearance in the case.

So instead of getting back to any of the reporters, I reached out to someone who really did matter—the assistant district attorney handling the case, Lisa Kaplan.

Assistant district attorneys usually answer their own phones because, by and large, they don't have secretarial support. The more annoying ADAs made a point of always letting calls go to voice mail so that they were never caught unprepared. At least Lisa Kaplan wasn't one of them, I thought, when she answered on the first ring.

Before dialing her number, I'd googled her, but because Lisa Kaplan is a common name, I couldn't tell if any of the thousands of hits was the one I needed on the other end of the phone. When I changed the search to "Lisa Kaplan ADA," all Google retrieved was two appellate briefs she filed ten years ago. As a result, I had no idea about the usual things you know about your adversary—age, pedigree, reputation. The fact that she was handling a high-profile murder case, however, most likely meant she was a veteran of the District Attorney's office and very, very good.

Nina was sitting next to me at my dining room table for this call. I told her I'd put Kaplan on speakerphone after I introduced myself.

"Hello. My name is Daniel Sorensen. I just entered a notice of appearance on behalf of Nelson Patterson."

"What can I do for you, Mr. Sorensen?" Kaplan said in an all-business tone.

"I called to introduce myself and my partner, Nina Harrington. She's actually here beside me, so, with your permission, I'd like to put you on speaker."

Kaplan didn't respond, which I interpreted to be tacit consent. "Ms. Kaplan, you're now on speakerphone." I expected her to say that I should call her Lisa, but she didn't. "Let me introduce you to my partner, Nina Harrington."

"Hi," Nina said enthusiastically into the speaker.

"What can I do for the two of you?" Kaplan said in a monotone, sounding like she had much better things to do than talk to the likes of us.

"We're going to ask the court for a reduction in bail," I said in what Alexa used to refer to as my "lawyer voice."

"Good for you," she said. "Now, is there anything *I* can help you with?"

"We'd like to examine the crime scene," I said.

"Fine. Tell me when and we'll meet you there."

"No. We'd like to do it unsupervised."

"I'm sorry, Counselor, but that's not going to happen. We have concerns about the integrity of the evidence."

I started to explain why her presence infringed on my client's rights and was about to cite case law that supported our position when Kaplan began talking over me.

"There's no need, Mr. Sorensen. I know you're trying to represent your client, but I'm very busy at the moment and I've already told you no. So if you want a different answer, it's going to have to come from Judge Pielmeier, because I'm not going to give it to you. Now, if you'll excuse me, I really have to go."

She hung up without saying good-bye.

After Kaplan, I tried Marcus Jackson's office again. But Jackson's receptionist repeated the same mantra I'd been hearing for the past three days—*Mr. Jackson is very busy, but I'll be sure to give him the message and he'll contact you as soon as he's got some available time.*

The time had come for me to take a stronger stand.

"Please convey to Mr. Jackson that, while I know he's a busy man, he also has a fiduciary duty to his former client. We have a court appearance before Judge Pielmeier tomorrow, and if I haven't met with Mr. Jackson prior to then, I'll have no choice but to raise the issue with the judge."

"I'll give Mr. Jackson your message," the receptionist said, sounding unfazed by my threat.

But it must have worked, because she called back at four thirty.

"I was able to get ahold of Mr. Jackson," she said, acting as if he was somewhere in the rain forest, rather than—as was far more likely—sitting in the office right next to her. "He is able to make some time available this afternoon, from five to five fifteen."

"He's going to give me fifteen minutes, and only if I drop everything and run over there right now?" I asked, straining to keep the annoyance out of my voice.

"I can only tell you what he told me," she said. "Are you available at five? If you're not, I'm supposed to give that slot to someone else."

11

To say that Marcus Jackson was a well-known criminal defense attorney would be akin to saying that McDonald's is a popular restaurant. For many in trouble with the law, especially African-American celebrities, he wasn't just on the short list of lawyers to consider—he *was* the list. That he was African-American himself had something to do with it, but there was no denying that he was magical in front of a jury.

Jackson practiced out of a town house in Greenwich Village. It was untraditional, but he had reached a point in his career when he could show up to court naked and have it described as just another aspect of the out-of-the-box thinking that got him results.

The parlor-floor reception area looked like Santa's workshop. Not only did a sixteen-foot tree sit in the center of the room, but there was actually fake snow on the ground and a model train set running a continuous loop around a Christmas village. The receptionist, a beautiful young African-American woman, even wore a green felt hat and pointy elf ears.

Nina and I arrived at 4:55, and we were left to cool our heels for another forty-five minutes. Apparently Jackson's five-to-five-fifteen window of availability was not as set in stone as we'd been led to believe.

At 5:40, Jackson's assistant, another gorgeous

African-American woman in an elf hat and ears, told us he was ready for us. We followed her up a sweeping marble staircase to the town house's second floor.

Jackson's personal office was probably more than fifty feet long. It had two roaring fireplaces, one opposite his desk under the window, the other anchoring the seating area near the door.

At first I didn't notice the woman seated in front of the fire. When I did, the yellow legal pad in her lap was a dead giveaway that she was his associate, and like everyone we'd encountered thus far at the firm, she, too, was African-American, and a woman, and beautiful. Fortunately for her, the elf getup was apparently not part of the dress code for attorneys. She was the first professionally attired person we'd encountered, and that included Jackson himself, who was wearing a silver suit, a shirt-and-tie combination of fifteen different colors, and a Rolex encrusted with diamonds.

"Please, have a seat," Marcus Jackson said.

He got up from behind an enormous desk and made his way over to the seating area. He was a mountain of a man, carrying what must have been close to three hundred pounds on his six-and-a-half-foot frame.

I introduced Nina, and Jackson pointed to the woman on the sofa and, in a deep voice, said, "This is my associate, Samantha Kingsley." As she extended her hand to shake mine, Jackson added, "Sam, these are the good people who mercifully replaced us as counsel for our favorite client, Mr. Nelson Patterson."

This bit of rhetoric was more for our benefit than for Ms. Kingsley's, something that Jackson didn't make much effort to camouflage by the way he glared at me as he said it. "Now, this fella here was getting ready to tattle on me to Judge Pielmeier," he continued, while pointing at me as if she had no idea to whom Jackson was referring. "But, Dan, as God is my witness, I will cooperate with you as much as possible."

I tried not to laugh. If one thing was certain, it was that Marcus Jackson was not cooperating with me as much as possible. But rule number one for a lawyer is to not piss off anyone from whom you want something, at least not until after you've gotten it. That's true whether you're talking to your client, a witness on the stand, or, as in this case, preceding counsel. If I started off too aggressively, Jackson would just shut down, and then I'd get nothing.

So I sucked it up.

"We certainly appreciate your cooperation," I said. "I apologize if I was too insistent, but we're before Judge Pielmeier tomorrow. As I'm sure you know, she's got a reputation for ripping the heads off lawyers who show up unprepared."

"I've been there," Jackson said, "so you have my unqualified sympathy." He looked at his watch. "And you've also got my undivided attention for the next few minutes. Unfortunately, I've got a client I have to meet out of the office at six."

That gave us, at most, ten minutes. Better get to it.

"I just need to ask you a few questions."

"Ask and ye shall receive," Jackson said, extending his arms out to suggest he was willing to reveal all.

"Did you and the ADA have any discussions? Either about the evidence or the possibility of a plea?"

"Ah, the lovely Ms. Kaplan," Jackson said as if he were recalling a college girlfriend. "The one and only time I spoke with her was after the arraignment. She didn't say anything beyond the usual DA blather—there wasn't much room to negotiate because her evidence was rock solid, and given the high-profile nature of the case, the DA would rather lose on a murder charge than be seen as soft on celebrities. I told her that L.D. wasn't much of a celebrity, given that the most celebrated thing the guy had done was to get himself charged with murder, but I took her point. And that was the sum total of my contact with her."

"Did you talk to L.D. about his past at all?" Nina asked.

"I'm not sure what you mean."

"Just background stuff. How he got his name. Where he's from. That kind of thing."

Jackson looked over to his associate. My guess was that he left the gathering of background information to her, which meant that he'd blame her if they'd missed something. She offered an almost imperceptible nod, suggesting she'd covered all the essentials.

"Sure we did," Jackson said, as if he knew firsthand. "What of it?"

That answered that question. L.D. apparently hadn't told Jackson the truth, either.

"Nothing," I said. "Just trying to make sure we're on the same page, that's all. L.D. also told us that you were pressuring him to take a plea."

I thought I'd said this nonchalantly, but it was clear that Jackson didn't take it that way. He leaned closer to me, challenge in his eyes.

"How many murder cases have you tried?" he said.

"Not as many as you, I must admit."

"What I hear is you haven't done as many as anyone who's ever done one, my friend. Now me, I've done thirty. All over this country. And I've got a pretty good winning percentage. So I don't appreciate being told by some guy who was formerly at the law firm of White Shoe and Tight Ass how to handle a murder case. And yeah, I know what you did for Darrius Macy. But rape ain't murder, and one case ain't a career. So if you really want to know why I wanted L.D. to plead, I'd appreciate it if you'd just ask me, you know, like a man would, rather than hiding behind what L.D. told you."

He stopped, as if this were a question that required an answer.

"Why did you want L.D. to plead?" I finally said in as strong a voice as I could muster.

"Because he told me that he killed her, and I thought a plea was the only way he'd ever see the sun again."

The words hit me like a punch to the gut.

"*What?*"

"You heard me right. Mr. Nelson Patterson told me that he beat Roxanne to death with a baseball bat."

"He confessed to you?" Nina asked, sounding like she was in shock.

"That's what I just said, isn't it? He sat right where Mr. Sorensen is sitting now and he told me that when Roxanne went down to see her family for Thanksgiving, she told him that he wasn't welcome. 'Disrespected' him, was the way he phrased it. That's a big thing with L.D.—not being *disrespected*. Anyway, when she came back, he said, he went to her place, they got into a fight, and he just lost it. He claimed that it was only after the press made the connection that he even thought about the 'A-Rod' song." Jackson let out a hearty bellow of a laugh. "So I guess that was one thing he was telling the truth about. He didn't mean the song to be about Roxanne."

I'm experienced enough to know that clients lie to their lawyers all the time, but even though I'd been told a day earlier how L.D. lied to us about his name, the fact that he'd confessed to Jackson and then lied to Nina and me took me completely aback. Most clients maintain the charade of innocence until the facts leave little other conclusion, and some hold on to it even after that.

Jackson kept talking. "I told L.D. that we had a triable case still, but it would be tougher to win now because putting him on the stand was no longer an option. I don't think he'd realized that confessing to me meant that he could no longer testify, at least about being innocent, because he kept telling me

that celebrities don't go to jail if they claim they're innocent. But like I told Ms. Kaplan, L.D. really wasn't
much of a celebrity, and that was now beside the point
because there was no way I was letting him take the
stand and commit perjury. He wouldn't budge. So I
told him to find someone else. And I guess that's you.
And here we are."

"You fired him?" I asked, sounding incredulous.

He smiled at me, a condescending gesture if ever
there was one. "Maybe it's something in your law
firm's water. You seem as hard of hearing as your partner over there."

Nina came to my defense. "L.D. told us that he was
the one who wanted to make the switch."

"Oh, *L.D. said*," Jackson said with a self-satisfied
smirk. "Well, no reason for you guys not to believe
the word of an accused murderer over me, a guy who's
been practicing law in this town for more than thirty
years."

Jackson laughed again, but I found nothing hu-
morous about the sudden turn of events. In fact, I
was pretty sick to my stomach right now.

He shook his head, more in sadness than in anger,
it seemed. "Look, I'm only telling you two because
the privilege remains when it's shared between lawyers for the same client. You don't have to believe
me, of course, and so if L.D. continues to claim he's
innocent, by all means, put him on the stand. I'm
never going to divulge his communications with me,
and even if he were to waive the privilege, you could

always say that you didn't believe me. So you're good to put on whatever defense you want. But you asked why I advised L.D. to take a plea, and that's why."

Jackson checked his watch, although I was relatively certain it was more for show than to find out if he was late for his off-site meeting. If he even had an off-site meeting, that is. He'd said his piece, and now there was no reason for him to spend another second with us.

"I'm sorry to have to cut this short, but I've got another appointment," he said, standing up. Ms. Kingsley rose with him, and so Nina and I had little choice but to follow suit. This meeting was over.

It was just as well. There wasn't much more for us to talk about now. I'd shown up at Jackson's office with one set of facts in my mind and was leaving with a completely different set.

Jackson walked us to the door of his office. "I'm sorry if we got off on the wrong foot, Dan. You know, so many of the decisions you make as a criminal defense lawyer are based on facts that no one knows about and you can never reveal. So sometimes you look like you haven't done your job when you let your client take a plea where he gets twenty-five to life, but that's only because no one knows that the only reason you're letting him do it is because he's already admitted to you about six other killings, and so you've spared him the needle. Like I always tell people, being a criminal defense lawyer is the only job there is where you can't brag about your greatest successes."

He extended his hand to me with an expression that said bygones should be bygones. After a slight hesitation, I took it.

"Sorry I was the one who had to be the bearer of bad news," he said, "but you honestly need to know who you're dealing with. You've heard his songs, right? Not just 'A-Rod' but the others?" I nodded to tell him we had. "Then you have a pretty clear picture of what he's all about. Some guys know the whole gangsta thing—you know, bragging about capping folks and ranting about bitches and hos—is all a put-on, but not him. L.D.'s the kind of guy . . ." Jackson paused, as if he was trying to think of the right words, and then he said, "No way to say it except the way it is—he's the kind of guy who would beat to death the woman he claimed to love."

12

I offered to hail a cab, but despite the fact that the weather was probably below freezing, Nina said she wanted to walk. Her pained expression told me that she was taking Jackson's revelation hard.

We walked in silence for a few blocks. When we'd reached Houston Street, Nina finally spoke.

"I don't believe him," she said flatly. "I bet you he's claiming that L.D. confessed because he's trying to save face about getting fired."

The frigid air caused her words to leave a trail of fog. She was shivering slightly, and I felt the cold chill run through my hair.

"Maybe," I said with skepticism. "It's an odd thing for him to say, though. I'm sure Jackson's been fired from other cases. There's no reason to drag your client through the mud on your way out."

"This is a very high-profile case, and it's going to look like L.D. fired him because he wasn't cutting it," Nina said. "And Jackson's a guy who clearly thinks a lot of himself. Besides, why would L.D. lie to Jackson about his backstory but confess to murder? It doesn't make any sense."

Unfortunately, it made perfect sense to me. I was all too well versed in the ancient art of lying to yourself. The things you say to be able to go on living the way you want to live. For me, it had been that work needed me more than my family did, or that I was doing the right thing when I pressed ahead with the Darrius Macy case. For L.D., it meant telling everyone he was shot and left for dead.

No, I didn't see anything inconsistent in sticking with the persona you've created for yourself, even as you confessed to murder. In fact, in some twisted way, L.D. might have even believed that the only way his killing Roxanne actually made sense was if Legally Dead had done it. No way Calvin from the Boston suburbs even gets close to a pop star, much less beats her to death.

Nina's shivering was becoming more pronounced, and I had the distinct impression that she wasn't going to move until I agreed with her. So I kept all this pop psychology to myself.

"Okay, I'm with you," I said, although my tone clearly told her the opposite. "Jackson's lying to us, and L.D. never confessed to him. Can we go inside now?"

"Thanks for nothing," she said with a grin. "Okay, let's go inside."

When we entered my apartment, I immediately went to pour myself a drink. I'd had a very rough day, by anybody's standards.

I actually had my hand on the bottle of scotch when Nina said, "Hold off, okay? Let me make us some cocoa instead."

I smiled. "It's not the same thing, you know?"

"I know. Cocoa is better. Especially when I make it. I don't use that powdered junk. I'm a purist. Milk and chocolate syrup, if you have it."

"I do."

"Excellent. And if you're lucky, I'll add a dash of cinnamon."

It occurred to me then that it had been two days since I'd had a drink. The last time being at lunch with Nina, after we'd met with Legally Dead for the first time. In other words, I hadn't had a drink since the case had begun.

Maybe cocoa would be better, I thought.

Apparently I was lucky, because I detected the cinnamon from the first sip. Nina was holding her cup with both hands, which was the way both Sarah and Alexa drank cocoa. Without making any mention of it, I changed my own grip. The warmth, first from the cup in my palms and then from the cocoa, spread throughout my body.

"Thanks," I said. "This is really good."

"You're welcome. Can we talk a little more about what Jackson said?"

"Sure."

Her brow was furrowed and her eyes narrow. For the first time since I'd agreed to take on the case, Nina seemed sincerely worried about the outcome.

I found it endearing. I'd learned the hard way that the outcomes of criminal trials don't turn on the truth. Never have, and never will.

"I hope it isn't going to change your view about

how we defend L.D.," Nina said. "He's got to testify if we're going to have any chance."

"Jackson's right about our ethical duty. L.D. hasn't confessed to us, so we're within our rights to believe that he's innocent, and that means we're not suborning perjury if we let him testify to that."

"Good," she said with obvious relief.

"Don't misunderstand me, though. I'm not saying we should put him on. Just that we're not ethically prohibited from doing so. It's still way too early to make the decision about whether he'll be able to stand up to a strong cross-examination."

"Okay," she said, sounding disappointed. "But we need to start developing a defense, don't we?"

"No worries there, Nina. There's only one type of defense that ever works in a murder case," I said with a sly smile.

She smiled back. "Yeah, what's that?"

"The tried-and-true SODDI defense."

"Is that Latin?"

"No, it's an acronym," I said with a chortle, pleased that she fell into the joke. "It means Some Other Dude Did It."

"Do you have another dude in mind?"

"No." I laughed. "But we better find one. In my mind, our only shot at an acquittal is if we give the jury enough so that they can blame someone else. In a high-profile case like this, I just don't think it's realistic to expect an acquittal based on reasonable doubt alone. I mean, do you see a juror appearing on *Dateline* after the trial explaining that he or she thought L.D. was guilty but still voted to acquit because the prosecution hadn't met its burden of proof? But if we can plausibly point the finger at someone else, they'll say, 'I thought that other dude might have done it.' Or, 'I was really troubled that the prosecution didn't focus more on that other guy. It seemed to me that they rushed to judgment on Legally Dead because of the song.'"

"Okay," Nina said. "That makes me feel better."

Despite what she said, she didn't seem to be at any greater ease. She sat with her arms folded, her legs crossed, as if she was wary. Although she didn't tell me what she was thinking, I had a pretty good idea: She was wondering whether, despite what I'd just said about our defense, I believed Jackson. If I thought we were representing the guy who did it.

The truth was, I didn't know.

13

A few days before Darrius Macy's trial, his wife came to my office to prepare for her testimony. I'd previously told Erica that a lot was riding on her, not only because jurors would be apt to think that if the wife believes the sex was consensual, then who are they to think otherwise, but also because Erica could directly rebut Vickie Tiernan's claim that she fought Darrius, scratching him to the point of breaking skin. Erica's testimony that she saw no such marks on her husband would go a long way to showing that there was no force used by Darrius.

I knew from the moment I met Erica's eyes, however, that she had a different agenda.

"I need to talk to you about Darrius," she said, closing my office door behind her.

A shrink might say that I knew what was coming, but I tend to think that it's just an occupational hazard to set ground rules before I talk to anyone in my office. Especially when my visitor makes a point of closing the door behind her.

"I'm happy to talk with you, Erica, but you need to remember that I'm not your lawyer, I'm Darrius's. The attorney-client privilege doesn't apply to what you tell me, and I have a duty to report it back to your husband."

In a cold voice, she said, "I don't care."

Since our first meeting the day Darrius was released on bail, I'd had only sporadic contact with Erica. Darrius usually came to our meetings alone, and so my interaction with Erica was in passing, when we said hello or chatted briefly on those occasions when she met Darrius at my office. Even so, I saw her enough to know that Erica was the worrier in the marriage. As a criminal defense attorney, I had probably seen as much marital tension as a couples counselor. If the indicted share a common personality trait, it's that they're not the kind of people who spend a lot of time pondering worst-case scenarios. Perhaps it's social Darwinism at work—or just plain irony—but they often marry people who spend a lot of time considering the downside risk.

"Okay, so . . . what's up?" I asked.

"I don't think I can go through with this."

I smiled, hoping to put her at ease. "Everyone gets nervous before they testify, but a few questions in, the butterflies go away. Then it just seems like a conversation."

"That's not what I mean. I'm not nervous. It's just . . . I've got to find a way for all of this to stop. If I don't, it's going to keep happening, again and again."

"I don't see what you can do to prevent this type of thing from happening, Erica. Sometimes people are falsely accused, and celebrities are natural targets for that sort of thing. Needless to say, Darrius should stay out of situations that might give rise to such a possibility, and he clearly made a mistake by putting himself in a compromising position with this woman, but given how badly he feels about it, I'm sure that's not going to happen again."

She laughed, but it was not because she thought anything I'd said was funny. Rather, it was to express contempt.

"You don't know?" she said. It was as much an accusation as a question.

"Know what?"

"You don't really think Darrius is innocent, do you?"

I didn't know what to say. Of course I thought he was innocent. He'd been telling me that nonstop for months, and she'd confirmed it the few times we'd spoken.

She looked at me like I was pathetic. "Well, here's a news flash for you: he's guilty. Guilty as they come."

My heart dropped like a rock, and I felt a cold sweat break out just below my hairline. I should have stopped her right there. There was nothing in it for me to find out that my client—who I was about to put on the stand to swear to his innocence—was actually an honest-to-God rapist.

But something inside me needed to know.

"What do you mean, he's guilty?"

"Do you have any idea how many women have accused Darrius of rape in the past two years?"

I just shook my head no.

"Three." Her faced tightened, and she bit down on her lip in an effort to hold back her rage. "Okay?

Three. And he always picked these poor little things, and so ten grand was like a million to them. Once he paid them off, they usually stayed quiet, and if one of them asked for a little more, he'd throw another few thousand at her. You know, I think Darrius thought of them as high-priced hookers. They'd say something nice to him or something, and maybe they were flirting, but he thought that meant that he could do . . . whatever the hell he wanted to do to them."

"Erica . . . hang on here. I can tell that you're very upset, but let's slow down a bit. I don't know anything about those other situations, but I've settled many cases, usually for a lot more than ten thousand dollars, and it was just to avoid having to go to trial, not because my client had done anything wrong. Nuisance value, it's called. Just because people make an accusation, and you pay them to avoid a lawsuit, that doesn't mean the allegation was true."

I knew instantly she wasn't buying it. From the look on her face, I could tell every fiber of her being knew what her husband really was.

I was getting the sinking feeling that I knew, too.

"When he came home after that night at the hotel," she began in a slow but steady voice, "he was so badly cut up that I knew what had happened. First he tells me that it was a bar scrape. Some misunder-standing with a drunk. Complete bullshit. Those were nail scratches. From a *woman*. So I tell him that he better not try to play me. I know what I know, and he's going to need my help, so he better tell me the truth. He looks like he don't know what to do, and then he finally starts telling me how sorry he is, and how much he loves me, but he had this one-night stand with some waitress. The same BS he's been giving you. The same shit he's going to say at the trial. But I know the difference between scratching somebody's back because you're feeling it and because you're trying to get away from something bad. *Real* bad. And I told him so. I told him that I wouldn't help him if he lied to me."

She began to cry. I looked around my office for tissues, but there were none. No one had ever cried in my office before.

"I'm still not following you completely, Erica. Are you saying that Darrius admitted to you that he raped her?"

"He told me that . . . I don't think he honestly understands what's rape and what's not, to tell you the truth. But what he described to me was her clearly trying to stop him, and his not giving a damn. So, yeah, that's rape."

We talked for another five or ten minutes, but nothing was resolved.

I told her I would explain to Darrius that we wouldn't call her to testify, but couldn't make any other promises to her, stressing that I had a duty to zealously represent her husband, even if I believed he was guilty. When I walked her to the elevator, I could tell that she felt she'd wasted her time by coming to see me.

As soon as the elevator doors closed, I went to Benjamin Ethan's office. He was on the phone, but I told Janeene that it was important, and she ushered me in.

When Ethan saw my expression, even before I said anything, he told whomever he was talking to that he had to go, and put down the phone. "Daniel, you look like you've seen a ghost. What's wrong?"

I told him what Erica Macy had just told me. About the other women who claimed Darrius had raped them and how he'd paid them off, the scratches on his back, what he'd told his wife about Vickie Tiernan resisting, and that Erica was convinced that her husband was guilty.

When I was done, we sat silently. Ethan's fingers clasped together under his chin, as if he were praying.

"I fail to see the problem, Daniel," he finally said with a smile to reinforce his belief that I was overreacting. "I suggest you mention the discussion to your client, but if he tells you that he's innocent, there's no prohibition to your letting him testify to that at trial. In fact, the opposite is true: he has the right to testify."

"But his wife is saying he's lying," I said, even though I knew the rejoinder I'd hear.

"She's not your client. There's only one question you need to answer: Do you know for certain that your client is going to lie on the stand?"

"Not for certain," I said.

"Then there's no problem."

I stared into space for a good thirty seconds. I knew

Ethan was right as an ethical matter and wrong as a moral one.

"I . . . I really had no idea," I finally said.

"And that's good, Daniel. I hate it when my clients lie in such a feeble way that it's obvious. If you know Macy is guilty because he tells you as much, then you should stop him from testifying, and even then, it's not that black or white. Some lawyers would still put their client on, and just let him testify in a narrative. But since it's your client's word against someone else's, there's no ethical dilemma at all here."

"It sure doesn't feel like that," I said.

"But it *is* like that. Nothing bad is going to happen because you do your job well. Believe me."

14

When I was at Taylor Beckett, a fleet of Lincoln Town Cars would line up along Madison Avenue, like a luxury taxi stand. You'd just get in the first one, hand the driver a voucher so the firm could charge a client for the ride, and that was it. When I became a partner, I learned that the firm also owned the car service, a little fact that was not disclosed to the clients as part of the billing.

The travel arrangements for Sorensen and Harrington were far less luxurious. We walked the fifteen or so blocks from my apartment to the courthouse. The moment we turned onto Centre Street, a caravan of news vans came into view, their weather vane antennae seemingly stretching on for blocks.

"We're definitely not in Kansas anymore," Nina remarked.

The Honorable Linda A. Pielmeier was something of a cautionary tale in state judicial politics. There was a time when she was considered United States Supreme Court timber, but that time was long past. She was elected to the bench in the late 1980s when she was only twenty-nine, the youngest judge in New York State history. That she was an African-American woman with a compelling biography—grew up in the Brooklyn projects; reared by a single mother;

scholarship to Columbia; law review at Harvard; and then eschewed Wall Street for public interest law—put her on every politician's radar.

Her star turn came when she took over the trial of the Chen-Tao Tong—universally acknowledged to be the most savage of the Chinatown gangs. She was the second judge on the case, her predecessor having been gunned down in front of his apartment building. The Chen-Tao trial lasted six months, during which Judge Pielmeier and her family were under twenty-four-hour security protection. In the end, all five defendants were convicted, and she gave each the maximum penalty. Rumor was that she had a security detail for years after.

The conventional wisdom after Chen-Tao was that Judge Pielmeier would get the next open appellate spot or the nomination for state attorney general. Neither of those things happened, however, and the Chen-Tao trial ended up being the high-water mark of her career. Whispers of crossing the wrong party boss about something. Whatever the reason, she was now a lifer in the purgatory known as the Criminal Division of the New York State Supreme Court. Of course, that didn't mean that Judge Pielmeier didn't want another turn in the spotlight, and the trial of Legally Dead might just be her last opportunity to bask in its glow.

In what she claimed with a straight face to be a nod to free speech, Judge Pielmeier got the chief judge to allow her to use the ceremonial courtroom for all Legally Dead–related matters. This increased the spectators from the fifty or so people who could fit in her courtroom to more than two hundred, nearly all of them members of the press. That still left hundreds more out in the cold, and so to curry favor with them, Judge Pielmeier devised a pool system, not unlike the one used by the White House, in which different reporters were permitted inside the courtroom each day, and then had to brief their colleagues on the day's events.

Judge Pielmeier entered the courtroom fifteen minutes after the hearing was supposed to start, which was more or less on time by judicial standards. Judges, as a group, show little concern for wasting the time of the lawyers appearing before them, even while most of them wouldn't think twice about holding a lawyer in contempt for returning the favor.

She was smaller than I'd expected, especially given her outsize reputation. Wearing the black robes, she looked something like a child in a witch's costume, a gavel in her hand instead of a wand. She was also older-looking than I'd imagined her, fully gray to the point of almost white, which contrasted sharply with her ebony complexion.

"Please be seated," she said in a soft voice after she'd sat down behind the bench. "First, allow me to welcome the members of the press. I'm also aware that we have a new counsel present today for the defendant."

I stood, buttoned my jacket, and said, "Good morning, Your Honor. My name is Daniel Sorensen. My partner, Nina Harrington, and I filed our notice of appearance yesterday."

"Sit down, Mr. Sorensen," she snapped. "I'll get to you in a moment. Before anything else is said on the record, however, I need to bring in the defendant. You do want your client to hear what's going on, don't you, sir?"

Perhaps it was out of bitterness over her stalled career, but among Judge Pielmeier's less admirable traits was that she was known for making lawyers feel utterly stupid. In this case, she needed to show me that I was a bit player in her courtroom; she was the one and only star of the show.

Legally Dead entered through the side door. From the moment he was visible, you couldn't help but think he must be guilty of something just by the way he looked. He was wearing an orange jumpsuit (gray must have been the home uniform, with orange worn on the road). His hands were cuffed behind his back, and his legs shackled around the ankles, which made him walk in a duck waddle. On either side of him were court officers, conspicuously displaying firearms.

The guards pulled L.D. toward our table the way you might drag a dog. When he arrived, his handcuffs were unlocked, but the ankle shackles remained.

Judge Pielmeier did not even give me the opportunity to say hello to my client. While the guards were still unlocking his handcuffs, she said, "Mr. Patterson, the Constitution of this great country guarantees you more than just a right to a lawyer. You are actually entitled to effective legal representation." She emphasized the word *effective,* using the long *e* sound. "While it is ultimately your decision whether Mr. Sorensen can provide such effective legal representation to you, I have been on this bench for too long not to know that if you are convicted of these charges, the first argument you'll make to the appellate court is that you didn't have adequate counsel before me. Now they tell me, Mr. Patterson, that you're something of a celebrity. I gotta be honest with you, I'd never heard of you before this case, but by the size of the media who want to watch this trial, I'm sure that there are lots of lawyers who would represent you solely to get their name in the newspapers. Let me be as clear as I can on this point: I have absolutely no reason whatsoever to think that's Mr. Sorensen's motivation here. It may well be that Mr. Sorensen is exactly the right lawyer to defend you in this case. But *you* need to be sure of that. Even more importantly, *I* need to be sure that you're sure. So I want you to state on the record that you wish to proceed with Mr. Sorensen as your counsel."

I placed my hand on L.D.'s arm, gently pulling on him to convey that he should stand. He did as he was told, but then looked at me for advice as to what to say. Given that we were in open court, my ability to communicate with him was limited, so I only nodded.

"Yes, Judge," he said in a weak voice.

"I'm not sure what you're agreeing to, sir, so I'm going to ask the question again. Do you want Mr. Sorensen to be your lawyer, in place of Marcus Jackson, who was your previous lawyer?"

"Yes," he said, this time a bit louder than before.

"Okay, then," Judge Pielmeier said, turning her focus back to me. "Mr. Sorensen, I accept your notice of appearance. I'll tell you this, though, you better have gotten whatever retainer you'll need to see this through to the end, because under no circumstances will I sign another substitution of counsel. Do you understand that?"

"I do, Your Honor," I said.

Judge Pielmeier waited for us to sit down before she began again. "You are the new kid on the block here, Mr. Sorensen. Is there anything you'd like to raise at this time?"

I stood again. It was a long shot to get bail, especially on a motion to reconsider, and I wasn't sure L.D. could meet even a minimal amount of bail. But clients who swear poverty when discussing their attorneys' fee have been known to find funds necessary to buy their way out of jail, and so it was worth a try.

Marcus Jackson had initially asked that Legally Dead be released without bail, the same released-on-recognizance request that I'd made for Darrius Macy. He must have figured it was a negotiating tactic—begin by asking for release without bail and meet somewhere at a reasonable number, just as Judge Ringel had done with Macy.

But Judge Pielmeier was very different from Judge Ringel, and she did not react well to Jackson's proposal. She found the request to be so out of bounds that she went 180 degrees the other way, denying bail altogether.

"We ask that the court set bail at an amount that is feasible for Mr. Patterson to meet," I said, trying to sound as reasonable as possible. "This defendant is not a flight risk because—"

Judge Pielmeier began to talk over me. Looking only at the court stenographer, she said, "No, I see no reason to reconsider my initial order denying bail. Nothing has changed concerning the nature of the crime alleged, or the motivation for this defendant to flee if released on bail. Accordingly, it's the order of this court that the defendant's motion is denied."

Damn. Even though the result was not that surprising, it still hurt. If L.D. had been out on bail, the entire dynamic of the case would be different. Time would be on our side, and there'd be no reason to rush to trial. Not to mention that I'd be a hero in my client's eyes. But now everything was going to be that much tougher.

The judge looked back to me and smiled. Then, in a syrupy-sweet voice, she said, "Anything else, Mr. Sorensen?"

"A few housekeeping matters, Your Honor," I said. "First, we'd like the court to impose a deadline for the people to provide us with discovery."

"Ms. Kaplan's a professional," Judge Pielmeier said with a dismissive air. "She doesn't need me telling her how to do her job. She'll get you what you need as soon as it's available. Isn't that right, Ms. Kaplan?"

Kaplan rose. She was actually much younger than I'd previously assumed—midthirties, at most. She was also very attractive, something that's never a good thing for a defendant. Her dark blue suit was well tailored, hugging her very trim figure. It looked expensive, the result of either family money or a rich husband, because no one bought designer clothes on an ADA's salary.

"Yes, Your Honor," Kaplan said, even though I had no doubt that she was going to hold back discovery until the last possible moment.

"But just so we're on the same page here, Ms. Kaplan," Judge Pielmeier said with a sly smile, "I'm assuming you won't have any difficulty getting Mr. Sorensen what he needs before Christmas, will you?"

Kaplan looked betrayed. "No, Your Honor."

"Good," the judge said as if it were a two-syllable word. "We done, Mr. Sorensen?"

"Your Honor, the defense would like to examine the crime scene, but Ms. Kaplan has insisted that both she and the police watch over our shoulder. As you can imagine, we'd rather not have the prosecution seeing what we think is important. Clearly, when the police investigated the crime scene, we were not permitted to be there and take notes."

"It seems to me that Mr. Sorensen is making a reasonable request," Judge Pielmeier said, with more surprise in her voice than I believed to be warranted. "What say you, Ms. Kaplan?"

"We have no objection, so long as it's just a counsel inspection. We would object if the defendant were also on the premises."

Kaplan had previously taken a hard line with me on the issue. Now, apparently sensing that Judge Pielmeier was going to grant our request, she decided to switch to the winning side, but not without trying to get something to make my life difficult.

"How about that, Mr. Sorensen?" Judge Pielmeier said. "That seems pretty fair to me, too, and I must say I do like it when the lawyers in my courtroom make my life easy. So, you get to go snoop around all by your lonesome, and then you can report back to your client about what you found."

"Your Honor, that would raise Sixth Amendment issues," I said.

"Since when?" she said with a mocking laugh.

"For effective representation to truly be effective, Mr. Patterson must be able to participate in all facets of the case. That includes helping us to see what's important at the crime scene and what's not."

"You see, Mr. Sorensen," Judge Pielmeier said in the belittling tone she seemed to reserve solely for me, "I throw you a bone and then you ask for the steak. So, here's what I'm going to do. You want to look around, just you and Ms. Harrington, that's fine by me, and I don't see the need for you to have a chaperone because I trust that, as officers of the court, you're not going to remove anything or disturb the scene in any way. But your client is not an officer of this court; he's—as Ms. Kaplan tells me at every opportunity—an accused murderer. So I'm not letting him roam free without a chaperone. The choice is yours."

"Your Honor, I appreciate the court's concern about maintaining the integrity of the crime scene, but, with all due respect, any such fear is unfounded. For one thing, the prosecution has numerous photographs of the scene, so they'd know if anything were disturbed. Also, Ms. Harrington and I will be with Mr. Patterson at all times. We're certainly not going to allow any disruption of the premises."

"Mr. Sorensen, are you having trouble hearing me? I made my ruling. You best move on to another topic, or I'm liable to end today's proceeding right now."

I was now 0 for 2. I decided to ask for something I was sure to get, if only to experience success for once.

"Last thing, Your Honor," I said. "I'd like the court's permission to have a few minutes with my client after the hearing. There's an issue that just came up recently that I'd like to discuss with him."

"Court time is my time, Mr. Sorensen," Judge Pielmeier said, sounding not unlike a pedantic schoolteacher. "Just like I don't write my decisions or hear other cases on your time, I don't expect you to be visiting with your client on my time."

This earned Judge Pielmeier some laughs from the gallery. She waited for the laughter to die down before continuing.

"Okay, then, since we have nothing else, I'm going to set our next conference for sometime after the New Year, at which time I'll set a trial date and hear from the parties if there are any discovery-related issues that require my attention." She turned to her clerk, who was sitting beneath her. "Eleanor, what's the first open day on the calendar in January?"

"The second," her clerk said without looking up. "At ten."

Judge Pielmeier stood. "See you all on the second at ten. And happy holidays, everyone." She then exited the courtroom through the door behind her chair, which led back to her chambers.

"Ain't she s'posed to bang that hammer thing?" L.D. said to me.

"Only on TV," I said.

By this time the corrections officers who had been standing a few feet from us throughout the hearing were already reapplying the handcuffs behind L.D.'s back. L.D. looked at me with wondering eyes, and it occurred to me he had no idea what had just transpired.

There was no way to raise Marcus Jackson's claim that L.D. had already confessed to the murder, or Matt Brooks's revelation that he wasn't who he claimed to be. Not in a crowded courtroom full of members of the press. That discussion would have to wait until we saw him next.

"L.D.," I began, talking quickly because I knew the guards would not wait for me to finish before removing him from the courtroom, "we weren't able to convince the judge to release you on bail. I'm sorry about that. We're going to get the prosecution's evidence by Christmas Eve, and we'll come in and see you on Christmas morning, okay?"

He looked at me in a way that caused Alexa to flash into my mind. An expression of such utter dependence that it made me swallow hard.

"Okay," he said with a forced smile. "But you don't need to ruin your Christmas."

"No, I want to see you as soon as we have the prosecution's discovery."

He was already a few feet away from me, with the gap increasing as the guards pulled him away. "Thank you," he called out before turning his back and leaving the courtroom.

15

Nina and I left the courthouse without sharing a word. The quiet didn't last long, however—the moment we stepped outside, the shouting started.

"Did he kill her?" called out the redheaded reporter from one of the local television news programs.

"Is Legally Dead guilty?" said a tall, thin man whom I didn't recognize, holding a microphone.

Others just yelled out my name, and occasionally Nina's.

I leaned in and whispered to Nina, "The trick is to walk by them fast and look like you didn't even see them. If you wave them off or say no comment, that's what they'll use on the news. And believe me, no one ever made their client look innocent by saying 'no comment.'"

We turned at the first corner and increased our pace slightly. A few blocks later we'd reached a playground in Chinatown filled with kids who must have been on recess, and I figured we were in the clear.

Ten minutes after that we were in Tribeca, standing in front of a restaurant that Nina said was great, although I'd never heard of it, despite the fact that it was only a few blocks from my apartment. Once inside, it didn't take me long to realize it was the kind of place where the waitstaff are all models. Our waitress fit the bill, a lanky blonde who asked us what we wanted to drink without ever making eye contact.

I'd now gone a third day without a drink. I was contemplating whether that show of willpower deserved to be rewarded when Nina said, "I'll have a seltzer with lime."

"Me, too," I said, feeling noble about not imbibing at noon, which, when I reflected on it, made me feel far less noble.

While waiting for our food to arrive, Nina and I engaged in the usual gossip that follows a court appearance. Nina said she wasn't too impressed with Kaplan, although I suspected that was a bit of wishful thinking on her part. The mere fact that Kaplan was assigned to the case meant she was the best they had. On top of which, I'd long ago learned not to discount the power of a pretty face with jurors, although sitting across from Nina, I realized we had that more than covered on our side.

We also disagreed about Judge Pielmeier. "She's going to be a nightmare for us" was the way Nina put it.

"We'll be okay," I said. "I'll take a smart judge who's pro-prosecution over a stupid one any day of the week. When you appear before a bad judge, it's like the Wild West. You never know what's coming in or what you can get away with. But with a smart one, you can anticipate the rulings, because nine times out of ten, they're going to be right. She's likely only going to be a problem for us in the ego department."

"She's funny, at least," Nina said with a chuckle. "That whole 'court time is my time' thing."

The idea of time made me think of Legally Dead.

He'd almost certainly be spending Christmas without seeing his daughter. That made two of us, I thought. And then, of course, Roxanne's mother made it a trifecta.

"I hope it was okay that I told L.D. we'd see him on Christmas," I said. "You don't have to come if you have other plans, but I figured we'd go in the morning and be done by noon or so anyway."

"No, it's fine. I actually think it was very thoughtful of you to say that we'd be visiting him on Christmas. It must be a hard day."

"They're all really hard."

"Are we talking about you or L.D.?" she said.

"Touché," I replied with a subtle nod.

"Well, given that we're spending Christmas Eve together looking at documents, and then Christmas morning at Rikers, care to come with me to Rich and Deb's for Christmas dinner?"

She looked at me hopefully.

"Thanks for the invite, but I think I'll pass."

"Unless you start telling me very convincingly about other plans, I'm not letting you off so easy."

"If you must know, I was going to order in some Chinese food and then maybe go to the movies."

"That just sounds too depressing for words, Dan."

I chuckled, an effort to show her that my plans weren't that sad. Her expression didn't change, however, which told me rather emphatically that it hadn't worked.

"It's not so bad," I said. "Sarah called it Jewish Christmas. She said that's what her family did growing up. Trust me, I'm not going to be alone. The movie theater will be filled."

"Not buying it, Dan. Come with me to Deb and Rich's. It'll be fun."

"Did you say it'll be fun? They write books about how painful Christmas with the extended family can be. And if you recall, the last time I spent any time at Deb and Rich's apartment, I had no recollection of it twelve hours later."

"Let me amend that, then. It'll be fun *after* dinner," she said with a sly smile. "If you go with me and provide some buffer from my family, I promise that we'll leave early and I'll buy you a really good glass of scotch. God knows, after a few hours with my family, I'll need a drink. More than one, I'm sure."

It was my turn to smile at her. "It's nice to know I'm not the only suffering soul in our law firm. So tell me, what's driving you to drink?"

"Dan, we all have our secrets."

"But we're partners. There should be no secrets between us. Isn't that in our partnership agreement?"

"We don't have a partnership agreement, as you well know."

I could tell she was thinking about how much to trust me. That she didn't stabbed at me, as I'd already come to think of Nina as the first friend I'd made since the accident, which, sadly, made her now my only friend.

Probably thirty seconds passed while she made the calculations, and then she said, "Do you really want to know?"

"I do, but if I'm prying, I'll be able to live with the disappointment of not knowing. So, only if you're comfortable sharing."

She squinted at me and then took a deep breath, almost as if she were going to swim underwater. "Okay, here it is. Rich and Deb are great, but sometimes they're like robots or something. Their lives are just too perfect. They have great jobs and that great apartment and a perfect little daughter. I mean, their family portraits look like freakin' Ralph Lauren ads. Add to that, my parents are going to be there, and the whole time they're going to be staring at me and wondering—*How'd we go wrong with her? She's thirty-three, never married, not even in a relationship . . .*"

"Somehow I don't think you have *that* much trouble finding a man, Nina."

"From your lips to God's ears. But I shouldn't complain, especially not to you. And I know many people have it much harder. Besides, I only have myself to blame. All my wounds are self-inflicted."

"I think everyone's wounds are self-inflicted," I said. "God knows, I should have spent more time at home, tried harder to be a better husband and father."

She didn't say anything at first, but then she reached over and patted my hand. Not a caress, exactly, but the way you might comfort a child. Her touch was nonetheless welcome, even if she removed her hand to her lap before it had turned into actual hand-holding.

"Thank you," she said in a quiet but serious voice.

"For what?"

"For letting me in. Even if it was only a little."

"No charge," I said, and smiled.

"Ah, there it is—the elusive Sorensen smile."

"Am I really that much of a sad sack?"

"Let me answer by saying that being around you is a little like living in London. It's not like the sun never comes out, but when it does, everyone is that much happier."

I chuckled. "Well, I guess it's nice to have your smile compared to the sun."

I didn't notice her hand until it was back on top of mine. This time she held it in place.

Our hand-holding lasted less than ten seconds, but it was long enough for me to realize that I was sad when she pulled her hand away.

16

I initially thought that the head of the Sex Crimes Bureau, a guy named Henry Ortega, would try the Darrius Macy case. Ortega had attended nearly all of the pretrial court conferences, and given his well-known ambition (he was gunning to be the next DA if the current occupant ever stepped aside), it made sense that he'd grab a high-profile case for himself. But when it came time to pick the jury, his deputy, Nancy Wong, was in the first chair. I got the sense that the switch was made recently, largely because Wong seemed somewhat unprepared.

By contrast, I'd never been better prepared for a trial. I'd been working nonstop for six months and knew every fact backward and forward. As Sarah would sometimes say, usually without humor, I knew more about Vickie Tiernan, Macy's accuser, than I did my own daughter.

It's a cliché that trials, like wars and athletic contests, are won in the planning. But clichés are such for a reason—they're usually true.

The trial lasted two weeks. Jury selection took almost half that time, mainly because Judge Ringel had an expansive view of what constituted good cause for dismissal. The experts testified for a day each—the prosecution's guy saying that Vickie Tiernan suffered a trauma consistent with forcible rape, and our guy saying the exact opposite—and the rest of the trial was the he said/she said that is the hallmark of all rape cases.

Vickie Tiernan was on the stand for two full days. You could hear her nervousness when she said her name, and I knew that no matter how she performed on direct, she'd be in trouble when I got my chance.

And that's exactly what ended up happening.

All modesty aside, I cross-examined the hell out of poor Vickie Tiernan. It was the kind of cross that you see on a bad Lifetime movie, where the defense puts the victim on trial. Not one of my proudest moments, but one of my best professional ones nonetheless.

The jury heard that she was a twenty-two-year-old high school dropout with two children by two different men, and she had no idea where either man lived today. After the rape charge against Macy, she'd filed an assault charge against her current boyfriend, and then dropped that charge, which opened the door to a series of questions in which I accused her of having a history of fabricating charges against men with whom she had willingly chosen to have sex.

Vickie Tiernan had testified on direct that she delayed reporting the rape because she needed two days to summon the courage to make the charge, given Macy's celebrity status. But on cross, I made the point, over and over again, that she was not summoning strength so much as calculating profit. She admitted she was deeply in debt and had been contacted by lawyers about filing a civil suit against Macy. Although she claimed that she had not retained any of them, she conceded that they'd advised her it would be that much easier for her to prevail in a civil suit if Macy was convicted. And while she vehemently denied that she'd ever had sex for money, the mere repetition of my questions on the subject made it impossible for the jury not to think that there might be some truth to the claim.

When Wong rested the prosecution's case, I thought we had a better than 50-50 shot at an acquittal if we didn't put on a defense. When I floated that idea to Macy—resting now, without his taking the stand—he shot it down without a second thought.

So, we put on our expert, who testified on direct that Vickie Tiernan's physical condition was consistent with consensual intercourse, and then conceded on cross that he could not definitively rule out the possibility of rape, especially if the assault had happened, as Tiernan claimed, a few days before she'd reported it. In other words, he offered the mirror opposite testimony of the prosecution's expert.

That meant it was all going to come down to Darrius Macy.

There's a school of thought among certain members of the criminal defense bar that your client should never take the stand. Benjamin Ethan was of that belief—I'd heard him say many times: "There's nothing the client can say that I can't phrase better in my closing, and the prosecution doesn't get to cross-examine my closing."

I'm of the other view, however—if you don't talk, you don't walk. But that works only if your client can sell it. To make sure Macy could, we held hours of mock questions, and a small army of consultants and lawyers would critique every word of his answer ("Call her Vickie, not Ms. Tiernan—and definitely never refer to her by a pronoun—to establish more of a feel that you actually knew each other"). Focus groups analyzed everything from his demeanor (sit forward in the witness chair so you look engaged) to whether he should wear a tie (yes, but monochromatic), and even whether his children should sit beside his wife in the gallery (no, they were too young and the testimony was too sexual). And because Macy was used to analyzing game film, we taped most of the sessions so that we could watch them together at the end of the day, while I offered further critiques.

By the end of our preparation, Macy's testimony was much more like a scripted play than a search for the truth, which is exactly what I wanted. Wong, obviously chastened a bit by Judge Ringel's rulings during the Tiernan cross, let me ask whatever I wanted without objection, and I took full advantage. At times it seemed as much like Macy was doing an ESPN interview as defending himself against rape charges. He went on about the struggles of his childhood, how his mother was a single mother like Vickie Tiernan, and so he understood how desperate such a situation could make you, and he spoke at length about his Super Bowl heroics, to the obvious pleasure of the eight male jurors who seemed to feel privileged to have such an intimate view of a superstar.

It was truly a virtuoso performance. I ended the direct examination with the million-dollar question. "Mr. Macy, did you rape Ms. Tiernan?"

And he hit it out of the park. "No. No, I absolutely did not. What I did was terrible, to my wife, to my children, to my teammates, and to this city. To them I have apologized and will make it my life mission to regain their trust. And while I am very sorry that Vickie seems to be so emotionally distraught about what happened, I know that I am not to blame for the misfortunes in her life. I take full responsibility for my conduct, which was terrible in its own way. I broke a vow I made to my wife and to God to be faithful, and as a result of breaking that vow, I have hurt people I love, who trusted and depended on me to be a better man. But something I learned on the football field is that we all get knocked down. What matters most is how you get up. I have pledged to Erica that I will never betray her again, and that I will seek her forgiveness through my conduct. And just as I have sought the forgiveness of those I have wronged, I am willing to offer such forgiveness to Vickie for making these false charges against me. It's not my place to judge the pressure she was under that caused her to do this, but I pray that she, too, can make amends and move on with her life."

The jury got the case late on Tuesday. We didn't hear a word from them on Wednesday. On Thursday morning they asked to hear the parts of Tiernan's direct testimony when she claimed that she had repeatedly screamed the word *stop*.

Macy asked me what I made of the jury's inquiry, and I told him that there was no possible way even to venture an educated guess. "They either want to hear it because they believe her, and that means they're going to convict, or because they don't believe her, and that means they're going to acquit."

At a quarter of five, we got word that the jury had reached a verdict.

There is nothing like awaiting a jury's verdict. The days the jury deliberates are spent doing nothing, holed up in the courtroom, knowing full well that if you leave the building for any reason, you'll be accosted by reporters. Arrival in the morning, leaving in the evening, and the back and forth from lunch are like running a gauntlet.

And if the waiting wasn't bad enough, when word comes back that the jury has reached a verdict, it's a thousand times worse. The fifteen or twenty minutes sitting at the counsel table in anticipation of the jury's arrival, followed by the judge asking aloud for the jury's verdict, the handing of a piece of paper from the foreperson to the bailiff to the judge and back again, the formality of the judge asking the defendant to rise and the foreperson to read the verdict, is like no other kind of pressure I've ever experienced. And I say that as defense counsel. I truly cannot imagine what it must be like for the defendant, knowing that in a matter of moments, freedom will either be returned or taken away.

"Madame foreperson, please read the jury's unanimous verdict," Judge Ringel asked.

The foreperson was a young African-American woman. She stood and declared in a shaky voice that the jury had voted "Not guilty."

I wish I could say that I had mixed emotions for my role in putting a rapist back into society, but I didn't. Sadly, my only thought was that with those two words—not guilty—my career, no, my life, was made.

How wrong I was.

Two days later my wife and daughter were killed.

I know that most people would view it as nothing more than an unfortunate coincidence, but I don't. In the law, there's a doctrine called the fruit of the poisonous tree. It holds that evidence rightfully obtained isn't admissible at trial if it was acquired as a direct result of evidence that had been improperly seized. So if the defendant confesses to the murder and also tells the police the names of his coconspirator, and the coconspirator later confesses, too, neither confession comes into evidence if that first confession was illegally obtained.

It's not a perfect analogy, but it's the prism through which I have always viewed Sarah's and Alexa's deaths. They didn't die because I represented a man I knew to be a rapist and got him acquitted, but if I hadn't done that, maybe everything in my life would have been different. Maybe if I'd stepped out of the case when I learned Macy was guilty, I would have been with them in East Hampton, and the accident would not have happened.

I know that the answer is that there are a lot of maybes in life. Maybe I would have been with them and an asteroid would have fallen on our house. I know. I've said it all to myself already. But when you help a rapist get acquitted and your wife and daughter are killed two days later, it's awfully hard to convince yourself that karma doesn't exist.

17

Assistant District Attorney Lisa Kaplan's promise in court to produce discovery before Christmas translated to 4:59 p.m. on Christmas Eve. It arrived in two banker's boxes. Apparently the DA's office had never heard of a thumb drive.

The production was 7,417 pages, each neatly numbered in the bottom right-hand corner with the legend "Patterson/People's Discovery." I gave Nina the first box and started to flip through the documents in the second one.

It didn't take long to realize that most of it was filler. Pages upon pages of irrelevant stuff—computer printouts of various searches that showed no hits, or notes of interviews of witnesses who didn't know anything pertinent to the crime, or if they did, it was information that had already been in the press.

After about an hour of review with nothing to show for it, Nina blurted, "Whoa, hang on. I've got something here."

"What?"

"This is really weird. If I'm reading it correctly, they produced a criminal record for Nelson Patterson."

"The Nelson Patterson that doesn't exist?" I said. "The one that Matt Brooks made up?"

"Maybe he does exist. I mean, whoever said that Brooks was the paragon of truthfulness?"

It's funny how easily I believed that my clients all lied. It hadn't even occurred to me that Brooks might be the liar here.

"But if Brooks created Nelson Patterson," Nina said, "he must have also made up a charge for gun possession. And look here, a mug shot."

I walked around to Nina's side of the table and bent down over her shoulder. There it was, a rap sheet, complete with photo. The fifteen-year-old in the picture could have been L.D., in that they shared a similar bone structure and coloring, but the skinny-looking kid from the picture certainly bore little resemblance to the scowling thug that was Legally Dead's public persona.

I flipped through some of the paperwork. It was a juvenile arrest, which under other circumstances should have been under seal. There were fingerprints attached to the file, which should have settled the question whether Nelson Patterson was our L.D. Of course, that raised an even bigger question: Why would Brooks lie to us, especially about something that was so easily verified?

"The charge was criminal possession of a firearm, which was a class D felony," Nina said, reading aloud. "It was pled down to an A misdemeanor. It looks like whoever this actually is served a year in juvenile detention."

When she made eye contact with me, Nina asked, "Do you think it's just a coincidence? They just pulled the wrong Nelson Patterson's sheet?"

"Didn't you just say that you thought Brooks lied to us?"

"I'm looking at different possibilities," she said with a shrug.

I scanned the arrest documents over Nina's shoulder. "It's standard operating procedure after an arrest to fingerprint the suspect and run the prints through all the various criminal databases. If you want to go with the Brooks-is-telling-the-truth theory, the only explanation I can come up with is that when they scanned for L.D.'s prior arrest, they must not have retrieved any matches. And although that should have been the end of it, someone at the DA's office must have thought to look at sealed cases, and that's where they found the juvenile arrest of this kid named Nelson Patterson."

"But why would they think that this Nelson Patterson was L.D.? There must be lots of Nelson Pattersons out there, and the fingerprints must not match."

I had no answer, which put me back in the Brooks-is-lying camp. But as I continued to read, a theory came to mind.

I extended my finger to show Nina where I was looking on the report. "Look here," I said, still thinking it through as I read about the circumstances surrounding the arrest. "This kid was shot four times. Maybe someone manually reviewed ten-year-old arrest records trying to find when a guy named Nelson Patterson was shot four times. They found this and figured it must be our Nelson Patterson. Of course, for that to make sense, you also have to believe they didn't bother to check the prints. Or maybe they figured there was some type of mistake in the old prints."

"I hear you," she said, with the same tone of disbelief I use when uttering the phrase.

We resumed the document review, and it wasn't long before I came upon the holy grail of criminal discovery—the CSU findings and the pathology report of Roxanne's murder. The analysis was crammed with technical jargon about fibers and fingerprints, but the long and short of it seemed to be that there was nothing connecting L.D. to the crime scene.

"There were two sets of fingerprints in Roxanne's bedroom, aside from Roxanne's," I said, reading as I spoke, "and neither of them matches L.D."

"Who do the other prints belong to?" Nina asked.

"It looks like they never made a match. So at least we have some reasonable doubt on that. We'll claim that they belong to the real killer."

"Mr. Soddi," Nina said with a grin.

I quickly flipped through the scientific study explaining how the conclusions were reached. It didn't take me long to realize that deciphering that stuff would require Popofsky's help.

But then I came upon photos of the crime scene. You didn't need a medical degree to know what they said. *Grisly* is the only word that sufficed.

"Jesus. You should see these," I said.

This time Nina came to my side. When she bent over to view the pictures, she noticeably recoiled.

"Oh, God."

"I know."

The first was of Roxanne's bedroom, shot as if you were entering, with the bed as the focal point. Beside it was an enormous mirror, obviously intended to reflect sexual activity for the enjoyment of the participants. Nina gave me a raised eyebrow and a smirk when she saw it.

My eyes were drawn to the blood, however. Deep purple, like a cabernet, and soaked into every surface—the headboard, the sheets, globs on the wall. There was even a spiderweb-like design visible on the mirror.

The next photo was from the other angle, capturing the fireplace that was opposite the bed. Above the mantel were two brackets, with nothing lying on top of them.

It had already been leaked to the press that Roxanne's housekeeper told the police she was sure the baseball bat was above the fireplace on the day of the murder. Now the crime scene photos showed that it was gone when Roxanne's body was discovered. Even if the police never found the bat, it would have been awfully hard to convince a jury that something else was the murder weapon. And with the "A-Rod" song, it was damn near impossible.

Toward the bottom of my box were seven eight-by-ten color photographs of Roxanne taken after her death. I'd only ever seen dead bodies at funerals. Even Sarah and Alexa were made available to me only after the mortician had cleaned them up. Morticians always make the deceased seem angelic, masking death's gruesomeness beneath white shrouds and waxy makeup. Roxanne's face, however, was bruised and covered in blood, and her hair was matted on top from where the blood had congealed. Her eyes were wide open and vacant.

"I have the autopsy photos," I said. "Not very pleasant."

Nina cringed when she saw the top one.

"Worth a lot more than just a thousand words, right?" I said.

She nodded. "So what do the words say?"

"That if someone beats you over the head a half a dozen times, you die."

"Seriously."

I began to read from the autopsy report. "Blunt force trauma to the cerebellum. No illegal drugs in her system. A little bit of alcohol. Roxanne color treated her hair, so in case you thought she was a natural blonde, she wasn't. She was on antianxiety medication, but apparently no birth control. No foreign fluids inside her."

I hesitated, not fully believing what I was reading.

"What?" Nina said.

"I think I got something from the crime scene report . . . but . . ."

"But what?"

"Apparently they found some hairs on Roxanne's bed. And if I'm reading this right, they're pubic hairs."

"So? L.D. left his pubic hair in her bed. It happens, Dan."

"They're not L.D.'s, though. They can't tell whose hairs they are because there was no follicle. So they couldn't do a full DNA analysis. The microscopic tests can only tell that it's pubic hair from a Caucasian."

I rolled around in my head what this meant, and kept coming back to the same conclusion. Roxanne had a lover who was in her bed right before she died. Maybe the evening she died.

"Nina, this is huge for us. Our SODDI guy might have just as well left his business card in her sheets."

"Is it definitely a man's hair?"

Damn. I hadn't thought of that. I scanned the report again, hoping that there would be some indication that the hair could not be from Roxanne. There wasn't.

"No," I said dejectedly. "All they could tell was that it's a Caucasian pubic hair. So it could be a woman's."

"You know that Kaplan's going to claim that it's Roxanne's," Nina said. "You've heard of Occam's razor, right?"

"Yeah, the simplest answer is usually the correct one. My mother used to tell us to think horses, not zebras. Same thing."

"So the most logical assumption is that Roxanne left behind her own pubic hair in her bed," Nina said, as if that ended the matter.

"But we used to always tell my mother that sometimes it is a zebra," I countered. "Zebras do exist, after all. Some people have seen them."

"Maybe at the zoo," she said with a chuckle. "But not in a pop star's bed."

18

For lawyers, there's probably no worse day to visit a jail than Christmas. At least I assume that to be the case, as this was my first Christmas visit behind bars.

There were lots of children and elderly people at Rikers that morning, which somehow made the surroundings even more depressing. The extra visitors also meant that the wait entering the facility was twice as long as usual. Nina and I were delayed another half hour or so because the prison officials literally flipped through every page of the document production we'd brought in to make sure there wasn't any contraband stuck to anything.

As counsel of record, we were now able to meet in a room without the glass barrier. The room they put us in, however, looked like a bus station bathroom, but without the facilities, and half the size. The tile was once white, but now would pass for gray. In the center of the room was a small metal table. The chair, also metal and without a cushion, was the most uncomfortable one I'd ever sat in. Needless to say, there were no windows.

We waited forty-five minutes for L.D. to arrive. When he finally appeared, he was wearing the same gray prison garb he had on the last time we'd visited

Rikers, and he was shackled around the ankles and handcuffed behind his back, just like when he entered and left court. The guard who accompanied him into the room, a large man whose only visible hair was a black goatee, unlocked the handcuffs, but, again, just like in court, the ankle shackles remained in place.

"I'm going to be right outside the door," the guard said to me.

"Thank you," I replied, probably not the proper response, given that Nina and I shouldn't be afraid to be in a room alone with our client.

After the guard left and shut the door, L.D. extended his hand to me. "Merry Christmas," he said with a broad smile. "I'm so glad that I got to see you guys today. I'm hoping Mercedes brings Brianna, but I know she ain't gonna. Christmas in here ain't fuckin' Christmas, you know what I mean?"

Nina and I each nodded, although it was obvious that neither of us really had any idea what it was like to spend Christmas in jail. At least not from the inmate point of view.

"Really nice for you to visit me when you got your own families. Did your little girl like her presents?"

My initial impulse was to continue the lie. A simple "yes" would have done it, but then I would be locked in to lying about Alexa for the duration, and I didn't think I could do that.

"I should have told you when we met the last time, L.D. My daughter died in a car accident. About eighteen months ago. Her mother, my wife, died too."

I could see the shock on his face, which caused me to smile at him, my effort to ease his pain and mask my own. With L.D., it didn't seem to work as it usually did with others. L.D.'s eyes actually welled up.

"Fuck," he said, and then he wiped his eyes.

Here he was, clad in the canvas gray prison jumpsuit, his legs chained together, denied his freedom, perhaps for the rest of his life—and if he was to be believed, all for a crime that he did not commit—and yet he felt sorry for me. And then I realized that he was right to do so. Certainly, if given the choice, I'd trade places with him in a second, all too glad to be imprisoned if it meant that Sarah and Alexa were alive somewhere—even if it meant that I had no idea where they were on Christmas.

"We have some things to discuss with you that are quite serious, L.D.," I said, perhaps too abruptly. The thought of my circumstances being worse than his was simply more than I could bear, and I wanted to get back on surer footing.

"First thing is that we met with Matt Brooks. He told us that your real name is Calvin Mayberry. That the whole Legally Dead backstory is a work of fiction."

L.D. chortled. "Fucking Brooks, can't even remember my goddamn name. It's Calvin *Merriwether*."

Damn. Our client was the liar. A little Occam's razor right there.

With all the seriousness I could muster, I said, "L.D., this isn't funny. You have to tell us the truth. About *everything*, okay? Or we can't represent you effectively."

"I know. I know. You gotta understand, and I know it sounds like some crazy shit, but I ain't Calvin no more. And I get that I should have told you because you guys are my lawyers and so I need to tell you everything, but ain't no thing. Everybody in show business uses a made-up name. You think Eminem is that dude's real name? Or Fitty's?"

"This is different, though," Nina said. "Those guys didn't also change their real names. Fifty Cent is Curtis something, right? And Eminem called one of his albums *Marshall Mathers*."

"That shit is all Brooks," L.D. said. "He said Calvin's gotta be dead and I gotta start over from scratch. Otherwise, you know, somebody would figure it out."

"Let me make sure I have this right," I said. "The rapper Legally Dead, who survived four gunshots, is really a kid from the burbs who never got shot? And you're saying that this was all Matt Brooks's doing?"

"Look," L.D. said, now sounding as serious as me, "it's true that I was never a gang member, and I was never shot and left for legally dead. But I am an artist and a musician, and as a part of my art, I play that role. And I do it twenty-four/seven."

"This is a major problem for us," I said with a shake of my head. "The prosecution thinks you're Nelson Patterson."

"So?"

"So the prosecution produced a juvenile detention record for Nelson Patterson," Nina said.

She pulled a red accordion folder out of her

briefcase. Within it she had arranged the key documents, each separated by a manila file folder. She handed L.D. the one with the tab marked "Juvie Records."

"Any idea who this is?" I asked.

L.D. studied the picture. After a few seconds of reflection he said, "Beats the hell out of me. Ain't me, though."

"I take it that Calvin Merriwether has no priors?"

"Always made honor roll, man," L.D. said with a smile.

"And you really have no idea who this other Nelson Patterson is?" Nina asked.

"Already told you. Never heard a him."

I knew from Nina's body language, the way her arms were folded across her chest, that she wasn't buying it. "This is an awfully big coincidence," she said. "Out of nowhere, the police just happen to pull the rap sheet of some guy named Nelson Patterson who was involved in a shooting just like the one Matt Brooks made up, at around the same general time frame, and this guy was about the same age as L.D. would have been then. And the real Nelson Patterson, this guy in the mug shot, he's never come forward and said that he's the guy who was shot and left for legally dead? I mean, c'mon."

"It's not that far-fetched," I said. "I bet you that somebody in Brooks's organization, or maybe even him personally, knew of this Nelson Patterson's story, and that's why they offered it up to L.D. Maybe they paid the real Nelson Patterson off, and that's why he's never come forward. Or maybe they knew he was dead. You know, there was this character in a Paul Newman movie called *The Hustler* named Minnesota Fats, who was this pool hustler. Totally fiction. But then this real-life guy, who was a real good pool player, and happened to be overweight, started calling himself Minnesota Fats, and soon enough, people just assumed that he was the guy the movie was based on. He made millions because people thought he was that character. I don't even think the guy was from Minnesota."

She nodded, the nonverbal equivalent of "I hear you."

"But," I continued, "no matter what the explanation, we're still left with something of an ethical dilemma here, L.D. Do we tell Lisa Kaplan that she's got the wrong Nelson Patterson? Do we tell her that your name isn't Nelson Patterson?"

"No," he said vehemently. "No fucking way."

"Did you legally change your name?" I asked, and then rattled off a few more questions before giving him the opportunity to answer the first one. "What's your driver's license say? Social Security card? What name do you file your taxes under?"

"Whoa," he said with a laugh. "Brooks handled all that shit for me. Maybe I signed some forms, but I don't know anything about that stuff. I got no license and I never made any money, so there was never no taxes needed to be filed."

"I don't think we have to do anything about the

name," Nina said. "Isn't it on them if they call him the wrong name?"

She was right, but only to a point. "Maybe in the first instance," I said, "but it's definitely going to be an issue if L.D. testifies. The first thing they say is 'Please state your name for the record.' What name is he going to give? And if he says Nelson Patterson, isn't that a lie, and won't we be guilty of suborning perjury?"

"It's the name I go by, man," L.D. said. "It fuckin' *is* who I am. And after all this shit is over, Imma go back to being Legally Dead. There ain't no life for me as Calvin Merriwether. The truth is, I rather be in here as Legally Dead than out there as Calvin Merriwether."

I looked over at Nina to see if she had anything further she wanted to add. Her expression registered that she was as concerned as me. She looked like she was smelling something bad, which in a way she was.

Recognizing that we weren't going anywhere on this, I said, "Among the other evidence the prosecution provided us with were a few pubic hairs in Roxanne's bed. There was no DNA material on the hairs, so they couldn't do the analysis you see on TV where they definitively determine whose hair it is, but they're from a Caucasian, which rules you out."

"But it could very well be Roxanne's hair," Nina quickly added.

"We've hired an expert," I began to explain, "a guy named Marty Popofsky. He's fresh out of the medical examiner's office and he'll do some analysis of the hair. We're hoping he'll give us an opinion as to whether the pubic hairs really belonged to Roxanne."

L.D. looked like he was somewhere else for the moment. Try as I might, I had no idea what was running through his head. Did he prefer that the alleged love of his life be cheating on him if it helped prove he was innocent of murder? Did he already know about her infidelity, and was that why he'd killed her? Or was he hoping that it all wasn't true, and that she had been faithful to him up to the end?

"What if they're not hers?" he asked in a weak voice. "Can you find out whose they are?"

"I don't know," I said. "If we had someone's pubic hair to compare it to, we might be able to get an opinion out of our expert about the likelihood of a match. You have any idea who?"

"Nah," he said flatly. "I'd be the last fucking dude to know."

"We're going to do our best to find out who this other guy might be," I said. "But you need to know going in that it's a risky proposition for us. There's definitely an upside to it. If there was someone else Roxanne was romantically involved with, we can point to that person as another suspect. And because we'd be the ones finding this other guy, and not the prosecution, we'll be able to score some points there, too."

"But," Nina chimed in, "it'll help the prosecution, too, because it brings a jealousy angle into it that they don't have right now. It basically gives them motive on a silver platter."

"How can that be if I didn't know there was another guy?"

I was tempted to laugh, although I knew he was being sincere. Why defendants think that because they say it, everyone believes it's true, I'll never know.

"L.D., no matter what you say, the prosecution will claim that you did know. It'll be your word against theirs."

"I don't know shit about some other guy," L.D. said.

"I hear you, L.D.," I said. "I do."

I turned to Nina, who offered a subtle shrug. The pubic hair subject exhausted, it was time to get to the most serious issue.

"Okay, let's move on. So . . . we also met with Marcus Jackson," I said without emotion, and then waited a beat to see if L.D. would provide some indication that he knew what we'd been told. He didn't so much as flinch, however.

"He told us that you confessed to killing Roxanne," Nina said in a similarly emotionless tone.

Legally Dead's response was a hearty laugh. It couldn't have been more misplaced.

"Do you find this funny?" I asked.

"If you believe him, then yeah, I find that pretty fuckin' hilarious. I've already told you guys, *I didn't kill her*. So that pretty much means I didn't confess, don't it?"

"With all respect, L.D., you also told us that your name was Nelson Patterson, and that wasn't true. So we're kind of in a gray area about how much to believe what you tell us."

"That's not the same fucking thing and you know it," he said with a flash of anger. "I wanted you guys because I thought you believed in me. If you don't, then fuck you both."

"L.D. . . . I think I need to give you what is a pretty standard speech in the criminal defense business. It goes something like this: as your counsel, we have an ethical duty to represent you zealously without regard to whether you're innocent or guilty—"

He held out his hand like a traffic cop, telling me to stop.

In a calmer voice, he said, "I know what you're going to say. I do. But I need *you* to hear *me*. I didn't kill Roxanne." I started to say something, but he interrupted me again. "Please, let me finish." I nodded that the floor remained his. "I know you're gonna give me that lawyer bullshit that you don't care if I'm guilty because you got a job to do. But what I'm sayin' is that I *want* you to care. I'm innocent and I need you to believe me. If I can't get you two to believe in me, some jury sure won't."

"Any idea why Marcus Jackson would lie to us?" Nina said this sharply, almost too much so, given L.D.'s heartfelt denial.

"No" was all he said.

"How'd you find Marcus Jackson, anyway?" I asked.

"Brooks got him for me. Like day one. I told him, I don't need no lawyer, but he said the boyfriend was always prime suspect, and with 'A-Rod' . . . well, I could see how it was gonna look, right?"

I took a deep measure of L.D. For a reason I couldn't quite comprehend, I believed him. The "A-Rod" song, the whole Calvin Merriwether thing, even Jackson telling us that he'd confessed, didn't change my view. I honestly believed that he was innocent of this crime.

Then again, I'd truly believed in Darrius Macy's innocence, and so my radar on this sort of thing was hardly what one would call foolproof.

19

At four o'clock Christmas Day, I was with Nina in her brother's living room along with Rich's wife, Deb, who had been Sarah's best friend, drinking a seltzer. Rich had offered me a glass of the same twenty-year-old Johnnie Walker Blue I'd had at their Christmas party a little more than a week before, but I declined. In part, that was because I didn't want to give Nina an excuse to renege on her promise of a later scotch, but also because I couldn't deny the benefits of my new sobriety. I hadn't had a drink since agreeing to take on L.D., and I could feel my mind and body beginning to respond.

Rich was going on and on about some deal he'd been working on, and from what I could glean from drifting in and out of his story, the client was a manufacturer of automotive parts acquiring over a hundred fast-food restaurant franchises in the Midwest, with the idea being that there would be a business synergy through drive-in services. Or something like that.

He must have noticed we were all glazing over a bit because he said, "I think it's time for someone else to tell a boring work story. Nina? Dan?"

"I don't know," Nina said with obvious sarcasm, "how could we possibly follow your story about the burgers and carburetors clause with our boring, front-page-of-every-newspaper-in-the-country   murder trial?"

"Just make it short and it might not be too painful," Rich said, and then he laughed.

Nina caught my eye, as if to ask which one of us would accommodate Rich's request, but before either of us said anything, cries of "Mommy, Mommy!" were heard, followed by Mia running into the living room. She was wearing a red velvet dress, with a white bow holding her soft curls off her face.

Just the sight of Mia made my heart lurch. I instinctively reached for my glass, only to realize it was filled with seltzer. God, I wish I'd said yes to that scotch.

"I'm hungry!" Mia said, with the urgency only a second grader can muster. "When are we going to eat?!"

"As soon as your grandparents get here, sweetie," Rich answered.

"When will that be?!" she demanded.

"Very soon," Deb assured her. "Mia, say hello to your aunt Nina. And do you remember Mommy and Daddy's friend Dan?"

Mia looked at me with inquisitive eyes. "Hi, Mia," I said, an octave higher than my normal voice. "You look so pretty. Is that a new Christmas dress?"

She nodded. "You're Alexa's daddy, right?"

I hesitated, not sure what tense to use. "Yes, I am."

"I miss Alexa."

"Me, too," I said, trying as best I could not to allow myself to tear up, at least not until Mia couldn't witness it.

"I'm sorry she died."

"Thank you for saying that. I am, too, Mia."

"Mommy says that I'm not going to die. Because Alexa died in an accident, and accidents don't happen to girls who are friends with a girl who died in an accident. So if one friend dies, the other one never dies until she's really old, like a grandma."

Rich's ears were turning red with embarrassment, and he started to say something to shoo Mia away, but I talked over him. "That's right, Mia. You're not going to die like Alexa. You're going to get to grow up, and so you're very lucky."

"Yeah," she said. "I don't want to die."

Mia turned and ran back into her room. Deb quickly followed, presumably to read her the riot act.

"Oh, God. I'm so sorry," Rich said.

"Don't be silly," I said, aware that I'd finally lost the battle to be tear-free. "She's really beautiful. Enjoy her."

I was about to tell Rich I'd reconsidered about the scotch, when Nina leaned over and whispered in my ear, "That was lovely, you know." Then her fingers brushed across the top of my hand, as if to emphasize the point.

Just the touch of her hand caused my nerves to settle, and a sense of calm slowly returned. When I looked back to her, she flashed that smile of hers, and for the first time in a long time, I actually felt a semblance of peace.

Dinner was nothing if not a true feast. Acorn squash soup, endive salad, rack of lamb, and more side dishes than I'd ever seen. Mia dictated the choice of topics, so they ranged from playing what she called the animal game—which was Twenty Questions, except instead of the answer being an animal, vegetable, or mineral, it was always an animal—to the type of pet we all wished we could be.

When everyone was sated, Deb directed us to adjourn to the living room while the table was being reset for dessert. Rich's father tried to get Rich to turn on football without being overt in the request ("Do you think the Auburn game is over?") as Mia tugged on his arm to play Polly Pockets.

"Not now, sweetie," Rich said.

"How about if Nina and I play Polly with you?" I said.

"What are pully sockets?" Nina whispered to me.

I smiled at her. The gap between parents and nonparents was wide indeed.

"Not pully sockets. Polly Pockets. They're these tiny dolls with rubber clothing. If we're lucky, she'll have Littlest Pet Shop, too."

I reached down to pull Nina up from the sofa. As it always had before, her hand felt warm in mine.

Mia's room reminded me of Alexa's, an unruly mixture of high-end furniture, an overindulgence of toys and stuffed animals, and the chaos of a child's imagination. Her bed had cat sheets that I remembered from the Pottery Barn Kids catalogue, and most of the artwork on the walls was Mia's. In the corner was the requisite bookshelf stuffed with the board books that

Rich and Deb had read to her before she could even open her eyes, while open on the desk was the third installment of the Harry Potter series, *The Prisoner of Azkaban*, which was bookmarked somewhere toward the middle.

"Are you reading this, Mia?" I asked, pointing to the Potter book.

"Yeah. Sometimes Mommy and Daddy read it with me. If I don't know some of the words."

I felt myself become choked up. Alexa had never gotten that far in her reading. She was able to read, but not a long book like Harry Potter. I couldn't help but think about how much I wanted to read to her again, and then told myself to stop it. There was just no point in thinking like that.

"So, do the Pollys have names?" I asked, plopping down on the floor next to Mia, in front of a large wooden dollhouse that appeared to be their home.

"I call them all Polly. This one is Red Polly because she has red hair," Mia explained while thrusting a red-haired figure in front of my face. "And this one is Brown Polly because her skin is brown. You can be her."

Mia created an elaborate backstory in which Red Polly was the mother of Brown Polly, and they were also apparently singers and had lots of pets. Nina's role was to make the animal noises for their "pets," although Mia was careful to explain to Nina that the pets were not actually Polly Pockets but came from Calico Critters.

"Mommy, Mommy," I said in a high-pitched voice intended to sound like a child's. "I'm scared."

"Don't be scared, my little baby," Mia said, maneuvering her doll closer to the one in my hand. "Your mommy is here and I'll protect you."

It continued on like that for about ten minutes. As we each played our parts, I could see Nina looking at me with a mixture of awe and surprise. It was as if I'd revealed fluency in some obscure foreign language, like Mandarin Chinese, but in this case it was little-girlese.

"I'm sorry to break up all your fun," Rich said, "but dessert is on the table."

Dessert was chocolate fondue and homemade cookies. Everything was delicious, but as it wound down, I whispered to Nina, "I think I'm about ready for that scotch."

"Right behind you," she murmured.

"Thank you so much," Nina said, rising from the table. "Everything was just perfect, but I'm afraid Dan and I need to go."

"So soon?" Deb said.

"Yeah, I'm really sorry, but we have a meeting first thing tomorrow morning with an important witness, and we need to finish prepping." A lie, which she delivered with an impressive degree of conviction. "So, duty calls."

"I can vouch for my partner on this one," I said, although even to my ear, I sounded less sincere than Nina had. "We really do have to be going."

After our escape, Nina and I walked south down

Madison Avenue for a few blocks before I suggested we get a drink at the Mark Hotel. I knew from experience that hotel bars are always open, even on Christmas, and I was not disappointed.

We took up residence in a corner booth. It was one of those tables with banquette seating, and so the place settings were catty-corner, directing us to sit next to each other.

The room was barely lit. It was so dark, in fact, that I had to tilt the drink menu against the candle on the table to ascertain the different varieties of scotch.

When the waiter came over, Nina said, "Two glasses of your best scotch."

He looked at me to confirm, and I was glad to have spent the time reading the menu. "Thank you, but we'll just go with the Macallan twelve."

"Are you telling me that I'm not worth their best scotch?" Nina said with a look of mock umbrage.

"That's right. Their best scotch is probably a couple of hundred bucks a glass. I thought we could make do with the twenty-dollar variety just fine. That okay with you?"

She nodded sheepishly, which caused the waiter to turn on his heel, apparently not happy that I'd just reduced his tip dramatically.

After he returned with our drinks, Nina lifted hers in a toast. "To surviving another Christmas," she said, but not without a subtle wince, which I attributed to her use of the word *surviving*.

"Oh my God!" she shrieked after the first sip. "It tastes like fire!"

"It's, as they say, an acquired taste."

"Agh! Why would anyone want to acquire it?" she replied, her eyes watering.

I flagged down the waiter. "My friend here is a bit of a lightweight, I'm afraid. Can she have a glass of . . ."

"Chardonnay, please, now," Nina said.

I nursed my one drink while Nina lapped me. After she had ordered her third, she began regaling me with the recent misadventures in her dating life. I can only assume it was because of the alcohol that I heard all about the anti-Semite ("No lie, he actually said, 'I thought only Jews were lawyers in those big law firms'"); the guy with the tiny penis ("He's lying on top of me, just about to enter, and says, 'I need to tell you something . . . I'm really small'"); and the guy who texted with another woman the entire date ("'Hang on, I'll be right with you,' he kept saying").

"Is this when I'm supposed to take out the world's smallest violin?" I said.

She looked at me hard, as if weighing whether she was going to commit to what she wanted to say.

"I know I can't go toe-to-toe with you in the tragedy department, Dan, but that doesn't mean that I haven't known heartbreak."

"I'm sorry, were you in love with the small-penis guy or the anti-Semite?"

Her pursed lip and rigid jaw left no doubt that she wasn't kidding anymore.

"No," she said. "Not them." She let out a sigh, and

then replaced it with a full gulp of air, and exhaled again. "But there was a guy and . . . I didn't just think he was the one, I *knew* it. The whole soul mate thing. And, of course, too good to be true always is. He was married, but he was going to leave her, just give him some time, and then we'd be together. . . . You know, the oldest story known to womankind. Anyway, I let it go on for far too long, and so I was good and hooked. I mean, the whole nine yards hooked. I had it so bad for him that it got to the point where I felt like I . . . like I had no free will at all anymore."

She ran her hand over her face in a rubbing motion, although I knew it was to wipe away tears. When our eyes met again, hers were fully moist.

"If I'm not prying, when did it end with him?"

"Hard to say with any precision. There's been some unfortunate backsliding . . . but we've managed to keep clear of each other for a little while now. We still talk every now and then, but I've been able to limit it to just that."

"You make it sound like a bad habit. Like you're trying to quit smoking, doing it one cigarette at a time."

"More like quitting crack cold turkey, and then maybe you'll have an idea."

For a moment I thought she was going to elaborate, but she seemed lost somewhere. I wondered if she was thinking about him.

"No, I take that back, it's worse than that," she said, "and here's why: even though I don't have too much experience about the effects of illegal substances, being a semi-good lawyer girl, I imagine that, with drugs, you know that they're bad for you, and so, even when you're addicted, you want to end it. But it's not that way when you're in love with someone who has that same power over you. When it actually happens, when you meet that guy who just takes your breath away, you think it's good for you, even if there are things about him—you know, like his having a wife—that you know are going to be a problem. You're really able to convince yourself that it's just part of the struggle that underpins all great love stories. That you're meant to be together, and so it's all going to work out in the end. It just has to, of course. What's the alternative?"

Nina was not looking at me as she said this, but her attention seemed to be off somewhere in the distance, as if she was delivering a monologue in a play and was speaking to the balcony. She had maintained a cheery facade during the soliloquy, suggesting that her remembrances were happy ones, but without any warning, her expression fell, and her eyes teared up again.

20

Although it's the oldest cliché of detective work, the next morning Nina and I returned to the scene of the crime. Or more accurately, *outside* the scene of the crime.

Given the choice Judge Pielmeier offered us, we decided L.D.'s presence was not necessary to our walk-through of Roxanne's house, and Nina and I would handle it on our own. If we thought there was something L.D. needed to see, we'd revisit the issue with Judge Pielmeier.

Roxanne lived in a brick Georgian town house in Greenwich Village, on an alleyway street. What that meant, aside from the fact that her place was worth eight figures, was that she had no doorman, the buildings around hers were also single-family homes without doormen, and the street was extra-quiet.

In front of Roxanne's house, behind a black wrought-iron fence, a makeshift memorial had sprung up, where fans had placed bouquets of flowers and lit candles. The full Princess Di treatment. Even today, a month after the murder, there were several flower arrangements in front of the door and three candles were burning. Next to them was a framed photograph of Roxanne. Her blue eyes glistened, a stark contrast to the lifeless eyes in the autopsy photos.

We were supposed to be there at noon for the walk-through. We'd gotten there early, however, to spend some time canvassing the neighborhood.

"Let's go a-knockin'," I said to Nina.

"Split up or together?"

"Together."

It is one of the Ten Commandments of criminal defense practice never to speak to a witness without a witness of your own. It's one of the most unfair aspects of criminal law: prosecutors are permitted to coerce witnesses with the threat of jail time, but if a defense lawyer even suggests some type of benefit to a witness in exchange for his cooperation—or worse, threatens the witness in any way—that's considered obstruction of justice, and the lawyer could find himself a defendant in a hurry. To guard against that happening, it's always advisable to talk to witnesses with a witness of your own, because it's harder later on for someone to claim that two lawyers are lying. Not impossible, but harder.

No one was home at the first house we tried. Or the one next to that. The house after that was at least occupied, but the middle-aged man who answered the door said he didn't even know Roxanne was his neighbor until after she died. The elderly, well-maintained woman who answered the door at the next home told us the same thing—she hadn't even realized that anyone famous lived on the block until after the murder.

"It was awful, just awful," the woman said. "All those television vans and people. This is a nice, quiet street, and . . . thank goodness, it's finally back to normal, although we still have the occasional tourist coming by taking pictures."

It was more of the same at the next few homes. Either no one was home or, if someone was, he or she had never seen Roxanne.

"Don't you find it strange that these people didn't know that Roxanne was their neighbor?" Nina asked me as we crossed the street to begin making our way down the other side.

"This is New York City," I said with a shrug. "Nobody knows their neighbors."

"I guess, but wouldn't there have been paparazzi camped in front of her house?"

"I think all that started after she died. From what I read, she only moved to this place a few months ago, and she'd been on tour for most of the time since."

We started down the other side of the street. The first house had a bright red door with a brass knocker, which I ignored, instead striking the door lightly with my fist.

A large black woman opened the door. Her hello was heavy with an accent, indicating she was from one of the Caribbean islands, and my prejudices led me immediately to assume she was an employee of the family that lived there.

"My name is Daniel Sorensen and this is my partner, Nina Harrington. We're lawyers working on the case involving Roxanne's murder. Did you know that Roxanne was your neighbor?"

She nodded that she did. "Dr. and Mrs. Collins are at work now. I'm just the housekeeper."

"Were you here the night Roxanne was murdered?" I asked quickly, realizing that our time with this woman was going to be short-lived.

"Yeah. I'm always here."

She said this with a smile, which I viewed as an opening. "May I ask your name?"

"Eugenia Tompkins."

"Ms. Tompkins, did you ever see Roxanne?"

"Not too much," she said.

Eureka! Someone who had actually spotted Roxanne, who I was beginning to believe was as elusive as the Loch Ness monster.

"So you did see her in the neighborhood?" Nina said.

"Not when she died. The police asked me about that, but a few weeks before, I'd seen her."

"Was she with anyone?" I asked.

"A man. At first I thought it may have been her father."

"Why'd you think that?"

"I dunno. I guess because he was older. I thought maybe they were going to church or something."

Tompkins looked back into the house. I figured I had one more question before she cut this off, so I decided to make it count.

"You said that you first thought he was her father. Did something happen to cause you to think he wasn't?"

"You could say that," she said with a mischievous grin. "They started to kiss. And it wasn't the kind of kiss you give your father."

She said this laughing, but when I was a beat too late joining in, she must have realized that she'd said too much. Even before I could get out another question, she said, "I think I hear the baby. I'm sorry, but I got to go," and then she slammed the door in our faces.

We knocked on the doors of the rest of the houses on the street, but no one else told us anything worth knowing. A few had seen Roxanne coming and going, usually getting into some type of black SUV, but no one had seen her with anyone, man or woman.

I was beginning to wish that paparazzi had staked out Roxanne's home. At the very least, we'd have photographs of the older man she'd been kissing.

By the time we made it back to Roxanne's house, two uniformed policemen were standing on her stoop, behind the wrought iron gates. They did not seem happy to be there, but I've rarely seen a cop happy to be anywhere.

"It's about time, Counselors," the older of the two cops said. He had a thick black mustache. The hair on his head was equally thick and also black as night.

"Sorry if we're late," I said, checking my watch to see that we were, in fact, on time.

"We're supposed to babysit you," said the mustachioed cop. "So we're going to stand out here and make sure you're not disturbed while you do your thing." He made little effort to hide that he found the assignment beneath him. "Then, when you're done, we're going to look through your bags and have you empty your pockets, so we can report back that you didn't take anything."

When the speech was finished, the other cop unlocked the gate, and then unlocked Roxanne's front door. "We'll be right out here if you need us," Mustache Cop said as we walked past his partner into the house.

Roxanne's house was far more classically appointed than I would have imagined. Her entry hall was done in black-and-white marble that reminded me of something out of an Edith Wharton novel. The furniture had a Victorian flair, as did the artwork, which was, by and large, oil paintings of landscapes.

"What are we looking for, exactly?" Nina asked.

"It'd be nice if some guy left a bloody wristwatch with his fingerprints all on it," I said, "but beyond that, we're just looking for something that doesn't make sense. It's like the old joke about pornography. Hopefully, we'll know it when we see it."

"Ha-ha."

We made our way quickly through the house. Aside from the television remote being on the floor of the media room, none of the other spaces looked like they'd been touched for months. That made some sense because Roxanne was in South Carolina the prior four days, and she had a full-time housekeeper.

All of which made the contrast with Roxanne's bedroom that much starker.

It was all white. Not just the walls but everything in it, too. Roxanne's king bed was upholstered in white leather, the facing sofas were covered in white chenille, and the throw pillows were white fur. Even the wall-to-wall shag carpeting was a bright white, which made the deep red around the bed pop out. You couldn't look at anything else in the room without your eyes being pulled back to those red stains on the floor.

The bed had been stripped not only of the sheets but the mattress, too, all of which now sat in an evidence room somewhere. The box spring remained, but the dust ruffle had been removed. On my knees, I got closer to the box spring but couldn't detect any blood. Not that it mattered, of course. Based on the crime scene photos, there was plenty of blood on the dust ruffle. It apparently hadn't soaked through to the box spring, however.

"So this is the famous mantel," Nina said, standing beside the fireplace. Behind her were the two empty brackets (of course, both white).

And wouldn't you know, they were precisely the right size for a baseball bat to rest upon.

21

I'd left four messages for Brianna's mother, Mercedes, at the number L.D. had given us. Her outgoing message didn't say her name, but at least it was a woman's voice, which indicated that she might exist after all. In the first message I stated my name, without any identification, a shot in the dark in case the fact that I was a lawyer was going to frighten her off. In the second, I said I was calling on L.D.'s behalf, and that it was important that she call me back. She didn't. The next day I revealed that I was L.D.'s defense counsel, but that didn't merit a return phone call either. Finally, I left a message saying that it was extremely urgent that she contact me at once, but she either never got the message or, if she did, she must not have agreed, because she didn't return my call.

I didn't think that knocking on the door at the address L.D. gave us would be any more successful than my phone efforts, but stranger things have happened than someone who was ducking your phone calls agreeing to talk to you face-to-face. With that in mind, Nina and I showed up at the Brooklyn address L.D. had given us, a run-down brownstone in the non-hipster part of Williamsburg.

Beside the front door were twelve intercom buzzers. In the middle was the one for apartment 4B, which had the name Mercedes Williams next to it.

"At least that's a good sign," Nina said.

"Want to place a bet on whether she still lives there?"

There was no answer when we buzzed. With no other option, I called the building's super, a man identified on the certificate of occupancy only as "Muki."

"Mr. Muki," I said when he answered.

"No, Muki's my first name," he said.

"Okay, Muki, my name is Daniel Sorensen. I'm a lawyer and I need to contact one of your tenants, Mercedes Williams. Have you seen her lately?"

"Nope. Unless she's got a leak or something, I wouldn't see her."

"Do you have any way of getting in contact with her?"

"No. I just knock on her door. The office may have a phone number."

"Okay, we'll ask them. If you do see her, will you ask her to call me? My name again is Dan Sorensen."

I left my phone number, but the fact that Muki didn't ask for a second to get a pen made it pretty clear that he hadn't written it down.

I was therefore understandably shocked when later that day, I received a call from Mercedes. I was equally surprised that she readily agreed to meet with us.

We were back at her building less than an hour later. This time when we buzzed the intercom, she answered and allowed us entry. I huffed my way up to the fourth floor. Nina giggled as I struggled, telling me that the staircase in her building was even steeper.

Everything about Mercedes was dark. Her eyes,

her hair, and her complexion were almost all the same hue, the color of a plum. She wore her hair straight, and long enough that it brushed her shoulders. Although she looked at us fiercely, it wasn't enough to hide that she was scared.

"Thank you for seeing us, Ms. Williams," I said. "May we come in for just a few moments?"

She nodded, and then led us into the apartment. We made it far enough inside for Mercedes to close the door behind us, but she stopped short of offering us a seat in the living room.

"Is Brianna at home?" I asked.

"No. She in school."

Of course she was. I really had no clue anymore about kids.

"I don't think I'm going to be much help to you all," Mercedes said, clearly wanting to move this along and get it over with. "It's not like me and L.D. talked much, you know?"

"Did he ever talk to you about his relationship with Roxanne?" Nina asked.

Mercedes hesitated for a moment. "L.D. know you here?"

"He does," I said. "That's how we got your phone number and address. We're his lawyers, and so nothing you say is going to go beyond us unless we think it's good for L.D., if that's what you're worrying about."

She nodded as I said this, presumably accepting its truth without requiring further proof of L.D.'s consent. But rather than reveal some bombshell that she only would have shared had she been sure L.D. wanted us to know about it, she just said, "None of my business who he with. Like I said, we didn't talk much."

"I get the whole not telling the ex-girlfriend about the new relationship," Nina said in a one-woman-to-another kind of way, "but you two must have talked about Roxanne sometimes. That's just normal."

"Maybe," she said, and then she took it back. "I really don't remember."

All of this seemed hard for me to believe. Roxanne was one of the most famous women on the planet. You'd think that there would be some discussion between them about her, if only about the impact on Brianna.

"L.D. told us that he had plans to see Brianna over Thanksgiving," I said. "This is very important to our defense. It's the prosecution's theory that L.D. killed Roxanne because they had recently broken up, right before Thanksgiving, which was the reason why he didn't go with her to South Carolina. But if we could put on proof that L.D. never intended to go, because he had plans to see his daughter, that would go a long way."

I couldn't have led Mercedes more with a GPS system, but from her scrunched-up expression, I knew that she wasn't going to help us out.

"What do you want me to say?"

That's the worst thing a witness can ever ask, at least to an ethical lawyer. There's only one response that's possible, and I gave it.

"We only want the truth."

She frowned, which made me frown, too. She didn't want to tell us the truth.

"I'll say whatever you want me to," Mercedes said. "Does L.D. want me to say we were together for Thanksgiving?" She sighed. "My momma was with me. If I say I was with L.D., they gonna ask my momma about it, right?"

"They will," Nina said.

"Please just tell us the truth," I said. "We know you want to help L.D., but the prosecution will check on your story, and if you lie, they'll be able to prove it with gas receipts or a photo showing you were someplace else. If that happens, it's not only bad for L.D., but it's really bad for you, too, because it's perjury."

Mercedes nodded. She saw the problem.

"Tell L.D. I wanted to help, okay?"

"Of course we will," Nina said.

"We weren't here for Thanksgiving. I got people in Boston, and we was up there."

"Do you know who L.D. was with over Thanksgiving?" I asked.

"If L.D. didn't tell you, I don't think I should."

"I understand that you want to help him, Mercedes," I said as compassionately as I could, given that I was furious that L.D. had lied to us. Again. "And I'm sure L.D. thought saying he was going to see his daughter over Thanksgiving would sound more convincing than whatever he was actually doing. But now that we know he wasn't with Brianna, we really need to know where he was and who he was with. Believe me, he's not going to be upset with you if you tell us. In fact, he'll be pleased because we're not going to be able to speak to him again for a few more days, and so you'd be saving us a lot of time, and in a murder investigation, time is really valuable."

I couldn't have blamed Mercedes had she decided to err on the side of not telling us. But she didn't.

"Have you spoken to Nuts?" she said.

"Who?" Nina said before I could.

"I'm not sure what his real name is. I think it's Milton, but L.D. always called him Nuts. I think L.D. was with him. Anyway, you can ask him yourselves. He lives in Brownsville. Tilden Houses, just like L.D. used to."

Brownsville was one of the city's most crime-ridden neighborhoods. Its history with the criminal element dated all the way back to the 1930s, when it was the birthplace of Murder, Inc., the forerunner to the Mafia. Today, the streets are a collage of burned-out buildings, vacant storefronts, and rusted cars stripped of anything that could be sold. It has the city's highest concentration of public housing and nearly half the families live below the poverty level. It was not a place that I'd ever venture to at night, and even during the day I felt like I was taking my life in my hands just by walking its streets.

The Tilden complex was actually eight buildings. Because Mercedes didn't know Nuts's building number, we had to walk up to each one and see if a Nuts or a Milton was listed.

It appeared that he lived in building three, apartment 8E. At least the name beside the intercom of that unit was Morris Milton.

The intercom didn't work, so we couldn't verify we had the right guy by buzzing up. On the bright side, the lock on the front door didn't work either, and so we were able to enter the building. We had to climb eight flights of stairs to get to apartment 8E, on account of the elevator also being out of order.

When I knocked on the door, Nina looked even more concerned than she had when we visited L.D. at Rikers. I didn't blame her—I felt safer in the prison, too.

"Who is it?" said a deep voice from behind the door.

"We're lawyers representing Legally Dead. Do you mind giving us a few minutes of your time?"

It was at that moment the thought occurred to me that he might not appreciate being called Nuts.

"Mr. Milton?" I asked when he opened the door.

"Yeah," he said, eyeing me up and down.

Nuts had the same general build as L.D., which is to say he was as big and strong as anyone I'd seen outside of an athletic arena. Like L.D., he was dark complexioned, and his head was shaved.

He differed from L.D. in one important respect, however. Nuts looked to be a stranger to human emotion of any kind.

"Th-thank you for seeing us, Mr. Milton," I stuttered.

"Call me Nuts," he said, which at least settled the issue of what to call him.

"Okay." I smiled, but that didn't cause him to recip-rocate. "Can we ask you a few questions?"

"'Bout what?"

"About L.D. and his relationship with Roxanne."

"You said you wuz L.D.'s lawyers."

"We are. We're looking for evidence that will show L.D. had plans to spend Thanksgiving in New York, and we were told to talk to you about that."

This didn't seem to placate him. "Who the fuck said that?"

Nina said, "Mercedes Williams."

Nuts must have recognized Mercedes's name because he didn't say anything more. I took the silence as an invitation.

"Did you spend Thanksgiving with L.D.?"

"You think I'm a fucking idiot?"

I reflexively took a step backward. I had the same feeling you get when in close proximity to a danger-ous creature. As if making a sudden movement could cause him to strike.

"Look, I understand that you don't want to be in-volved in a murder trial. Nobody does, but—"

"You want me to hurt you?"

"No," I said, and left it at that.

"Then there ain't no reason for you to still be stand-ing there."

After we left Brownsville, Nina suggested we go to Bubby's, another restaurant around the corner from my apartment to which I'd never been. Once inside,

Nina said what I was thinking. "It seems pretty clear that Mr. Nuts is not going to be our star witness."

"That depends. If we need someone to scare the hell out of the jury, I think he's the perfect guy."

"Our client may be enough to do the trick all by himself," she said with a chuckle. "Two incredibly scary guys might be overkill. Pun intended."

When our food arrived, Nina was telling me about her New Year's Eve plan, which was to attend a very private party being held at a club that I'd never heard of. "The way it works," Nina explained, "is that you get an invitation email with a passcode. You use the passcode to find out where the party is, how many people have confirmed, and who invited you, but that's all you know about it. You don't get the guest list or anything else. So all I know is that it's being held at this club on Stanton Street, and there are going to be about five hundred people there."

"So who invited you?" She broke eye contact. "Oh no, not Mr. Married Man?"

"I know, it's pretty messed up, right? He won't be there, of course. I'm sure he's out with the wife, but this way he still gets to exert some type of control over me."

"Why go, then?"

"Because it'll be fun. Hold on, let me rephrase. It'll be more fun than just sitting at home doing nothing. One of my girlfriends is going to come with me. She's got nothing better to do either, apparently. Which brings me to my next question: What are your plans for tomorrow night?"

"I'm still weighing several very enticing invitations," I said.

"Yeah, sure. Rich already told me that he invited you to go out with him and Deb, and you made some bullshit excuse about needing some time alone to reflect on all that's happened in the past year."

"Did he tell you that the party they're going to is being thrown by the parents of Mia's friend? Some guy who's a hedge fund guru. And if that isn't bad enough, it's black tie. Sorry, no thanks."

She laughed. "I guess I'd rather stay home alone than do that, too. Hey . . . why don't you come with me? I can probably get you into my highly exclusive little soiree."

"That sounds tempting, but I'm still going to pass. I'd really be no fun."

"What are you going to do instead?"

"If you must know, my New Year's Eve plan is to order in the greasiest food I can think of from the diner down the block and watch the James Bond marathon on Spike."

She laughed. "That actually sounds like fun. Just don't drink too much, okay? We have our meeting with Popofsky the next day."

Now I laughed. "That's not until four, but I get your point. I'll be a good boy."

22

Last year, I spent New Year's Eve alone, drinking myself into a stupor that I hoped would last the entire year, if not longer. My revelry ended shortly after midnight, however, when I vomited all over myself.

At least this year I was not going to do that. Progress.

New Year's Eve had started off pretty much as I'd predicted. I ordered a half-pound burger stuffed with Roquefort cheese, French fries and onion rings, and a brownie sundae, and wolfed them down in front of *Goldfinger*.

At eleven fifteen, in the middle of *Dr. No*, and while I was still nursing my first glass of scotch, my intercom buzzed.

"You have a visitor," Mario, the night doorman, said.

When I opened the door, Nina was standing there smiling ear to ear and holding a shopping bag. Through her partially open overcoat, I could see that she was wearing a very tight and very short black dress, which was so low cut that it was difficult for me to maintain eye contact.

"Happy almost New Year," she said, the smell of alcohol on her breath.

"Um . . . you, too. Come on in," I stammered.

"I wanted to surprise you and just barge in, but you've got a different doorman at night."

It took me a second to realize she meant that when she came over in the morning for work she wasn't buzzed up, but the evening doorman wouldn't let her go up without notifying me first. "So, to what do I owe this unexpected pleasure?" I said.

I thought I said this teasingly, but she must not have taken it that way. "Are you sorry I came over?"

"No, of course not."

"Okay, then, I will take off my coat and stay awhile," Nina said loudly.

"I-I'm sorry," I stammered again, realizing my bad manners. "Would you like something to drink?"

"Yes, please."

"I'm having scotch, but I'll get you some wine."

"No, I'm going to try the firewater again. I've already had two or three Cosmos at the party, so I think I'm ready."

After I confirmed that she was serious, I went into the kitchen and poured Nina a glass of scotch. When I reentered the living room, Nina had stretched out on my sofa. She wasn't lying down, but sitting on enough of a diagonal that she occupied more than half the seating area. Her shoes were off.

I handed her the glass and sat down beside her. She immediately raised her glass to eye level.

"To . . ." She hesitated.

"A happy and prosperous New Year?"

"If you like," she said, and then clinked her glass against mine.

She took a sip. The effect of having downed several

Cosmos must have worked, because she didn't seem to be in pain, as she had been the last time she'd tried to swallow scotch. "Mmm," she added with a smile.

"You sure it's okay?"

"Better than okay." And then, as if she'd been startled, she jumped up and said, "I almost forgot, I come bearing gifts."

She grabbed the shopping bag she had brought and walked back to the kitchen, returning a few moments later with two cupcakes on a plate. One was green and the other looked exactly like a Hostess cupcake, down to the white swirl of frosting on the top, except that it was twice as large.

"I thought we'd share. One's mint and the other is just what it looks like."

"Did you bring a knife?" I asked.

She laughed. "A cupcake should never be sullied by a knife or a fork. It's to be eaten from hand to mouth, and when shared, the same rule applies. So, have a taste."

She brought the green cupcake to my mouth and I took a bite. It was sweeter than I had expected, and not very minty at all. After my bite, Nina followed, swirling the green crème filling around her tongue.

"You have to taste the crème," she said. "That's the part that's minty."

We finished the mint cupcake first, alternating bites, and then dug into the Hostess-looking one.

"I think we're both really due for some good luck in the New Year," Nina said, now swirling the white crème on her tongue. "Don't you think?" Before I could answer, she said with a start, "What time is it? You don't think we missed the ball drop?"

"Now that would be a bad way to start the New Year," I said. "But no worries, it's only a quarter to."

I turned the television on to see Ryan Seacrest. The little timer in the corner of the screen was counting down to midnight and showed ten minutes remained in the old year. From the shearling overcoat Seacrest was wearing, you would have thought he was standing in Siberia.

At the stroke of midnight, Nina kissed me.

"What's that about?" I said, pulling slightly away, but not so far that I couldn't still feel the heat of her breath as well as smell the sweet scent of scotch.

"It's time," she whispered, and moved back toward me without any hesitation. As a near fluid motion, her tongue took over my mouth and her weight pushed me back onto the sofa, demanding surrender from the rest of me.

It would be a lie to say I hadn't been fantasizing about this very moment. But that didn't mean that I actually thought it was going to occur. I fantasize about a lot of things these days—Sarah and Alexa being alive, my having lived a different life before their deaths, playing center field for the Yankees—and I know those things are never going to happen.

"Come with me," Nina whispered in my ear. Without waiting for a response, she stood, and I felt an ache when she peeled her body off mine.

It wasn't until we were kissing again in my bedroom that it finally registered completely that I was about to have sex with someone other than Sarah. I didn't feel as guilty as I'd thought I might when this moment finally arrived. It reminded me of my more drunken nights, when I reveled in the warmth of intoxication, even as I knew in the back of my brain that there would be a reckoning when the euphoria subsided.

"God, Dan, I want you so much," Nina moaned in my ear the moment I put my hand on her breast.

Everything was how I remembered it was supposed to be, but it was still vaguely foreign, like when you revisit a place after a long absence. Nina's body differed from Sarah's in almost every way—her breasts were more than a full cup larger, while the rest of her was smaller, from her mouth, which seemingly fit inside my own, to her neck, which seemed impossibly narrow as I kissed its length.

We were like this—kissing and groping—for what seemed like a very long time. For some of it, we were undressing each other, and each time another part of Nina's flesh came in contact with my own, I'd lose myself that much more. It was ironic, considering the benders I've had, but I couldn't recall ever feeling so out of control. Even so, I held back the ultimate goal. It was as if I couldn't be the one to initiate the act, so Nina would have to take control to bring us to that point.

As if she could read my mind, Nina rolled around me, so smoothly that I didn't quite realize it had happened, until I saw her on top of me, her breasts still in my hands. She reached behind her, clutching me in her hand, and then guided me inside her.

I had been watching her, almost curiously, wondering what was going to happen next, but the moment I felt her wetness, my eyes closed, and there was nothing but blackness, which only heightened the sensation that everything was happening in my head as much as anywhere else. I didn't know how much time passed, but it seemed to me that virtually from the moment I was fully immersed in her, Nina's pace quickened.

When Sarah and I made love in this position, I always knew when she was about to climax because she'd angle her body away from me. Like everything else so far, Nina was the opposite. She bent completely toward me, locking her mouth on mine so tightly that for a moment I couldn't breathe. And then it felt as if she was breathing for me, and I could hear her pleasure, the sounds coming directly through her mouth into mine.

When I felt what I thought was the rush of her orgasm, I clasped her elbows tightly, holding her quivering body in place, but then I realized that I might have been wrong, because a new wave came over her that was far more intense.

A millisecond later, I heard my own groan as I ejaculated. Almost simultaneously with that joyous release, I experienced the sadness that I'd been expecting.

23

Marty Popofsky showed up fifteen minutes early for our four o'clock meeting. When the meeting was originally scheduled, I apologized for asking Popofsky to work on New Year's Day but explained that we needed to see him before the January 2 court conference, and it made sense to give him as much time before then to do the work he needed to do. He didn't seem to care at all.

"Happy New Year," I said.

"You, too," Popofsky said. "I made sure not to overdo it last night so I'd be good and ready for today."

The very idea of Marty Popofsky overdoing it on New Year's Eve made me chuckle.

Popofsky methodically removed his coat, and then his scarf, rolling it in a ball and tucking it into the sleeve, the way they teach you to do in kindergarten. After that, he tucked his Mets cap into his coat pocket.

When he was finally ready, I led him into the apartment, where, like seemingly every man, everywhere, he lit up when Nina came into view.

"So what do you have for us?" I asked, if only to snap Popofsky back to reality.

"Something quite interesting, actually." He put his beat-up briefcase down on the table and started to rummage through it. "Now, if I could only find the report . . . Okay. I got it here."

The report we'd sent him had been fastened together by a black binder clip, but now the pages were loose and folded in every which way. He began to rearrange them again, smoothing over some of the more crinkled pages with his hands. Most pages were covered in yellow highlighter.

"I've read through the report," Popofsky finally said. "Several times, in fact. And I've done some preliminary work, but don't hold me to what I'm going to tell you because other factors might come into play. First thing is that I don't have much quibble with the estimated time of death being around midnight. As I understand it, that's not a critical issue for your client because he's home from about eight p.m. until the morning, right?"

It didn't escape my notice that Popofsky referred to L.D. as "your client." As a technical matter, that was correct—Popofsky's retention was by Sorensen and Harrington, and not by L.D., which was done purposefully so that his conclusions would be within the attorney-client privilege until such time as we decided to waive it. At the same time, I couldn't rule out that his choice of language wasn't just him being precise but was a way of distancing himself from Legally Dead.

"Yeah, that's right," I said.

"So there's not too much help I can give you on that front," he continued. "I also took a shot at trying to figure out the approximate height and weight of the murderer. You can do that through an analysis of the blood spatter. To a point, anyway. It's never exact, but juries eat that stuff up because it's like what they see on television."

"So were you able to do that?" I asked, undoubtedly sounding exasperated at Popofsky's roundabout way of getting to the point.

"Not to a certainty, because you're not certain of the murder weapon. The way you do the calculation is that you look at the blood spatter and you can determine the velocity with which it hit the wall. It's funny because most people think it's based on the *speed* the blood hits the wall, but that's actually not the way you do it. It's the splash that's important. So I'm not looking at the blood that flew off Roxanne's body and then stuck. I'm looking at that blood's splash onto another part of the wall."

He had the expression that experts sometimes get when they think the minutiae of their findings is fascinating in every way. Jurors, however, like lawyers, and like everyone else for that matter, want to know the conclusion first. Expert testimony is a lot like journalism in that way—you should never bury the lead.

"Marty . . . can you give us the bottom line, please?" I asked.

"That's what I'm trying to tell you." Now *he* sounded exasperated, as if any idiot would have figured this out already based on his discussion of blood spatter. "I can tell you the speed with which the blood hit, but all that tells you is the force with which the victim was struck. To extrapolate that back to figure out how large a person would have to be to create that type of force, you got to know what she was hit with. And what she was hit with is inconclusive." He paused and looked around, as if this simple point needed a visual aid. "Okay, let me try it this way. I could tell you that if the injuries were caused simply by someone's fist, your murderer would have to be enormous. So that tells you the killer either has a place in *The Guinness Book of World Records*, or a weapon of some sort was used. But what kind of weapon? Now, that's critical. Because a five-foot-tall woman might be able to create the same impact with a golf club as a six-foot-tall man would generate with a baseball bat. And that, in a nutshell, is the problem."

"Assume a baseball bat," I said. "How big is the guy?"

"Five ten to six two. Reasonably strong, too."

"So you're telling us that you've excluded women and short men. And that's it?"

He chuckled. "I can't even say that, I'm afraid. A strong woman, although she'd have to be very strong . . . an athletic woman, sure, she could have done it, too."

"Okay. I hope you don't mind my saying this, Marty, but we already knew all that."

"Yeah, I know," Popofsky said, seemingly oblivious to my frustration with him. "But you know the way there were Caucasian pubic hairs found on Roxanne's bed?"

He actually paused to get our acknowledgment. As if we might have forgotten that minor detail.

"Please tell us you know who they belong to," I said, if for no other reason than to avoid another dissertation on the science behind Popofsky's findings.

"I already told you, I can't do a DNA analysis without the follicles, which these samples don't have. If you get me a hair to compare against those found in the bed, I can offer an opinion as to whether they match. But it'll still be a qualified opinion. Without the follicle, you can never say with certainty that it's a dead-on match. The way it'll be is that I'll tell you that the victim's hairs and the hair we're comparing it to have certain matching characteristics. There are twelve comparison points in all. So if one or two of the characteristics match, that likely means they're not from the same source. If five or six of them match, it's a maybe, and if ten or more match, I'll be able to say it's likely, but I couldn't rule out that there might be some others that match, too. A twelve-point match is pretty conclusive, but there's also a lot of judgment that goes into determining what's a match and what isn't. What I think is a ten-point match our friend Harry Davis may turn around and say is a six-point match. You see what I'm saying?"

I truly felt like shaking him.

"Forgive me, Marty, but did you find out who the hair belongs to or not?"

"No, no, no. Like I said, I can't tell you who they came from." He paused, and then a smile came to his lips. "But I think I can tell you whose hairs they *aren't*."

Popofsky said nothing else, milking the suspense. Everyone likes being the center of attention.

"I'm not following you," I said. "Who *don't* they belong to?"

"They're not Roxanne's," he said triumphantly.

"How do you know that?" Nina said.

"It's on page seven of the autopsy. Hang on . . ."

He shuffled a few of his rumpled pages until he came upon one that had, in addition to extensive yellow highlights, a paper clip stuck to the side. "Right here," he said, pointing to the highlighted portion.

I'd already read the section when we reviewed the discovery on Christmas Eve, but I must have missed something. I started through it again, slowly. All I saw, however, was a sea of medical jargon that meant as little to me as it did the first time.

When I looked back up, it must have been clear to Popofsky that I didn't fully understand, because he said, "What that all means, in layman's terms, is that she waxed her pubic region." I knew what that meant, of course, but Popofsky must have thought it was possible I was confused because he then offered: "Roxanne didn't have any pubic hair at the time of her death."

Like my joke to Nina when we searched Roxanne's house, although our SODDI guy hadn't left a bloody wristwatch with his fingerprints all over it, the pubic hairs were a close second. But that didn't mean it was all good news. For one thing, we still had to match the pubic hair to the proverbial haystack of male genitalia out there.

Nina didn't see that as much of a problem, however.

"We've got evidence that she was having sex with another guy," she said, "and that the guy was in her bed right before she was murdered. So what difference does it make if we can't identify the guy by name?"

"I doubt L.D. is going to conclude that Roxanne's sleeping with another guy is really a good thing for him," I said.

"The fact that she was cheating on him is the least of his worries right about now, don't you think?" was Nina's response.

Which led to the second issue.

"I assume you've considered the potential downside of proving another lover?" I said. "That we're giving them strong evidence of a jealousy motive."

Nina chuckled. "You're really a glass-is-half-filled kind of guy, now, aren't you," she said.

Nina shared my bed that evening for the second night. There wasn't much discussion about it. After dinner, we watched television for a little while, and then she announced that she was going to bed, and I followed her into my bedroom.

"You're going to have to bring some clothing over here," I said.

"No worries." She smiled. "I don't like wearing pajamas anyway."

Intellectually, I realized that there was no reason for me not to be with Nina; in fact, many people would have said I should have rejoined the living much sooner. But each moment with her felt like I was letting go of Sarah a little more, as if my brain had limited memory and I was overwriting my recollections of making love with Sarah with these new experiences.

I lasted longer this evening than the two times we'd gone the previous night, the jitters gone, I suppose. And for parts of it, I could almost rein in my thoughts, focusing on how beautiful Nina looked below me, her eyes tightly shut, a wide, unabashed smile across her face.

After we were finished, our bodies glistening in sweat and the musty scent of what we'd just done permeating the room, Nina nestled her head on my chest. "Thank you," she said. "That was . . . I don't know what word to use. Magical?"

In the moments before I dozed off, as I went back over in my mind exactly how Nina looked at her highest peak, the irony of my life struck me with full force. I had stopped one descent and replaced it with another, for there was no denying that I was falling hard for Nina.

24

Judge Pielmeier never took the bench until everyone was present and she had finished whatever else she needed to do. On January 2, that meant ten forty-five a.m., for a conference originally scheduled for ten.

The judge's law clerk knocked three times on her desktop. "All rise!" she cried out. "Please come to order. The Supreme Court of the state of New York, for the county of New York, the Honorable Linda A. Pielmeier presiding, is now in session. All present before this court appear and you shall be heard."

Some judges seem embarrassed by the pomp of their office, choosing to have court meetings in their chambers, or immediately telling counsel to sit when they enter the courtroom. Judge Pielmeier was at the other extreme. I got the sense she wouldn't have minded if a marching band played some type of judicial equivalent to "Hail to the Chief" whenever she entered.

"I apologize for the delay," Judge Pielmeier said, looking past the lawyers to the gallery, and without providing any explanation for her tardiness. "I'm going to ask the corrections people to bring the defendant in, unless there's something we need to discuss prior to that."

Assistant District Attorney Kaplan and I stood in unison to tell her that there was not.

Judge Pielmeier nodded, a signal for the clerk to open the court's side door. Just like before, L.D. was accompanied by two guards and was wearing the same orange jumpsuit, complete with the wrist and ankle accessories. When they approached counsel table, the guards once again unlocked only the handcuffs, leaving L.D. restrained about the ankles. Then they took their position about six feet behind us.

"What's this about?" L.D. whispered to me as he entered.

"We've made a few discovery motions," I told him. "Stuff we need to get on the record."

L.D. nodded. It wasn't clear to me whether he knew that the record mattered only in the event he was convicted, in which case it was what the appellate court reviewed.

"We're now on the record," Judge Pielmeier said, ending my conversation with L.D. "We're here on several discovery motions filed by the defense. . . . I've read the papers, so you can assume I'm familiar with the facts. Mr. Sorensen, it's a defense motion, so why don't you go first?"

"Thank you, Your Honor," I said. "My partner, Nina Harrington, will make the argument for the defense."

Nina had written our briefs, and so we'd agreed that she'd make the argument. The first point she'd address was what we wanted most, the prosecution's witness list. With it, we had a road map for the prosecution's case. Without it, we'd be trying the case in the dark.

We knew, however, it would be an uphill battle. Witness protection was something of a paranoia for Judge Pielmeier, a vestige of her Chen-Tao experience, where she actually lost a witness midtrial. As a result, she was probably the worst judge we could have pulled on this issue.

"A criminal trial should not be an ambush," Nina began, a prevetted line that we thought would be a good sound bite for the press. "We have absolutely no idea of the identity of the witnesses the people intend to rely on at trial. We cite in our briefs the case law setting forth the right of defense counsel to get a witness list sufficiently in advance of trial."

Kaplan rose without Judge Pielmeier prompting her to respond. I couldn't help but think I would have earned a judicial rebuke had I done the same thing.

"Your Honor, we have serious concerns about the safety of our witnesses if we provide the defendant with a witness list. This case involves a brutal murder."

"Thanks for that reminder, Ms. Kaplan," Judge Pielmeier said with her tongue in her cheek. "I'd almost forgotten what the people are claiming happened here." The gallery laughed, and Judge Pielmeier let them without interruption. When quiet returned, she continued, "But you need to remember that although we can all agree this was a brutal murder, the issue for us is whether this defendant committed that brutality. I'm not locking you up just because this was a brutal murder, now am I, Ms. Kaplan?"

The gallery laughed again. For once I was enjoying

Judge Pielmeier's sense of humor, seeing that this was a rare occasion when the defense wasn't the brunt of it. But it didn't take long for her to put Nina back on the hot seat.

"Now, Ms. Harrington, I know life would be a whole lot easier for the defense if the defense knew ahead of time who was going to testify for the prosecution, but I need to balance that against the possibility of witnesses being intimidated or coerced, or something worse. What do you have for me that says I should give you what you want on this one?"

Although it sounded like she was asking for a bribe, I understood that the judge wanted Nina to cite some legal precedent to support our contention. I also knew we didn't have anything. At least nothing directly on point.

"The defendant's rights should outweigh the prosecution's unfounded fears," Nina said. "The appellate court stated in the *Hutchinson* case—"

"Oh, that's not right, Ms. Harrington. Not right at all," Judge Pielmeier interrupted. She did it with a smile, indicating that she was looking forward to showing Nina how wrong she was. "Now, I could go through the reasons why you're wrong, not the least of which is that *Hutchinson* was a white-collar prosecution—and before you start with me on this, I'm not saying white-collar defendants get more rights than blue-collar ones, even though from what I've seen of your client's professional wardrobe, he's a no-collar worker, or should I say, a no-shirt worker." She laughed at her own joke, getting the expected support from the gallery. "But there's a great difference between letting an accountant know who is going to testify against him about fraudulent tax returns, which was the issue in *Hutchinson*, and allowing a self-professed"—she looked down at her notes—"'meanest dude there is' to know the identity of the people who stand between his freedom and a lifetime of incarceration. So if that's the best you got, I'm denying the request for a witness list."

Although not completely unexpected, that one hurt. Having a witness list would have gone a long way. Without it, we'd have to prepare for every conceivable witness.

"What else you got for me, Ms. Harrington?"

Dwelling on failure served little purpose, and so like a pitcher who had just given up the go-ahead homer, Nina turned to face the next batter. Unfortunately for her, it was still Judge Pielmeier.

"We'd also like a ruling that Mr. Patterson can wear nonprison clothing at trial," Nina said. "And for the corrections officers to be seated in the gallery, also wearing civilian clothing, so as not to call attention to themselves as guards."

This was truly a no-brainer. Nothing was more prejudicial to a defendant than a prison jumpsuit and uniformed officers holding guns sitting behind him. Kaplan could have easily conceded the point, but true to form, she made us work for it.

"The people take no position on the issue of the

defendant's wardrobe, Your Honor," Kaplan said, "but decisions regarding the safety of the court and court-room personnel are extremely serious. We believe that the defense should make an application to the prison officials with regard to that request."

Judge Pielmeier took the bait. "Mr. Patterson can wear whatever he wants, so long as he's got a shirt on." She paused to allow the gallery time to laugh, which they did, as if on cue. "But I'm going to reserve judgment about security until after I consult with the corrections people. You got anything else on your list, Ms. Harrington?"

I wished she did, but I knew she didn't. "No, Your Honor," she said.

"Okay, then. So let's talk about when we're going to do this," Judge Pielmeier said.

How quickly to go to trial is one of those issues on which clients almost always disagree with their lawyers. From the defense lawyer's perspective, time is almost always an ally. The more time that passes, the more recollections dim, key evidence might be lost, or, if you're really lucky, a witness or two dies.

Clients, however, are like little kids—they want to jump to the end as quickly as possible to see how it all turns out. They talk about how terrible it is that people *think* they're guilty, without much recognition that being found guilty itself is much, much worse.

There's one caveat to that rule of delay, however. If you know your client is guilty, and a key piece of evidence has not been found by the prosecution—the body, or a witness, or the murder weapon—then you want to get to trial before the prosecution can find it.

Nina favored going to trial as soon as possible. When I asked her why, she said it was because our client was already incarcerated. I couldn't help but wonder, however, if it was more because she believed that if the bat was found, L.D.'s prints would be all over it.

If Judge Pielmeier had asked me, I would have requested a trial date four months from now, around mid-May, but that would have been a negotiating position. I expected Kaplan to ask for three months before whatever date I picked in order to take advantage of the prosecution's built-in head start—she'd been engaging in fact finding and evidence gathering well before the indictment. Judge Pielmeier could be expected to split the difference. So asking for mid-May translated into a trial date toward the end of March, which is where I really wanted to end up.

Judge Pielmeier, however, never even broached the subject.

"I'm afraid April is off-limits for me," she said, looking at a computer screen that I presumed had her trial calendar. "And I have another matter that is already scheduled for much of May. Can we push this out until June?"

I turned to L.D. He was vigorously shaking his head. Completely unacceptable. June meant another six months in jail.

"Your Honor, the defense would object to that," I said. "Given that the court has denied Mr. Patterson an opportunity at bail, every day he's incarcerated is a gross miscarriage of justice. Under the speedy-trial rules—"

"Don't quote basic criminal rules to me, Mr. Sorensen," Judge Pielmeier snapped. "You gonna play hardball with me? Okay, then, I'm going to play hardball with you. Let's say January twentieth."

This time I didn't even consult with L.D. "Your Honor, while we greatly appreciate the court making time on its schedule so soon, I'm not sure the defense can be ready by the twentieth, which is little more than two weeks away."

"I know when it is, Mr. Sorensen, but let me remind you why we're here. You said you wouldn't waive your right to a speedy trial. You said you wanted to go to trial as soon as possible. You said that every day your client is incarcerated is—I think the term you used was—'a gross miscarriage of justice.' How gross a miscarriage of justice is acceptable to you?"

Over the giggles in the gallery, I said, "If Your Honor had time in February or even any time in early March, that would be preferable."

"My courtroom is not a restaurant that takes reservations, Counselor. If you are invoking your speedy-trial rights, it's January twenty. And I appear to have misspoken about my availability in June. So your choice, Mr. Sorensen, is to proceed on January twentieth to avoid the gross miscarriage of justice that you are so concerned about, or to waive your speedy-trial rights, which will put this matter in line for sometime during the summer, although now I'm thinking it might be as late as September. Perhaps even October. So, Mr. Sorensen, which one will it be?"

"We'll be ready to go on January twenty," I said in utter defeat.

Judge Pielmeier announced that we were adjourned even before I could ask her for the opportunity to speak to Legally Dead. I could have shouted out to her as she left the bench, but I knew she wouldn't grant the request, and I didn't want to be told again how court time was her time and that I should speak to L.D. on my time.

"L.D.," I said as the guards started to cuff him again, "we're going to try to see you tomorrow about something important."

"I'll be home," L.D. said just as he was being led away.

God, we were so screwed.

25

The Christmas decorations had already been re-moved when we returned to Rikers the following morning. I doubted they were getting ready to put up the Valentine's Day stuff.

Legally Dead was brought in to see us by a different guard than last time, but this one also subscribed to the grooming regimen of a big bald head and a black goatee. He followed the standard operating procedure with respect to the restraints, unlocking L.D.'s hand-cuffs but keeping his legs shackled.

L.D.'s eyes lit up when he saw us. I wondered if that was because of Nina, given that he didn't see any women other than when she visited. But even if that was the reason, L.D. was always respectful toward her. More so than Brooks or even Marcus Jackson. At least L.D. didn't stare at her breasts when he was talking to her.

"Tell me you got some good news for me," he said.

"Let me tell you the news, and then we can talk about whether it's good or bad," I said. "I hate to just blurt it out like this, but we have pretty good evidence that Roxanne was involved with another man." I stopped to check his reaction, but there really wasn't one, and so I pressed on. "First, one of her neighbors saw her kissing somebody, although that's a very shaky

ID because she doesn't remember when it was, but she did think that it was an older, white man. The bigger thing we found out was through the autopsy report. You remember I told you we hired some guy who just left the medical examiner's office to be our expert witness?" L.D. nodded. "Well, he hit us with a bombshell." I waited a beat. "Apparently, Roxanne didn't have any pubic hair when she died. She'd waxed it off. So the pubic hairs found in her bed must belong to some other Caucasian."

He waited a moment, seemingly taking in this information. A good ten seconds later he still hadn't shown any emotion. His subdued reaction didn't match up with L.D. beating a woman to death in a jealous rage. Then again, maybe that's why he was acting subdued.

"I'm assuming you didn't know that she had . . . a Brazilian," I said.

He shook his head. "No."

"Did she ever tell you she'd done that before?" Nina asked.

L.D. shrugged. "Not something we ever talked about, be honest with ya."

"Did you know the name of the place where she gets her hair done?" Nina followed up. "She might have had the waxing done there."

This time L.D. laughed. "Nah. She never mentioned shit like that. I doubt she just walked into some place, though. You know what I mean? Somebody probably came to her."

"And what about this older man?" I asked. "The only ID we got was that he looked old enough to be her father. The witness who told us about him shut us down before we could get a decent description, but I'm assuming he was white and had gray hair or was bald, or just somehow looked twenty or thirty years older than her at a distance. Any idea who it might be?" "

L.D. laughed. "You?"

I shot him a look of disapproval. "I'm not that old, L.D. But seriously, any idea who the guy might be? It's important because that could very well be the guy who killed her. And, even if it's not, he could still be your best shot of getting out of here."

The smile fell off his face. "No idea, man. I'd be the last guy on earth to know if Roxanne was fucking somebody else, you know?"

That was probably an understatement.

He scrunched up his face. "But if some guy fucked Roxanne like right before she died, wouldn't he have left behind . . ." He looked at Nina. "Shit with his DNA?"

"Not if the guy used a condom," Nina said. "There was no semen found as part of the autopsy."

"And we really don't know when the hairs were left. We'll argue that it had to have been after the last time you had sex with her." He looked at me as if he didn't follow my logic. "I'm assuming, L.D., that if Roxanne didn't have pubic hair when you were last with her, you would have told us that," I explained. "Especially because we were assuming that the hairs found in her bed could be hers." He still offered me a blank look, and so I said, "So when was that, the last time you were with her?"

"I dunno. A couple of days before she left for South Carolina."

"So that means that our timeline is something like . . . she leaves for South Carolina on Wednesday, so let's assume your last time with her was Monday, just for the sake of argument. She could have had the waxing on Tuesday and that's when the guy was with her. Or she could have gotten the wax while she was in South Carolina, and then the guy was with her when she came home on Sunday night."

"Yeah, but if some dude was with her Sunday night, don't that mean he killed her? I mean, she was killed sometime Sunday night, right?"

"Like we told you before, L.D., the fact that there was another lover cuts two ways," I said. "It's good because, like you just said, it gives us another possible murderer to parade in front of the jury. And we can make some hay out of the fact that, at least as far as we know, the prosecution didn't go out of its way to find out who left those hairs. So we can push a rush-to-judgment angle. But there's a downside, too. The presence of another lover means that it supports a jealousy theory of motive. I mean, even what you just said, that somebody else might have been in her bed on Sunday evening, the prosecution could turn into a story where that guy leaves at eight or nine o'clock, and then you come over, and there's some evidence of her being with somebody else, and you just lose it. Hell, they could say maybe you caught Roxanne in the act and lost it."

"And," Nina added, "we're still not able to completely disprove they're not Roxanne's hairs. I mean, if the sheets weren't changed for a while, they could be hers from before she waxed." As if she just had another thought, Nina continued, "This may be a little TMI, Dan, but Kaplan's a woman, so this is going to occur to her, too. I bet you anything that she argues you do that kind of thing—you know, waxing—when you have a new man in your life. That's going to play right into their jealous-rage theory. Maybe they're going to claim that L.D. found out about the waxing and went crazy."

"I fucking hate it when you talk about me like I'm not here," L.D. said. "I didn't know she'd done it. Doesn't the truth matter at all to you guys?"

"You really want to talk to us about the truth, L.D.?" I said sharply. "We caught up with Mercedes. You weren't going to see Brianna over Thanksgiving. So when you told us you were, that was a lie. So yeah, the truth does matter. It matters a lot."

That knocked him off the high ground sufficiently for him to look away, and the anger drained out of his face. I expected him to say something but heard Nina's voice instead.

"She would have lied for you," Nina said soothingly, as if the moment required a touch of compassion. "But she couldn't. She went out of town, so there was no way she could claim she was with you. Too many people saw her in Boston. She told us that you actually spent Thanksgiving with a guy named Morris Milton, who apparently has the catchy nickname of Nuts."

"Yeah," he said. "That's the truth."

"Nice to know that sometimes you tell us the truth," I said.

He gave me a disapproving glare, but it was only fleeting. He knew he was the one in the wrong here.

"I was gonna see Brianna," he finally said, "but then at the last second, Mercedes tells me she's gonna go see her people. Nuts got no family, so we hung and watched some football, brought in some KFC."

"There was nobody else for you to spend the holiday with?" Nina asked, sounding sorry for him. I didn't dare mention that I spent Thanksgiving alone, too.

"Nah. Don't got no family. I mean, I gots an aunt and uncle who still live in Everett, that's near Boston, but we ain't real close, and I didn't feel much like hiking up there neither."

"Don't you have a manager or PR person?"

"You spend Thanksgiving with people who work for you?" L.D. said with a grin. "Besides, not like them dudes are longtime friends or nothin'. They just people Brooks got to look after me. And Nuts . . . Nuts is good people, so why not chill with him, you know."

"If he's such good people, why didn't you tell us

that you were with him?" I asked, my tone much sharper than Nina's had been.

L.D. looked away from me when I said this, further admission that he knew that he'd screwed up. "Yeah, I'm sorry 'bout that. I shoulda told you. I guess . . . I guess I knew he wouldn't help, and I thought, you know, maybe Mercedes would."

"Well, you were right about that," I said. "He didn't help."

"You guys actually talked with him? What he say?"

"Besides threatening us, he didn't say anything," I said.

He shook his head, deflated. "Figures. You know why he got the name Nuts?"

"No," I said.

"Because he *is* nuts. You know, like a psycho."

Nina glanced over at me. She had a look of confusion and disgust and I felt the same thing in the pit of my stomach.

"We're back at square one, L.D.," I said. "We got nothing. No evidence that you weren't planning on going to South Carolina for Thanksgiving, which means that we can't rebut the prosecution's argument that you were disinvited at the last minute, and then flew into a murderous rage when you confronted Roxanne after she returned. To the extent that we have something about Roxanne having an affair with someone else on account of the pubic hairs, we don't have the first clue as to who that somebody else might be, and as we keep saying, I'm not sure we even want to go that way, because the most logical conclusion to be drawn is that you killed Roxanne in a fit of jealousy."

We waited for L.D. to respond. He didn't for a good ten seconds.

In a measured voice, he finally said, "I know it looks bad, but I didn't kill her."

"I hear you," I said.

26

It was a direct flight from LaGuardia to the Greenville-Spartanburg Airport in South Carolina, and so it took less than four hours, door to door, for us to arrive in Stocks. The place where Roxanne was born and raised.

The plan was to see if anyone from Roxanne's past knew anything about her present. It was a long shot, but, quite frankly, we didn't know what else to do.

The Old Westerbrook Hotel. The reason we'd picked it was because it was the only lodging within a forty-minute drive of Stocks that didn't have the term *motor inn* attached to it.

Upon our arrival, we discerned that the Old Westerbrook was a series of cottages situated around a golf course. The posters in the lobby indicated that the course had hosted the LPGA U.S. Open a few years earlier and was still a regular stop on the women's tour. Why anyone would put a championship golf course in Stocks, South Carolina, however, was beyond me.

The woman at the front desk was fresh-faced enough that the term *girl* would have applied. She was wearing a dark red blazer with a white shirt and a large name tag telling the world that her name was Lysette and she was from Charleston, South Carolina.

"That'll be a nonsmoking room with a king bed," Lysette said to me after I gave her my name.

Nina had actually made the reservations, but I nonetheless turned to her to confirm that sharing a bed was what she had in mind.

"I don't smoke, if that's what you're wondering," Nina said with a sly grin.

"That'll be fine," I told Lysette, and handed her my credit card.

We were given cottage fifteen, which Lysette told us had a nice water view. Not that it mattered. It was pitch-black outside, and so the only things we saw in the windows were our own reflections.

Cottage fifteen was more nicely appointed than I had anticipated. There was a reasonably sized living room, furnished in a Southern wicker motif, and a stone fireplace. The bedroom had a four-poster bed with cream-colored linens.

"It's pretty nice," I said, looking around. "I expected . . . I don't know what I expected, the Bates Motel, maybe."

Nina chuckled and plopped down on the corner of the bed. "This is the size of fifteen hotel rooms in New York. And at one-third the price."

"I wouldn't know," I said, "having never stayed in a New York hotel room, on account that I actually live there."

My comment struck a nerve. She knew that I was referencing the married man of Nina's past, for why else would she have any experience with the size of New York hotel rooms?

Nina's expression instantly grew colder, and I was

about to apologize when she spoke first. "What's going on with us, Dan?"

Of course I knew what she meant. And equally predictably, I said, "What do you mean?"

"I mean, I realize that you must have a flood of stuff going on in your head, but that doesn't excuse you from sharing it with me. What is this for you? Are we just law partners with benefits? If that's the way you want it, I guess I can deal, but, frankly, I didn't think that's where we were heading."

"No. That's not what I want."

"Then what?"

I sat down beside her and took her hand. She leaned in to me slightly, her arm rubbing against mine. When our eyes met, she looked sincerely concerned that she might not like what I was about to say.

I had to fight a laugh, for this was certainly not the time. But I couldn't understand how she could be so unaware about the way I felt about her.

"I'm still trying to get my arms around this a little bit," I said. "I don't mean that as an excuse, although it probably is one. But you're the first person I've felt . . . this kind of closeness with since Sarah, and so there are a lot of conflicting feelings that come along with it. I guess I should have made it clearer to you that the strongest of those feelings is . . . what I can only assume is happiness, and I say that I can only assume it because it's been so long since that particular emotion registered with me at all. So, thank you. Really, I've been very happy since we've been together, and given how my mental state has been over the last year or so, that's really saying a lot. And I don't just mean since New Year's Eve. Since you hauled my ass out of bed after Rich and Deb's party. You were right, this has been really good for me, and I truly believe that a big part of why it's been so good is because of the time I've been able to spend with you."

I kissed her, at first with a closed mouth, but it wasn't long before our tongues were all over each other's. I assumed that we had finished the talking part of the program, but after a few moments of necking, Nina pulled away.

"You need to know, Dan, that you're not the only one who's vulnerable here. I know that my story has none of the overt tragedy of yours, but it doesn't mean that I'm not every bit as gun-shy. I promised myself that I was done falling in love with unavailable men. So I don't think I'm asking too much of you to just be honest with me. If this is a . . . I guess *rebound* isn't the right word, but you know, a getting-your-feet-wet kind of thing, but you're not up for a full-fledged relationship, just tell me now."

I had seen Nina in many different looks—confident and sexy were the main ones, but she could also be charming and inviting. This was the first time I saw insecure and uncertain.

"I'm sure that my James Bond approach to life has confused you," I said with self-deprecation, "but I'm not a love-'em-and-leave-'em kind of guy. The truth of it is, Sarah was my first serious relationship, and even though it's only been a few days, I already consider you my second. I can't guarantee how it's going to end, but I know that I don't want it to end."

I looked into Nina's face, questioning if I should say more. She answered by kissing me again. Now the talking part of the evening was over.

27

We had rented the cheapest car they had at the first rental counter in the airport, a Nissan Sentra, two-door. The moment I turned it on the next morning, the "A-Rod" song came through the speakers. And it was right at the good part:

> *Gonna stop you when you sing,*
> *gonna give it til you scream;*
> *don't like what you said,*
> *gonna go A-Rod on your head.*

"That's an unfortunate coincidence," Nina said.

"Not much of a coincidence. I bet they play that every ten minutes down here, and on virtually every station."

We headed directly to Roxanne's high school. The hope was that someone there might be able to tell us who Roxanne's friends were from back then, and they might know something about her life now.

The school's principal was, unfortunately for him, named George Clooney. Even more unfortunate, this Mr. Clooney looked much more like a high school principal than a former two-time *People* magazine Sexiest Man Alive, right down to the plaid shirt, cheesy mustache, and ten-years-out-of-style glasses.

He was kind enough to show us Roxanne's senior yearbook, however. Pulling it off a top shelf, he immediately flipped to the pages covering the senior show, which had the banner headline "Beauty and the Beast."

"This is Carolyn Anton," he said, pointing down at one of the pictures. The girl he was indicating was wearing a beast costume from the ballroom scene. "I would have said she was Roxanne's best friend. They were the two stars of the show. Roxanne played Beauty, and Carolyn was the Beast. They did three shows, and on the last night, they switched parts."

"Any idea where Carolyn is now?" I asked.

"She still lives in town, so she probably isn't that hard to find. I don't know her address. Her mother died right after graduation, so she's not at home anymore."

"Do you know where she works?"

"No, sorry."

George Clooney seemed much more interested in the yearbook photo than where Carolyn Anton was today. He chuckled, almost to himself, but loud enough that I felt obliged to ask him what he found amusing.

"I always thought that Carolyn was the more talented one. Guess I made the right call not becoming a talent scout."

"What about Roxanne's mother?" Nina asked. "We understand that she still lives in Stocks."

"Yeah. New house, though. She moved to the nicer part of town right after Roxanne hit it big."

"Do you have her new address?"

Nina followed this request by flashing him her gold-standard smile, and George Clooney smiled back. I'm sure if I had asked the question, I would have gotten a lecture about student confidentiality, but for Nina, he said, "Sure. We update student addresses, you know, for alumni purposes."

George Clooney then put down the yearbook and walked out of his office until he was hovering over one of the secretaries. "Can you get me Andrea Wells's new address?" Clooney asked her.

We decided to try Carolyn Anton first. As luck would have it, locating her address wasn't very difficult at all. She was listed in the phone book, or in this case, on Google. Finding her house, however, was a bit more challenging. It required several turns down unpaved roads, and more than once the female computer voice on my phone GPS seemed to be leading us away from civilization altogether.

Although I didn't recall actually passing over railroad tracks on the way to Carolyn Anton's home, she definitely lived on the metaphoric wrong side of them. Most of the structures along the roadside were little more than wheel-less trailers, usually with some type of rusted car parked on the small patch of grass in front.

Her house was just such a double-wide. In the front wasn't a car, but a tricycle, the red paint peeling in most places.

A woman came to the door just after we'd gotten out of the car, likely because she heard us coming up the gravel driveway. On her hip she was holding a girl who looked to be about two. In her other hand was a cigarette.

If this was Carolyn Anton, the few years since she'd graduated from high school had not been kind to her. She was at least thirty pounds heavier than in the year-book pictures, and the bags around her eyes made her look a decade older than the twenty-one or twenty-two years she'd actually lived.

"Hello," I said as we approached the door. "Are you Carolyn Anton?"

"Yeah. Who are you?"

She said this with hostility, even though she had no idea that we were there on behalf of the man accused of murdering her former best friend. To her, we were just two people wearing dark suits in a trailer park, and that was bad enough. I had little doubt that Carolyn Anton assumed we were there to take something from her.

"My name is Dan Sorensen and this is Nina Harrington. We're lawyers from New York City, and we would like to ask you some questions about Roxanne Wells. We understand that you were her best friend in high school. In fact, we heard that a lot of people thought *you* were the one who was going to be the big star."

Carolyn smiled at the compliment. I couldn't help but think that compliments didn't come her way too often anymore.

"Are you reporters?"

"No. Like I said, we're lawyers. From New York City."

"There were lots of reporters down here right after Roxanne got murdered. But most of them have left by now. I guess it's not such big news anymore."

"Would you mind if we asked you a few questions?" I asked.

"Sure," she said, too eagerly, I thought.

She opened the door, and her daughter jumped out of her arms and scurried away. "Come on in," Anton said.

From the looks of the inside of her double-wide, Carolyn Anton didn't do much entertaining. *Filthy* was the word that first came to mind. Dishes in the sink from at least three meals ago, dog hairs on the furniture, and the smell of cat urine so strong that I assumed she must have become immune to the odor long ago.

Out of my peripheral vision I caught Nina grimace at the squalor around her. This was every woman's worst nightmare. Every person's, really. Alone, broke, with no real possibility of it being better tomorrow.

I decided we didn't need to bother introducing ourselves again. I asked, "Do you know anything about Roxanne's life in the weeks leading up to her death?"

"I saw her over Thanksgiving," Carolyn said with obvious pride, as if it supported her status as Roxanne's closest friend.

"Did you visit her at her mother's house?" Nina asked.

"No," Carolyn said, looking a bit sheepish. "But I saw her at the Old Westerbrook."

"Was she staying there?" I asked.

"I guess so. They hire hourlies over the holidays, and so I was there doing some cleaning, and ended up seeing her. She was real nice and was happy to see me. I asked her if we could get a drink or something before she left, but she said she was real busy. I gave her my email and she said she'd friend me on Facebook, but then she died right when she got back."

This didn't make sense. Why would Roxanne stay in a hotel when she was coming to visit her mother? Then again, maybe that's what celebrities did. What did I know?

"Did you talk to her at all about anything going on in her life? Specifically, about men?" Nina asked.

"No. Just what I already said. That's all. She said she was late to something and had to go."

"Do you remember which cottage?" I asked.

"It was number eighteen. That's the nicest one, and so I thought, you know, only the best for Roxanne."

"Was she with anyone?"

"No. I mean, who would she be with?"

A lover, her murderer, her mother . . . but I let the question drift away without answer.

"When was the last time you spoke to Roxanne before seeing her that time over Thanksgiving?" Nina asked.

"Oh, it'd been a really long time. Right after graduation, maybe. She went to New York that summer and . . . and I got pregnant. I invited her to my baby shower, but she didn't come."

That pretty much indicated we were wasting our time. Carolyn Anton didn't know anything more about Roxanne's life than we did.

"Kind of strange, isn't it?" Nina remarked as we were driving away.

"How so?"

"If Roxanne hadn't been able to sing, this probably would have been her life, right? She'd be a waitress or whatever the women who aren't waitresses down here grow up to be. She would have married young and pushed out a baby or two by now. Who knows if the husband sticks around. And instead of that, she was royalty."

"Makes you realize why our guy was willing to do all he did to become Legally Dead."

"And why he's willing to risk going to prison to keep it," she added.

As Principal Clooney had told us, Roxanne's mother lived in a much nicer part of town. Her home was at the end of a tree-lined street like the kind you imagine when you think of a Southern town, grand homes with well-manicured lawns. Her house fit right in, a yellow Victorian with a white, wraparound porch.

I knocked lightly on the screen door. Just getting Andrea Wells to open the door would be something of a victory. Luckily for us, she was the trusting sort who preferred to ask us face-to-face to identify ourselves, rather than calling out behind the door "Who is it?"

The moment she opened the door, the resemblance to her famous daughter was apparent. Roxanne had clearly inherited her large blue eyes and inviting smile from her mother's side of the family. Andrea Wells was an attractive woman, but there was a strain in her face that made her look older than I had expected.

It was a look I knew all too well. She was in mourning.

"Mrs. Wells?" I said.

"Yes," she answered cautiously.

"My name is Dan Sorensen. I've come all the way from New York City. I'm a lawyer representing Legally Dead, and I'd like to talk to you for a few minutes."

Nina and I had actually scripted the introduction. We'd debated whether to reveal that we were representing L.D., and concluded we didn't want to be accused of tricking a woman whose daughter had recently been murdered.

"Who are you again? The police?"

"No," I said, following it with a smile. "We're lawyers. We represent Legally Dead . . . L.D. Like you, we just want to make sure the police arrested the right man."

It all clicked for her then. She knew we were the enemy.

"Please leave. Now," she said sternly.

"We're very sorry for bothering you," Nina said, and turned and began to walk away.

I turned around, too, but only for a moment. I didn't even realize what I was doing until I'd begun speaking, and by then my eyes were filled with tears.

"Mrs. Wells, I lost my daughter recently, too. I know what you're going through and I am sincerely sorry for your loss. I wouldn't be here to talk to you about a subject that is so painful unless it was very important. All we want is to be sure that another family doesn't suffer the pain that you're going through now."

She took a deep breath. One that said she didn't know quite what to do.

"People keep telling me it's going to get better," she finally said.

"Yeah," I said, realizing that it wasn't much of an answer.

"Can I ask how your daughter died?"

"It was a drunk-driving accident. My wife died with her."

Andrea Wells started to tear up. I did, too.

"She was six years old," I said.

Wells said, "Every day, when I wake up, it's like Roxanne just died."

It was a feeling I knew all too well. And while under normal circumstances I would have kept that fact to myself, I knew that approach wasn't going to get Andrea Wells to open up to me.

"Sometimes I'll see something in a store and think that Sarah, my wife, would like it, or I'll hear some silly joke that I think Alexa, that was my daughter's name, would find funny, and then there's the awful feeling again when you realize that the first thought you had, that happy feeling about sharing something with someone you love, it just wasn't real because they're not there anymore."

"How long has it been?" Wells asked.

"Eighteen months. And I suppose I can give you a little bit of good news. I can't say it gets better, but it does get easier. For a long time after, I just couldn't do anything, and then Nina approached me about this case, and I met with L.D., and I . . . I truly believed him when he said that he loved your daughter and did not hurt her. And I thought, wouldn't Sarah and Alexa be proud of me if I was able to save an innocent man? I understand how you must feel. Believe me, I do. The man who killed my wife and daughter died at the scene of the accident, and to this day, I only wish he'd suffered more for what he did. So I understand completely that you want whoever did this to your daughter to pay for his crime. But the thing is, so does L.D. And it would be a tragedy if the person who actually murdered your daughter is not punished for what he did. All we're asking, and I know it's a lot, but still we need to ask, is for a few minutes of your time, so we can be sure that the right man is going to be punished. I promise, we won't be long."

She hesitated for a moment, clearly not sure what to do. But then she pushed open the screen door. After she stepped inside, she motioned for Nina and me to follow.

The inside of the home was as well maintained

as the exterior. In fact, it looked a little like a page from a magazine, the way everything belonged with everything else, without matching too much. Like her famous daughter, Andrea Wells preferred light colors. The living room sofa, love seat, and easy chair, as well as the curtains, were all slightly different variations of a pale yellow.

I imagined the home was the result of the cliché you always hear about how the first thing a pop star does with the advance off her first contract is buy her parents a house. This was that house, and everything in it had likely been purchased with Roxanne's advance. I suspected Roxanne's childhood home, while perhaps not as grim, was still closer to Carolyn Anton's trailer than this place.

"Mrs. Wells, like I said, we understand that you want your daughter's killer to be punished. And the truth is, we want that, too. We're just not sure that our client is the man who killed her. We know the police have told you that he's guilty, but we want to make sure."

Perhaps it was wishful thinking, but I thought I saw a nod of support. As if Roxanne's mother had her doubts, too.

"So, could you tell us whether Roxanne ever said anything about problems in her relationship with L.D.?"

"She actually didn't talk about him much at all. You know, when Roxanne was in high school, she wasn't allowed to go out with any boy until I'd met him. But after she moved to New York City . . ."

Mrs. Wells didn't finish the thought. Instead, she broke off eye contact and was now staring at the floor. I got the sense that she was embarrassed to admit how little she knew about her daughter at the end, which was apparently another thing we shared.

"Were you expecting Roxanne to come for Thanksgiving with L.D.?" I asked.

"No," Mrs. Wells said, still looking away. "It wasn't until the last minute that Roxanne even decided to come. She first said that she had to work. I was so happy when she called and said she could get away."

If Roxanne hadn't planned to come to Stocks until the last minute, then she couldn't have invited L.D. and then disinvited him. But that still didn't address why L.D. hadn't gone with her, especially since his own plans had fallen through at the last moment, and that meant there was still room for L.D. to feel, as Marcus Jackson had so eloquently put it, *disrespected*. Besides which, I suspected Roxanne's mother would not end up being our star witness, and her story would undoubtedly change after Kaplan had some time with her.

But, as L.D. said, the truth matters. Or at least it should.

As I was mulling this over, Nina said, "Did Roxanne stay with you over Thanksgiving?"

"Of course. Where else would she stay?"

I felt a jolt of enthusiasm, like when you realize you've hooked a fish. We had something. I just wasn't sure what exactly, or how big.

"Roxanne was seen at the Old Westerbrook," I said. "Do you know why she was there?"

"She was at the Old Westerbrook?" Wells said, as if she might have misheard me. "Well . . . maybe she was visiting a friend who was staying there."

"I take it, though, that you didn't know she'd done that? Or who she might have been visiting?"

When Wells didn't answer, Nina said, "We also spoke to a witness who thought she might have seen Roxanne kissing an older man. Do you know who that might be?"

From the look on Wells's face, I knew Nina's approach had been too aggressive. Wells kept shaking her head, as if she were trying to convince herself it wasn't true. It wasn't clear to me what she found more disconcerting—that her daughter might have been involved with an older man, or that she knew so little about Roxanne's life. What I could discern from her expression, however, was that she regretted letting us in, and that meant we were running out of time.

"I don't think that would be true," she said. "If Roxanne had a man in her life . . . she would have told me."

"Even though you just told us that she didn't tell you much about L.D.?" I said, trying not to sound argumentative.

"That was different."

"Can you explain to us how it was different?" Nina asked.

Wells paused, turning from Nina to me. "I'm

sorry," she said, "but I shouldn't be talking to you, I think."

I tried my best to salvage the situation. "We meant no offense, Mrs. Wells, and we're very sorry if we upset you. It wasn't our intent. We just wanted—"

"You need to leave," she said, and then stood up to walk us to the door.

28

When Nina and I arrived back at the Old Westerbrook, a different woman was behind the front desk than the one who had checked us in. She looked to be just out of college, if such higher education was a prerequisite to man the front desk at a rural South Carolina hotel with a championship golf course. Like her morning counterpart, she wore a dark red blazer with a name tag. The afternoon desk clerk was named Jodi and she hailed from Farmington Hills, Michigan.

With an inviting smile, Jodi asked if there was anything she could do for us.

"There is, actually," I said. "We're interested in knowing who was staying in cottage eighteen over Thanksgiving weekend."

Jodi from Farmington Hills, Michigan, suddenly had the look of someone who didn't quite get the joke. "Pardon me?"

"Could you please tell me the name of the guest who was in cottage eighteen over Thanksgiving weekend? It was November twenty-eighth through December second, if that helps."

I offered a smile that suggested my request was nothing out of the ordinary. Unfortunately, Jodi was too smart to be taken in by it.

"I'm sorry, sir," she said with a frozen smile. "We're not allowed to give out that type of information."

"Jodi," I said, "we're lawyers from New York City. My name is Dan Sorensen, and this is my partner, Nina Harrington. We're representing Legally Dead, who I'm sure you know has been accused of murdering Roxanne. We heard from a witness that Roxanne was visiting the guest in cottage eighteen over Thanksgiving. That means that the person who was staying in cottage eighteen is an important witness in the upcoming murder trial."

Jodi from Farmington Hills, Michigan, looked suddenly less happy to be in Stocks, South Carolina. "Like I said, sir, I'm not allowed to give out that type of information. I'll get my supervisor, if you'd like."

"Jodi, did you work here that weekend? Do you remember seeing Roxanne?"

I could tell that Jodi was weighing whether she could answer. She must have figured she could because she said, "I worked some of that weekend, but I don't remember seeing Roxanne. Somebody probably would have said something to me if she'd been in the restaurant or on the golf course or something."

"But if she came in and went straight to cottage eighteen, you wouldn't necessarily know, right?" Nina said.

Jodi must have felt like Nina was helping her. A sisterhood thing, perhaps, because she sighed and answered Nina in a more relaxed voice.

"That's right. I don't know who visits the guests

staying in the cottages. I only know about the people who check in."

"And that's why it's so important for us to know who checked in to cottage eighteen," I said.

Jodi held her ground, however. "I'm sorry—I'm just not allowed to give out the names of our guests. I don't think any hotels are."

"Please, Jodi," Nina implored.

"No. I'll get fired."

Seeing that Nina's good-cop routine had run its course, I decided to go all in on the bad-cop side of the equation.

"Jodi, the choice is yours. You can either punch a few keys and then whisper a name to us, and your involvement in this matter comes to an end, with no one ever knowing you were even involved. Or, you can say no, which means that I appear before a judge and get a subpoena with your name on it, and that makes the newspapers. That subpoena will require you to come to New York City and testify at the biggest criminal trial of the decade, and that's going to make all the newspapers, too. And on top of that, we'll make your boss come, too, and we'll be sure to tell him that the only reason he's being inconvenienced is because you made us do this the hard way. As you can see, that's a lot of aggravation for you, and that's a lot of bad publicity for the Old Westerbrook, and it can all be avoided if you just whisper to us the name of that guest."

Jodi looked to Nina and then back to me. Neither of us offered her any help.

Nina finally said, "This way will be so much easier for you. Believe me."

Jodi looked past us to see if anyone else could witness what she was about to do. Then, nostrils flaring, she quickly jabbed at the computer.

She took a deep breath, like someone about to jump off a high board might, and then took the leap.

"Matthew Brooks," she whispered.

Now we had a theory: Matt Brooks was our SODDI guy. We'd tell the jury that he was having an affair with Roxanne, and for whatever reason, things turned bad. Maybe she threatened to go to his wife, and he killed her to keep her quiet. Or maybe she ended it, and he was the one who flew into the jealous rage.

All in all, it wasn't a terrible defense, although it was far from foolproof, a point Nina made to me several times.

"She couldn't have ended it with him, Dan," Nina said on the plane back from South Carolina. "Our theory is that he was in her bed right before she was killed."

"You never heard of breakup sex?"

"So our theory is that they had sex, and then Brooks killed her?"

"Yeah. Why not?"

"Are we just dismissing out of hand what Marcus Jackson told us?"

"Actually, it's just the opposite. I think Brooks put Jackson up to telling us that L.D. confessed to him."

She came pretty close to rolling her eyes at me. "Really?"

"Yes. Really. Think about it for a second. When does Marcus Jackson ever take on a case pro bono? My guess is that he did it as some type of favor for Brooks. Maybe Capital Punishment is throwing him business, or he's getting paid some other way."

"Then why did he pull out?"

"What choice did he have? The client fired him. So he decided to do Brooks a final favor on his way out the door by getting us to think that L.D. was guilty, probably so we'd continue his work of pressuring L.D. to take a plea, and thereby completely insulate Matt Brooks from liability."

She smiled at me. "Look who's the true believer now."

Nina and I agreed that our first order of business upon our return home was to serve a subpoena on the Old Westerbrook for the guest registry over Thanksgiving weekend. That would give us admissible proof of Brooks's presence, while keeping our promise to Jodi from Farmington Hills, Michigan, to keep her out of it.

"We'll need Carolyn Anton, too," I said. "The hotel registry puts Brooks there, but only Anton puts Roxanne with him."

"I don't see that being a problem," Nina said. "I bet she's already wondering if she could play herself in the television movie of the trial. Of course, that still doesn't give us proof that Roxanne and Brooks were lovers. He could have been meeting her for some business reason."

Now it was my turn to roll my eyes.

"C'mon, Dan. You know that's what Brooks is going to say."

"So let's see if he does. Brooks is now back from wherever he was, and he did say that he'd be happy to help. Let's see if that happiness extends to his giving us a sample of his pubic hair."

29

There were fewer flowers in front of Roxanne's house upon our return visit, but not by much. I wondered when the vigil would finally be over. The day the last flower was picked up and no one came to lay down another. Just like when I stopped getting casseroles from Sarah's friends.

We were here to button down Eugenia Tompkins. If she could confirm that the older man she'd seen Roxanne kissing was Matt Brooks, or even if she said it might have been Brooks, we'd be very close to proving they were lovers, no matter what cock-and-bull story Brooks came up with as to his reason for being in Stocks over Thanksgiving.

We knocked on her door armed with a glossy photograph of Matt Brooks that I'd pulled off the internet. It ran alongside some puff-piece article in *Vanity Fair* that discussed him as if he was equal parts Warren Buffett, Houdini, Mother Teresa, and Jesus Christ. The picture captured Brooks in all his glory—silver hair shining, double-breasted suit, crisp white shirt, and bright yellow tie and matching pocket square.

The woman who answered was another heavyset woman from the Caribbean, but it was not Eugenia Tompkins.

"Is Eugenia Tompkins here?" I said.

"She went back to Saint Lucia."

Goddammit. We were too late.

"Do you know how we can contact her?" asked Nina.

"No, I'm sorry."

"Are the owners of the house at home?" I said.

She stepped aside and a smaller man came front and center. At first I was surprised, given that it was business hours, and so, if this was the man of the house, he should be at work. Then again, his Gucci loafers were a clear statement he wasn't the hired help.

"Is this your home?" I asked.

The way he squinted at me said in no uncertain terms that he'd be no more helpful than his new housekeeper. "Who are you?" he said.

"My name is Dan Sorensen, and this is my partner, Nina Harrington. We're lawyers representing Legally Dead. We're here because—"

"I know why you're here," he interrupted. "I would appreciate it if you did not come by again. Eugenia's mother has taken ill, and she went back home. I don't know what she told you, but neither my wife nor I ever saw Roxanne on our street."

"Is there any way that we could contact Eugenia? It's extremely important that we reach her."

"I'm sorry, but I don't have any contact information for her."

"She must have left a phone number or something."

"Well, she didn't," he said forcefully.

"We'll pay all expenses for her to travel back here for the trial," I said, "if you could just let her know."

"I can't let her know," he said. "I don't know where she is right now, so I can't help you. I'm sorry."

He didn't seem sorry at all, though.

Standing on the other side of the closed door, I said, "How do you figure Brooks found out?"

Nina grimaced, the look you give someone who has just finished telling you that the moon landing was a hoax. "Nobody wants to be a witness in a murder trial, especially for the defense. Maybe Eugenia just got cold feet and decided to take some vacation."

That was possible, of course, and yet I knew it was untrue. Nina apparently could tell that I wasn't buying it, because she said, "Mind if I play a little devil's advocate?" She didn't wait for an answer. "I'm beginning to think that we might be playing into Kaplan's hands. Why are we knocking ourselves out trying to prove that Brooks was the guy Roxanne was sleeping with? Aren't we better off saying that L.D. wasn't jealous of anyone rather than identifying the guy who made him crazy enough to kill Roxanne? Besides, Brooks may have an alibi, and then we're in real trouble, pointing at a guy who can prove he didn't do it."

"I understand what you're saying, Nina, but the jury is already predisposed to believe L.D. killed Roxanne because that's who the police and the prosecutor say did it, as well as a hell of a lot of people who heard the 'A-Rod' song. For us to convince them that the cops were wrong, we need to show them who really killed her."

"Look, I'm not saying that Brooks didn't have an affair with her. Maybe he did and it's his pubic hair in her bed. But it's also possible the pubic hair belongs to some bartender Roxanne picked up that night. Who knows? But what I do know is that we're running out of time. I just wonder if we're being smart by focusing so much effort on trying to prove an affair with Brooks when, even if we can do it, I'm not sure that helps the defense, and it might really hurt."

I didn't answer, which caused Nina's eyes to drop to the pavement, as if she was embarrassed by what she'd just said. When she looked back at me, it was with something of an expression of pity.

"It's just us, Dan," she said soothingly. "Do you still think L.D.'s innocent? I mean, *really*? Based on everything you and I have seen recently? You knew that I was the original true believer, but after all the lies . . ."

My first impulse was to lie to her. It would have been easy for me to argue that I just disagreed with her view of the evidence. But what was the point of falling in love with someone if you couldn't be honest with them? If they didn't understand exactly what you were feeling, deep down?

"I don't know," I said slowly and softly. "Sometimes, though, it feels like it's not so much that I *believe* he's innocent as much as I *need* him to be innocent. Does that make any sense?"

"It does," she said, a strong current of sadness in her voice. "A lot, actually. But, Dan, you have to remember, the jury, they're not going to need L.D. to be innocent. In fact, the opposite is going to be true. They're going to need him to be *guilty*, because that way, Roxanne's murderer will be punished."

30

Capital Punishment Records was housed in the Time Warner building at Columbus Circle. At the height of the internet bubble, back when the company was called AOL Time Warner, business was flush enough to justify building two sixty-story towers. The bottom three floors are filled with high-end designer stores and restaurants, including one where a prix fixe dinner runs $350 per person, before drinks, tax, and tip. The twenty uppermost floors are corporate offices with among the highest per-square-foot rents in the city.

When we got off the elevator on the sixtieth floor, a waterfall was where I expected the reception desk to be. I followed the running water with my eyes until an impossibly proportioned Asian woman with stick-straight platinum blond hair that fell past her waist came into view.

"They're all waiting for you," she said with a British accent.

Nina and I followed her down the length of the hallway to the corner of the office space. Once there, she opened an unmarked door and told us to enter.

Matt Brooks's office was even more over-the-top than the reception area. A life-size nude photograph of his supermodel wife hung on the only wall that wasn't a window, along with no fewer than six television screens. Every piece of furniture was fire-engine red, including Brooks's desk, his chair, the guest seating, and even the rug.

"So nice to see you again, Dan," Brooks said. "And you, too, Nina."

Brooks looked Nina up and down, just like he'd done in Atlantic City. It was only upon his return visit to her face that he extended his hand to me.

"Allow me to introduce you to my brain trust." Brooks motioned toward the seating area. "This is Jason Evans, who is my chief of staff, and next to him is our general counsel, Kimberly Newman."

Evans was as large as a refrigerator, and I assumed that among his chief-of-staff duties was to serve as Brooks's bodyguard. Newman was at the other extreme, waif thin. She was around my age, I assumed, still on the young side to be the general counsel of a company generating a billion dollars in annual revenue.

Brooks settled into the red leather club chair next to Newman, and Nina and I were directed to the red leather sofa opposite them. Looking like a man without a care in the world, Brooks said, "So, what can I do for you legal eagles today?"

"We'd like to know more about Roxanne," I said. "What was she like? What did you observe about her relationship with L.D.? That type of thing."

Nina and I had agreed that this was the way to approach Brooks. Go in softly, getting him to give up as much information as we could, and then hit him hard with the evidence we'd obtained down in Stocks.

Brooks looked at Newman as if he was asking her to give him consent to continue. Either she did or her silence was deemed approval, because he said, "You can't swing a dead cat and not hit some diva prima donna in this business, but Roxanne wasn't that way at all. She was just an angel."

"Was that just with you because you were the boss, or did she have that reputation with everyone?"

"As far as I know, everyone."

"How did you feel about her relationship with L.D.?" I asked.

"They were consenting adults."

I didn't say anything. Sometimes silence is a better inquisitor.

"Look," he said, "no boss wants fraternization, but what can you do? That kind of thing happens when you're on the road. You just hope everyone can stay professional after it ends, because, you know, it always does."

Nina looked back at me, as if to say, what now? There was really only one other thing I wanted to know and so I asked it straightaway.

"Mr. Brooks, were you having an affair with Roxanne?"

Newman spoke quickly and loudly. "He doesn't have to answer that."

"I think he may just have done so," I said with intended snark.

Newman started to argue with me, but this time Brooks spoke over her. "It's fine, Kimberly. I don't mind telling Mr. Sorensen what he wants to know."

He shifted his gaze from her to me, and with the change of position came a change in expression, from happy-go-lucky to controlled vengeance. "No" was all he said.

"So you're denying that you and Roxanne were lovers?" I said, although that was clearly what he'd just said.

Newman had had enough. "Matt, as your legal adviser, I must insist that we end this now."

"Only a fool disregards his lawyer's advice," Brooks said with a broad smile. "And whatever else you may think about me, I hope that at least you have come to the conclusion that I am not a fool."

Nina knew this meant we weren't going to get anything else, and so she reached into her briefcase and handed Newman a subpoena. Newman looked at it quickly, grimacing as if she were reading an off-color joke.

"We've provided all our records concerning your client to the DA's office," Newman said. "You'll need to take it up with them."

Kimberly Newman was clearly not very well versed in criminal practice. In civil litigation, subpoenas are always about documents. Emails, letters, drafts of agreements, and the like. There's no end of paper that a civil litigator can produce.

"We're not looking for documents," I told her. "As

you'll see, the subpoena calls for Mr. Brooks to provide us with samples of his fingerprints and a few strands of his pubic hair."

Brooks chortled. "You've got some balls, Dan."

I stared at him, not sure whether to acknowledge his statement as a compliment, and then I stood to signal that, to my mind, the meeting was now over. Nina rose with me, and that caused Brooks's flunkies to follow suit. Finally, Brooks, too, got to his feet.

Still wearing that big smile, Brooks reached out and literally grabbed my hand to shake it. He squeezed so tightly that I could actually feel his fingernails cut into my flesh. His eyes darted, looking wildly about. I pulled back, but that only caused him to force me toward him, so that we were standing only inches apart.

So close, in fact, that when he leaned in, his whisper was not heard by anyone but me. What he said was: "Let me give you a piece of advice, *Counselor*. If I ever hear another word out of you about me and Roxanne, nobody, but nobody, is ever going to hear from you again."

Nina didn't say anything until we were out of the building. The moment we were back on the street, however, she said, "What did Brooks say to you when we were leaving?"

"Nothing," I said. "Just . . . school-yard stuff."

"C'mon, Dan. Now's not the time for bravery. Tell me."

From the look on her face I realized that if I tried

to downplay it so she wouldn't be worried, I'd likely just make her more concerned. "He said that if I made a thing about his affair with Roxanne, he'd kill me. Not that blatantly, but that was the gist of it. Like I said, just school-yard threats. I'm not worried." With a chuckle that might have been confused with whistling by a graveyard, I added, "Nobody kills defense attorneys."

She didn't laugh.

31

At seven thirty the next morning, the phone woke me. I didn't want to answer, but Nina kept nudging me.

"It might be someone important," she said.

"I don't want to give you an excuse to get dressed," I said as the phone rang for the second time.

"At least check the caller ID," she said in the middle of the third ring.

She was right. It was important.

"Hello, Daniel," said the distinctive baritone of Benjamin Ethan.

My first thought was *Damn*. My second was about how I could have been so stupid as to not see this coming.

"Hi, Benjamin . . . to what do I owe the pleasure?"

"I'm calling on behalf of Matthew Brooks, whom I've been retained to represent. I understand you met with my client and Kimberly Newman yesterday and served a subpoena. Unfortunately, I've been on the run, but I wanted to reach out to you right away so that we could set up a time to meet."

That's why Taylor Beckett was a no-go when I asked for office space. Even as early as then, Ethan must have already been retained by Brooks.

And that meant Brooks, unlike me, saw this coming weeks ago.

I wasn't taken in by Ethan's "aw shucks, I'm not sure what's going on" presentation. He was famous for being one of the hardest-working lawyers in the city. There was no way he would ever have made this call without full command of the facts.

"There's really no reason we need to meet," I said, "unless you want to hand over Mr. Brooks's pubic hairs and fingerprints in person."

He chuckled. "Now, now, Daniel, let us not get ahead of ourselves. And yes, I understand what you are seeking in the subpoena. I have to tell you, though . . . off the record and as a friend, you are making a major mistake, and I hate to see you look foolish."

His tone actually conveyed that he thought he was doing me a favor. Of course, that made it all the more condescending.

"All I'm asking, Daniel, is to allow me the opportunity to talk to you for about twenty minutes. At worst, I'll be giving you free discovery. No reason to turn that down, right?"

I couldn't argue with that logic. If I refused to meet for the sake of scoring points in my passive-aggressive struggle with Ethan, I'd be shortchanging my client.

"Okay, Benjamin," I said. "What time?"

"Thank you, Daniel. I do appreciate it. I'm not available until four today. Can we meet then, at my office?"

Not available. Right.

"No problem. I'll see you then."

Nina must have known it was bad news from the

look on my face. Tentatively she asked, "Who was that?"

"Benjamin Ethan." I shook my head. "You're not going to believe this, but Matt Brooks has been lawyered up since day one."

"Nothing but the best," she said. "So now what?"

"We're seeing him at four. He said he was busy until then. What he really meant was that he needed the time to get a protective order."

Taylor Beckett moved into its current space two years before I joined the firm. It was actually one of the reasons I had picked it over its equally prestigious competitors. Unlike, for example, Nina's old shop, Martin Quinn, Taylor Beckett had enough space so that first-year associates immediately got their own offices. Funny how things like that can shape your life. I'm sure that if I'd gone to another law firm, things would have progressed pretty much the same way—long hours, same accident—but you never know.

Everyone refers to Taylor Beckett's building as the Pyramid Building because the top of the tower resembles something of a pyramid, albeit one made out of black glass and sitting atop a fifty-floor office tower. As I walked into the Pyramid's lobby, I thought about how much I'd changed since the last time I'd entered this place.

I was a sadder man now, that much was undeniably true. At the same time, I was a more hopeful one, too. The day before the accident, I had no reason to believe that my life would look any different ten years from then, or twenty, or ever. Now I was definitely a work in progress, and although I had no expectation that my grief would ever fully subside, for the first time since the accident I could envision a future in which I was happy.

"Good to see you again, Mr. Sorensen," the guard in the lobby said the moment Nina and I approached the front desk. I was embarrassed that I had absolutely no clue as to his name. Then again, I never stopped at the front desk when I worked in the building.

"We're here to see Benjamin Ethan," I said.

"Yes, we were told to send you right up. Forty-seven," he said with a smile.

"Yeah, I remember," I said, smiling back.

"Is this really strange for you?" Nina asked as we made our way to the elevators.

"Not as strange as I think it's going to get," I said.

When the doors opened on the forty-seventh floor, Janeene was there to greet us. If I thought she had come out to say a friendly hello, she made it a point to disabuse me of that notion immediately.

"Please follow me," she said coolly. "You will all be in conference room A."

Once we arrived at our designated location, she said, "Please make yourselves comfortable. I'll tell Mr. Ethan you're here, and he'll be down in just a moment."

Taylor Beckett, like most large New York City firms, had two types of conference rooms. There were a host of interior rooms designated as "war rooms" that were usually filled floor to ceiling with boxes containing "hot docs," the 10 percent of documents that were the most important in a case. I had been practicing long enough to recall the days when the other 90 percent, which might be more than a million pages, were kept off-site somewhere in a warehouse, but nowadays they would more often be kept on a thumb drive in the lead partner's desk.

In contrast to the war rooms, the conference rooms that visitors were allowed to see were the most opulent spaces in the firm. Usually twice the size of a partner's office, they had museum-quality artwork with plaques beside them indicating the artist and the year they were created. Conference room A was a case in point, with an Adam Fuss photograph of a baby suspended in blue liquid on one wall and an equally striking Miró print facing it. I was on the art committee when we purchased both, a hundred thousand dollars hanging on two hooks.

A long, white marble table surrounded by twelve high-back leather chairs sat in the center of the room, and a matching credenza held a collection of sodas and bottled waters. The coffee station, as it was called, was on the other side of the room.

Ethan arrived wearing a gray glen-plaid flannel suit with a vest, and his customary bow tie. No matter what his daily wear, however, you couldn't mistake Benjamin Ethan for anything other than an old-line WASP. He was tall and thin, creased around the eyes and nowhere else, and he hadn't lost a single white hair.

A step behind him was a beautiful woman, probably no more than a year or two out of law school. Ethan was known at the firm for always working with someone who fit that bill. Looking at Nina, however, reminded me that I lived in a glass house on this issue.

"Daniel," he said, shaking my hand.

Ethan had one of those voices that were made for a defense lawyer. Not only deep but serious, and he manipulated his inflection so that each word could have a different meaning depending on his emphasis. The way he said my name told me immediately that we were not friends.

"Good to see you again, Benjamin. This is my partner, Nina Harrington."

Ethan introduced the woman as his "associate," as if all non-partners were fungible commodities that could easily be replaced by another, which, truth be told, they were.

Not that it mattered. The associate wouldn't say a word at this meeting. Her entire job function was to take notes. And, of course, look good while doing it.

"To be absolutely frank, I am disappointed in you, Daniel," Ethan said just seconds after we'd been seated. "What on earth makes you think that you have the right to compel Mr. Brooks to provide you with a sample of his pubic hair?"

"Not just his pubic hair, Benjamin. The subpoena also requests a copy of his fingerprints for our expert to analyze. Both are relevant because we believe they're going to put your client at the scene of Roxanne Wells's murder."

Ethan didn't respond at first. Rather, he sat there impassively, as if my request had dumbfounded him. If it weren't for the scratching sound of his associate trying to take down what I'd just said, the silence would have been deafening.

After an exaggerated sigh, Ethan finally said, "Please, Daniel, we are both experienced enough lawyers to know that unless you have some evidence of a romantic relationship between Mr. Brooks and Ms. Wells, there's no basis for the subpoena."

Among his many other skills as a lawyer, this was one of the best. Ethan never gave any information, but he was able to get the other side to give him plenty of it. In this case, he wasn't confirming or denying that Brooks was sleeping with Roxanne but was trying to figure out whether we had any evidence that proved it.

"Then you have nothing to worry about," I replied. "But it seems to me that you're turning what should be a nonevent into something quite significant."

"Enlighten me as to how I am doing that, Daniel."

"Well, I take it that Mr. Brooks is denying he had a sexual relationship with Roxanne." I stopped, trying to gauge Ethan's reaction, but he didn't betray any response. His associate didn't even look up. "If that's true," I continued, "then there's no way his pubic hair could have ended up in her bed. And if that were the case, well, then there'd be no reason not to give us a sample. We'd do the test, the hairs wouldn't match, and then we'd leave Mr. Brooks alone. Done, end of story. But you're not going that way . . . and that tells us an awful lot."

Ethan didn't answer. Instead, he looked at the beautiful, anonymous associate, the cue for her to reach into her bag and pull out a stack of papers at least a foot high. Then she pushed them across the conference table to me.

On the first page, in all capital letters and bold type, it stated: "MOTION TO QUASH FILED UNDER SEAL." Just as I'd expected.

"Judge Pielmeier set the hearing for tomorrow at two," he said.

"I guess we'll be seeing you in court, then," I said.

"That went well," Nina said to me on our way out of the building.

"What do you think was my best moment?" I deadpanned back. "When Ethan told me I was an idiot or when he dropped the motion to quash on us?"

"I was being serious, Dan. You were right about what you said in there. There's got to be something there about Brooks or they wouldn't be taking such a scorched-earth approach."

I chuckled. "I'm glad you're on my team, Nina."

32

To ensure secrecy, Benjamin Ethan's motion wasn't on the court calendar. As a result, the one camera crew on the sidewalk was there for another case, and we walked by them without being recognized.

It also meant that the courtroom was empty, except for the six of us: Kaplan and her number two, a bald guy named John Something-or-Other who looked older than her; Nina and me; and Benjamin Ethan and the same very attractive female associate Ethan introduced as "my associate" during the meeting in his office.

Judge Pielmeier never actually took the bench. Rather, her law clerk invited us all to come back to the judge's private office. Without an audience, she must have figured there was no reason to put on a show.

When we entered, the judge was sitting behind an antique desk. A court reporter was seated next to the judge, at the ready.

Even off the bench, Judge Pielmeier wore her judicial robes. It made me wonder if she wore them at home, too.

"Come in and sit down," she said. "Pull some chairs in from the conference room so there's seating for everyone."

No one asked why we didn't meet in the

conference room, which had more than enough chairs. Instead, the men got chairs from the next room—thick wood and covered in a red vinyl with exposed nail heads that were as heavy as they looked—while Kaplan, Nina, and Ethan's associate took their places in the chairs already in the judge's office.

When everyone was seated, Judge Pielmeier said, "On the record," which prompted the court reporter to begin typing. "We're here on the motion made ex parte by a nonparty witness requesting that I quash a subpoena duces tecum seeking a sample of pubic hair and fingerprints. Before we begin, because we're in chambers, there's no need for any of you to stand when addressing me. Also, Mr. Sorensen, as I'm sure you will understand, given the emergency nature of the motion, the court did not have the opportunity to arrange for your client to attend this conference. Although I'm sure you will consent to our proceeding without him, just this one time, I still need to have that stated on the record."

There was little point in delaying the proceedings, and Judge Pielmeier was now making abundantly clear to me that there would be blowback from her if I tried. "No objection, Your Honor," I said, hoping that it might buy me some goodwill.

"Okay, then, now that that's out of the way, we can begin. Mr. Ethan, the floor is yours."

Despite Judge Pielmeier's instruction, Ethan stood and then buttoned his jacket, just as he would have done in court if he were twenty feet away from her, instead of the three feet that actually separated them. "Thank you, Your Honor. We ask the court not to permit the defendant to destroy the reputation of a highly public man in what is, plain and simple, nothing more than a fishing expedition. New York State law is very clear that a criminal defendant is not permitted to require innocent people to have to produce their pubic hair. I know Your Honor is well versed regarding the scope of discovery to which a criminal defendant is entitled, but because Mr. Sorensen has made this request, it is possible that he's not as familiar with the criminal procedure rules. So if the court will indulge me for just a moment, section 240.20 only permits a defendant to obtain statements made by him and/or his coconspirators, photographs of the crime scene, scientific reports and the like, and exculpatory evidence under *Brady* and its progeny. And, Your Honor, that's it. There is nothing in the law that permits the defendant to obtain any other evidence, such as pubic hairs from nonparties."

I tried to take advantage of the pause. "Your Honor—" But Judge Pielmeier wouldn't hear of it. She interrupted me with a wave of her hand.

"It's not your turn yet, Mr. Sorensen. Just like in kindergarten, you have to wait your turn. Now, Ms. Kaplan, do you have anything to offer us in this enlightened discussion about pubic hair?"

So much for my buying goodwill.

Kaplan followed Ethan's script, so much so that it

occurred to me he likely drafted it for her. Right down to her standing when she addressed the judge.

"The prosecution has no dog in this fight," she began, a phrase that didn't seem natural coming from a woman wearing what I'd wager were five-hundred-dollar shoes. "Nonetheless, we certainly agree with both points made by Mr. Ethan. First, as Mr. Ethan said, the criminal procedure rules do not permit a defendant to obtain this type of discovery. And purely as a matter of decency and fairness, there's no reason for someone of Mr. Brooks's standing in the community to be humiliated—to have his marriage threatened—on nothing more than the unsubstantiated allegation that he was having an affair with the victim. In fact, Your Honor, allowing the defendant to pursue this type of discovery would sully two people's reputations without any basis. Not only will Mr. Brooks's reputation be irrevocably compromised, but Roxanne's will be damaged as well. Many young girls looked up to her, and it would be a true tragedy if in death she was turned into some type of home wrecker, especially when there is absolutely no evidence of any sexual relationship between Mr. Brooks and Roxanne."

The moment Judge Pielmeier turned to me, I knew I was in deep trouble. Her eyes were narrowed, like she was about to go for the kill.

"You got to admit," the judge said, "they make a strong point. There's no evidence you've presented that suggests Mr. Brooks and the victim were even intimate. You could just as easily be asking for *my* pubic hair now, couldn't you, Mr. Sorensen?"

Even though I felt foolish doing it, I stood. "Your Honor, we have evidence that the hairs found in Roxanne's bed came from a non–African American—"

"Congratulations, you've narrowed it down to ninety percent of the population, or thereabouts," Judge Pielmeier said.

"That may be true, but what's important is that it eliminates the defendant as a potential match."

"But it doesn't mean that person is Mr. Brooks, now, does it? And that's all we're talking about."

"That's precisely why we're asking you to enforce the subpoena," I replied. "If the hair belongs to Mr. Brooks, that proves the point. And if it doesn't, then that also proves the point."

Judge Pielmeier actually looked to be enjoying the back-and-forth. "How about that, Mr. Ethan?" she said. "Mr. Sorensen is telling me that all it'll take is a few yanks of your man's privates, and we'll know for sure whether your man left this little gift in the victim's bed."

"Not to be disrespectful, Your Honor, but after Mr. Sorensen concludes that the pubic hair in Ms. Wells's bed was not left by Mr. Brooks, why isn't the same argument he makes now equally applicable to his asking for anyone else's pubic hair? Just think about it for a second: he's got as much basis for asking Mr. Brooks to provide a sample as he does you, as Your Honor just suggested."

"Well, not mine, Mr. Ethan," Judge Pielmeier said with a chortle. "He needs a white person's hair. Maybe yours, though."

"The court has driven home the point for me," Ethan said, a triumphant smile on his face. "The exact same argument Mr. Sorensen makes now with regard to Mr. Brooks is equally applicable to my pubic hair, and to everyone's pubic hair he decides he wants to test. 'What's the harm?' Mr. Sorensen will say. If it matches, then it was a good thing he was able to get the hair. And if it's not a match, then he will move on to the next person. I submit, Your Honor, that is precisely why the legislature expressly limited the kind of discovery that a defendant can obtain, to avoid these types of fishing expeditions that do, indeed, harm innocent third parties. No matter what Mr. Sorensen says, news of his request will get out into the media, and that will forever follow Mr. Brooks. The only way to avoid that is for this court to quash the subpoena."

Judge Pielmeier turned to me. "What's your evidence of this sexual relationship?"

I knew I needed to really sell it. Unfortunately, I also knew I didn't have much to sell.

"We have evidence that Mr. Brooks was with Roxanne at a hotel only a few days before the murder," I said.

"What hotel? Where?" the judge asked.

"In South Carolina. That's where Roxanne was staying over the holiday. Mr. Brooks was also there."

"Your Honor," Ethan interjected, coming to his feet. Although I was hoping that Judge Pielmeier was going to tell him that it was my turn now, I knew that she wouldn't. "This is the first I've heard of this, so I cannot, at this time, confirm or deny the truth of Mr. Sorensen's claim. However, it does not matter. Even if Mr. Brooks was there, and I reiterate that I have no reason to believe that to be the case, it would hardly be surprising, given that Mr. Brooks and Roxanne Wells did work together. It is entirely possible that Mr. Brooks was in South Carolina on business."

Judge Pielmeier gave him a raised eyebrow. It emboldened me.

"Your Honor," I said, "we also had a witness that saw a man matching Mr. Brooks's description kissing Roxanne in front of her home."

"You're getting warmer with the kissing part," Judge Pielmeier said, "but what do you mean you *had* a witness?"

"We spoke to this witness a week or so ago, at which time she told us that she observed Roxanne kissing someone who matched Mr. Brooks's general description. At the time, we had no reason to suspect Mr. Brooks was her lover, because we didn't know about Mr. Brooks and Roxanne being together at a hotel in South Carolina over Thanksgiving. The other day, however, we returned to the witness's home to ask whether the man she saw Roxanne kissing was Mr. Brooks, but we were told that she was no longer in the country. We are trying to track her down, but we're not sure we're going to be successful on that front."

Ethan was quick to respond. "In other words, Your Honor, they have nothing. No evidence of a sexual relationship whatsoever. And as I said before, the law is quite clear on this issue. Even if there was a sexual relationship, the defense is still not entitled to obtain this type of discovery. The legislature has already weighed in on this subject and, with all due respect, Your Honor, it is not for the courts to override the legislature."

"You have anything for me on that, Mr. Sorensen?" Judge Pielmeier asked.

Ethan was right on the law, which didn't give me much leeway to convince Judge Pielmeier that he was wrong. So I played the fairness card.

"This defendant is being charged with a crime that, if he were to be convicted, could likely send him to prison for the rest of his life. Surely he's entitled to obtain evidence to defend himself against such charges."

Judge Pielmeier smiled at me, and for once I didn't feel like she did so in a mocking fashion. This was worse, however. She felt sorry for me. She knew that I should be right, and yet I wasn't.

She looked down at her notes, which suggested that she had decided the outcome of this hearing well before anyone said a word. Then she turned in the direction of the court reporter and began to read her decision.

"Defendant's subpoena requesting fingerprints and pubic hair samples from Matthew H. Brooks is hereby quashed. Pursuant to the rules of criminal procedure, specifically section 240.20, the type of discovery sought by defendant's motion is not permitted to the defense."

Ethan stood again. "We request that this hearing be filed in the court's records under seal, and that the court further order counsel to refrain from discussion of the motion or its result."

"That seems to be a reasonable request. So granted."

I looked over at Ethan, who stared right back. At least he was enough of a professional not to smirk in triumph.

33

As soon as we got out of the judge's chambers Benjamin Ethan sidled up to us. "We should talk."

"Whenever you want," I replied, trying my best not to seem too deflated by the events in court.

"No time like the present. We can borrow the witness room." He turned back to the others. "Lisa, do you have a few minutes to join us?"

I wasn't sure what I found more disturbing: that Ethan invited the ADA to a meeting, that he was on a first-name basis with her, or that she immediately agreed with an "Of course."

We all assembled in the witness room. Ethan took a seat at the head of the table, as if he was chairing this meeting.

Kaplan spoke first. "I've got a belated Christmas gift for your client. I've been authorized to make a very generous plea offer. Man one, with a sentencing recommendation of fifteen. With good-time credit, he'll be out in ten."

Kaplan delivered the offer with a grimace, which told me she was clearly not happy to have had her case hijacked by Benjamin Ethan and the powers that be in the DA's office. And she was right—the offer was a gift. The statutory sentence for the top count of the indictment, murder in the second degree, was twenty-five to life. Kaplan's offer meant the difference between L.D. attending Brianna's high school graduation and possibly never seeing the outside world again.

The first rule of negotiating is never to accept the opening offer. So I pushed back a little, mainly to see if Kaplan might shave off a couple more years.

"It sounds to me like we're getting close to the truth about Mr. Brooks's role in all of this," I said. "We all know that Judge Pielmeier's ruling isn't going to stop us from calling Brooks at trial. What's he going to say under oath when we ask him if he was having an affair with Roxanne? And we're going to have evidence of the affair. We'll find that witness, or another one. Believe me, someone will talk."

Kaplan said, "You should know that I am not a supporter of giving your client such a sweetheart deal. So if you want to roll the dice, be my guest. But be advised, this is our best and last offer, and it expires the moment we see Judge Pielmeier again."

Ethan, however, was not so cavalier. In his Dutch-uncle voice he said, "Daniel, you are missing the bigger picture here. Just because Mr. Brooks might—and I say *might*—have been engaged in a sexual relationship with Ms. Wells, that doesn't mean your guy didn't kill her. You know that, right?"

34

The next day we were back at Rikers. It was "Come to Jesus" time.

"I didn't expect to see you guys until the trial," L.D. said when he waddled into the small visiting room. His usually smooth complexion was marred by a creased forehead. He knew something was up.

I didn't say anything as I watched the guards do their thing. When they were done and had left the room, I said, "A lot's happened since we saw you last, L.D."

"Yeah, like what?"

All of a sudden the sheer magnitude of just how much L.D. didn't know hit me. We'd never even told him we were going to Stocks, no less that we'd found out that Brooks had been there over Thanksgiving. Last but not least, there was the plea offer.

I stuttered, trying to find a suitable place to begin. Then I just spit it all out.

"After we visited you, we went down to Stocks, South Carolina. We were hoping that someone down there might know something about Roxanne's love life. What we found out was that Matt Brooks was there over Thanksgiving."

"Brooks was there? With Roxanne?"

In a flat voice I said, "We believe that Matt Brooks was having an affair with Roxanne at the time she was killed."

"That motherfucker, cocksucking—"

I'm sure that the string of profanity would have gone on longer, but I cut him off. "Let me tell you all of it, okay?"

"What else I need to know but that Matt Brooks is setting me up to take the fall for killing Roxanne?"

I assumed the question to be rhetorical, but Nina took it at face value. "We don't have any proof of the affair, L.D., and we have absolutely nothing linking him to the murder."

"What about the pubes?" L.D. asked. "Are they Brooks's?"

"I was getting to that," I said. "Brooks refused to allow us to test his pubic hair, so we went to the judge to ask her to force him to give us a sample. Unfortunately, we got shut down. That was yesterday. And remember I told you that we had a witness, a housekeeper for one of the families who lived on Roxanne's block, who saw Roxanne kissing an older man? Well, we went back to her place the other day to see if she could identify that man as Brooks. No good news there, either. She's left the country."

"I'm gonna fucking kill that motherfucking Brooks my damn self."

"That's not going to help things," I said.

"Just so there's another point of view represented here," Nina said, "it is also entirely possible that Brooks was down in Stocks for some business reason and the man the housekeeper saw was someone else. And in that case, the pubic hair could belong to the guy the housekeeper saw, or just some random guy Roxanne picked up or something. We just don't know, L.D., so that's another reason why making threats of murdering Matt Brooks isn't the thing to do right now."

"Besides," I said, "that's not even the most important thing we came here to talk to you about. After the hearing, we met with Kaplan and with Benjamin Ethan."

"Who's he?"

"He's Matt Brooks's lawyer. He, or rather Kaplan, with a strong push from the Brooks camp, made us a very attractive plea offer."

"No," L.D. said firmly. "No fuckin' way."

"L.D., you need to hear me out," I said, trying to be equally resolute. "She offered a jail term of fifteen. That means you'll likely be eligible for parole in ten, maybe even less than that."

He was already shaking his head that this offer, and I suspect any offer, was completely unacceptable. Then he put a point on it: "Fuck you."

"We're not the enemy here," Nina said. "We're trying to help."

"If you want me to say that I killed Roxanne when I didn't, then you fuckin' *are* the enemy. You sure as hell ain't friends."

No one said anything for a few seconds.

"You're right, L.D.," I finally said. "We're not your friends. But we are your lawyers. And as such, we have a duty to tell you the truth. Not what you want to hear, but the truth. And so here it is: You were Roxanne's boyfriend and you have no alibi for the night she was murdered. The prosecution is going to claim that she dumped you, and that's motive. And that goddamn song . . . everybody on earth has heard you say—some people would say *brag*—that you're going to beat a singer to death with a baseball bat." I stopped and shook my head at him, as much in sadness as in anger.

Nina said, "That's why it's our professional opinion that you should take this deal. We don't think we can win with what we have."

I expected something of a tirade in response, but L.D. seemed to be in complete control of himself. Almost too calm, given the circumstances.

"So lemme ax you something, then, Dan. If I take this deal, and I do whatever you said, ten years, fifteen years, do you get to spend that time at home in your bed?"

There was no emotion to the question. No sarcasm at all. It was like he really wanted to know the answer.

"Yes," I said.

"And if I don't take no deal, and we go to trial, and I lose, and that motherfuckin' judge, she throw the book at me and I do life, no parole, fifty or sixty years, what happens to you then?"

I knew where he was heading on this, and felt obliged to play along. "Nothing," I said. "I'm still going home to my own bed."

"That's right. And so that's why I don't give a fuck

what you think I should do. Because I know I didn't kill Roxanne, and that's all that matters to me."

"That's all that *should* matter," I said, "but you know that it's not all that *does* matter. You don't need me telling you about the real world, but, just in case you might have forgotten, innocent men do go to jail. Especially if they're black and are accused of killing white women. We're not saying that we think you're guilty. But we are saying that, based on the evidence as we know it right now, a jury will find you guilty. *That's* what matters here. I know that ten years seems like an eternity, but it's not. You won't be much older than Nina when you get out and a lot younger than me. Look how much life there is to be had after that. How can you give all that up?"

He shook his head again, looking almost betrayed. It was as if he'd been trusting that I'd understand why he was making this decision, and now he was all alone.

"You really don't get it, do you?" he finally said. "I can live with a bad result, even if I have to live with it in prison for the rest of my life. But I can't live with myself anywhere if I say I beat Roxanne to death. Which. I. Did. Not. Do."

35

Our last pretrial conference was held four days before the real deal was to begin. Judge Pielmeier had made it clear that she wanted to get right to jury selection on Monday morning, and so she had scheduled this appearance for the parties to voice whatever last-minute issues had arisen.

For us, that meant being heard on our motion in limine, which was our effort to keep the "A-Rod" song from the jury. Nina pegged the odds of our success at roughly the equivalent of L.D. nabbing the Nobel Peace Prize.

Never shy about milking her moment in the spotlight, the judge put the appearance on her regular calendar, and so the courtroom was filled with reporters. Then she outdid herself, making us all wait more than an hour.

When she finally took the bench, the standard operating procedure began: Judge Pielmeier called for Legally Dead; after a few minutes, he entered through the side door, doing the duck waddle with the usual contingent beside him.

Judge Pielmeier began by going over the ground rules for jury selection, which she referred to by its Latin name, voir dire. She would question each prospective juror and then give both sides a turn. She made clear her view that her questions would be the most pertinent, and therefore she didn't want the lawyers to plow the same ground she did.

After she made this same point at least three different ways, Judge Pielmeier finally opened the floor to someone else. It was Kaplan's turn first.

"We don't have any issues to raise," she said.

"That leaves you and your in limine motion, Mr. Sorensen," Judge Pielmeier said. "I've read your papers and listened to the song in question. So tell me, Mr. Sorensen, why isn't the jury better informed if this song is admitted into evidence?"

"I'm going to be making this argument, Your Honor," Nina said.

The judge clearly didn't care. With a bored expression she said, "Then you tell me, Ms. Harrington."

"For the simple reason that it's not evidence," Nina said. "It's a song lyric. Jurors might be confused into thinking that someone who is creative must really believe the things he writes, but the truth is that song lyrics aren't evidence of anything but creativity. If Stephen King were on trial, the court would not permit the reading of passages from *The Shining* to show that he had homicidal tendencies. The same rationale must surely apply to hip-hop artists as it does to novelists. Simply put, the 'A-Rod' song is a work of fiction. For this reason, we plan to question the jurors closely during voir dire on their knowledge of Mr. Patterson's music and seek to exclude any who are very familiar with his song. All of that work will be for naught if the court then allows Ms. Kaplan to simply play the song for the jury during the trial."

"Okay," Judge Pielmeier said, and it looked as if she was trying to come up with a one-liner and couldn't. "Let me try to unpack what you're saying here, so we can deal with your objection in a systematic way. First off, on the jury issue, good luck to you finding twelve people who are not aware of Mr. Patterson's music. I tell you, I'd never heard of him before his arrest, but I can't turn on the radio now without hearing that noise he calls music." She broke eye contact with Nina and looked directly at Legally Dead. "No offense, sir, I'm sure you have many fans. I'm just more of a Luther Vandross kind of person."

I knew that L.D. had no idea who Luther Vandross was. Nina probably didn't either.

"My second point," Judge Pielmeier continued, "is that the lyrics in question concern the defendant bragging that he is going to beat to death a singer with a baseball bat."

"That's not what it says," Nina replied. "The 'singer' referenced in the 'A-Rod' song isn't Roxanne. The lyric in question doesn't even refer to a singer in the musical sense. It's about a *snitcher*, involved in a gang situation. If you listen to the preceding line—"

Judge Pielmeier interrupted her with a loud laugh, which stopped Nina in her tracks.

"Ms. Harrington, what all this tells me is that you may be right about one thing—if this song is art, as you claim, then it's subject to various interpretations. So maybe your interpretation that it's about . . . whatever you just said it was about, will carry the day with the jury. I'm not in any way preventing you from arguing that interpretation, or that your client is one of the great creative geniuses of our time. But I'm also not going to prevent Ms. Kaplan from telling the jury that the song means what *she* says it means. So the bottom line is that the jury *is* going to be able to hear the song and make up their own minds on what it means."

I thought that was it, but then the judge said, "Now, off the record . . ." The court reporter lifted her fingers from the machine in front of her in a Pavlovian-like response.

I couldn't help but turn around. *Off the record* meant that what she was about to say would not be included in the court transcript, but there were more than a hundred reporters behind me that would certainly publish what she was about to say, and the prospective jury pool would no doubt read those stories.

But, of course, Judge Pielmeier couldn't resist a good sound bite. "Mr. Patterson, I'll tell you this. If you wrote a song about killing a singer with a baseball bat, and then you went out and killed a singer with a baseball bat, you are, quite simply, the stupidest human being on the face of the earth."

And right on cue, the courtroom, of course, exploded with laughter.

36

That evening, Nina suggested we take the night off. The idea was, in her words, to be like normal people.

"I'm a little out of practice," I said. "What do you normal people do?"

"I'm far from an expert," Nina said, "but I think they watch TV. Some type of guilty pleasure, maybe."

"Like a singing competition, or do you want something more *Real Housewives*–ish?"

"You choose. But nothing involving the legal system. So, no *The Good Wife* or *Law and Order* reruns."

We settled on a block of sitcoms. I sat on my sofa, feet on the coffee table, with Nina nestled under my arm, her head resting against my chest.

We bantered about gibberish, a welcome change from our usual discussion topics of pubic hair and blood spatter. Nina told me that her favorite TV show of all time was *Saved by the Bell*.

"You're kidding, right? The Saturday-morning thing?"

"Very good," she teased. "Yeah, I loved that show. That to me was what being a kid was like. I was positive I was going to marry Zack."

"Wouldn't the one who was in *Showgirls* have gotten jealous?"

She shot me a snarky look. "Figures that that's your connection to TV's gold standard. And for your information, Zack's girlfriend on the show was Kelly, not Jessie."

"I stand corrected."

"So what are your favorites? Movie? Book? Television?"

I rattled off my answers. "TV show: *Seinfeld*; movie: *The Godfather*; book: *The Great Gatsby*."

"My God," she said. "How old are you, anyway?"

"What? These are classics."

"C'mon, you're flipping the channels and you have the choice between watching *Godfather* or . . . one of the Batman movies. You're not telling me that you watch *The Godfather*."

"Christian Bale Batman I'll watch, but not the Schumacher ones. No way."

"My point exactly," she said with obvious self-satisfaction.

"Are you going to rag on *The Great Gatsby*, too?"

"No, that I saw coming from the day I met you. A romantic who lives in the past . . . might as well have your picture on the cover."

"Am I that predictable?"

"We all are, I'm afraid. My favorite book is *Anna Karenina*. Feel free to insert your own jaded-about-love joke."

She slid into me even more, like a cat nuzzling. I reciprocated by rubbing the small of her back, occasionally slipping my hand under the waistband of her sweatpants, tickling her soft skin.

"This is really nice," she said, a purring sound that matched her feline movements. "It's been a really long time since I spent a night like this."

"No cuddling with the married man?"

I must have said this too sharply, or else Nina was right and I was utterly predictable, because she knew what I was really thinking.

"Are you jealous, Dan?"

"No," I said, sounding unconvincing even to myself.

"What a sorry pair we are," she joked. "I'm jealous of your dead wife, and you're jealous of some guy who strung me along."

"Please don't be jealous of Sarah," I said.

My mind flooded with what I wanted to say next. I tried to think about how I'd said it before, and I couldn't remember. For some reason I knew that this time I'd always remember.

Nina must have thought I had nothing more to add, because she'd returned to her position under my arm. I ran through the words in my head.

"I know it hasn't been very long, but I'm pretty sure that I'm in love with you, Nina."

"Pretty sure?" Nina said.

Even though I knew she was teasing, I felt like an idiot. It was the kind of thing to be said without any qualifier, or not to be said at all.

"Let me try that again. I know that all I think about is how happy I am when we're together, how grateful I am that you came into my life, how much better a person I am than the day before I met you, and how I never, ever want this feeling to stop."

She pulled herself up, so her face was inches away from mine. I could smell the lilac scent of her shampoo.

"That was much better," she said. Then, after a beat, "I'm not pretty sure, I *know* that I'm in love with you, Dan."

37

The first day of trial is like picture day during grade school. Everyone is wearing their best clothing. For me that meant the same charcoal-gray Brioni suit I wore when Nina and I visited L.D. for the first time, which now seemed a lifetime ago.

Two lifetimes ago, in fact.

There was the life I led with Sarah and Alexa, the life in which I was a partner at Taylor Beckett. Then there was the life after that, where I was, more or less, a recluse and a part-time drunk. And now, at forty-three, I was beginning my third life. For all intents and purposes, it might have looked like a replay of the first one—respected lawyer—but I knew that everything about me was different now. If Nina and I were going to have a life together after the trial, I'd be a different man than I'd been with Sarah. Better, in every way.

Nina wore a dark suit that hugged her figure and a light blue shirt. Lisa Kaplan must have shopped in the same store because she had on pretty much the same outfit.

The law clerk called out: "*People of the State of New York vs. Nelson Patterson,* criminal case number 085572."

In the end, we hadn't said anything about Calvin Merriwether not being Nelson Patterson. Nina had done the legal research on the issue and concluded that making that kind of revelation would implicate L.D.'s Fifth Amendment rights against self-incrimination. "Besides," Nina had said, "what difference does it make? It's not like what they call him is really going to matter. If he's found guilty, he's going to jail either way."

"Good morning, all," Judge Pielmeier said after only a short twenty-minute wait. "Please be seated. And let me extend a warm welcome to those of you in the gallery. I know you all are packed in there pretty tight, and for that I'm truly sorry. But better to be cramped in here than to be outside in the corridor with lots of elbow room."

The huddled masses behind me gave the judge her sought-after laugh, which was also apparently the cue for the judge's law clerk to notify the prison officials to bring Legally Dead into the courtroom. A minute later, L.D. entered through a side door marked "Do Not Enter."

It was the first time I'd ever seen L.D. without restraints of some type. That he was still rubbing his wrists indicated he had not been free for very long.

I'd bought him a suit, rejecting the ones he already owned as way too flashy. The one I picked was from Brooks Brothers, figuring it didn't get more conservative than that. It was a light gray, which I thought would contrast with the darker hues Nina and I were wearing. He'd told me that he was a 44 jacket, but I'd bought a 46, for fear that if the suit was cut small, it would give him a more imposing look, like he was about to burst out of it, Incredible Hulk–style. Instead, it swam on him a little, and he seemed less than comfortable in it.

The guards were dressed in suits, as per the judge's order. They looked more like undertakers than spectators, however. For a moment I wondered if it wouldn't have been better to have had them wear their uniforms. They weren't fooling anyone.

Nina caught me taking a deep breath. "It'll be okay," she whispered.

"I know," I said back, but in reality, I was far less certain.

In the trials I'd done while at Taylor Beckett, we always relied on high-priced jury experts and focus groups to help us decide which members of the jury pool to select. But the advice always boiled down to the same thing—defendants want jurors who will empathize with them, and that means people like them.

The obvious juror for Legally Dead, therefore, was a young African-American man. After them, I favored older African-American men and younger white men. Women of any race or age came with the risk that they might identify with Roxanne. Last on my list were older, white males, who I feared would view themselves as fatherly protectors of Roxanne.

When the first pool of fifty entered, I couldn't believe that any random collection of New Yorkers could be 90 percent white. I scanned the faces and it wasn't until nearly the end of the second row that I saw someone who I thought might be under thirty-five, and even then I wasn't sure. To add to our bad luck, the pool appeared to be more than 50 percent female.

Judge Pielmeier gave the prosecution six peremptory challenges and our side nine—the free lives of jury selection. Each peremptory represented a pool member who could be removed without cause, which meant that if the prospective juror's answers didn't reveal a preconceived bias, we could still dismiss that juror. Unfortunately, we'd need a lot more than nine to get a decent jury out of this group.

L.D. saw the problem immediately, too. He leaned over and whispered in my ear, "Damn, it looks like a fucking country club over there."

There were only two black men in the entire pool. One was the first prospective juror, who, according to the questionnaire he filled out, was twenty-nine years old and worked in the warehouse of a paint manufacturer. He was our ideal juror, and so it was no surprise that Kaplan barely paid attention to his answers regarding his ability to adjudicate L.D.'s fate without prejudice. When it was time to vote, Kaplan used her first peremptory to excuse him.

The second prospective juror was exactly the kind Kaplan wanted: sixty-two-year-old white male, middle management at Time Warner Cable. I thought hard about using one of our challenges to strike him, but the sea of people who looked just like him in the jury pool caused me to conclude I'd better keep my powder dry.

He was seated as juror number 1. Eleven more to go, and judging from the potential jurors we had to choose from, we might lose the case before it had even begun.

As luck would have it, the only other African-American male was next up. I knew from the get-go he was a keeper, but to make something of a show of it, I asked about five questions before telling Judge Pielmeier that this juror was acceptable to the defense. Kaplan didn't even ask one before using her second peremptory to strike him.

That's when I opened my mouth and objected.

"Mr. Sorensen," Judge Pielmeier said, sounding surprised, "what's the problem with Ms. Kaplan using one of her challenges to strike this prospective juror?"

In a very loud voice, I announced, "The prosecution is obviously eliminating jurors on the basis of their race. They are illegally preventing African Americans from serving on this jury."

Judge Pielmeier shot me the disgusted look I deserved. An objection like that should have been done at sidebar, so as not to poison the entire jury pool. Of course, that was precisely why I didn't do it at sidebar. I needed to create some luck here or L.D. was finished.

After a sigh so loud the people in the back of the gallery undoubtedly heard it, Judge Pielmeier said, "Unfortunately, due to Mr. Sorensen's objection, which he knows very well that he should not have voiced in front of you all, and which Mr. Sorensen and I will discuss in just a moment, I have little choice but to dismiss all of you from consideration for serving on this case. Please go back to the general sitting room. Perhaps you'll be called for another case." She looked down at the paper in front of her. "Mr. Anderson," she said to the one juror who had already been seated, "I'm afraid I'm going to dismiss you as well."

Kaplan looked positively horrified by this turn of events. "Your Honor, the prosecution does not believe the prejudice is sufficient to justify dismissal of the entire jury pool," she said in a pleading voice.

"I know this one hurts, Ms. Kaplan, and I sympathize. And believe me, Mr. Sorensen will *not* go unpunished for his conduct. But despite some of the nastier things being said in the court of public opinion"—she glared at the reporters in the gallery as she said this—"I will not allow race to play *any* part in this trial, and I'm not going to allow people to second-guess the verdict based on the racial composition of the jury like they did in the O.J. Simpson case."

During the few minutes it took the first jury pool to file out of the courtroom, I tried not to make eye contact with Judge Pielmeier, but I knew she was bearing down on me. I had butterflies in my stomach, and it felt a lot like when I was a child awaiting my parents' punishment.

When the last member of the first jury pool had left, Judge Pielmeier finally had the opportunity.

"This is not going to happen again, Mr. Sorensen!" she thundered. "Do you understand me? If you are going to say anything—anything—that might even remotely prejudice . . . No, I'm not even going to assume you're capable of making that determination. From now on, all your objections shall be explained with only one word. So you'll say, 'Objection—relevance' or 'Objection—hearsay.' If you need more than one word, you are to ask for a sidebar, or by all that I hold holy, there will be dire consequences. Understood?"

"My apologies, Your Honor."

"Save it for someone who believes you, Mr. Sorensen," she said with a note of disgust so pronounced that had she not been in court I'm sure her words would have been laced with profanity. "Now put your *Batson* objection"—and with that she rolled her eyes—"on the record, so I can tell you, on the record, just how ridiculous I think it is. And, Mr. Sorensen, you'd be wise to remember who you're appearing before in this case."

"Thank you," I said, as if I had received an honor rather than a tongue-lashing. "Put simply, in the *Batson* case, the United States Supreme Court held that, even though peremptory challenges can be made without cause, they cannot be racially motivated. In this case—"

"That's enough, Mr. Sorensen."

I had more to say, but Judge Pielmeier had already heard enough. More than enough, I'm sure she would have said.

Seeing it was her turn, Kaplan rose to respond, but Judge Pielmeier gestured that she should resume her seat. "Ms. Kaplan, there's no need for you even to waste your breath on this one."

Then, turning back to me with anger still all over her face, Judge Pielmeier continued, "This is the ruling of the court. Defendant's *Batson* challenge is denied and deemed frivolous. I have, off the record, explained to Mr. Sorensen that this type of conduct will not be tolerated in my courtroom. But more than that, no one is more opposed to racial profiling than me. I have written opinions on the subject and testified before Congress about it. It does a disservice to allege racial profiling without any basis, which is precisely what this court believes the defendant's counsel has done. I understand that lawyers are duty bound to zealously advocate for their clients, but I do not believe that extends to a blatant attempt to contaminate what counsel believes to be a demographically unfavorable jury pool by yelling 'Racism!' when there's absolutely no evidence to support such a serious charge. To erase any doubt that Ms. Kaplan acted in anything but a completely appropriate manner, I would have struck those jurors, too. Let the record therefore show that it was with serious reservations that I dismissed the first jury pool and the one already-seated juror, but I did so because continuing with a possibly tainted jury pool was not in the best interests of justice. I'm going to give the prosecution back their two peremptories, and I'm taking two peremptory challenges away from the defense as punishment. So the prosecution has their six back, and Mr. Sorensen and Ms. Harrington, you are now down to seven, and I'll keep chopping away at that if I have to. Now . . . we're going to bring in a new pool, and we're definitely going to seat a jury today. Does everyone understand?"

"Yes, Your Honor," Kaplan and I said in unison.

"I know *you* understand, Ms. Kaplan," Judge Pielmeier said, "but I'm not sure that Mr. Sorensen does. So, Mr. Sorensen: let me be absolutely clear. This is when I might tell you that the next time you pull a stunt like that, I'm going to hold you in contempt, but that would suggest there might be a next time. Rather, I want you to understand, in no uncertain terms, that there will *not* be a next time. Is that clear, sir?"

"Yes, Your Honor," I said, trying hard not to show even the hint of a smile.

And wouldn't you know, the next jury pool turned out to be as good for us as the previous pool had been bad. Even with our side having two fewer peremptory challenges, the jury that was seated was better than we could have hoped for. Seven of the twelve were African-American men under forty. Among the other five, there wasn't a single white male over fifty.

We actually had a shot now.

38

I knew Nina disapproved.

She didn't say anything about it during the walk back to my apartment after court, beyond a cryptic comment that I "must be pleased with our jury," but I could tell by her body language that she was unnerved by my conduct.

We ordered in Chinese food for dinner. One thing we had agreed upon was that we shouldn't be seen in restaurants during the trial. A photo of Nina and me smiling or canoodling over glasses of wine would undo our effort to portray ourselves as single-minded in our devotion to Legally Dead's innocence.

After a bite of steamed vegetable dumplings, Nina finally made reference to the elephant in the room.

"Just so I'm clear, Dan . . . is this one of those 'we're going to do whatever it takes to win' kind of things? Or was today a onetime detour from the world of ethics?"

"We didn't have a chance with that jury pool, Nina."

She frowned at me. "That's not an answer, and you know it. Besides, Kaplan now has as bad a jury for her as we originally had for us. Do you think she's got no chance? Did you hear her yelling 'racism'?"

"Her client doesn't have a constitutional right to a trial by a jury of its peers. Our client does."

She put down her chopsticks. It looked like she was

debating with herself whether to let the issue go or take another stab at it.

Apparently she decided to give it one more try.

"It scared me a little bit. Seeing you that way."

The sentiment surprised me. I had anticipated her saying that she was disappointed in me, claiming that I should have more faith in myself or the legal system than to feel like I needed to put my thumb on the scale.

But scared?

"I don't understand," I said.

"I'm worried that this case has made you desperate. You know, it isn't lost on me that our client—who may end up spending the rest of his life in prison—seems to be at peace with that, so long as he's true to himself. I worry sometimes that . . . well, that that's not the case for you. That you won't be at peace with yourself if we lose, and that's making you betray who you are."

I dismissed the suggestion with a shake of my head and a smile.

"No, that's not right," I said. "Believe me. I'll be fine, win or lose."

But even as I said this, I knew Nina was right. Although I had told myself repeatedly that L.D. could be found guilty, and I could go on to lead a very happy life, with Nina at my side, for some reason, I couldn't see it unfolding that way. The lesson I took away from Darrius Macy was that I'd been punished for my role in allowing a rapist to go free. To undo that required more than L.D. being found not guilty. He had to be truly innocent *and* he had to be acquitted.

This meant, when you parsed through it all, that Nina was right. There would be no peace for me if we lost.

Later that evening, as I worked on my opening statement, Nina appeared to be working just as hard on distracting me from working on my opening statement. I was hunched over my laptop while Nina was kissing my ear.

"Are you already bored with me, Dan? Is that where this relationship is going?"

"So you don't subscribe to the rule adhered to by football players—no sex the night before the big game?"

"I've dated more than my fair share of football players, and most of them claimed to have had the best games of their career *after* having sex with me. So, you may want to keep that in mind."

She said this with laughter, but I had little doubt it was true. I also knew that, like with most issues pertaining to Nina, I was going to give in.

Afterward, we both dozed off. When I awoke about an hour later, Nina was breathing softly beside me. I decided to let her sleep, and turned back to the opening. I wasn't working long before she was awake.

"Hey. Come back to bed," she cooed.

"Soon. I need to do a little more work."

"How's it coming along?"

"Okay, but I'm struggling with that age-old debate about our SODDI guy. Do we go after Brooks in the opening or hold fire?"

"You know my view," she said with a yawn. "It's just too risky."

Nina was sitting up in bed. She held the top sheet over her breasts, like they do in the movies, a bit of modesty that seemed out of character for her.

"I'm just worried that we'll lose some of the jury from the get-go," I said. "Once that happens, you never get them back. They're *expecting* us to argue that L.D. didn't do it, which means that someone else did, and so they're just going to glaze over when I make that point. What they're not expecting is for us to identify the murderer. If we name Brooks, then they'll be attentive for the whole trial, waiting for evidence linking to him."

"That's the problem, though, isn't it?" she said, smoothing her hair. "We don't have that evidence. You may be right that if we pin our whole case on proving that Brooks did it, the jury won't jump to the conclusion that L.D. is guilty during the opening. But so what? When our case is over and we *haven't* proved that Brooks did it—or offered much even to suggest that he did—the jury is going to feel bait-and-switched. Besides, even if you're right about needing to give the jury another person to blame, it doesn't mean that you have to give them a specific someone else in the opening. If you feel we need to go that way, leave the SODDI guy nameless. So, you'll say, 'Ladies and gentlemen of the jury, Roxanne had another lover and he's the real killer.'"

And if her logic weren't enough to persuade me, she let the top sheet drop, exposing her perfect, full breasts.

"Now you're playing unfair," I said.

"All's fair," she replied coyly. "Now, hear me out on this. You have to remember, we have no idea where Matt Brooks was the night of the murder. I bet his wife alibis him, whether he was with her or not. And if we go after Brooks in opening, we give Kaplan time to see if Brooks's prints match the ones left at Roxanne's house, and maybe she'll even have her expert do the match on the pubic hair."

I shook my head in disagreement. "If we put L.D. on, Kaplan will call Brooks in her rebuttal case. And if she needs time to run tests on the pubic hairs, do you think Judge Pielmeier won't give it to her?"

Nina shrugged. "That's a good argument for keeping L.D. off the stand. But it's not a reason for going after Brooks in the opening."

I was still thinking about how that would play out, and whether it was even possible to convince L.D. not to testify, when Nina got out of bed. Still naked, she walked over to me, not the least bit self-conscious. When she knelt beside me to kiss the back of my neck, I could feel the softness of her breast along my back.

Her hand started at my chest, but in no time it was beneath the elastic on my pajama bottoms. For a moment I wasn't sure if this was because she'd convinced me with regard to our trial strategy, or if she thought I needed a little more encouragement.

Either way, it was enough for me to forget anything about the opening.

39

The next day, we all waited forty minutes before Judge Pielmeier took the bench. She welcomed the gallery back, and then called for the guards to bring in the defendant. That's what she always called L.D.— the defendant.

L.D. entered wearing the same exact suit, shirt, and tie as the day before. Nina leaned over to me. "Let's remember to bring him a new tie tomorrow."

After L.D. took his seat, and the guards took theirs behind us, Judge Pielmeier called for the jury. To a person, they looked dead tired. Yesterday was exciting, the whole waiting-to-be-selected thing, but now, even before the trial had begun, they looked no different from anybody else at the start of a workweek.

When the jury was ready, Judge Pielmeier went through the standard pretrial speeches. First she explained that L.D. was innocent until proven guilty, offering a circular explanation of reasonable doubt.

"It doesn't mean 'no doubt,'" she said, "but it also doesn't require that you be certain of the defendant's guilt. The standard is that if you have doubts that are *reasonable* as to whether the defendant is guilty, you must vote not guilty."

After that, she instructed the jurors that they should consider as evidence only what the witnesses said. "Now, these lawyers, they're smart and they know all the tricks, but not one of them knows anything about this case except what other people have told them. And guess what, that's what you'll know, too, after the evidence. So my instruction to you is this: listen to the lawyers, but understand that what they tell you should only be used as a road map showing the evidence that is about to come up. And like any road map, it should only serve as a guide. Don't let it overrule your eyes and ears and good judgment. If one of the lawyers tells you something is true, but none of the evidence supports that conclusion, then you should not believe it, any more than you should keep going on a road that you can see out your windshield is a dead end. Which is a long way of saying, ladies and gentlemen of the jury, trust your own judgment."

The jurors nodded in unison, which was enough for Judge Pielmeier to get down to business. "Ms. Kaplan," the judge said, "we're ready to hear your opening statement."

Kaplan walked in front of the jury, introduced herself as "Assistant District Attorney Lisa Kaplan, representing the people of the state of New York," and then walked back to counsel table and sat down. She waited long enough to build some suspense, but not so long as to allow anyone's mind to wander. Then she pressed a button on the laptop beside her.

L.D.'s voice blared through the courtroom's speakers:

Gonna stop you when you sing,
gonna give it til you scream;
don't like what you said,
gonna go A-Rod on your head.

Then the music came to a dead halt.

All eyes were on Kaplan, and she milked it but good. She didn't move, remaining in her seat for about ten seconds, and then, still without saying a word, she walked in front of the jury as deliberately as she had before.

Once she was facing them again, she repeated the lines, somehow managing to make them sound even more frightening than when L.D. rapped them.

"Gonna stop you when you sing,
gonna give it til you scream;
don't like what you said,
gonna go A-Rod on your head.

"This isn't a confession," Kaplan said. "Confessions come after the crime. This, ladies and gentlemen of the jury, was a threat—a threat of murder, made by the defendant"—she pointed at L.D., just like they teach you on the first day of ADA school—"Nelson Patterson, aka Legally Dead. Then, when he didn't like what Roxanne said, Legally Dead made good on that threat by brutally bashing in Roxanne's beautiful face. In other words, he went A-Rod on her head."

Kaplan told the jury there were some things

about which there could be no doubt, so much so that not even the defense—and then she pointed at me—would claim otherwise. Among these indisputable facts, Kaplan included that Roxanne and L.D. were lovers, that L.D. had written a song in which he bragged about beating to death a singer with a baseball bat, and that Roxanne was a singer who was murdered by being beaten to death with a baseball bat.

"These facts," she said, "leave no doubt that Legally Dead murdered Roxanne. No doubt."

Then she played the audio again, to emphasize her point.

> *Gonna stop you when you sing,*
> *gonna give it til you scream;*
> *don't like what you said,*
> *gonna go A-Rod on your head.*

I figured that was going to be her closing flurry, but as Kaplan made her way back to the counsel table, John Something-or-Other, the bald guy second-seating her, handed her a baseball bat.

"Objection!" I shouted, mindful of Judge Pielmeier's admonition not to say more than one word.

"Overruled," she replied without even asking me to state the grounds.

Kaplan then showed me how formidable an adversary she would be. Picking up on the fact that the jury undoubtedly didn't follow what had just occurred, she put herself in the role of their friend.

"Ladies and gentlemen, Mr. Sorensen objected because, as our witnesses will explain to you later, the murder weapon in this case has not been found. Legally Dead was way too clever to leave behind something that would link him to this crime. But you'll hear that Roxanne was given a baseball bat as a gift when she sang our national anthem at the first game of the World Series, a bat signed by the players on both teams. Roxanne kept that bat in her bedroom, and it was there on the last day of her life. And you'll hear that when the police arrived after her death, it was gone, and it has never been found. And, of course, the song clearly threatens a brutal beating with a baseball bat. But, ladies and gentlemen, at the end of the day, it matters very little what weapon killed her. Certainly it didn't matter to Roxanne. No, what matters, what you must always remember when you're hearing evidence, is that the last moments of Roxanne's life involved her being violently struck by a powerful object until her body could no longer withstand the blows."

She walked over to the jury box, holding the bat in her hand. I knew what she was going to do and my mind raced through the possible objections I could make. None seemed to apply and my quick calculation was that by saying anything, I'd only make things worse.

"Just imagine," Kaplan continued, now only inches away from the jury foreperson, "what that must have been like for Roxanne. There she was, alone in her bedroom with the man she had been intimate with, and he stood over her holding a baseball bat." Kaplan raised the bat over her head, and as she did, each juror's eyes pointed toward the bat. "And then Roxanne saw that weapon come crashing down on her," and with that Kaplan struck the wooden rail hard enough to make the jurors jump back.

Pure theatrics, but my God, was it effective.

"Let's start with the name," I said when it was my turn.

Once Nina and I had decided not to come clean about L.D.'s birth name, we'd still had to figure out what we were going to call him. We were fairly confident that the prosecution would call him Legally Dead, unless they could pin some other, more offensive, moniker on him. I gave some thought to asking Judge Pielmeier to require the prosecution to refer to him as Mr. Patterson, a tactic often used in mob cases when the defense doesn't want the defendant referred to as Johnny the Rat or Jimmy the Axe, but I ultimately concluded that the jury would find it disingenuous to portray L.D. as someone different from the man they'd read so much about in the news. I also doubted that Judge Pielmeier would rule in our favor.

"You heard Ms. Kaplan refer to our client over and over again as Legally Dead. But that's just a stage name. Like Lady Gaga or Pink or Eminem. No one actually calls him Legally Dead in real life. His friends call him L.D., and that's what we're going to call him.

"I'd be the first to admit that his lyrics are often harsh, but even hip-hop artists fall in love," I told the jury, trying to wax poetic. The reference to L.D. as a hip-hop artist, rather than as a rapper, was deliberate, our attempt to conjure a softer image, more Drake or Bruno Mars than 50 Cent. "L.D. loved Roxanne, and for that simple reason, no one wants justice for Roxanne more than he does. But there can be no justice for Roxanne unless L.D. is found not guilty. He is innocent of this horrible crime, and the only way Roxanne's murderer will be brought to justice is if you find L.D. not guilty."

I went through the mirror opposite of Kaplan's opening, listing the evidence that wasn't there. "Keep focused on what the prosecution cannot prove," I said, trying my best to suggest that something sinister was afoot. "The prosecutor, Ms. Kaplan"—and then I did the pointing thing right back, extending my arm in Kaplan's direction—"is going to ask you to *assume* all sorts of things. But assumptions aren't facts or evidence. So don't be tricked by them.

"The biggest assumption the prosecution is going to ask you to make is also the most unfounded, and that's about the song Ms. Kaplan played for you. She says it's about Roxanne, but what evidence does she have for that? Zero. Nada. Zilch. The truth is, it's just a song. It doesn't reflect L.D.'s innermost feelings. Do you think Elvis really owned blue suede shoes? Did the Beatles really all live in a yellow submarine? These are made-up stories set to music. So is the song that Ms. Kaplan played for you. It's a work of brutal fiction."

The last five minutes of my opening were all

SODDI. But I followed Nina's advice, not once naming Brooks as our SODDI guy, just in case we needed to go in a different direction after we saw the evidence.

"If L.D. did not commit this crime, then who did?" I said, my voice rising. "If I were sitting where you are, that's what I'd want to know. After all, we've all watched enough cop shows to know that the boyfriend is suspect number one, right? But what if there was more than one boyfriend? The prosecution doesn't want you to know about Roxanne's *other* lover. Ms. Kaplan never said a word about that, now, did she? But the evidence will tell you that. The evidence says that loud and clear. We'll show you evidence that several pubic hairs were found in Roxanne's bed that could not possibly have come from L.D. Those pubic hairs came from a Caucasian, and that Caucasian was in Roxanne's bed right before she was murdered. Maybe even on that very day. So . . . who was it?"

I stopped and tried to make eye contact with each juror before going on. Some of them looked away, but most of them didn't.

Benjamin Ethan called it the nod poll. "If I get a nod during opening statements, that juror is mine through deliberations," he'd say. Kaplan had a few nods during her opening, but she would ultimately need twelve votes to convict. So far I had maybe one headshake, but no nods.

"What do we know about Roxanne's *other* lover?" I said. "One thing we know for sure is that the police didn't do anything to find him. Another thing we know for sure is that this man didn't come forward to publicly acknowledge that he'd been in Roxanne's bed, perhaps as recently as the day she was murdered."

I stopped, offering the jury another dramatic pause.

"Why didn't the police find him? They had his pubic hairs and possibly his fingerprints, and yet they did nothing to locate him. Why? Again, the answer is simple. It's because the police had already arrested L.D., and so they didn't want the embarrassment of admitting that they were wrong. And why didn't this man come forward on his own accord? If you were in a relationship with someone who was killed shortly after you'd been naked in their bed, wouldn't you come forward? Wouldn't you realize that you might have critical information to share with the police?" Another pause. "You already know why he didn't do that, don't you? The man who shared Roxanne's bed that last time did not come forward for one reason and one reason only: he's the man who murdered her."

And there it was. Two jurors nodded.

40

The prosecution's first witness was a police detective named Boyle. He was a big, burly Irishman with doughy features and a ruddy face. The prototypical grizzled cop straight out of central casting. Just one look at him made you think he was the kind of guy you'd want to buy a beer and hear his stories because you knew he'd pretty much seen it all.

Kaplan made sure the jury knew that Boyle didn't just look the part.

"How many years have you been a police officer, Detective Boyle?"

"Twenty-two."

"Is this your first murder investigation?"

"No, ma'am."

"Your second?"

"No, ma'am. Far from it."

"How many murder cases have you handled, Detective?"

"I'm sorry to say, it's been thirty-seven."

"Anyone on the NYPD handle more murder cases than you?"

"I don't know for a fact, ma'am, but I've never met a cop who has."

Kaplan turned away from her witness and toward the jury. She smiled, and held the pose when I caught her eye.

Boyle's direct testimony held no surprises. Kaplan's questions were more or less limited to "And what happened next?" but that was enough to get Boyle to tell the jury everything Kaplan wanted them to know.

She started with the crime scene.

With an actor's cadence, Boyle said, "The first thing that I noticed when I got to Roxanne's house was that there was no evidence of forced entry. That's very important because it usually means that the victim allowed the murderer entry into the home. In this case, you had a situation where Roxanne was killed between eleven p.m. and three or four in the morning, and in her bedroom. That told me that she not only knew her murderer but was likely intimate with him, because she allowed him not only into her home late at night but also into her bedroom."

This made perfect sense, but it was also riddled with holes and assumptions. Contrary to Boyle's conclusions, the murderer could have tricked Roxanne into letting him in, pretending to be a neighbor or even the police. Or the murderer might have entered the apartment much earlier, held Roxanne hostage for the day, and forced her up to the bedroom hours later to kill her. But that's the thing with direct examination. You have no choice but to sit helplessly by while the other side makes its points, no matter how misleading, and wait until cross-examination to correct them. Of course, by then, most of the damage has already been done.

"Please tell the jury what you observed in Roxanne's bedroom, Detective Boyle?" Kaplan asked.

"Roxanne was lying facedown, beside her bed. Her white, silk comforter was completely soaked red with blood. The walls were also covered in blood. In my twenty-two years on the force, this was probably the most gruesome crime scene I'd ever seen."

I would have bet twenty bucks that with the dead body of a famous pop star in front of him, Boyle hadn't spent time analyzing the fabric of Roxanne's comforter, and I'd have gone double or nothing that he didn't even know what fabric his own comforter was made out of. These were undoubtedly little verbal cues supplied by Kaplan to paint a more vivid picture of the crime scene. "Blood on her covers" just doesn't hit you like a "white, silk comforter that was completely soaked red with blood."

Kaplan handed me the crime scene photos, the standard protocol before passing them on to the jury. I'd seen them dozens of times by now. So often, in fact, that I'd become inured to their shock value. But so much of a trial is theater, and I knew that the jurors would draw conclusions based on my reaction, and so I did my best to look horrified.

L.D. knew the drill, too. Showing no emotion would make him seem like a sociopath, but false emotion would cast him as a liar, which wasn't much better.

He looked stoically at the first picture, lingering on it for a few seconds, and he held that pose through the second. By the time he'd reached the third, however, he shed a tear, something he'd never done when we looked at them in private, not even the first time. He then pushed the stack back to me without looking at the rest, as if he couldn't bear to see another one. As far as I knew, L.D. had never done any acting outside of his videos, which hardly qualified, but this was an Academy Award performance.

I handed the photos back to Kaplan, expecting her immediately to pass them on to the jury. Unfortunately, she still had a little more lily gilding to do.

"I have to caution you in advance, ladies and gentlemen," she said, "I'm now going to distribute photographs of the crime scene, which include pictures of Roxanne shortly after she was murdered. I wish there was a way that you could fulfill your service without having to see the horror depicted in these photographs, so that you could all remember Roxanne as the beautiful young woman she was in life, and not the disfigurement of her death. I apologize in advance for having to give them to you, but it is very important that you see these pictures to fully understand the brutality of this crime."

Not a word of Kaplan's little speech was true. There's nothing ADAs like better than showing juries gore, and juries don't have to see the victim lying in blood to understand that a murder occurred.

When they finally got hold of the photos, each juror seemingly went through the same process. First they'd excitedly take them, the way you look forward to seeing the car accident that's caused all the traffic, but as soon as they'd made it to the second one, their expression changed abruptly, as if they'd just realized that this was a real person. A murdered woman. Then each juror stared right at L.D. with utter revulsion.

When the last of the jurors had performed this exercise, Kaplan finally broke the silence. "Detective Boyle, was there any evidentiary matter in Roxanne's bed?"

This settled a side bet between Nina and me. Nina thought Kaplan wouldn't address the pubic hairs at all during her direct examination. I disagreed. "If she doesn't," I said at the time, "she's undermining her credibility with the jury." It was smart of her to do it right after showing the photos because the jury would still be thinking about what they'd just seen.

"Yes," Boyle said, "we found three hairs."

"Did you later learn anything more about those hairs?"

"Yes. I learned from the crime investigators that they were pubic hairs."

"What assumption, if any, did you reach concerning who the pubic hair in Roxanne's bed belonged to?"

"The most obvious assumption was that Roxanne left them, naturally."

Nina kicked me under the table. Was it possible that Harry Davis hadn't seen what Popofsky did? Did the prosecution not realize that Roxanne didn't have any pubic hair?

Kaplan told Judge Pielmeier that she had no further questions for Detective Boyle. When she turned to walk back to counsel table, her confident bearing made clear that she thought it had gone very well.

Before I began my cross, Judge Pielmeier gave the jurors a fifteen-minute midmorning break, which she never failed to refer to as a leg stretch. She prohibited the lawyers from leaving the courtroom for the first ten minutes, so we wouldn't run into jurors in the bathroom.

"What do you think is going on?" Nina whispered to me as we watched the jurors file out. "Do you think Kaplan doesn't know about the waxing?"

"Popofsky says it's obvious from the autopsy," I replied, "but who knows? Maybe they just weren't focused down there. It's not like there are any wounds on that part of her body."

"Are you going to cross Boyle on it?"

"Let's see how it goes," I said.

41

When it was my turn with Boyle, I began by playing up the rush-to-judgment angle.

"Detective Boyle, did you ever consider any other possible suspects?"

"Everyone is a suspect at the beginning," he said, the standard police line.

"For how long were you open-minded to the idea that someone other than L.D. may have committed this crime?"

"Until the evidence indicated that your client killed her."

The smug look on his face made clear that Boyle viewed this as some type of competition, and he thought he'd scored first. If that was what he believed, he was sorely mistaken. The witness-interrogator battle is hardly a fair fight. If I did this right, I wouldn't ask Boyle any question to which I didn't already know the answer. That meant I'd always have the upper hand.

"Of course, Detective," I said with a dismissive tone, my signal to the jury that I didn't believe him. "But how long was it before, in your opinion, the evidence pointed to L.D. as Roxanne's killer? Was it days? Or hours? Minutes?"

"I don't remember the exact moment, Counselor.

But it wasn't immediate, if that's what you're trying to imply. We considered the facts for some time."

"Some time," I repeated. "That sounds like more than a day, then, right?"

"Yes," he said, as if I must be the stupidest person on earth not to know that *some time* meant more than twenty-four hours.

His tone didn't matter, however, because now I had the poor bastard. He just didn't know it yet. It felt good to be on top of my game again. After the months of wallowing with a bottle, I was finally back.

"Let's see, now, Detective Boyle," I said, making little effort not to telegraph I was going to thoroughly enjoy this. "You knew pretty much from the start that L.D. was the victim's boyfriend, right?"

"Yes."

"As an experienced police detective with twenty-two years on the force, is it common for you to focus on someone that the victim was having a relationship with—such as a husband or boyfriend?"

He paused. His eyes said he realized where this was heading.

"The statistics bear that out."

"But it's your testimony that the fact that L.D. was Roxanne's boyfriend did not cause you to suspect him from the start because you considered the facts for *some time*—which you just testified is more than twenty-four hours—before focusing on L.D. as a person of interest."

"I don't believe I said that, Counselor."

He was right. He hadn't said that, but what a witness actually says doesn't matter. Although jurors can ask for some portions of the trial transcript to be read back to them during deliberations, they usually don't, which means that what the jurors *think* has been said matters much more than the actual testimony. The questions lawyers ask can change what the jurors recall about the testimony, much the way that political punditry sometimes alters people's recollection of the actual event being pontificated about.

"Well, it's true that you just testified that it took *some time* before you concluded that L.D. was guilty. You're not changing your story on that, are you, Detective?"

"No, Counselor. As I said, we arrested the defendant after some consideration."

Boyle had the tricks down, I had to give him that. He never referred to L.D. by name, always calling him "the defendant" or "your client." It was subtle, but it reduced L.D.'s humanity, making it easier for the jury to convict. It's also why I never used such terms and invoked L.D.'s name as much as I could. Boyle's other little verbal tic was to call me "Counselor." It was a nice touch, actually, because it reinforced the idea that I was there doing a job, and not that I actually believed in L.D.'s innocence.

"There was no evidence at the crime scene linking L.D. to the crime, was there, Detective?"

"We believe your client wiped the scene clean of his fingerprints. Given that he was Roxanne's boyfriend, his prints should have been in her house. As a result, the fact that his prints were not there was actually an indicator of guilt, not the other way around."

"That's very interesting," I said, my hand on my chin, as if I was actually pondering this information. "So, if I understand what you're saying, it's your testimony that the fact that there was *no* evidence of L.D. being anywhere near the crime scene was interpreted by you to be actual evidence that he was, in fact, there."

"Objection!" Kaplan called out. "Your Honor, the question is argumentative."

"Mr. Sorensen, please move on to something else," said Judge Pielmeier, her way of saying that she agreed with Kaplan, but not so much as to sustain the objection.

"Of course, whoever wiped the crime scene would have removed L.D.'s prints. It didn't have to be L.D. who did that, now, did it, Detective?"

"Was that a question, Counselor?" He chuckled and gave a nasty little smirk.

"You'll find this question more straightforward perhaps, Detective. Did you find the murder weapon in L.D.'s possession?"

"You know that we didn't, Counselor." Boyle punctuated this thought with a loud sigh, his signal to the jurors that the very fact I was daring to ask him questions was a waste of his precious time. I decided to call him on it, for little reason other than to show him who was really in charge here.

"That's right, Detective, I do know that. But I asked you the question so that the jury would know, too."

"No, we never found the baseball bat. Are you happy now, Counselor?"

I was happy. I'd called it the murder weapon. He'd called it a baseball bat.

"No, I'm not happy about that, Detective. Because if you had found the murder weapon, be it a baseball bat or something else, it would have proven that L.D. is innocent of this crime. But, by your testimony, it seems pretty clear that you were looking for a baseball bat, which I take to mean that you ignored all the other possible murder weapons, doesn't it?"

"Objection!"

"Sustained. Mr. Sorensen. Please."

Kaplan had done us a favor. Had Boyle been allowed to answer, he would have undoubtedly given a long explanation as to how they checked for every conceivable weapon. Now the jury assumed the premise in my question was correct.

I walked from the podium until I was standing directly behind L.D., and placed my hands on his shoulders. "Detective," I continued, "you just told this jury, under an oath to tell the absolute truth, that it took you *some time* to believe that the evidence pointed to L.D. as the murderer. You swore to these jurors that you were thoughtful in your investigation. That you did not rush to judgment solely because the easiest thing to do in a high-profile case is to arrest the boyfriend. That was your testimony, wasn't it, Detective?"

"Objection!"

Whereas just before she shouldn't have objected at all, this time she objected too late, allowing me to get through my speech. Judge Pielmeier said, "Your job is to ask questions, Mr. Sorensen. We all know what was said."

The gallery laughed, but I noticed that Kaplan didn't. Although it was most likely inadvertent, Judge Pielmeier's quip supported my claim that Boyle had actually testified as I'd recounted.

"Detective, what did you learn in days two, three, and four of the investigation that led you to believe that L.D. was guilty of this crime that you didn't know on day one?"

"Look, Counselor, I'm not sure when exactly we came to the conclusion that your client was guilty, but we ultimately reached that decision."

"I know you reached that conclusion," I said. "That's why L.D. is sitting here. But it doesn't mean you were right." Before he could say anything, I added, "Let me ask the question this way: Did you still have doubts that L.D. was guilty even after you knew he was Roxanne's boyfriend? After you saw the baseball bat in Roxanne's bedroom was missing? Doubts that caused you to wait another four days before arresting him?"

"Objection! That's three questions, at least, Your Honor."

Judge Pielmeier seemed to think about it for a moment, but then she said, "Sustained. One at a time, Mr. Sorensen."

Kaplan couldn't win for losing. If she'd let Boyle fend

for himself, I had little doubt that he would have said he had no doubt about L.D.'s guilt from the get-go, but he just wanted to make sure his case was airtight.

"Let's talk about those three pubic hairs, Detective Boyle."

"Okay, let's," he said, regaining some of his swagger from earlier.

"You cannot say definitively that they came from Roxanne, can you, Detective?"

"As you know, Counselor, the hairs were without the root. The experts told me that without the root, they couldn't make any definitive determination."

"That's not exactly true, is it, Detective?"

"Excuse me?"

"You just swore, under oath, that without the root, you can't make any determinations, and I'm saying that's not true. For example, you know that the hairs came from a Caucasian, don't you?"

Boyle looked annoyed, but for once, at least, it was probably more at himself than at me because this one he just missed. "I'm not an expert in pubic hair analysis, Counselor. I'm only telling you what the investigators told me. I think you'd call it hearsay. But what they told me was that the only things they could tell for sure about the hairs are that they are from the pubic region and from a Caucasian."

"And by deduction, you concluded that they did not belong to L.D. because he's African-American, correct?"

"Yes."

"And is it also your sworn testimony that you concluded that the pubic hairs you found in Roxanne's bed belonged to her, and not to someone else?"

"As I previously testified, Counselor, that was the most logical assumption based on the evidence. You see a hair in the bed, and you assume it belongs to the person who slept in that bed every night."

I had the next question on the tip of my tongue— *Did Roxanne have any pubic hair at the time of her death?*—but I held it back. That was our one bullet in the chamber. The one surprise we held, and I needed to fire it at their expert.

I leaned my head between L.D. and Nina. "I think I'm going to stop it there," I whispered. "What do you think?"

"I agree," Nina said.

"L.D.?"

"Yeah, man, that was great."

"No further questions, Your Honor," I said.

As soon as we stepped inside the apartment, Nina and I were at each other like teenagers. For me, the time after was as wonderful as the act itself. Nina laid her head on my chest, and neither of us said anything, the silence filled only with the sound of heavy breathing. My mind replayed each moment, a kind of highlight reel. More than anything else, I reflected on the fact that this must be what the phrase *utter contentment* meant.

42

I expected Kaplan to lead off the next day with the coroner, Harry Davis. Instead, she announced that the people's next witness was Andrea Wells.

There was a gasp from the gallery when her name was called. And then everyone's eyes followed Wells from the back of the courtroom to the witness chair, as if she was some exotic animal that no one had ever seen before.

L.D. leaned over and whispered in my ear. "What's she going to say? I never met the woman."

My best guess was that the prosecution was going to use Roxanne's mother to establish motive. Somebody had to explain to the jury that Roxanne ended things with L.D., which led to L.D.'s enraged attack. Who better than the victim's mother?

I decided not to share any of that with L.D. "No idea," I whispered back.

Dressed in an expensive-looking cream-colored suit, with enough jewelry to remind the jury of Roxanne's success without being over-the-top about it, Andrea Wells looked much better on the witness stand than she had when we dropped in on her in South Carolina unannounced. Her blond hair was loose and her makeup made her appear five years younger than I had estimated previously. I now wondered if she was much older than me, and concluded she likely wasn't, a fact that was confirmed when she testified to being only nineteen when Roxanne was born.

I chose not to object to Wells's testimony about how she learned of her daughter's death and how that made her feel. Although not in any way relevant, jurors like to hear that stuff, and I thought they might hold it against L.D. if I denied the victim's mother the opportunity to share her grief.

But when Kaplan asked, "Mrs. Wells, what was your understanding of the nature of your daughter's relationship with Legally Dead at the time of her murder?" I got to my feet and, still careful to obey the judge's one-word rule, shouted, "Objection!"

"On what grounds, Mr. Sorensen?" Judge Pielmeier said.

"May we approach, Your Honor?"

She curled her fingers on both hands, summoning us forward.

Judge Pielmeier held sidebars literally at the side of the bench farthest from the jury. Because the judge was a short woman, probably not even five feet tall, and her bench was significantly elevated, she got up from her chair and walked around to the side so she could be heard without having to raise her voice.

"What is it?" she said to me after we'd all assembled.

"Ms. Kaplan, we believe, is trying to establish that the defendant and the victim were no longer in a relationship at the time of her death."

"And what's wrong with that?" Judge Pielmeier asked.

"Whatever Mrs. Wells could say on this topic was told to her by Roxanne, and therefore is going to be hearsay."

Judge Pielmeier obviously hadn't thought of that because she gave me a subtle nod. She then shifted her gaze to give Kaplan her chance at rebuttal.

Kaplan followed the primary rule for a trial lawyer in this situation—never look concerned. "Mrs. Wells's testimony on that issue meets the present-sense-impression exception to the hearsay rule," Kaplan said.

The present-sense impression was the biggest loophole in the evidentiary rules. It permitted hearsay testimony if the statement at issue was made at the same time the event was perceived. The idea was that the speaker wouldn't have had enough time to formulate a lie, and therefore the statement was reliable.

I waited until Kaplan was finished before saying, "Your Honor, there was nothing contemporaneous in Roxanne's statement. If—and I say if—she and my client had broken up, the prosecution's theory is that it occurred days before Roxanne saw her mother in Stocks. Although Ms. Kaplan should get points for originality, this is just not a situation where the present-sense exception even remotely applies."

Kaplan had begun to offer a response, saying something about Roxanne's statement being contemporaneous with her present mental state, when Judge

Pielmeier held up her hand, signaling that she'd heard enough.

"Here's what I'm going to do," the judge said. "The witness's statements about what Roxanne told her about the breakup are hearsay. However, Ms. Kaplan, I will allow you to question the witness about what she perceived, and the conclusions she reached from those perceptions."

Judge Pielmeier might as well have been Kaplan's personal GPS system for the directions she was giving her. With the latitude the judge was offering, Kaplan would have no trouble getting the evidence she wanted before the jury.

"Your Honor—"

"I don't want to hear it, Mr. Sorensen. Now, step back."

I stalked off, attempting to maintain my composure.

When she resumed her direct examination, Kaplan asked, "Mrs. Wells, would you please tell the jury about the last time you saw your daughter?"

"She visited me for Thanksgiving at my home in Stocks, South Carolina. She stayed for a few days, and on the night she returned to New York, she was murdered."

That was another sign of Kaplan's witness preparation. Not one prosecution witness ever said Roxanne was *killed*. She was always *murdered*.

"Did the defendant accompany Roxanne to South Carolina for Thanksgiving?"

"No, he didn't."

"Did you draw any conclusions from the fact that the defendant did not come to your home for Thanksgiving?"

"Yes. I believed that Roxanne had recently ended her relationship with him. If they were still a couple, I'm sure Roxanne would have insisted that he come for Thanksgiving."

"Mrs. Wells, could you please describe for the jury Roxanne's general demeanor that weekend?"

"She was happy. Very happy, in fact."

"Did you draw any conclusions from Roxanne's happiness that weekend about who had ended the relationship?"

"Yes. It was my strong belief that Roxanne ended the relationship."

And just like that, the prosecution had established motive. After all, who wouldn't believe the victim's mother's ability to read her own daughter's moods?

"Roxanne's mother is just not going to contradict herself," Nina said to me during the midmorning break. "Cross-examining her will only make the jury feel even more sympathetic toward her, which is only going to make them hate L.D. even more than they do now."

"But if I don't, we lose the opportunity to get before the jury that Roxanne only decided to go to Stocks at the last minute."

"Dan," Nina said in a somewhat exasperated voice,

"she's going to deny it. You know that. So what's the point?"

"The point is that the question puts the issue out there, so the jury's thinking about it. Besides, I'll ask her who Roxanne was visiting at the Old Westerbrook, and when she says that she doesn't know, we've established she wasn't so knowledgeable about what Roxanne was doing, which undercuts her claim that she knew that Roxanne had ended the relationship with L.D."

"Dan, do you really think that's the way it's going to play out? I bet you, whatever you want, that Roxanne's mother comes up with some reason that Roxanne had to sign papers or something and that's why she met Brooks at the hotel, and she'll claim she knew all about it."

"If we don't try, we're not going to have any other way to get this information into evidence."

"We have Carolyn Anton; she puts Roxanne in the hotel room."

"I know, but she doesn't indicate that Roxanne's mother didn't know Roxanne was going there."

Nina frowned. "This is a bad idea," she said.

I began the cross-examination by establishing that we'd already spoken to Andrea Wells, and Wells began her answers by making it clear to me that she would be a hostile witness.

"Mrs. Wells," I said in as cheery a tone as I could, "we've met before, correct?"

"Yes. You came to my home, without any advance notice, and tricked me into speaking with you."

"I don't recall it that way, but let's focus on what you told me at that time. Do you recall telling me that you had not expected Roxanne to visit you over Thanksgiving?"

Kaplan objected, rightfully so. I needed to establish the predicate before I used Wells's prior statement against her.

Before Judge Pielmeier ruled, I said, "Let me withdraw that and ask it a better way. Isn't it true that your daughter first made plans to visit you for Thanksgiving only a day or two before the holiday?"

"No, that's not true."

Andrea Wells showed me a smug smile. It made me wonder for a moment whether I'd lie under oath to convict the man who I thought killed Sarah and Alexa. I wondered only for a moment, however, because I knew the answer was a resounding yes.

"Mrs. Wells, I take it that you do not recall telling me and my partner, Nina Harrington, that Roxanne had initially told you she had other plans for the holiday, and then at the last moment decided to visit you?"

"I don't recall it because it isn't true."

"And do you know whether your daughter visited anyone at the Old Westerbrook hotel over that weekend?"

"I know that she went there. She told me that she needed to go there for business."

"And I take it that you are also claiming that when we visited with you a few weeks ago, you did not tell us that you had no knowledge your daughter had ever made such a visit."

"Once again, that's a lie."

"And who was it that she was visiting?"

"She told me, but I don't remember."

"Was it Matt Brooks?"

"I don't remember."

"Wouldn't you have found it odd if she met with her married boss in a hotel room over a holiday weekend?"

"Not if she had to sign papers or do something for business."

I paused, and looked back at the counsel table, where Nina looked at me with I-told-you-so eyes. The next question in my head was *Did you know that your daughter had another lover?* Or maybe *Was your daughter in a sexual relationship with Matt Brooks?* And the answer I imagined Andrea Wells giving ranged from not helpful to devastating.

So I looked up at Judge Pielmeier and said, "Your Honor, I have no more questions." And then, before returning to counsel table, I said to Roxanne's mother, "Mrs. Wells, please accept my sincerest condolences for your loss."

"It's a good thing they don't serve liquor here," I said, referring to the court cafeteria. I'd just brought over my tray, which carried a turkey club, a bag of chips, and a diet cola. Nina's lunch looked to be the same thing, without the chips.

"You don't drink when things are tough anymore, remember?" Nina said. "Besides, it really wasn't as bad as you think. The jury knows she was testifying as a mother, not as a witness. What else is she going to say?"

"Okay, but next time you need to tell me that I'm about to make a big mistake," I said with a serious voice.

"Okay, next time," Nina said.

"My guess is that she calls Harry Davis to the stand next," I said.

"That's where you need to be sharp, Dan. Let this one go, and rip him to shreds."

43

When Kaplan called Dr. Harry Davis to the stand, Marty Popofsky took his place next to me at the counsel table, and L.D. and Nina slid over one. And my heart started to beat a bit faster. It felt like before I crossed Vickie Tiernan in the Darrius Macy trial—this was a make-or-break moment for our case. Perhaps not *the* make-or-break moment, not if L.D. and maybe Matt Brooks testified, but after Davis had his say, we'd have a pretty good idea if we were winning or losing.

Either Kaplan worked with Davis to create his appearance, or he'd testified enough to know how to play the part. He was right on the money—dark suit, white shirt, red tie, and rimless glasses. Even his thinning gray hair looked professorial, cropped very tight, as if his head had been dusted with snow.

It only got worse for us when Dr. Davis took the oath. He said his name in a voice so deep he reminded me of the guy who narrates movie trailers.

"Are you currently employed, sir?" Kaplan asked.

"Yes. I am the chief medical examiner for the city of New York."

"Tell the jury about your educational background, Dr. Davis."

"I'm a product of the New York City public

schools," he said, earning me an I-told-you-so jab in the ribs from Popofsky. "After that, CUNY Queens and Harvard Medical School."

"Thank you, Dr. Davis. Very impressive. Can we talk for a few minutes about the findings of the Roxanne Wells murder?"

"Certainly."

"What can you tell us about the time and cause of death?"

"The victim's time of death was between eleven in the evening and three in the morning. The cause of death was a blow to the head, most likely with a heavy object. About the size and weight of a baseball bat."

"Can you tell whether the person who murdered Roxanne was right- or left-handed?"

"Yes, the blood spatter and angle of the wounds indicates a right-handed assailant."

"Please tell the members of the jury whether you reached any conclusion concerning the likely height and weight of the person who murdered Roxanne."

"Based on the force of the blows, the murderer was of considerable strength. Also, from the angle of the blood spatter, I concluded that the attacker was between five foot ten and six feet three inches tall."

Popofsky scribbled on a notepad "Assumes that weapon = bat," and I nodded that I understood. It would have to wait for cross, however.

"Your Honor, could you please instruct the defendant to stand?" Kaplan asked, a little bit of showboating that prosecutors just love to do.

I didn't wait for the judicial order. Instead, I whispered for L.D. to rise. He knew enough on his own to look defiant.

"In your expert opinion, Dr. Davis, is the defendant of sufficient size to have caused the injuries Roxanne suffered?"

"Definitely."

After Dr. Davis established everything that Kaplan needed, she turned her focus to a preemptive strike against what she knew would be our line of attack—the pubic hairs.

"Dr. Davis, the jury has heard testimony concerning pubic hairs that were found in Roxanne's bed. Did you study those hairs?"

"I did."

"Did you do a DNA analysis?"

"No."

"Why not?"

"The hair samples that we had did not contain the hair root. Without the root, you cannot perform a DNA analysis, like you often see in the movies. Instead, all that can be done is an examination of certain characteristics about the hair."

"Did you study the hairs for those characteristics, Doctor?"

"Yes, of course. Based on that study, we concluded that the hairs came from a Caucasian and were from the pubic region."

"Is Roxanne a Caucasian, Doctor?"

"She is."

"Is it therefore possible that the hairs on Roxanne's bed were hers?"

"Yes."

"Thank you, Doctor," Kaplan said, resuming her seat. "No further questions, Your Honor."

I began my cross focusing on Davis's conclusions about the size of the murderer. Popofsky concurred in the estimate Davis had given, so I wasn't going to challenge Davis's conclusions, but I wanted to start to lay the groundwork so the jury could see that L.D. wasn't the only right-handed person on earth between five foot ten and six foot three.

"Your range, Dr. Davis, five-ten to six-three, that covers an awful lot of men, doesn't it?"

"Yes," he said matter-of-factly.

"In fact, you fit that description, do you not, sir?"

"I do."

"And me, too, correct?" I said.

"Yes."

Davis was as good a witness on cross as Boyle had been bad. The first rule of cross-examination is to keep your answers as short as possible while still answering the question. The standard joke was that if a cross-examiner asked if you knew the time a certain event occurred, the best answer was to say only "Yes" and wait for the next question before saying, "Two o'clock."

"You can't even rule out that the murderer is a woman, can you?"

"It would have to be a very strong woman, but statistically, it's possible."

Davis said this without concern, with almost an "anything is possible" air. I needed to get to an area where I could do some damage to his authority, and so I turned to the pubic hairs.

"Dr. Davis, you testified on direct examination that three hairs were found in Roxanne's bed. Do you recall that testimony?"

"I do."

"And you said that you could not conclusively link that hair to any specific person."

"That's right."

"But you could exclude certain people as the source, right?"

"Yes."

"Whom could you exclude?"

"As I said before, non-Caucasians could be excluded."

"African Americans, in other words."

"Yes. And people of Mongoloid descent." He turned to the jury. "That's the scientific term used to identify people who trace their ancestry back to Asia and the Pacific Rim."

"And L.D. is African-American, is he not?"

I took advantage of Davis's initial hesitancy on such a simple question by adding, "L.D., stand up so Dr. Davis can get a better look at you. He must have been so focused on your height and weight when he testified on direct that he failed to notice your skin color."

This earned me my first gallery chuckle and a gavel strike from Judge Pielmeier.

"Calm down," she said, making it clear that playing to the crowd was exclusively her province.

"Yes, he is African-American," Davis said in a bored tone.

"So, one thing we know without any shadow of a doubt is that they weren't L.D.'s pubic hairs in Roxanne's bed. Right?"

"That is correct."

I had the first half—Davis was conceding that they weren't L.D.'s pubic hairs. Now I needed to push him hard on the second half—getting him to admit they weren't Roxanne's either.

"Was there anything—anything at all—that led you to conclude that it was possible that the hairs did not belong to Roxanne?"

Davis's gaze went beyond my shoulder, so that he was looking straight at Kaplan. They must have been hoping that we'd missed it. Now the jig was up.

As much as thirty seconds of silence followed, which in court time feels like an eternity. He finally said, "At the time of her death, Roxanne did not have any hair in her pubic region."

So they *did* know.

The giggles from the gallery that followed Davis's revelation were loud enough for Judge Pielmeier to use her gavel again.

I felt like a boxer whose opponent had merely been stunned. I went in for the kill but tried to do so carefully, so that Davis couldn't land a knockout punch while my guard was down.

I scrolled through the next series of questions in my head, thinking through Davis's likely answers as well. I didn't see any immediate danger, and so I forged ahead.

"Dr. Davis, did you examine Roxanne as part of the autopsy?"

"I did."

"And in that examination you saw that she did not have any pubic hair?"

"That's correct."

"And that led you to conclude, did it not, that the pubic hair in her bed was from someone else?"

"No," he said.

No? How could that be? Roxanne doesn't have any pubic hair, and yet Davis was nonetheless claiming that she left her pubic hair in the bed?

My curiosity got the better of me. "Really? Why not?"

"It's possible that she had recently removed her pubic hair," Davis said matter-of-factly. "So the hairs in the bed could easily have been hers from before she had her pubic hair removed."

There's a story lawyers tell each other about the dangers of asking one question too many in a cross-examination. Supposedly it happened to Abraham Lincoln during his lawyer days. A witness testified that he was certain that Lincoln's client had bitten off the ear of the victim. On cross, Lincoln got the witness to admit he didn't see the biting. Then Lincoln asked the one question too many—"If you didn't see my client bite off the ear, how can you testify with such certainty that he did?" And the witness said, "I didn't see him bite it, but I saw him spit it out."

I'd fallen into that same trap, allowing Davis to plant the idea that it still might be Roxanne's hair after all. That meant I had some backing and filling to do.

"If I understand what you're telling us, Dr. Davis, the only way the pubic hair found in the bed could belong to Roxanne is if she left it in her bed, and then before the sheets were changed or washed or the hairs were otherwise brushed away, she removed all of her pubic hair. Do I have that right?"

"Yes."

"If, contrary to your conclusion about the recent removal of Roxanne's pubic hair, if, in fact, she had her pubic hair waxed long before the murder, then would you agree with me that another man was in her bed shortly before she was killed?"

"If I understood your question, the answer is no because it could also be a woman."

That was probably the closest I was going to get to an admission out of Davis, and it was more than a little convoluted. I briefly considered plowing the ground again to get a better sound bite to repeat to the jury during closing, but thought better of it, fearing that it might give Davis time to take back the little progress I'd made.

"How long could pubic hairs stay on her bed like that?"

Davis chuckled. "I'm sorry, Counselor, but my

expertise in the field of forensic medicine does not give me insight into routine housekeeping matters."

The gallery laughed with him, which caused Judge Pielmeier to get in on the act. "You're going to need to call an expert maid if you want someone to testify about clean sheets, Mr. Sorensen," she said.

I had no choice but to wait for the gallery's laughter to subside. When it did, I decided to try a different tack.

"Let me ask you this, Dr. Davis: Did you do anything, anything at all, to determine whether the pubic hairs found in Roxanne's bed belonged to someone other than Roxanne?"

"There was nothing to do."

"Why—strike that. Did anything prevent you from comparing the hairs to someone else's hairs?"

"That assumes we knew who to compare them to," he said.

I smiled, and when I did, I saw Davis realize he'd stepped in it. "Thank you, Doctor. I take that to mean that if you *did* know whose hair it might be, you would have conducted a test to ascertain, one way or the other, whether that person might be the real murderer."

"Objection!" Kaplan shouted, clearly upset. "Dr. Davis is a medical examiner. He does not direct the investigation."

"Once again, Mr. Sorensen, you are beyond the scope of this witness's expertise," Judge Pielmeier said. "The objection is sustained."

It didn't matter. I looked over at the jury. Half of them were now nodding.

44

The prosecution put up a host of single-issue witnesses over the next two days. Thursday began with Roxanne's housekeeper. She testified that there had been a baseball bat hanging over the mantel in Roxanne's bedroom since shortly after the first game of the World Series, and she was sure it had been there the last time she had been in Roxanne's home, which was the morning of the murder.

On cross, I tried to get her to admit that she had changed the sheets right before Roxanne's death. That her English was less than perfect only made it that much more difficult.

"When did you last change the sheets in Roxanne's home?" I asked.

"It was a long time ago, I don't remember," she answered.

"You regularly changed the sheets in her home, did you not?"

"*Sí*. I mean, yes."

"Did you do it a few times a week?"

"One time a week, usually. Unless she asks me to do it another time."

"The regular change of sheets, did you do that on a specific day? For example, did you usually change the sheets on a Monday, or a Tuesday, or a Wednesday?"

She shook her head, and I assumed she would say that she did not know, but instead, the words "Usually Tuesday" came out.

We now had the timeline. On Tuesday, Roxanne's sheets were changed, and she slept in her bed that evening. The following morning she left for South Carolina. Four days later, on the Sunday after Thanksgiving, Roxanne returned to her bed, and sometime during that evening she was murdered. If Matt Brooks—or someone else, for that matter—had been in that bed and left his pubic hair behind, he would have done so on either the Tuesday before Thanksgiving or the night Roxanne was murdered.

The autopsy report had not found any semen inside Roxanne, but that didn't mean she hadn't had sex the night she was killed. A condom wouldn't prevent the wearer from leaving some pubic hairs, however.

We knew from the subpoena to the Old Westerbrook's spa that Roxanne hadn't made an appointment there to have a Brazilian, but that didn't mean very much because there were plenty of other places in the area that might have done it, or, as L.D. had suggested, Roxanne could have brought someone in to do it in private. For a while I held out hope that Roxanne's waxer would show up on *TMZ* or *Inside Edition*, revealing when she stripped Roxanne of her pubic hair, but she never did. Like Nina said about Roxanne's neighbor's housekeeper, some people don't want to be involved in a murder case.

The truth was that it really didn't matter when she'd

waxed. She still could have had it done in New York on Wednesday, before she went to Stocks, or even sometime Sunday after she returned, and the prosecution could therefore still claim that it was her hairs in the bed.

In other words, the pubic hair was a dead end. We couldn't prove that those weren't her hairs, but the prosecution couldn't prove that they were hers either, certainly not beyond all doubt.

The rest of Thursday was consumed with the mind-numbing science that was a big part of the government's proof, but barely anyone could understand. Carpet fiber analysis, the art of retrieving blood spatter, chain of custody. Very little, if any of it, was disputed by us, and the jury didn't seem to care at all. In fact, the only time I saw any emotion from them the entire afternoon was when Judge Pielmeier announced that we were done for the day.

On Friday, Kaplan closed the loop on the baseball bat. First came a young police officer who testified that he was first on the scene and did not see the baseball bat hanging over Roxanne's bedroom mantel. He was followed by an older cop, who explained the lengths the NYPD went to in their search for the murder weapon. Nearby garbage cans, sewers, the subway tracks.

After him, Kaplan called a representative of Major League Baseball, who told the jury that Roxanne received a baseball bat for singing the national anthem at the first game of the World Series. He even slipped in that Roxanne told him she was going to put the bat in her bedroom, a half second before I made my objection.

When he stepped down, Judge Pielmeier asked Kaplan to call her next witness, at which time, in a clear, confident voice, Kaplan said, "Your Honor, at this time, the people of the state of New York rest their case in chief."

The prosecution had proven everything it needed— the old troika of means, motive, and opportunity. And by dragging out her case until Friday, Kaplan also got the collateral benefit of denying the defense the opportunity to put on any witnesses until Monday. That was more than enough time for the jury's position to harden. Perhaps irrevocably.

"Very well," Judge Pielmeier said. She turned to the jury. "I'm now going to dismiss you all for the weekend. I will see you back here on Monday morning, and until then, remember to follow the rules I've established: Don't talk to *anyone* about the case. Stay away from the media. Keep an open mind."

After the prosecution rests, the defense always makes a motion for a directed verdict, because failure to do so precludes certain arguments from being raised on appeal. As a result, no matter how convincing the prosecution's case, the defense lawyer stands up and tells the judge that the prosecution has not met its burden of proving guilt beyond a reasonable doubt— no thinking jury could ever vote to convict on the evidence presented.

So after the jury left, I made the best show of it that I could.

"Your Honor, the prosecution has failed to establish any of the elements that could give rise to a reasonable jury voting to convict. All they have established is that Roxanne was murdered. They have not provided this jury with any evidence linking the defendant to the crime—"

"Mr. Sorensen," Judge Pielmeier interrupted, "let me save you some time so we can all get a jump on the weekend." The gallery provided her with the sought-after laugh. "I know you need to make this motion to preserve your record. You've made it. Now I'm going to deny it."

She struck her gavel.

"Court is adjourned until Monday morning at nine thirty."

That evening, over a pepperoni pizza, Nina and I discussed what our case would look like. There was actually very little mystery involved. The only evidence we had was the guest registry at the Old Westerbrook and Carolyn Anton's testimony that she saw Roxanne coming out of cottage eighteen. With that, we could put Matt Brooks in South Carolina over Thanksgiving weekend and Roxanne in his room.

The question on the table, however, was whether that was enough for an acquittal. My vote was no.

"I think we have to put Matt Brooks on the stand," I said.

She grimaced. We'd served a trial subpoena on

Brooks the previous week, and at that time agreed to disagree about whether we'd actually use it. Now, however, we had to make a decision.

"It's going to be Roxanne's mother all over again," Nina said. "Brooks isn't going to admit to the affair."

"He'll have to admit to being in Stocks over Thanksgiving."

"The registry already proves that. Brooks will say it was business."

"What's he going to say when we ask him why he refused to give us a pubic hair sample??"

"Judge Pielmeier never lets that in. And even if she does, he says that he didn't refuse, it was a decision of the court."

She was right about that, but it didn't mean I thought she was right about whether we should call Brooks to the stand.

"There's a reason Brooks didn't testify for the prosecution," I said.

"So that's why we're calling Brooks to the stand? Because Kaplan didn't?"

"No," I said, although I stopped to think if that wasn't part of the reason. "I've been saying this from the beginning: I just don't think we can win a reasonable doubt acquittal. Our guy has the only motive the jury's heard and then there's that goddamn song. And what are we saying in response? That there *might* be another lover? There *might*? I bet you that the jurors aren't even convinced of that after Harry Davis testified, and that was our best piece of evidence.

Now they think that Roxanne just had a lousy house-keeper."

Nina must have known that this discussion wasn't going anywhere because she didn't respond. At least not verbally. The mournful shaking of her head told me everything, however—she thought we'd be making a huge mistake if we went after Matt Brooks as our SODDI guy.

45

On Saturday morning, I got up early, and much to my own surprise, I decided to go for a run. My running sneakers hadn't been called into service in more than a year, and although I worried that I might not have even packed them when I moved, they were hiding in the back of the closet.

When I stepped outside, two thoughts hit me simultaneously. The first was that it was freezing, and I laughed to myself about all the spring days I stayed inside drinking rather than exercise. The second was that I had no idea which direction to go. In my previous life my running had been in Central Park. I was lost downtown, off Manhattan's grid, with no clear path to follow.

I walked west to the Hudson River Park and began running north. I set a goal to make it to Chelsea Piers. I couldn't remember its precise cross street but thought it was below Twentieth Street, which meant I had a modest goal of about a mile up and another mile back.

Even out of shape, two miles seemed doable. At the very least, I thought I could make half that distance, which meant just making it to Chelsea Piers and walking back.

From the first stride, I could feel my extra weight. Even though I had begun to slim down over the past few weeks, my shirt still clung to my belly, rather than hang loosely over it, as I recalled it doing when I ran in my pre-accident life.

I tried to let my mind wander, but for the first few minutes I couldn't think about anything other than that my knees hurt every time my feet hit the asphalt. When I passed the large serpentine sculpture that told me I was at Watts Street, which was less than five blocks from where I started, I began bargaining with myself. *Just five more blocks, and then you can stop.*

To focus on something other than my labored breathing, I began to fantasize about Nina. In my mind's eye, she stood before me, slowly unbuttoning her blouse, and then we were kissing, and then making love. I could hear Nina's moans in my head, drowning out my own panting as I struggled forward.

The Holland Tunnel signage appeared before me, indicating I'd gone half a mile. Suddenly I felt strong enough to continue, at least through SoHo.

At Morton Street, I caught a glimpse of the glass condominiums built by the architect Richard Meier, which Sarah, ever the modernist, loved. I imagined her looking down at me, wondering what she would think of my relationship with Nina.

Sarah was not the jealous type, and she would have wanted me to go on with my life, to be happy, but I was reasonably certain that she'd be surprised at how overwhelmed I'd become by Nina. I suspected Sarah thought of me as like her in that regard, able to look rationally at love and not to be taken in by the sweeping passion of it all.

No one was more surprised than I was that I turned out not to be that way at all. I'd fallen harder and faster for Nina than I had ever thought possible. There were times when I had to actually count back how long we'd known each other—a little more than a month—and remind myself that no one truly falls in love that fast. And then, of course, I played my own devil's advocate, noting that it wasn't a typical month of dating but nonstop, 24/7 being together, under pressure. That speeds up the timeline, doesn't it?

But the bottom line to it all was that it didn't matter how long I'd known Nina, or how long normal people take before they think they're in love. I knew how I felt. And though it embarrassed me to admit it, I felt a passion for Nina that I couldn't remember ever experiencing with Sarah, and it imbued me with a sense of being alive that I'd been without even before the accident. While my descent began on the day Sarah and Alexa were killed, the truth of the matter is that I wasn't really alive before that, either. More like in some type of zombified state, just going through the motions of a life.

And now, with Nina, my life had meaning. It was just as she had predicted that first day we visited L.D. at Rikers. By agreeing to try and save L.D., I'd actually saved myself.

Before I realized it, I was approaching Chelsea Piers, which began on 17th Street and stretched for about five blocks. I made one last bargain with myself—to go to the taxi stand at the northernmost point of the complex. I picked up my pace until I was actually sprinting the last hundred yards or so.

After a short breather, I began to walk back, intent on enjoying each step of the return to an equal degree that it was painful on the way there. The sweat on my face was evaporating quickly, creating a light mist, and the chilled air now felt refreshing rather than painful.

The thought continued to swirl in my brain. *I saved myself.* I had. And while that caused my chest to swell, I realized that I had to deliver that same salvation for L.D. I just had to. And that meant I had to prove that Matt Brooks killed Roxanne.

When I came into the apartment, I immediately removed the fleece sweatshirt I'd been wearing to run. The T-shirt underneath was soaked in perspiration and sticking to my body.

Nina was still in bed, but my entrance stirred her awake.

"Where have you been?" she said sleepily.

"I went for a run."

"Really?"

I laughed. "Yes. Only don't ask how far or how fast."

"Doesn't matter. I'm proud of you. And you look damn sexy dripping in sweat. Come here."

She reached out her hands, beckoning me back into the bed.

"Let me shower first."

"And waste all that sweet sweat? Not on your life."

• • •

We fell asleep afterward but were awakened by the phone. My caller ID revealed it was none other than Benjamin Ethan.

"To what do I owe the pleasure of a Saturday-morning call, Benjamin?"

"Daniel, I would like to meet with you today. Are you available this afternoon?"

"You may not have heard, Benjamin, but I'm actually in the middle of a trial," I said with the deadest of deadpans. "In fact, I'm scheduled to question this very squirrelly character named Matt Brooks, and I'm spending today preparing."

Ethan said, "I was hoping you'd give me the opportunity to talk you out of calling him, which would save us the trouble of bothering Judge Pielmeier with a motion to quash."

"You do what you have to do, Benjamin, but I don't see Judge Pielmeier quashing a trial subpoena. Last time, you had the better argument because, as you so ably told the judge, the criminal code doesn't permit a defendant to take that kind of discovery. But she's not going to deny my guy his Sixth Amendment right to call your guy. No way that happens."

"Well, if you are so sure that Mr. Brooks will end up taking the stand, perhaps you will accept my invitation to hear a preview of his testimony. I assume you do not have any aversion to free discovery."

As the great Yogi Berra purportedly said, it felt like déjà vu all over again.

46

Even though it was a Saturday, a receptionist was situated on the forty-seventh floor, and Janeene came out to greet us. That was pure Benjamin Ethan. If he was at the office, everyone who worked with him needed to be there, too.

Ethan had one of the prestige offices at Taylor Beckett. The corner on the forty-seventh floor of the building's west side, which gave him a dead-on view of Central Park. The space was large enough to have a sitting area, and that was where everyone was situated.

The whole gang was there. The beautiful associate Ethan still hadn't introduced sat on one end of the sofa, and Capital Punishment's general counsel, Kimberly Newman, anchored the other end. In the chair next to them sat the guest of honor, as it were, Matt Brooks.

Being that it was a Saturday, there was a casual dress code for this meeting. That meant jeans or khakis for everyone, including Ethan, who nevertheless looked like a New England prep school teacher in a tweed sports jacket with patches on the elbows. Of course, Matt Brooks adhered to his own dress code, meaning that, like always, he was attired in a dark double-breasted suit, white shirt, and matching yellow tie and pocket square.

Ethan wasted no time getting into it. Even before we had completed the handshaking ritual, he said, "Daniel, we think it is in everyone's best interest for you to withdraw the trial subpoena you served on Mr. Brooks."

"I've already told you that's not going to happen," I said in my most assertive voice. "So let's get on to the real reason for this meeting, shall we? We only took time out from our trial preparation because you promised a preview of what Mr. Brooks is going to say on the stand. So, let's hear it."

Ethan rubbed his chin, as if in deep thought. After a subtle shrug to his client, as if to say, *I tried*, he said, "All right, then. Matthew, please tell Daniel what you told me."

If ever there was a man who looked comfortable as the center of attention, it was Matt Brooks. In a strong, confident voice, he said, "As I've told you before, I didn't kill Roxanne. And I know you don't want to hear this, but the truth is that your man killed her."

"I'm sure you understand why I don't find your self-serving denials particularly compelling," I replied. "The same goes for your efforts to throw blame onto L.D."

He laughed, not unlike a cartoon villain, actually. He was enjoying this far more than he should have.

"You don't understand, Counselor," Brooks said with a cat-that-ate-the-canary expression that I wanted to smack off his face. "If I testify, I'm not just going to tell the jury that L.D. killed Roxanne, I'm going to tell them *why* he killed her."

I knew he was baiting me, but I also knew I had to ask. "And that is?"

"She found out who he really was."

"What, the Calvin Merriwether story again? Nobody's going to believe that's a motive for murder."

Brooks laughed again, this time sounding as if I'd said something truly amusing. "So . . . you mean he still hasn't told you?"

"Told us what?" Nina said.

"Damn," Brooks said, shaking his head in disbelief. "I mean, I understood why he didn't tell you on day one. He needed to make sure you guys were in for the long haul before he started telling you what's what. But I just can't believe that he still hasn't told you."

My heart sank. I could feel every inch of my body tighten, as if preparing to receive a blow. As much as I'd convinced myself that I truly believed in L.D.'s innocence and Brooks's guilt, at that moment I couldn't deny that I believed that Brooks actually had proof that Legally Dead was Roxanne's murderer.

"Well, maybe, then, you should tell us what you claim our client's been keeping under wraps," I heard myself say.

Benjamin Ethan interrupted. "How about if we show you, Daniel?"

The beautiful, anonymous associate handed Ethan a manila envelope, which he, in turn, slid across the table to me. It wasn't sealed but simply closed with a metal clasp. After twisting back the prongs, I slid out three eight-by-ten photos.

For a moment, my mind flashed onto the autopsy photos, but unlike those, which were too crisp for comfort, these were grainy black-and-whites. They were most likely shot with an infrared camera, and at a long distance.

The first was of two men, both of whom were naked. I couldn't see either of their faces—one was out of the shot altogether and the other was buried in his partner's private area—but I knew the man on his knees was Legally Dead by virtue of the large dollar sign tattoo on his back. The other two photographs were even more graphic and left no room for doubt that one of the two men was L.D., even though his lover's face wasn't visible.

"You can do wonders with Photoshop," I said, somewhat weakly.

"Oh, not these," Ethan replied. "We had an expert—a Taylor Beckett expert—check them out. You can have your own guy verify it if you want, but if nothing else, I would hope that you trust me enough to know that I would not manufacture evidence."

"I don't know what to think, Benjamin. But I'll tell you this much—I thought you held yourself, and this law firm, to a slightly higher standard than being a conduit to extortion."

"No one is extorting you, Daniel," Ethan said. "We showed you the pictures because they are very relevant to the case."

I didn't answer right away, my mind whirling. "Well . . . I guess that's right, Benjamin. They *are* relevant. Because if L.D.'s gay, as these pictures suggest, then he doesn't have any motive. The prosecution's whole theory is that L.D. was so devastated after being dumped by Roxanne that he killed her. I don't see him being too upset about it if he prefers men. So, as far as I'm concerned, you've just made our case for us, Mr. Brooks. I can't wait to put you on the stand to tell this story to the jury."

"Nothing is ever so simple in a criminal trial, Daniel," Ethan said. "You know that. If you call Mr. Brooks to testify, he will explain to the jury your client's true motive for committing this crime."

"And that is?"

Brooks answered. "L.D. killed Roxanne to keep her from outing him. Plain and simple. Roxanne walked in on L.D. while he was entertaining a gentleman friend. He thought that if anybody found out he was gay, that was it for him. There's no such thing as a gay, hard-core gangsta rapper."

"That just doesn't make much sense," I said. "If—"

"Look, I don't care if you believe me," Brooks said, "but those twelve folks on the jury are going to believe me when I tell them that Roxanne came to see me and gave me these photos. She said she was so humiliated on account of his claiming that he loved her and all, that she was going to go public with them. Then I'm going to say that I tried to talk her out of it, but she wouldn't listen, and so I gave L.D. a heads-up that this was coming." He smiled at me. "Imagine me saying this with tears in my eyes"—he rubbed his face with his hands, like an actor getting into character. "'I blame myself. I should never have told L.D. I just had no idea that he'd kill her to keep her quiet.'"

When he was finished with this performance, Brooks laughed. That son of a bitch actually laughed.

"You're going to let this happen, Benjamin?" I said.

Ethan didn't blink. "My client says it's the truth. You know my position on this issue, don't you, Daniel? It's the same thing we discussed with that other case. There's no ethical prohibition to allowing your client to tell the truth. But don't focus on Matthew, Daniel—focus on your case. Right now, you still have an excellent chance of an acquittal. That goes away the second you put Matthew on the stand. Your client will not survive his testimony. You really don't have a choice. You have to withdraw the subpoena."

"Not just that," Brooks said. "I don't want to hear my name come up at that trial again unless it's in praise. On account of my generous nature, I'm going to give you one for free, and you already had it with Roxanne's mother. But from here on out, if you make any reference to my relationship with Roxanne, I'll make it my personal mission to see that your man goes down."

When we left Taylor Beckett, Nina tried to show me the bright side, but I was in no mood to hear her arguments about how this might all be for the best. We were being played, plain and simple, and that's never good.

Later that night, Nina decided to give it another try. Perhaps because we were in bed she thought I'd be more receptive.

"We can win without pointing at Brooks," she said. "We have enough already to suggest another lover, and that alone might give us reasonable doubt."

I still didn't want to talk about it, but I knew that now I had little choice. We had our final meeting with our client first thing the following morning, and L.D. was going to want to know what type of defense we'd be putting on.

"You know Brooks is lying, Nina. He didn't get those pictures from Roxanne. He must have hired someone to take them himself. And he did it because this is his play to avoid having to testify, and to make sure we don't put on evidence of the affair he was having with Roxanne."

"Then why doesn't he just say that L.D. confessed to him? If he's going to lie, why go through the whole *L.D. is gay and Roxanne was going to out him* charade?"

"Because Brooks is smart. If he just pointed the finger at L.D., without any corroborating evidence, we'd be able to cross him by saying that he's the real killer, and he's just throwing blame onto L.D. This way, Brooks has got proof in the photos, and he's not *saying* that L.D. killed her; he's just reporting what he said to L.D. It's a much more convincing story, even though every word of it is a goddamn lie. Besides, he doesn't care if L.D. is convicted or not, he just wants to make sure that his affair with Roxanne stays under wraps—because that destroys his marriage, which in turn destroys his empire. That's a pretty strong motive for murder."

She looked at me with pity. "Dan, you know as well as I do that it doesn't matter if he's lying. Our job here isn't to bring Roxanne's murderer to justice. It's to make sure that our client doesn't get convicted. And I don't think there can be much question that if Brooks says what he told us today, the jury will believe him. And that means L.D.'s going to be convicted."

"L.D. wants to testify," I said, "and it'll come out then, so—"

"You're not going to actually put L.D. on the stand, are you, Dan? It'll be legal suicide. What's he going to say that helps his defense?"

"Oh, I don't know. That he didn't kill her."

She rolled her eyes. "Yeah, him and every other murder defendant in history. I suppose the better question is, what's he going to say on cross? He's got no alibi. No, he's got worse than no alibi, because he might say that he was with . . . you name it, Mercedes or that Nuts character, but neither of them will corroborate him. That makes it worse than no alibi in my mind because it looks like he's lying. He's got the explanation about the song, but you can make that point more effectively in your closing argument than L.D. could ever do on the stand. Think about it, what does his testimony really do for us?"

I'd been checkmated. There were simply no more moves to play.

"L.D.'s going to be one unhappy camper if we tell him that he's not testifying," I said.

That was an understatement. If there had been one constant in L.D.'s story, it was that he wanted to tell the jury he was innocent.

Unfortunately, that was virtually the only thing he'd been consistent on.

47

Legally Dead walked into the visitors' room with his usual wide-eyed grin, but it vanished the moment he caught my expression. He knew instantly that he had a serious problem.

Without even exchanging pleasantries, I said, "We met with Benjamin Ethan yesterday. He wanted to take one last shot at talking us out of calling Matt Brooks. And he gave us this."

"What is it?" L.D. asked without even looking at the envelope.

"They're photographs of you having sex with a man."

The muscles in his face tightened, but beyond that he didn't show any emotion. He methodically opened the envelope and slid out the photos, glancing quickly at the first one—the one where only his tattoo was visible. He lingered slightly longer on the second, and then flipped to the final picture, all without a change of expression.

"How'd Brooks get these?"

"So they're real?" I asked.

"Any chance we can claim they're not?"

Nina's expression was what I'd expected. *He's such a goddamn liar,* it said.

"Benjamin Ethan told me that they were checked out by one of his people and they're legit," I said. "We can do a check ourselves, but I think it'll be a lot easier if you just tell us the truth. For once, I mean."

He nodded. "So that's Brooks's response—he's going to tell the world I'm gay? Fuck him. I really don't care anymore."

"It's not that simple, L.D.," I said. "Brooks told us that if he testifies, he'll say that you killed Roxanne to keep her from outing you."

"*What?!*" L.D. said with utter shock on his face.

Nina told L.D. what Brooks had said, laying out the way the testimony would come in if we put Brooks on the stand. She also explained the risk that if we told the jury about Brooks's affair with Roxanne, Kaplan would call Brooks as part of her rebuttal case, and then he'd hammer us that way.

When she was finished, L.D.'s face was a picture of murderous rage.

"Can't you see what's actually going on here?!" he said, his voice rising with every word. "Brooks fucking killed her and he's setting me up! Roxanne *knew* I was gay. I told her. And she didn't care, and she sure as shit wasn't going to out me. Christ, half her fans and practically all her backup dancers are gay. The idea that Roxanne and I were dating—that was all Brooks's. He said it would be good for both our images—soften me up and give her some edge—so we went along. You're not that fucking stupid that you believe what Brooks is saying, are you, Dan?"

"Calm down, L.D.," I said.

"You never believed me! You talked shit when we

first met, but you never really believed that I didn't kill her!"

I wanted to scream back at him. To shout how much I needed to believe in him, and how utterly impossible he made it for me to have that faith. All I had riding on him, and how his conviction would be a tragedy for me, too.

But I caught myself. In a soft voice, I said, "L.D., I don't believe what Matt Brooks is saying. I don't. But whether it's true or not, he's going to say it if we put him on the stand. So the question for us is: If that is his testimony, how bad will it be for us? And I'm not sure there's any other conclusion but that it's going to be pretty fucking bad. Remember, he's going to come off as someone who was a friend to both you and Roxanne, and so what reason does he have to lie?"

"What fucking reason? Dan, he's lying because he killed her. He was the one fucking her, not me."

"I know. I know. But we don't have any proof of that. All we have on the affair is that he was in South Carolina over Thanksgiving, and she visited his room. Brooks is going to say it was for business, and we have nobody who's going to contradict that."

Nina came in for further support. "We should rest our case now. We shouldn't even put Popofsky on. They've already conceded Roxanne's lack of pubic hair at the time of the murder, and that's all he was going to say anyway. Dan will make the other points we have—about 'A-Rod' not being about Roxanne, about there not being any credible evidence that you two even broke up—during his closing. We think that'll be enough for reasonable doubt."

"No, you don't," L.D. said. "You just think I've got no shot the other way, and this way I got . . . I don't know, a fuckin' prayer."

That pretty much summed it up. None of us said anything for a good minute. We all just sat there.

"Just answer me this, Dan," said L.D. "Honestly. Okay?"

"Okay."

"Do you think I'm innocent and Brooks is guilty?"

I thought about saying that what I thought didn't matter. Then I thought about saying that what I thought shouldn't matter to him.

"Yes" was what I said instead.

When I turned to Nina, she looked away. Clearly she disagreed.

More silence followed.

"It's my choice, right?" L.D. finally said.

"What is?" I asked, although I knew.

"Testifying. If I say I'm going to do it, you have to put me on, right?"

I nodded.

"I got to do it. I gotta tell them that I didn't kill her. I don't give a fuck about Brooks, but I just can't let the jury decide without them hearing me say that."

Nina was now staring at me, imploring me to say something to change L.D.'s mind. It came as something of a surprise to me, but I realized, in that moment, that I didn't want to change his mind.

"You understand that you'll have to testify truthfully?" I said. "About everything? The gay stuff. That you were never shot four times. All of it."

"Yeah."

"Okay. When you take the oath, you'll tell them that your name is Calvin Merriwether?" He nodded that he would. "Then I'll ask you a couple of questions about why you called yourself Nelson Patterson, and you'll answer them truthfully. From there, I'll ask you about your relationship with Roxanne, and what will you say to that?"

"That we were friends, but not lovers. That Matt Brooks asked me to go on tour with her, and I did."

"And why did you pretend to be her lover?"

"Because Matt Brooks said it would help my sales."

It was actually going pretty well so far. Better than I had expected, in fact.

When I looked over at Nina to see if she shared my reaction, however, it was clear to me that she did not. She was sitting with her arms crossed and a dissatisfied expression. Not too dissimilar to when I decided to cross-examine Roxanne's mother.

"Then we'll do 'A-Rod.' You're okay on that."

"I'll say that if you listen to the entire lyrics, you'll hear that it's about men. Gang members. That the singer in the song isn't Roxanne. The reference is to someone who's a snitch to the police."

It wasn't lost on me that he sounded like an entirely different man. The street lingo and profanity were gone. In their place were the measured phrasings of a man who was focused on the job at hand.

He just might be able to pull this off. More than that, it just might be true what he was saying.

"Where were you on the night Roxanne was killed?"

"I was home alone. No one can alibi me, but that's not surprising since I lived alone. I was home alone the night before she was murdered, too, and I can't prove that, either."

"Nina," I said, "do you want to do some cross with L.D.? See if you can shake him."

She nodded but looked defeated even before she began. "You claim that 'A-Rod' is about killing a man with a baseball bat?"

"Yes."

"So you don't deny that you wrote a song about killing someone with a baseball bat, do you?"

"No, but I've written a lot of songs, and most of them have some violence in them. Just like a horror movie. People die in all sorts of ways in my songs. That one involves a baseball bat."

"And so it's just a coincidence that you wrote a song about a singer getting killed by a baseball bat, and that Roxanne, a singer, had a baseball bat in her room that is now missing, and she was killed by being beaten, most likely with that bat. Is that what you want this jury to believe?"

L.D. didn't answer at first, and then he smiled. It reminded me of the first smile I'd seen, that day in the jail, through the glass. Dimples popping on both sides.

"No, it's not a coincidence," he said in a steady voice. "Matt Brooks killed Roxanne, and he's been setting me up to take the fall. He's the one who insisted that I put 'A-Rod' on the album. I never thought the song was any good. He's also the one who told me to go on tour with Roxanne, and then he said we should pretend to be a couple. I couldn't see it then, but I do now. He wanted me to pretend to be Roxanne's boyfriend to throw his wife off the scent, so she'd think Roxanne had someone else, you know, other than him. Then when he decided that he couldn't be sure Roxanne would stay quiet about the affair, he killed her, and he did it in a way that would throw blame on to me, by using a baseball bat."

When he was finished, L.D. smiled at me. It was obvious it felt good for him to get all that off his chest.

That night, I had a sense that something was wrong. Even though Nina's actions belied that she was upset—she let me work on my direct of L.D. in peace, even going so far as making a supermarket run so that she could cook while I worked—she was uncharacteristically silent all evening.

"What's the matter?" I asked when we got into bed. "You've barely said two words to me tonight."

"I was letting you work." She looked back at me.

I shot her a suspicious look. "Since when have you ever let me work?"

"I'm nervous," Nina conceded.

"You and me both. Tomorrow's going to be some day."

"And then what?"

"What do you mean?"

"I mean, with us?"

"What's gotten into you?"

"I'm just worried that . . . when the trial is over . . . everything will change."

"I hope so," I said with a smile. "I hope it gets even better. Think about how great it will be when we're not working twenty hours a day."

"Promise."

"I promise," I said, and kissed her.

And then, as we did every night, we made love, which only reinforced in my mind what I'd said. I never wanted to spend another night away from Nina.

48

Judge Pielmeier took the bench at exactly nine thirty, the time court is supposed to start each day. If that wasn't enough to make me think something was amiss, she immediately said, "I'd like to see all counsel in my chambers."

My first thought was that there must be an issue with one of the jurors, and that would be a big problem for us. The next alternate, and the two alternates after her, for that matter, were all undesirables from our point of view.

Unlike the last conference, this time there were enough chairs for everyone in the judge's office. We all took our seats—the prosecution sat to the judge's left and us to the right, just like we line up in court.

In a slow and steady tone, Judge Pielmeier said, "A few minutes ago, I was informed that just before your client was to be transported to court this morning, he was involved in some type of altercation with another prisoner. I'm sorry to be the one who has to tell you, Mr. Sorensen and Ms. Harrington, but he was stabbed to death."

It felt like when I'd heard that Sarah and Alexa had been killed. That it just couldn't be true. I was waiting for Judge Pielmeier to laugh and say she was only kidding, but, of course, she didn't.

"Do they know who did it?" I asked.

"No," Judge Pielmeier said, with a shake of her head. "They're doing a full investigation down at Rikers, but I'm told that unless a guard sees it, which wasn't the case here, it's very difficult to find out what happened in a prison fight."

I walked back into the courtroom in something of a stupor. There was a buzz that immediately fell silent upon our entry. The somber looks from the gallery were all I needed to realize that word of L.D.'s death had already leaked out, at least to the press.

It seemed to take an eternity for the jury to enter the courtroom and then assemble in the jury box. When each was finally in his or her place, Judge Pielmeier took a deep breath and repeated to them what she'd told us in chambers.

Almost as a collective, the jurors gasped. The relative quiet from the gallery, however, confirmed my initial suspicion that news of L.D.'s death was by now widespread.

"As a matter of law, Mr. Patterson is not guilty of these charges," Judge Pielmeier said, sounding almost as if it mattered. "And so, ladies and gentlemen, on behalf of the people of the state of New York, I thank you for your service. You are no longer under my jurisdiction and so you are free to talk with whomever you wish, including members of the press. If you choose not to do so, the guards will ensure that you can leave the courthouse without being accosted."

Then she gaveled twice and said, "We're adjourned."

I stood as the jury made their way out for the final time, but Nina did not. She seemed to be in another world.

"Stand up, Nina," I said. "The jury's leaving."

She slowly came to her feet. When she did, I could see she was weeping.

49

L.D.'s funeral was a mysteriously arranged affair. Perhaps that was poetic justice, given how enigmatic a life he'd lived.

I received a call the night before from a man who claimed to be L.D.'s relative, without specifying the actual relation. He told me the particulars of the funeral, the where and when, and then asked if I'd be good enough to inform Nina. I told him that I could speak for her as well, and that we'd both be in attendance.

As soon as I hung up, however, Nina told me that I'd been wrong in my assumption about her inclination to pay her respects.

"I just don't think I can handle it," she said. "One day we're talking to him about testifying, the next day he's gone. I've never known anyone who died before. I mean, even my grandparents are still alive. So I'm more than a little freaked out by everything."

I understood what she meant. Many people had expressed similar sentiments about Sarah. That she was the first friend of theirs who'd died, and how it made them face their own mortality. That kind of thing. It was something that I was well past, however. I knew how fleeting life could be long before L.D.'s death.

• • •

At the cemetery's main entrance stood a small African-American man dressed in a black suit, bright white shirt, solid black tie, and a gray fedora. He looked like a civil-rights leader from the 1960s, like one of the men standing beside Martin Luther King Jr. in a history book photograph. I pulled my car beside him and lowered the window.

"Mr. Sorensen," he said, as if we'd met before, even though I couldn't imagine how he recognized me.

"Yes," I said tentatively, and then added, "I'm sorry but Nina Harrington sends her regrets."

"That's quite all right," he said. "We're glad that you could pay your respects."

He handed me a map of the grounds. The route to the grave site was highlighted in yellow.

He said, "Please, go on ahead. We'll be starting soon." Then he stepped back from the car window.

L.D.'s plot was as far away from the entrance as you could get, and I wondered if the remote place-ment was intentional. But even though the map made it seem as if I was driving to the next county, it was barely a minute before I came upon a lineup of cars. Up the hill were about a dozen people surrounding the burial plot.

In the center of the group was an older man. He was tall and thin, looking too frail to be out in the cold for even the twenty minutes or so I estimated the service would take. Upon closer inspection, I saw that he was wearing a clerical collar.

The priest was flanked by two even older-looking African-American women, both of whom were crying, which led me to make the obvious assumption that they were relations of some sort. Next to them were men of about the same age, husbands, most likely.

Off to the side was Mercedes. A little girl was hiding between her legs. Brianna, I assumed. Seeing L.D.'s daughter brought an instant smile to my face, even as I recognized it was a misplaced emotion. There's nothing about a girl losing her father that's worth smiling about, but it felt like I was looking at L.D., just for a second.

On the opposite side from Mercedes stood Nuts, looking as defiant as the time I'd visited him in Brownsville. If he recognized me, he didn't show it.

I scanned the rest of the mourners. The only white face I saw belonged to Matt Brooks. He was flanked by Jason Evans, his wardrobe-size chief of staff.

Brooks smiled at me when we made eye contact, that son of a bitch.

The priest delivered a short sermon in which he spoke about loving God even in times of grief. He referenced Brianna, saying that L.D. would live on through her.

"I did not know Calvin," the old priest said, using L.D.'s real name, "and so it's appropriate that the man who knew him best say a few words."

And with that, Matt Brooks stepped forward and began to speak.

"L.D., your family and friends are here today to say good-bye," Brooks said as if he was speaking to the man and not to his mourners, "and while we all are saddened that your time on earth was much too short, we take comfort in the fact that through your music, you will truly be immortal, and someday your musical genius will be recognized."

There was more, but I tuned it out after that. Instead, my mind swirled with the things I wanted to say to Brooks as soon as the service was over.

As a technical matter, the professional rules governing attorney conduct prohibit a lawyer from communicating with someone represented by counsel. And had L.D. been alive, and there was a chance gathering in which both Brooks and I were in attendance, I would not have spoken to him.

But now that L.D. was dead, I no longer had a client. Besides, I didn't see much chance of Brooks turning me in to the committee on professional responsibility. More to the point, I didn't much care.

"Mr. Brooks," I called out in what I thought was my most serious voice.

He was shaking hands with the priest. Jason Evans stood beside him, looking into the distance as if he were scouring for potential snipers.

"Dan," Brooks said, walking toward me, Evans a step behind. "I thought we were on a first-name basis."

I ignored his effort to invoke familiarity between us. "That was quite a performance," I said.

"I don't know what you mean."

"It's a rare man with balls so big that he'll eulogize a man he murdered."

"Is that what you think you just heard?" Brooks's smile told me that he recognized it wasn't a denial.

"You knew that L.D. was going to testify," I said. "That's why you had him killed."

"Dan . . . I know you want me to be the villain of this story, but it's just not so. The truth is that getting killed in prison just isn't all that hard. Especially if you're a goddamn hothead, like L.D. You know, somebody killed Jeffrey Dahmer in prison, too. That doesn't mean he didn't eat all those people. The simple fact is that L.D.'s death had nothing to do with me. He got in the wrong guy's face, and he paid for it. Simple as that."

He smiled again at me, and I would have punched that grin off his face but for the fact that Evans would have killed me and that, being this was a funeral, it was hardly the place. "It's not over," I said.

"Yes, Dan, it is," he replied.

Brooks pushed past me, and Evans followed, deliberately bumping me with his wide body. They walked down the hill to Brooks's waiting Bentley. Evans opened the back passenger door, and shut it behind Brooks. Then he walked around to the driver's side and they drove away.

50

The time just after trial has its own rhythm. Of course, its cadence will differ markedly based on whether you've won or lost.

At Taylor Beckett, a successful verdict always merited a weeklong series of high fives, and a lavish celebratory dinner with the trial team, which included anyone who billed a tenth of an hour to the case. Congratulatory emails would come from friends and firm elders, reporters would call for a pithy quote, and the firm's PR machine would place articles in legal journals touting your genius. And if all that weren't enough, you also had the undying love and admiration of your client.

Losing went the other way, but with ten times the force. Every judgment was called into question, and the firm treated you like something of a pariah, with the joke being that instead of paying millions of dollars for a Taylor Beckett defense, the client would have achieved the same result with a legal team comprising monkeys. Worst of all, the client blamed you, and only you, for his plight, as if the conduct in which he'd engaged bore no relationship to the verdict.

Technically, the result here was a mistrial. The legal equivalent of a tie. But no loss ever felt as empty.

When I returned from the funeral, I called out Nina's name. Nothing.

For a moment I panicked, but then I saw a note on the dining room table. It was sitting on top of a Redweld filled with trial exhibits.

> *D—I headed home for a little bit. Need*
> *to see what my apartment looks like, pay*
> *bills, drop off dry-cleaning. The stuff I*
> *haven't done in forever. Be back soon.*
>
> > *Love you*
> > *—N.*

I stared at the closing *Love you*. Nina loved me.

For the first time in a long time, I was again alone. It seemed reason enough to pour myself a scotch.

When I poured myself a second one, I decided that this was as good a time as any to purge my living space of L.D. The files covering my dining room table weren't going to go away by themselves, and as long as they were out, it was like L.D. was still here, too.

When a case ended at Taylor Beckett, a team of legal assistants cataloged all the documents and prepared an index so if the files were ever needed again they could be easily retrieved. Then the guys in the mailroom boxed everything up and sent them to one of the several off-site, long-term storage facilities the firm used. Before 9/11, the firm used one facility in New Jersey, but after the Trade Center attack, the firm spread out the files, just in case al-Qaeda decided to strike a warehouse in Weehawken next. I'd never had occasion to actually visit any of the storage facilities, but I'd been told they looked similar to the final scene of *Raiders of the Lost Ark*, nothing but aisles and aisles of identical boxes.

The process of closing a file at Sorensen and Harrington amounted to my throwing everything into a giant box. What I was going to do with the giant box after it was full was still undetermined.

First I threw the Redwelds and exhibit folders into the box without a second thought. Our case research—all the stuff about exclusion of evidence we'd gathered for the motion in limine—went in next. God, Nina had really done a lot of research on that, all for naught, of course.

When I grabbed the pathology report, I stopped short before adding it to the heap. I sat down at the dining room table and started to flip through the pages. I suppose I wanted one last look at Roxanne before closing her up in the box.

The image of her vacant eyes in the autopsy photos was as haunting as ever. It occurred to me that L.D. was not the only person I'd failed in this case.

Underneath the forensic photos was the juvenile record for the other Nelson Patterson. The mug shot was staring up at me. I was about to toss it in with the rest when something occurred to me.

I couldn't believe it. I stared down at the photo of this fifteen-year-old Nelson Patterson.

Why hadn't I seen it before? But Nina and Kaplan had apparently missed it, too. And, of course, it wasn't something L.D. told us, although he undoubtedly knew as well. Ironically, it wasn't a lie that angered me. If anything, this lie made me proud of L.D.

I drove straight to Brownsville and headed directly for the Tilden Houses, building number three. The door was still propped open and the elevator still didn't work. The smell in the staircase hadn't improved either.

"Remember me?" I said when Nuts opened the door.

"Lawyer dude, right? Where's the hot chick?"

"Just me today."

"Don't know why you here, but you better get to the point fast."

"I know that you're the real Nelson Patterson," I said in a flat but sure voice.

He hesitated for a moment, which I took to be a good sign. It meant I couldn't be that off base.

"Do you mind if I come in?" I said. "There are some things I need to talk to you about that require privacy."

He didn't say anything, but when he stepped aside, I walked by him. Then he shut the door behind me, still without saying a word.

"How'd you find out?" he asked, all bravado vanished.

"The mug shot," I said.

He laughed, a borderline maniacal cackle. "Shit. I figured all black guys look alike to white dudes."

"After I saw you at the funeral this morning, I was putting away the file and I came upon the mug shot, and it clicked. But it's not the only picture of you that I have, Nelson."

"Don't call me that."

He said this with anger. For a moment I thought he might lash out, even before I got to the stuff that I thought might actually make him take a swing at me.

I slid the manila folder out of my coat pocket and handed it to him. "These were taken by Matt Brooks. Long lens, probably infrared."

He opened the clasp, his hands moving almost in slow motion. I watched his eyes carefully, looking for any type of tell.

It was very minor, but he twitched at the first picture. It was the kind of reaction that would have been a full-fledged flinch but for my presence. He flipped through the last two, and when he was finished he let the subtlest smile slip through.

The smile gave it all away. He was pleased that his face wasn't visible.

"What the fuck do I care if L.D. liked to suck cock," Nuts said.

"Not going to fly anymore, Nuts. I know."

"Yeah? What the fuck you think you know?"

"Changing your name doesn't change the way things are." I waited a beat. "I know that's you with L.D."

"Like fuck it is."

He took a step toward me. At that moment it occurred to me how ill conceived my plan had been. No one even knew I was here.

He pushed me against the wall. His massive forearm was under my chin, pressing against my throat.

"Hold on. I'm not the enemy here."

He pushed in even tighter, and I could feel his weight against me, my throat even more constricted. He snarled, spraying spit in my face.

"I'm pretty much your best friend right now," I managed to squeeze out.

"How you figure," he said, spitting as much as speaking.

"The way I see it, the best thing you got going for you is that, right now, I know you and L.D. were lovers, but Matt Brooks doesn't."

There was a momentary standoff. I could almost see the wheels turning inside Nuts's head. How sure was I that it was him in the photos? Would I really tell Brooks? And if I did, what would Brooks do?

The increased pressure on my larynx made me realize that he might just conclude that the safest out for him was to eliminate that possibility by killing me right here.

"Brooks gave me these pictures," I said, finding it difficult to speak with his forearm crushing against my windpipe. "It was his effort to convince L.D. not to testify. When L.D. wasn't persuaded, Brooks had him killed. What do you think will happen if I tell him that you were L.D.'s lover? You think he won't figure that you and L.D. shared secrets? Some pillow talk? And that means that he's coming for you next. You're just as much a threat to him as L.D."

"That's reason enough for me to make sure you don't tell him."

His forearm pressed harder against my throat.

"Back the fuck off me!" I barked. "You think my partner—the hot one—doesn't know I'm here? You think I didn't tell her to tell Matt Brooks and then the cops everything—in that order—if I don't call her in ten minutes?"

I pushed him hard. He felt like iron, and barely budged. But then, having nothing to do with my effort, he stepped back.

I swallowed a few times in rapid succession, and then rubbed my throat. I could feel my heart rate begin to settle down, my fight-or-flight response returning to normal.

From the look in Nuts's eyes I could tell that he'd folded to my bluff. He wasn't going to attack me again.

"So what do you want?" he said in a defeated voice. "Money?"

"No, I don't want your money. I want your help. I want you to make things right."

51

When I got home, the apartment smelled like garlic. Nina was in the kitchen, wearing one of my old T-shirts and my blue sweats. Her hair was unruly, and she didn't have on any makeup, a look that led me to conclude that she hadn't yet showered. And wouldn't you know it, she looked spectacular.

"I'm making lasagna," she said. "I knew today was going to be tough for you, and I was feeling a little guilty about bailing on you . . . so I figured that the least I could do was make you some comfort food for dinner."

"Thanks," I said.

"Do you want some wine? I bought a nice bottle of Chianti."

"Thanks, but do you mind if I pour myself a scotch?"

"You're back to that? I was kind of hoping I'd weaned you off the hard stuff."

"Like you said, today was kind of a tough day."

She didn't acquiesce, but didn't say no either. That was good enough for me.

As I was pouring, she said, "I'm sorry I didn't go with you. I just couldn't."

"No, you were right. Brooks gave the eulogy. I wanted to throw up."

Nina smiled at me, and my mind flashed on the day I met L.D., the first time I took true notice of Nina's smile. It still made me weak.

Love you —N.

"It wasn't a total waste," I said. "I got us a new client."

"Really?"

"Yes, really. I figured we either had to get a new client or go out of business."

"So you just went out and picked one off the client tree? Who is it?"

"A gentleman you know by the name of Nuts."

"Whoa. L.D.'s Nuts?"

"How many guys named Nuts do you think there are?" She rolled her eyes at me. "And what are we doing for this fine citizen?"

I laughed. "Give you one guess as to the identity of L.D.'s mystery lover?"

Her eyes widened. "No."

"Yes. But wait, there's more. Guess who's really in that old mug shot of L.D.?"

"That's Nuts? You're kidding, right?"

"Far from it. They go back a lot of years. Even before L.D. and Mercedes. Nuts told me that after Mercedes got pregnant, L.D. asked her to marry him, but she already suspected that he was gay, even if he hadn't fully admitted it to himself yet. Apparently, he and Mercedes were together during that period when he thought he could will himself out of it. She told L.D. that the best thing for her, for their baby, and for him was that he be true to himself. And so L.D. went back to Nuts to live happily ever after. Fast-forward a few years, and Matt Brooks tells him that he couldn't be Calvin Merriwether and be a rap star, and so L.D. and Nuts agreed that L.D. would just take his name and backstory."

"And Nuts just admitted all of this to you?"

"First he thought about beating the hell out of me. And he nearly did, too. But I suggested a way he could avenge L.D.'s death, and then he calmed down."

"How can he do that?"

"By giving Lisa Kaplan proof about Matt Brooks's affair with Roxanne."

"What proof?"

"He wouldn't say. But what he did tell me was that he had it and it was ironclad."

"And L.D. didn't know about it?"

"Nuts said that he did." I chuckled. "When all is said and done, L.D. turned out to be quite chivalrous. He wanted to keep Nuts out of it, even if that made it more likely he'd be convicted."

"So why'd Nuts tell you?"

I smiled at her. "Because I threatened him."

"With what?"

"I think the technical term is bluffing," I said with a sly grin. "I told him that I knew he had proof of Brooks's affair with Roxanne because L.D. had told us that he did. His reaction told me that it was actually true. So then I told him that he had one of two choices: tell the DA everything he knew and live out a happy life in the witness protection program, or

I'd make sure word got out to Brooks about what he knew, and then he was a dead man."

"And Nuts didn't tell you what he had?"

"Nope. I told him that I didn't want to know until we were with the ADA. I didn't want anyone claiming that he'd been coached. But whatever it is, he said that only he knows about it, and apparently he's got some corroborating proof too."

"Even if Nuts can prove Brooks was sleeping with Roxanne, what does it matter now?"

"Our favorite assistant district attorney thinks it matters a lot. While I was sitting with Nuts, I called Kaplan and told her what Nuts had told me. She was *very* interested to hear all about it. So much so that if Nuts's information stands up, she'll empanel a grand jury and get Brooks's pubic hair. And once that happens, a lot of pieces are going to fall into place."

"So what are we doing in all of this?"

"We're escorting Nuts down to Lisa Kaplan first thing tomorrow morning. Eight thirty."

Dinner tasted as good as it smelled. I took seconds on the lasagna, and before I had swallowed the last bite, the bottle of wine was empty.

After dinner, before we cleaned up, Nina led me by the hand to the bedroom. We stood at the foot of the bed, then Nina took a step back and pulled the T-shirt over her head. In a fluid motion, she kicked off the sweatpants.

"Isn't it my job to undress you?" I said.

"Are you complaining?" she said back.

"A little. It's couples in a rut that don't undress each other."

She favored me with a seductive smile. "I didn't know that. Then permit me to undress you."

I was awakened by Nina's rustling. When I opened an eye, she was pulling on her shirt.

"Where are you going?" I asked.

"I need to run to my apartment to get clothes for tomorrow. I'll be back in a flash."

"Don't go," I whined. "Get them in the morning."

"You said we're meeting at eight thirty. You want to wake up at six?"

"We're just going to the DA's office. Wear what you have here."

"Your stained undershirt and sweatpants? Go back to sleep. You won't miss me at all, and when I come back, I'll make it worth your while." Then she flashed that smile.

It took her less than forty-five minutes to make the round-trip. I was at the computer when she returned. She entered the bedroom wearing the suit I suspected she'd put on again in the morning, and wasn't carrying anything else.

"You travel light," I said.

"As you know, I don't do pajamas. What are you looking at?"

"Travel sites. I was thinking that maybe we should go away. I'd originally thought we'd take a trip after the trial was over . . . and now maybe we just push it back a little bit and go as soon as the Nuts situation is finished."

"I'd like that," she said.

She looked like a woman with something on her mind. Her brow was furrowed, her lips pursed.

"You okay?" I asked.

"Yeah, I was just debating whether to raise something with you."

"Now I think you have to."

She didn't, however. At least not right away. Instead it looked like she was running through what she wanted to say, a dry run, just to see if she should say it out loud.

"Okay, just remember, you asked. I know we haven't been seeing each other for that long, but when I was making my mad dash across town, I was thinking that maybe we should figure out a way to stop all this back-and-forth. Over the last few weeks I've been here twenty-four/seven anyway, and today when I said that I'm going home for an hour, you got all 'No, stay here and go to the DA's office naked' on me, so I was thinking maybe I could bring some of my stuff here. I'm not saying we should get married, or even that I'm moving in. I'll keep my place, so there'll be no pressure, but—"

"That sounds like an excellent idea," I said with an ear-to-ear smile.

52

The alarm went off the next morning at six forty-five. As was our usual routine, Nina took the first shower, opting for the additional time to get ready over sleep. By the time I got out of the shower, Nina was already dressed.

"I'm not going to dry my hair," she said with a laugh, "not for Lisa Kaplan."

I reached into my closet and hesitated before pulling out the same charcoal-gray Brioni suit that I wore to visit L.D. that first time. The suit I wore to bury my wife and daughter, and to do my opening in the Macy trial, as well as L.D.'s.

It fit looser than it had back when I visited L.D. Even with the daily grind of trial, I was taking better care of myself. Not consuming at least three scotches a day probably had something to do with it.

I spied Nina watching me from the reflection in the mirror as I smoothed the hair out of my face. Her smile was broad, and her eyes shimmered. It's a silly word to use, but I thought she seemed proud of me.

And that's when I decided that I wasn't proud of myself.

I undid my tie and unbuttoned the top of my collar.

"What's wrong?" Nina asked.

I took a deep breath. "We're not going down there."

"What do you mean?"

I had thought about teasing it out, just to see whether Nina would lie to me. But I needed to get this over with.

"If we go to the DA's office today," I said, looking her square in the eyes, "you're going to be arrested, Nina. The Nuts thing, it was a setup. Not of you so much as Matt Brooks, but I couldn't set him up without also setting you up."

"I don't understand, Dan. What are you saying?"

She didn't sound confused. Cold comfort, but at least it was something. She understood and just wanted me to explain the steps more clearly.

"You told Brooks that L.D. was going to testify," I said, "and that's why L.D. was killed. And then, last night, you told Brooks that Nuts had evidence against him, full knowing that he was going to end up just like L.D."

She didn't betray any emotion. No head-shake denial, but no slumped shoulders of admission either.

"Is he dead?"

"If you mean Nuts, no. He's fine. He was nowhere near his home last night. He's been under heavy police protection since I called Kaplan yesterday. Kaplan texted me this morning that Brooks hired some guy to do it, and they arrested him at Nuts's apartment last night. Kaplan didn't say whether the gunman had already given up Brooks, but I don't think he's going to hold out too long when they start mentioning the death penalty. Murder for hire and all that."

"And you're supposed to bring me to Kaplan?"

"I made it part of the deal. I told Kaplan that I didn't want cops coming to my house and I'd surrender you this morning. For your sake, I hope you didn't call Brooks from your home or cell."

She didn't respond, but instead stared at the floor. It was as if her head had become instantly heavy, unable to look anywhere but down.

"So long as you didn't," I said, "you should be fine. Without me, there's no link between you and him."

"Thank you," she said, and stepped toward me.

She would have kissed me if I'd let her. Probably would have done more than that.

"Don't," I said in a stern enough voice that she must have feared there was a possibility I'd change my mind. "I don't have it all figured out yet," I continued, "but I got far enough along to realize that Matt Brooks is the married guy you were seeing."

She still showed me nothing. It was like looking at a corpse.

"How'd you meet?" I asked.

She continued to stare at me. Through me, almost.

"Nina, come on. I need to know. You saw me get dressed. I'm not wearing a wire. It's just you and me."

Her face screwed more tightly. I could almost hear her teeth grinding.

"I'm about to give you a very significant gift here,

Nina. It's called freedom. The least you can do to repay me is fill in the blanks."

"If I'm paying something, then it's not a gift," Nina said with a sad smile.

I knew she was trying to lighten the moment, but she was right. This wasn't a gift. We were negotiating.

"Okay, then consider it a bargain," I said, "but I need to know everything."

In my mind, she was now someone else entirely. Not my lover or even my law partner.

Someone already much more my past than my future.

"We met at Martin Quinn," she said, her voice barely above a whisper. "About a year ago. There was some fund-raiser I went to, and he was there. It's not what you think, though."

I smiled, meaning it sarcastically, as if to say, *Oh, of course not.* There was no doubt in my mind that it was *exactly* like I thought.

"Tell me why it isn't what I think," I said.

She wasn't going to say anything, that much I knew. Not until I had told her what I knew.

"Let me make it easy for you. I'll tell *you* what I think, and then you can just say yes or no. The way I figure it, you fell hard with Brooks and, like you told me, you just had no willpower when it came to what he asked you to do. When L.D. cut Marcus Jackson loose, you came in to pick up the slack. You told Brooks that you knew me, and you could get me to take the case. I bet you worked L.D., too, telling him about Darrius Macy so he'd want to hire me. And then you fed Brooks information about our defense. That's how he was always one step ahead of us with the witnesses. And I guess that sleeping with me, that was . . . well, whatever it was, it worked. You got me to lose my judgment when it came to you."

Midway through what amounted to my closing argument, she had begun to cry. Not sobs, but enough tears to have an effect on me.

For a moment I felt sorry for her, but then my resolve stiffened. Murderers shouldn't cry, I told myself. Even if you were just aiding and abetting, crying should still be a right that you lose, like voting privileges for felons.

"Were you really so far gone, Nina? So much in love with the man that you were willing to help him commit *three* murders? And even when you knew he was also screwing around with Roxanne? Is that how lost you became?"

"Like I said, it wasn't like that," she said, choking through tears. "Things ended between Matt and me before Roxanne was killed, and I didn't know that there was anything between them until much later. I wanted to marry him, and he said he wanted that too, but we had to wait until after the IPO. He was worried that if he asked Chiara for a divorce, she would scuttle the deal, but apparently there was something in their pre-nup that gave him more control over a public company than a private one. He promised me that right after the IPO, we'd be together for real. I told him that I was tired of being strung along, and he should just call me when he was ready, and we'd see if that's what I wanted then too. Then a month or so later, Roxanne was murdered, and a few weeks after that, Matt called. I swear, I had no idea that he'd killed Roxanne. I still don't know if he did. He told me that he thought L.D. killed her. He said that after we broke up he was devastated, and he started seeing Roxanne on the rebound. He said it was only a few times, and he'd ended it before she died. But he was afraid L.D. knew about his affair with Roxanne and would use it to pin the murder on him. He said that all he wanted me to do was to stay close to L.D., so I could keep an eye out for him."

"And when L.D. decided he was going to testify . . . you set up the hit," I said.

"No! I didn't know that was going to happen. I swear it. I told Matt that L.D. was going to testify, but I wouldn't have said anything if I'd thought Matt was going to have him killed. "

"Bullshit. If that were true, you would have come clean after L.D. was killed. At the very least, you wouldn't have arranged for Brooks to kill Nuts, too."

Her eyes dropped to the floor. She was crying in spurts now, while still trying to defend herself in between sobs.

"You don't understand, Dan . . . you really don't. After L.D. died . . . Matt called me and said we were in this together. He said that if he got caught, he'd take me down with him. And he could have. I mean, y-you believe that I was in on L.D.'s murder, right?

Who wouldn't? So he told me that I needed to tell him if anything else was hap-happening. When you came home saying that Nuts was going to give up Matt, I . . ."

"You told Brooks, even though you knew that he'd kill Nuts."

"I told him, yeah, but I didn't think he was going to kill Nuts. You have to believe me. I thought he was going to pay him off, like he did with that housekeeper, or that they'd just steal whatever evidence Nuts had. I didn't think Brooks would have him killed. I swear, I didn't. But think about it from my perspective. What choice did I have?"

"I think you know the answer to that," I said coldly. "You should go, Nina. Right now. Find someplace without an extradition treaty with the U.S. I hear Venezuela is the place of choice for fugitives these days."

"What are you going to do?"

"Me? I'm going to start over. Again."

53

As soon as Nina left, I boxed up the few personal items that mattered to me—which amounted almost entirely to family photos—and took them to the storage place around the corner. It was the same one that held all of Sarah's and Alexa's items that I couldn't eliminate from my life.

"How long are you going to need to store this stuff?" the guy behind the desk asked me.

"I don't know. At least six months, but maybe longer," I said.

The bank visit came next. I was able to do the entire transaction with a teller I'd never met before and would never see again. All it took was a single form, identifying the routing number of the receiving bank.

Years before, on the advice of the tax partner at Taylor Beckett, I'd set up an offshore account. I never saw the need to keep funds there, and so I'd only maintained the minimum balance. But by the time I'd left my local bank branch, I'd arranged for enough funds to be at my disposal that I'd be able to live well for a very long time without having any contact with the United States.

Next, I called my sister. I told her that I needed to clear my head a little bit, after the trial and everything, so I might be off the grid for a little while, but that she shouldn't worry. She offered a rueful laugh before saying that she was already worried about me.

My last call was to Mercedes.

"I'm going to be out of pocket for a little while," I said, "and while I'm away you're going to hear some things about me and my partner, Nina Harrington, and about L.D. I wanted to make sure that you knew the truth. L.D. did not kill Roxanne. I'm sure of that. And he loved Brianna. Of that I'm also certain. One of the last things he said to me was that the truth should matter more than anything else. When she's old enough, please make sure that Brianna understands that's how her father felt. That at the end, he wanted the truth to come out, and he was unwilling to save himself if it meant living a lie anymore."

"Where are you going?" she asked.

"It's better if you don't know," I said. "Just like I think it's better that you do know what I just told you."

As soon as the call ended, I threw my phone in the trash. Then I jumped in a cab and headed straight to JFK.

After a maze of flights—Mexico City to Rio; Rio to São Paulo; São Paulo back to Mexico City—I ended up in St. Martin, on the French side.

My hasty vacation to St. Martin was not a criminal act, at least not as far as I know. Of course, the fact that I didn't tell anyone of my plans, and haven't contacted anyone since I've gotten here, not to mention my circuitous travel route, all suggest that I'd rather not test that hypothesis.

I didn't spend a lot of time in my selection process. The weather in St. Martin is warm, the living expenses are low, and most people speak English. Of course, I could have ended up in dozens of other places that fit the same description.

I'd visited St. Martin with Sarah, almost fifteen years ago. It was before we were married, and we stayed at a five-star resort. I don't recall too much about the trip, other than that Sarah was particularly fond of the hotel's fish tacos, and I bought a silver box from the gift shop, which sat atop my night table in the apartment Sarah and I shared, as well as the place in Tribeca. Ironically, the silver box is where I kept my passport.

Reflecting that my stay this time would be open-ended, I eschewed a hotel and rented a small, one-bedroom cottage about a hundred yards from the beach.

The silver box sits in its rightful place next to my bed, my passport inside.

It is there that I've begun again the long process of starting over.

Matt Brooks's arrest was front-page news all over the world.

The district attorney held a flashy press conference in which Lisa Kaplan stood right behind him. The DA explained that Brooks hired a contract killer to murder a witness who had damaging evidence that linked Brooks to other crimes, and to prevent his wife from finding out about his affair with Roxanne. The name of that witness was being withheld for security purposes, and the DA said that the witness himself was safely in the witness protection program.

The case against Brooks would be based almost entirely on the testimony of the hired gun, a guy named Romanow, who some press outlets were reporting had a connection to the Russian mob. Romanow had a long rap sheet and no obvious connection to Brooks. From what I could discern about the evidence, I figured that Brooks had a better than fifty-fifty shot at acquittal.

Benjamin Ethan is still representing him. He's been a near nonstop media presence, telling any news outlet that will listen that Brooks is innocent, and champing at the bit to have his day in court. The lawyer in me knows Ethan is posturing. Brooks hasn't invoked his speedy-trial rights, and the flurry of procedural motions that Ethan's filed reveals that he's trying his best to stall Brooks's day of reckoning. Perhaps he hopes that Romanow will end up on the losing end of a prison fight.

L.D.'s murder remains unsolved. As Judge Pielmeier predicted, the investigation of who actually put the shiv in L.D. ended without an arrest. Not that it mattered much, given that L.D.'s killer, like Nuts's would-be assassin, was almost certainly a hired gun anyway, and one who was already in prison to boot. And while there has been press speculation that Brooks was behind it, none of the media or enterprising bloggers have come up with any proof to support that charge, but I have no doubts that Brooks ordered the hit. There have also been the press reports that the DA is considering reopening the investigation into Roxanne's murder, and that Brooks was required to provide a sample of his pubic hair. The results of that test have not been made public, but I'd bet my life that they were a perfect match for the ones in Roxanne's bed.

Brooks was right about how damaging it would be for him if news of the affair became public. Shortly after the DA's press conference, Chiara filed for divorce and Capital Punishment's IPO was shelved. Although the divorce proceedings are just beginning, it's a safe bet that Chiara's settlement will be one for the record books.

There hasn't been any public disclosure of L.D.'s true identity, his sexual orientation, or his relationship with Nuts. If Matt Brooks goes to trial, which I consider almost a certainty given that I can't envision him agreeing to a plea that includes the lengthy prison term that the DA's office will undoubtedly demand, the whole story will come out. But just like I told Mercedes, I think L.D. would have been pleased that, in the end, the public will learn who he really was and what he was really all about.

Mercedes hired a lawyer to file suit against Capital Punishment. The lawsuit was brought in the name of L.D.'s estate, noting that any recovery was to be held in trust for L.D.'s only living heir, his daughter Brianna. The complaint sought more than $4 million in royalties, and the case settled right before Brooks was scheduled to give a sworn deposition. Although the settlement terms were confidential, my guess is that L.D.'s estate got every penny it was owed, and then some.

As for the last player in this drama, as I suspected, Nina was never charged.

The DA's office initially described Nina as a "person of interest," but in the weeks following Brooks's arrest, her name appeared less and less frequently in the press. I run a Google search now once a week, and it's been a while since there's been a hit.

Without my testimony, the DA won't be able to make a case against Nina. Nuts never did have any evidence of Brooks's affair with Roxanne, which meant that no one else could have tipped off Brooks except either Nina or me. By making myself unavailable, I've destroyed the prosecution's case against Nina because she can now plausibly claim she knew nothing about Nuts's connection to L.D., or my claim that he had evidence against Brooks, without fear of contradiction. Nuts might tell Kaplan I told him Nina knew about my visit, but that's not admissible, and even if it were, it doesn't prove that I told Nina that Nuts had incriminating evidence against Brooks.

Of course, Brooks could still do her in, but I sincerely doubt he will. Giving Nina up would mean acknowledging his own guilt, and I just don't think Brooks is built for that.

And that's probably the best explanation for my conduct, too. I'm just not built to destroy the life of someone I loved, no matter what crimes Nina committed.

Three months into my self-imposed exile, I received an email at my Sorensen and Harrington email address.

The fact that I continued to check that account puts the lie to any claim that the message took me by surprise.

The sender's address was unrecognizable, and it was unsigned, even electronically. The contents were sufficiently ambiguous to allow a denial of authorship, if it ever came to that. But I had no doubt that it was from Nina.

> *My Dearest Daniel:*
> *I hope you have found a place that makes you happy. I know you'll understand if this note is short and doesn't address all that I'd say if given the opportunity to do so in person. Are there any more insincerely uttered phrases in the English language than "I'm sorry" and "Thank you" and "I love you"? How can I convey that all three are true?*
>   *Love*

Love. There was that word again.

Sometimes I tell myself that it was more like lust than love. I was a starving man and Nina presented me with the opportunity to feast. But other times, truer moments, I accept that I was in love with Nina. It was a different type of love than the kind you experience in a decade of marriage, but it was love nonetheless.

When I arrived in St. Martin, my goal was to stay long enough to devise a plan about how to start my life over. It didn't take me that long, however, to realize that starting over is not a possibility. There's just no reset button in life.

Perhaps a better way of looking at it is that I've already started over. I'm now content with the days drifting into weeks without any accomplishment to mark the passage of time. Simply taking time for myself. To think. To appreciate what I once had and to contemplate what still lies before me.

I've started running again. Not too often or that far, but a few miles along the sand every couple of days. Although I keep a bottle of scotch in my kitchen, it's the only bottle I've bought down here, and it's still more than half full.

I can't help but think that Sarah would approve of my new life. I'm only sorry I didn't reach this realization sooner, so I could have shared this version of myself with my wife and daughter. But all I can do is take comfort that I've discovered this path now, and not later, or never at all.

And I know Alexa would have loved living so close to the ocean.

I began with the question "Where should I start?" and so I suppose it's fitting to ask, "Where should I end?" I've chosen this point, which I also believe to be the middle.

ACKNOWLEDGMENTS

A Case of Redemption is my second novel, and people sometimes ask if writing the second book is more difficult than the first. The answer is yes, although perhaps not for the reason people think. I have the sense that readers and friends alike assume that an author's first book is autobiographical and the second requires more creativity. At least in my case that's not actually true (both are very loosely autobiographical, and other than that, completely made up). However, the second book *was* more difficult to write for me because I knew from the outset that people other than my friends and family would read it, and that put pressure on me to make it as good as it possibly could be.

It is my great hope that such pressure made my second effort superior to the first. And like with *A Conflict of Interest*, if that is the case, it has much to do with the people I'm about to thank, all of whom were instrumental in shaping the book.

I am greatly indebted to everyone who reads my work. One of my favorite things about publishing *A Conflict of Interest*, and something I'm already looking forward to after *A Case of Redemption* comes out, are the emails I receive from readers. Whether they are short notes of praise or longer discussions about things that made them angry or that I got wrong, I truly enjoy reading every email, and encourage all readers to share their thoughts with me at adam@adammitzner .com. I answer them all, so you'll hear my views, too.

Heartfelt thanks to the troika that took my work from my family and friends to a readership beyond my wildest dreams: Scott Miller, my agent at Trident; Ed Stackler, a freelance editor who reviews the early drafts; and Ed Schlesinger, my editor at Simon & Schuster's Gallery Books imprint, who does the hard work after I think the book is finished to make it so much better. In addition to all their good advice and counsel, there are others who work with them to whom I'm equally grateful: Scott's assistant, Stephanie Hoover, and all the people at Simon & Schuster and Gallery Books, including the wonderful people in PR, Jean Anne Rose and Stephanie DeLuca, and my copy-editor, Stephanie Evans.

I also am indebted to the team at FSB Associates, Fauzia Burke, Leyane Jerejian, Julie Harabedian, and Courtney Elise, for getting the word out to the blogosphere about my books and for being great supporters of my work.

Another big difference between the first and second novels is that it is much easier after you're a published author to get people to read your manuscript. The following people, however, were readers even before they knew that their names might someday appear in the acknowledgments of a published book, and I am deeply appreciative of their early insight and comments: Anna Gryzmala-Busse, Clint Broden, Jane Cleary, Gregg Goldman, Sofia Logue, Margaret Martin, Natasha Mayer, Debbie Peikes, Ted Quinn, Elisa Reza, Kevin and Jessica Shacter, Ellice Schwab, Linda Sansotta, Lisa Sheffield, Marilyn Steinthal, and Jodi Siskind.

There is an old joke about how, in an egg-and-bacon breakfast, the hen is involved but the pig is truly committed. In that vein, perhaps even greater thanks must go to those who contributed their names to this book. In each and every instance the character is completely fictional, but it is still fun for me to be able to use names of people I know and shape the character in some way around them. In *A Case of Redemption*, I thank the following for letting me fictionalize them: Linda A. Pielmeier, Jordan Ringel, Steven Weitzen, Marty Popofsky (and his family, who purchased the naming right at a school auction), Kimberly Newman, Nancy Wong, and Lisa Kaplan.

Special thanks in this category to Matt Brooks, one of my closest friends for nearly thirty years. He was helpful in shaping the Matt Brooks character (filling me in on, among other things, the particulars of private helicopters and blackjack), and I'm only disappointed that the storyline did not permit more of the real Matt Brooks to come through, for there is an entire novel (if not a series of books) that could be built around his real-life persona.

Although some people might think that having two jobs is the worst of all worlds, for me it is truly a blessing. By day I am a partner at the law firm of Pavia & Harcourt, and I am very grateful to my partners and all the lawyers and staff at the firm for being supportive of my nighttime activities as a writer.

My parents, Linda and Milton Mitzner, both died before my first novel was published, but I am grateful that they lived long enough to know that such a day would arrive. Shortly before my father's death, he introduced me to his roommate in the hospital as "my son, the author," the first time anyone referred to me that way, which is a memory that I will always cherish.

The major life event for me between the publication of *A Conflict of Interest* and *A Case of Redemption* is that I got married, which has enriched my life in more ways than I could have ever imagined. Among them is that I am grateful to be the stepfather to Michael and Benjamin, who bring enormous joy to my life and who never fail to have insightful comments when we try to work out plot points over dinner conversation.

My daughters, Rebecca and Emily, continue to be my greatest inspiration, and nothing quite matches the feeling of knowing that your children are proud of you.

Our puppy (who is three years old, so not quite a puppy anymore), Onyx or Nixie, does not help my writing in any way, but we love her, and so she deserves mention just for that.

Most of all, I want to thank my wife, Susan, to whom *A Case of Redemption* is dedicated, for so many more reasons than I could ever mention. Being a writer's wife is different than I think she imagined, both in the amount of time I'm focused on my work and the number of times I ask her to read the book in draft. Susan has always been and remains my toughest critic, most ardent supporter, and the best editor and sounding board I could ever imagine. Beyond her help in making this book, and everything I'll ever write, much better than it would have been without her input, I know that without her in my life, I would have never been able to write a word, and with her, it truly does not matter if I ever write another word, for my life is fulfilled beyond what I could have ever imagined.

Pick up a
blockbuster thriller
from Pocket Books!